GABRIEL FAURÉ

GABRIEL FAURÉ

Robert Orledge

Revised Edition

EULENBURG BOOKS
LONDON

Ernst Eulenburg Ltd
48 Great Marlborough Street
London W1V 2BN

Copyright © 1979 Robert Orledge

First published in 1979 by Ernst Eulenburg Ltd
Revised edition published 1983

ISBN 0 903873 41 9 (paperback)

Printed and bound in England by
Page Bros (Norwich) Ltd

CONTENTS

Contents

For Charles McFeeters

'For me, art, and especially music, exists to elevate us
as far as possible above everyday existence.'

(Fauré to his son Philippe, Lausanne, 31 August 1908)

(*See plate XIX*)

PREFACE
to the first edition

Since Hugues Imbert's critical profile in *L'Indépendance Musicale et Dramatique* in 1887, and Louis Vuillemin's slightly longer appraisal in 1914, there has been less written about Gabriel Fauré than about almost any major composer. The present book is only the second in English and the first for over 30 years since Norman Suckling's volume in the Master Musicians series, excluding Leslie Orrey's contemporary translation of Charles Koechlin's short but perceptive study. Since 1946, many letters, manuscripts and other documents have been recovered, causing dates and opinions about this reticent and enigmatic composer to be substantially revised. The most significant contribution to our understanding of Fauré was the publication of his *Lettres intimes* to his wife in 1951 by his son Philippe Fauré-Fremiet, though this collection is now sadly unavailable and has never been translated into English. Wherever possible, Fauré's own words and manuscripts form the basis of the present study, and it is only fair to say that the bulk of this pioneering work has been carried out with inspiring devotion and scholarly awareness by Jean-Michel Nectoux of the Bibliothèque Nationale in Paris, whose 1972 study proved a landmark in Fauré research.

The aim of the present volume is to make the facts available in English in a comprehensive reappraisal that will interest both the layman and the musical scholar. It deals in some detail with Fauré's English connections, which are more extensive than is generally realised. It would be both foolish and presumptuous to assume that this book represents the last word on Fauré, and there are doubtless many more letters and manuscripts in private collections around the world which will cause some of the facts and opinions it contains to be revised yet again. The opening biographical chapter is deliberately summary for this reason, and I should like to direct readers towards a further collection of letters, edited by M. Nectoux, entitled *Gabriel Fauré: Correspondance* and published in 1980 by Flammarion, Paris.

I have included analyses of Fauré's more important works, and his compositional processes and the extant sketches from the collection of Madame Philippe Fauré-Fremiet are discussed in some detail for the first time in chapter 6. The compositions are divided into three periods, subdividing into genres for easy reference: songs, piano music, chamber music, secular choral music, religious vocal music, orchestral music, and Fauré and the theatre. The order within each section is chronological, except where a major work or collection imposes itself on a series of lesser ones, as is the case with *Prométhée* or *La Bonne Chanson* in chapter 4. The early compositions of the École Niedermeyer and Rennes periods are discussed together as separate groups within chapter 3. Where there is a marked change of style within a period, as in the third, I have subdivided further, though I have resisted the temptation to make five periods out of Fauré's career, as this would unbalance the structure of the book and make it appear as if Fauré's development had suddenly accelerated out of all recognition. Equally, I have resisted the temptation to dispense with the division into periods altogether, as the removal of these familiar guidelines would, I feel, do Fauré's case more harm than good.

Appendix A gives a chronological list of works which is as complete as possible, and includes unfinished sketches. I have also included a chronological list of the major works by genre to complement the sectional subdivision of the chapters. I have not included a discography for two reasons. First, Fauré is now becoming increasingly widely represented in the various record catalogues, and it is an easy matter to consult these and make a personal selection: tastes differ widely, and I would hate to impose my own choices as in any way definitive, or simply catalogue hundreds of records, not all of which I have heard, merely because they exist. Secondly, a complete discography (1900–77) by M. Nectoux is due to appear in 1979, published by the Bibliothèque Nationale. Any attempts to match this massive undertaking here would make the cost of this book prohibitive, and a select discography is only of value in the years immediately following publication.

Robert Orledge
Liverpool, September 1977

PREFACE
to the revised edition

A revised edition of *Gabriel Fauré* has proved necessary for several reasons. First, to incorporate the results of recent research and many inevitable factual corrections. Second, to provide precise manuscript references to the extensive collection of Mme Philippe Fauré-Fremiet which is now in the Bibliothèque Nationale. Third, to delete information concerning the songs *Les courlis dans les roseaux* and *Cette fille, elle est morte* (in the Humanities Research Center at the University of Texas at Austin) which are now known not to be by Fauré, even if their authorship has yet to be established. As a result, Exx. 62–3 have been omitted, though all other examples are numbered as in the first edition. Lastly, to further acknowledge my debt to the original research of Jean-Michel Nectoux who has been an unfailing source of inspiration to me in my work.

Robert Orledge
Liverpool, August 1982

ACKNOWLEDGEMENTS

During the preparation of this book over the past few years, I have been assisted by many institutions and individuals and have received only kindness and willingness to help from all concerned. I hope that this study may help to repay my debt of gratitude, if only in part. My research in Paris was greatly facilitated by grants from the University of Liverpool Research Fund, and I was most fortunate to have an understanding head of department in Professor Basil Smallman, who helped me in every way possible. I should also like to thank Rollo Myers, Mervyn Horder and Sir William Glock for their initial help in making this study feasible. It could not have been completed in its present form without M. Jean-Michel Nectoux, to whom I am deeply indebted for practical help with Appendix A, as well as a great deal of other information and advice, and permission to quote from his extensive published material on Fauré. I am also indebted to Mme Philippe (Blanche) Fauré-Fremiet, who has always welcomed me warmly into Fauré's final home in the Rue des Vignes in Paris, as well as kindly allowing me to consult and quote from original manuscripts in her extensive collection, now donated to the Bibliothèque Nationale. She also allowed me to reproduce photographs in her possession, as did Mme Emmanuel Fauré-Fremiet, Robert Cecil and Richard Ormond.

I should also like to thank the publishing houses of Hamelle (now merged with Leduc), Heugel and Durand for permitting me to consult autograph manuscripts in their possession and to quote from published music by Fauré. I am grateful too to the tolerant music staff at the Bibliothèque Nationale; the Paris Opéra Library; the Pierpont Morgan Library, New York; Yale University Library; the Library of Congress; and the Humanities Research Center at the University of Texas at Austin who have sent me, or allowed me to consult unpublished material in their collections and given me permission to cite extracts from it.

For information on Fauré's English activities I should like to thank Sir Adrian Boult, Robert Cecil, Florence Clayton, Ronald Crichton, Michael Kennedy and Richard Ormond; also David McKibbin, who kindly sent me copies of Fauré's letters to Mrs George Swinton, and the publishing house of J. B. Cramer and Co Ltd, who allowed me to consult their London archives.

Acknowledgements

For other assistance of various sorts, I am grateful to Dr Roy Howat, John Barrie Jones, Dr Ralph Locke and Dr Norah Nicholls. I should particularly like to thank Dr Michael de Cossart for his help and encouragement in the various stages of preparation of this book, and my editors, Sir William Glock, Paul Inwood and Brian Bowen, for their patience and invaluable advice during its publication.

ABBREVIATIONS USED IN THE TEXT

1. BOOKS

FF	Fauré-Fremiet, Philippe: *Gabriel Fauré*, Paris, Albin Michel, 2/1957
K	Koechlin, Charles, transl. Orrey, Leslie: *Gabriel Fauré*, London, Dennis Dobson Ltd, 1945
LI	Fauré, Gabriel: *Lettres intimes* (presented by Ph. Fauré-Fremiet), Paris, La Colombe, 1951
N	Nectoux, Jean-Michel: *Fauré,* Paris, Éditions du Seuil, 1972
OM	Fauré, Gabriel: *Opinions musicales,* Paris, Éditions Rieder, 1930
Su	Suckling, Norman: *Gabriel Fauré,* London, J. M. Dent and Sons Ltd, 1946

2. ARTICLES (also in Appendix C)

BAF	*Bulletin de l'Association des Amis de Gabriel Fauré*
ML	*Music and Letters*
MM	*Music and Musicians*
MQ	*Musical Quarterly*
MT	*Musical Times*
RdM	*Revue de Musicologie*
ReM	*La Revue Musicale* (*ReM,* 1922 means the special edition of 1 October 1922; *ReM,* 1945 refers to the special publication *Le Centenaire de Gabriel Fauré (1845–1945)*).

3. GENERAL

BN	Bibliothèque Nationale, Paris
La	autograph letter
ms	manuscript

n	footnote
n.d.	undated
OS	orchestral score
SMI	Société Musicale Indépendante
SN	Société Nationale (de musique)
VS	vocal score

Also

d	d minor
D	D major
op. 95/2	opus 95, number 2

In the case of the piano and chamber music, any page numbers used refer to the Hamelle, Heugel or Durand separate printed editions. Those of the first eight Nocturnes refer to the collected Hamelle edition fingered by G. Thyssens-Valentin (1958).

In the music examples, A_1 is the sign for a derivative of theme A, or an idea closely associated with A. The letter I is omitted in the lists of themes to avoid confusion.

LIST OF PLATES

Front cover Gabriel Fauré at Stresa, September 1906? (Coll. Mme Emmanuel Fauré-Fremiet; Photo Bibl. Nat. Paris)

(Detailed descriptions will be found with each plate)

INTRODUCTION

It is easy to despair of finding a clear line of development in Fauré's music in the Germanic sense: he quite happily incorporated piano miniatures written in Rennes in 1869 into both the *Huit pièces brèves* (op. 84) at the turn of the century and the divertissement *Masques et Bergamasques* of 1919. He re-used material from one *Ave Maria* of 1877 in another twenty-nine years later. The modal Lydia theme (op. 4/2, c.1870) crops up in all three periods in a variety of guises from *La Bonne Chanson* to the Second Quintet, and Appendix B shows the perhaps unexpected extent of Fauré's self-borrowing. As Aaron Copland observes (*MQ*, 1924, p. 576): 'It is the *quality* of the inspiration that has most changed. The themes, harmonies, form have remained essentially the same, but with each new work they have all become more fresh, more personal, more profound'. This is evident from a comparison of songs like *Nell* (1878) or *Le Secret* (1880–81) with *La Mer est infinie* and *Diane, Séléné* from the *Horizon chimérique* cycle of 1921: the outward similarities are obvious but the inner content is profoundly different. The quality of constant renewal within an apparently limited range is one of the more remarkable facets of Fauré's genius. If the self-discipline seems severe, the professional mastery is complete.

In addition, many of the works written before 1900 have twentieth-century counterparts: the First and Second Violin Sonatas; the *Ballade* and the *Fantaisie* for solo piano and orchestra; *La Bonne Chanson* and *La Chanson d'Ève*; *Prométhée* and *Pénélope* spring immediately to mind. There are numerous stylistic features common to all three periods of Fauré's career and, whilst it is obvious that songs like *Puisque l'aube grandit* (op. 61/2) and *L'Aube blanche* (op. 95/5) belong to different periods, it is difficult to see exactly where a change of style takes place. The most noticeable change of style actually comes in the *middle* of the third period with the almost violent wartime compositions of 1915–18.

Fauré's gradual evolution as a composer took place in harmony rather than in texture or form: in the syntax rather than the language of music. He revitalized the tonal system from within by fusing it with modality, and in so doing he stretched enharmonic change to its farthest limits

1

without making his music feel tortured or contrived. Just as the first few modal chords of Debussy's *La Damoiselle élue* betray their author instantaneously, so the first modal phrase of the First Piano Quartet bears the powerful imprint of Fauré's musical personality. His compositions have a decisiveness, reassurance and strength of character that the genial Fauré himself lacked; and to some extent he exemplifies Romain Rolland's dictum on Wagner's *Siegfried*[1] that:

> One goes astray in trying to interpret an artist's life by his work, for it is exceptional to find one a counterpart of the other. It is more likely that an artist's work will express the opposite of his life. . . . .The object of art is to fill up what is missing in the artist's experience.

Fauré's awareness of day-to-day political events had little or no direct bearing on his music: he sought in his art to transcend reality, and the relevance of his music lies in its capacity to take its audience outside themselves whenever it finds one that has ears to hear. Too often, however, the search for perfection resulted in Fauré's music simply going over its audiences' heads; its superb continuity makes it all too easy to listen to superficially and even the enharmonic complexities can appear paradoxically untroubled. It is easy to see how the criticism of Fauré as an 'ivory tower' composer arises, but this is as erroneous as the belief that his main skill lay in writing charming miniatures for salon consumption.

As Jean-Michel Nectoux shrewdly observes (N, p. 4): 'Fauré's work is a work of transition; he is a musician of the nineteenth century, but also a classic of the twentieth'. Increasing restraint and classicism are features of his final period from *La Chanson d'Ève* onwards, although both attributes are in evidence before 1906, as might be expected. Fauré's allusive and subtle art revels in craftsmanship and precision, but is at the same time expressive and sensual. He was even more aware of French traditions than Debussy or Ravel, and his music is the fluent and distinctive quintessence of Gallic civilization.

I do not propose to include here a detailed chronicle of the chequered history of France during the lifetime of Fauré; this can be found in any standard textbook. But it is interesting to consider that he was born in the reign of Louis-Philippe at a time when France was only just beginning to take tentative steps in industrial development and educational reform, and real power was still monopolized by a small political élite as it had been in the days of the Ancien Régime. Before he died in 1924, France, under the Third Republic, had emerged as a domineering nationalist State; Prime Minister Raymond Poincaré's occupation of the Ruhr in January 1923 to guarantee the full German payment of reparations for the war left no doubt as to the international standing of France. Before Fauré died, the atonality of Schoenberg's *Pierrot Lunaire* had been rationalized in the twelve-note method in opp. 24–6, and surrealism had supplanted cubism and expressionism in art. At the time of his birth in 1845, art was dominated by Delacroix; Chopin, Schumann and Mendelssohn were still active, and Liszt had not yet started writing orchestral music, nor Wagner conceived the idea of his Ring cycle. Poets later set by Fauré, like Leconte de Lisle (1818–94) and Baudelaire (1821–67), actively supported the 1848 Revolution, and Alphonse de Lamartine (1790–1869) actually proclaimed the short-lived Second Republic on 24 February 1848. Yet, apart from Émile Zola's intervention in the Dreyfus affair in 1898, artists by and large stayed out of the French political limelight during Fauré's lifetime, and the dream of a socialist utopia in 1848 was replaced by a general feeling of hostility between artists and society in the second half of the nineteenth century, typified in the embittered writings of Victor Hugo (1802–85). A yawning chasm existed between the serious artist and his uneducated public, and he suffered from distrust in influential circles as well as from obtuse critics. 'Not one of the many millionaires in Paris thinks of doing anything for serious music', Berlioz wrote as early as 1854; 'the composer who would produce substantial works in Paris outside the theatre must rely entirely on himself'. Thus it was that Fauré expended so much effort before the turn of the century in cultivating social patrons and on trying to find a suitable opera libretto. So-called 'realism' was the hallmark of art in this period, but the predilection of the Second Empire, in which Fauré was stretching his wings, was for elegant rubbish. Many saw the age as one of decadence, with some justification. The best-selling novelists were Ernest Feydeau (1821–73) and Octave Feuillet (1821–90); Offenbach's new *opéra-bouffe* dominated the fashionable musical scene and blended ideally with the developing cosmopolitanism and moral licence of France under Napoleon III.

The chain of short-lived artistic movements which plagued France in Fauré's lifetime hardly affected him at all; even Wagnerism made little impact on his music, though he was a fervent Wagnerite for a time. Only Romanticism, whose death-knell was sounded by the failure of Victor Hugo's *Les Burgraves* and Berlioz's *Damnation of Faust* around the time of Fauré's birth, and finally by the 1848 Revolution, is visible in his music, which prolonged the influence of Chopin and Schumann into the second half of the nineteenth century. Like Beethoven, whose late flowering of chamber music is often compared with that of Fauré, he is something of a romantic classic. But whereas Beethoven scaled the greatest heights as well as descending to some depths which enthusiasts prefer to forget, Fauré's music maintains a consistently high level. If it never attains the peak of the Choral Symphony, then equally it has no equivalent to the so-called Battle Symphony or *Wellington's Victory*.

After the disruptive war of 1870–71 and the establishment of the Third Republic, Fauré's active participation in current events ceased. The continual changes in Government, and scandals like the Dreyfus affair only wearied him as he struggled to make his living as a professional musician; they affected him less than the problems of reforming the Paris Conservatoire or diplomatically maintaining the uneasy balance between the SN and the SMI (see p. xv). Fauré remained a creature of the nineteenth century in his lack of concern for the development of electrical recording techniques and the gramophone and telephone, preferring to continue with concerts and letters and the occasional piano-roll recording. But he was deeply concerned by the progress of the First World War and, as with Debussy, a reflection of this concern can be seen in the changing focus of his music, as well as in his efforts to raise money for the war effort through concerts. Fauré also kept abreast of the latest developments in French poetry and, to bring the story to a full circle, one of his first compositions after the declaration of peace in 1918 was the song cycle *Mirages* to texts by Baroness Renée de Brimont, the great-niece of the poet and liberal democrat Alphonse de Lamartine.

Footnotes to Chap. 1
1. Essays on Music (ed. David Ewen), New York, Dover Publications, 1959, p. 324.

I

THE FACTS OF LIFE

> Your character is definite and clear-cut. Mine is not. I shall die the same elusive person I have always been. . . .I have been reserved all my life, even as a child, and have only been able to let myself go in certain situations.
>
> (Fauré to his wife Marie, Nice, 24 March 1921, LI, pp. 270–1)

There is no trace of music in Fauré's ancestry. His paternal grandfather and great-grandfather were highly respected butchers in the department of Ariège, the former settling in Foix. The southern dialect (*langue d'oc*) pronunciation of the family name 'Faouré' suggests that they might once have been smiths. Fauré's maternal grandfather Germain Lalène (1759–1851), from the village of Gailhac-Toulza, was a captain in the Imperial army who, Philippe Fauré-Fremiet tells us (FF, p. 9)[1], retired early because he did not relish marrying his colonel's daughter. After the downfall of Napoleon he resumed his links with the lesser nobility by readopting his family name of de Lalène-Laprade.

Fauré's father, Honoré Toussaint (later Toussaint-Honoré: 1810–85) was the first to break away from family tradition and, whilst a young schoolmaster in Gailhac-Toulza in 1829, he married Germain's daughter Marie-Antoinette-Hélène de Lalène (1809–87). Promotion seems to have been fairly rapid, for by 1839 the solid and industrious Toussaint-Honoré was Deputy-Inspector of Primary Education at Pamiers. Here, on 12 May 1845 at 17 Rue Major, his sixth child was born, and named Gabriel after his grandfather, and Urbain after a maternal uncle. He seems to have been an unexpected addition to the family—the Benjamin of the tribe, so to speak—and he was sent away for his first four years to a nurse at Verniolle, to whom he returned in the summers of 1849–54 after he had rejoined his family.

This came about when his father was appointed head of the Mont-gauzy Teacher Training College at Foix. Most of Gabriel's childhood was therefore spent alone for his four brothers, Amand, Paul, Fernand and Albert were all at school during the day, and his sister Rose, who married her father's successor Casimir Fontes, was fifteen years his senior. As his mother was doubtless preoccupied with domestic matters and his father was strict, conscientious and, I suspect, rather reactionary and unyielding, it is little wonder that Fauré grew up reticent, self-reliant and reluctant to divulge his innermost feelings to anyone. 'According to my parents I was silent and bound up in myself as a child', Fauré told his wife on 26 April 1907 (FF, p. 37), and we know that he found communication with his father very difficult. His main solace was the large garden at Montgauzy where he could escape from the austere family house into another world of mediterranean trees— pines, cypresses, magnolias, cedars, and beautiful flowers, which made a lasting impression on him and must surely have been in his mind when he wrote the exquisite *Le Jardin de Dolly* (op. 56/3) in 1895 or *Le Jardin clos* in 1914. He was also impressed by the sounds of hammering from the Catalonian forges of the Arget and the evening bells from nearby Cadirac. The latter were clearest when the wind was in the west, and Fauré later recalled the bells at the start of the Adagio of his Second Piano Quartet 'almost involuntarily' (LI, p. 132).

The College at Montgauzy was built on the ruins of an old convent and naturally possessed a chapel. Here Gabriel received his introduction to music in the form of plainchant accompanied on the harmonium. He also had access to the school piano, but does not seem to have had any music lessons; quite naturally he 'had neither the fabulous precocious-ness of Mozart nor the early virtuosity of Saint-Saëns' (FF, p. 29). His keyboard proficiency was nonetheless sufficient to impress the member of the Assembly for Ariège, M. Dufaur de Saubiac, on a visit to Montgauzy in 1853. He advised Toussaint-Honoré to send his son to the new school in Paris founded by the Swiss Louis Niedermeyer (1802–61), where thirty or so pupils were trained as future organists and choirmasters. Had it not been for de Saubiac's official intervention it is doubtful if Fauré would ever have gone into music, as his father did not approve of any sort of hazardous career for his offspring. Amand, his eldest son, enjoyed a brilliant career which included being a prefect of the Republic; Paul was decorated for his army service in Algeria and China; Fernand continued in his father's footsteps, becom-ing an inspector for the Académie; and Albert became a naval officer. A letter of 6 July 1854 (FF, pp. 19–20) makes it clear that, if Fauré's father had been unable to obtain a full grant for him, he would not have gone to Paris, though Toussaint-Honoré followed his son's career with interest, never failing to offer sound advice and signing his letters 'ton père et ton ami'.

Fauré reached the École Niedermeyer at 10 Rue Neuve-Fontaine-Saint-Georges (now Rue Fromentin, Paris 9) in October 1854 and stayed there till 1865. After a period in the Papal chapel, Niedermeyer had resolved to devote his life to the 'rediscovery' of the music of the

sixteenth and seventeenth centuries and his 'career reads like an anticipation of that of Charles Bordes' half a century later (Su, p. 11). In
1843 he founded a 'Société de musique vocale religieuse et classique'
which, although shortlived, made its presence felt with eleven published
volumes of its magnificent repertory. Niedermeyer then focused his
attention on the low standard of church music, which Fauré tells us was
then the rule rather than the exception (*ReM*, 1922, p. 6). He considered
that the best way to remedy the situation would be to found a model
school. So in 1853 began the celebrated 'École de musique religieuse
et classique' where selected pupils were taught history, geography,
literature and Latin by the clergy of the nearby church of Saint-
Louis-d'Antin, as well as music, which for plainchant meant St Gregory,
for sacred music Palestrina, and for the organ J. S. Bach.

Fauré later remembered that his first musical education was 'exces-
sively rigorous. We were not allowed to play Schumann or Chopin:
Niedermeyer did not consider this suitable music for young people'
(*Excelsior*, 1922, p. 2). Niedermeyer was famous for his setting of
Lamartine's poem *Le Lac* and as the composer of successful operas
such as *Marie Stuart* and *Stradella*, but the sort of prizes Fauré won at
the school reflect the seriousness of Niedermeyer's educational purpose:
Handel's *Judas Maccabaeus* (solfège prize, 1857); Haydn's *Seven Last
Words* (harmony prize, 1860); Bach's keyboard works (piano distinction
prize, 1862); and orchestral scores of Mozart's *Don Giovanni* and *The
Magic Flute* (first prize for musical composition, 1865). Fauré was taught
the organ by Clément Loret, counterpoint and fugue by Joseph Wack-
enthaler, and harmony by Louis Dietsch, whom Fauré tells us wrote
'a score for *The Flying Dutchman* from the actual libretto of the opera
sold by the impoverished Wagner in Paris' (*ReM*, 1922, p. 8). Niedermeyer himself taught singing, piano and composition, and the *Traité
théorique et pratique de l'accompagnement du plainchant* by Joseph
d'Ortigue and Niedermeyer (1857) and the *Traité d'harmonie* by
Niedermeyer's successor and son-in-law Gustave Lefèvre give some
idea of how much less dogmatic their harmonic teaching was than that
of the Paris Conservatoire. Passing notes and enharmonic modulation
were treated in a freer and more enlightened manner, and the tonal
language was frequently enriched by modal elements. All this greatly
influenced Fauré who saw that the modes had a wider application than
plainchant accompaniment. From necessity he also acquired the ability
to work anywhere, amidst any sort of distraction, for limited space at
the school meant several pianos in one room. Although he was kept
short of funds and conditions at the school were far from being luxurious,
Fauré and his friends Gigout, Périlhou and Koszul got up to all sorts
of antics: their orchestra, which included 'four pianos, two violins,

several pairs of tongs, some shovels, coal buckets and the lid of a stove' (*ReM*, 1922, p. 9) sounds as if it might have been a joyous forerunner of the ensembles of John Cage!

The death of Louis Niedermeyer on 14 March 1861 was a sad day both for Fauré and for his school. But the appointment of Camille Saint-Saëns (1835–1921) as piano teacher in his stead came as an important compensation. Although ten years Fauré's senior, an intense teacher-pupil/father-son relationship began which happily developed into a lifelong friendship, for Saint-Saëns's homosexuality in later life was little short of notorious. Fauré's sexual proclivities however were strongly in the opposite direction, though he must have been aware of the usefulness of his swarthy good looks when seeking entry to Paris and London society through men like Comte Robert de Montesquiou or Frank Schuster.

Fauré particularly admired Saint-Saëns's ability to achieve excellence in all types of musical composition and, as late as 1922, he still maintained that 'among the modernists I find Saint-Saëns superior' (*Excelsior*). It was Saint-Saëns who introduced Fauré and the other pupils at the École Niedermeyer to the 'modern' music of Schumann, Liszt and Wagner at the piano[2], which they otherwise would not have known, for the official teaching repertoire did not go beyond Beethoven and Mendelssohn and was mostly concerned with music written before 1750.

After Fauré finished at the École Niedermeyer in July 1865, Gustave Lefèvre arranged for his appointment as organist at the church of Saint-Sauveur in Rennes in January 1866. Relatively little is known about this period except that Fauré disliked provincial life. Fernand Bourgeat says that he took up lodgings with very religious, upright folk where he was obliged to retire each evening at 8 o'clock and was condemned to an almost monastic existence (N, p. 14). Other reports tell of the priests at Saint-Sauveur complaining of his smoking in the church porch during sermons, and of his being sacked for appearing in the organ-loft in full evening dress after spending the previous Saturday night at a ball in the town (Su, p. 14).

In August 1866 Saint-Saëns came to Rennes with a group of friends on their way to the shrine of Sainte-Anne-la-Palud in Brittany[3], as a result of which Saint-Saëns probably wrote his *Trois Rapsodies sur des cantiques bretons* (op. 7) for organ, which he dedicated to Fauré (Nectoux, *RdM*, 1972, p. 201 nl). Fauré gave lessons in Rennes to various young girls and was received into the homes of some of them as a friend. It was thus that many of the pieces written in 1869 come to be dedicated to the de Leyritz sisters Valentine and Laure. In 1868 Fauré acted as accompanist to Madame Miolan-Carvalho for a concert tour of Brittany, as a result of which she agreed to sing his Victor Hugo setting *Le Papillon et la fleur*, written whilst at the École Niedermeyer in 1861. But Fauré remained unimpressed with Rennes. When circumstances forced him to spend a day there thirty years later on his return from a holiday in Saint-Lunaire, he recalled this unhappy period when he 'could think of *nothing*, having a mediocre view of myself, a total indifference. . .without a shadow of ambition' (LI, p. 23).

Early in 1870, Fauré returned to Paris as assistant organist of Notre-Dame-de-Clignancourt, but he soon left to participate in the start of the war with Prussia, being placed in a regiment of light infantry soldiers in the Imperial Guard on 16 August 1870. From there he progressed to the 28th Infantry Regiment. M. Nectoux has discovered that, because of his youth, Fauré was placed at the advance posts and served as a liaison agent during the siege of Paris (N, p. 15). In this capacity he took part in the skirmishes aimed at relieving the capital: first, in October 1870, at Champigny; then, in November-December at Le Bourget; and finally at Créteil. By this time food was at a premium in the city with cats fetching six francs a carcass, rats one franc and dog-meat one franc a pound! Fauré helped the soldiers forget their problems temporarily with improvised recitals in abandoned houses in the Paris suburbs.

Following the capitulation of Paris on 28 January 1871 and the agreement between Thiers and Bismarck, Fauré's military role came to an end. One of the main reasons behind the events leading to the Paris Commune of April-May 1871 was the disbanding of the National Guard, ending the only regular wage many Parisians had. Fauré was briefly employed as organist at Saint-Honoré-d'Eylau on 19 March 1871 but during the Commune he escaped to Rambouillet with the aid of a false passport (K, p. 3) and spent four months that summer at Cours-sous-Lausanne in Switzerland where he was entrusted with the composition class of his old École Niedermeyer, which had sought refuge on the Niedermeyer estate of Champ-d'Asile. Here, Fauré formed a strong friendship with his first pupil André Messager which lasted throughout his life.

Returning to Paris, Fauré was appointed second 'accompanying' organist to Charles-Marie Widor at Saint-Sulpice in October 1871. In the early 1870s, Saint-Saëns helped considerably to launch Fauré's musical career, compensating for his former pupil's lack of ambition and acting as his passport to society and later to official recognition. On 25 February 1871 the 'Société Nationale de musique' (SN) was founded by Saint-Saëns and Romain Bussine, a professor of singing at the Conservatoire, with the assistance of Franck, d'Indy, Lalo, Massenet, Bizet, Guiraud, Fauré and Duparc. Their motto was 'Ars Gallica' and their aim 'to make known published or unpublished works of

French composers forming part of the Society, and to aid the production and popularization of all serious musical works'. Formed in the wave of nationalist feeling following the establishment of the Third Republic, French music in the closing decades of the nineteenth century. Works were democratically selected by the voting committee that met on Sundays at the house of Romain Bussine, where their authors were called on to perform them in reduction at the piano. The first secretary was Alexis de Castillon, and after his unfortunate early death Fauré took over his post in November 1874. He was not penalized for his frequent unpunctuality and many of his works were introduced to the public through the SN, like the Violin Sonata (1877) and the First Piano Quartet with its original finale (1880). In his *Excelsior* interview in 1922, Fauré observed that the SN was the main venue for the performance of chamber music in France and that 'at first they found my music noisy and discordant'. But he added that 'they even found Gounod barbaric and reproached him for being unmelodic'! It was only after Franck's death, however, that the SN took on a marked bias towards the works of the newly founded Schola Cantorum, though d'Indy's efforts in this direction met with considerable opposition from Saint-Saëns.

Fauré's introduction to Parisian society by Saint-Saëns began around 1872 with the Viardot family. It is not difficult to imagine how impressive the soirées of the celebrated Spanish contralto Pauline Viardot must have been to the young Fauré. Recalling them in 1922, he wrote:

> This was 'something else'. There we performed charades with Turgenev and Saint-Saëns as actors and Flaubert, George Sand, [Ernest] Renan and even Louis Blanc as spectators. George Sand was at this time a grand old lady. Turgenev was the great panjandrum himself, handsome and with a gentleness that was even more attractive. I still remember the sound of his voice to the extent that, when I read one of his books, it seems to me that I can hear him talking. Gustave Flaubert took great delight in our jesting, but it was Renan who amused him most.[4]

These soirées took place on Thursdays at 28 Rue de Douai, Paris 9; the musical ones, which undoubtedly encouraged Fauré's inclination towards song writing in the 1870s, took place on Sundays. His duets for two sopranos *Puisqu'ici-bas* and *Tarentelle* (op. 10) are dedicated to Pauline's daughters Claudie (Madame Chamerot) and Marianne, as is his *Ave Maria* of 1877. The *Chanson du pêcheur* (op. 4/1) and *Barcarolle* (op. 7/3) are dedicated to Pauline Viardot.

In the 1870s Fauré was also on extremely good terms with the family of the rich industrialist Camille Clerc; being poor he was naturally 'very attracted towards the materialistic life' (*Excelsior*, 1922). The Clercs' soirées in Paris were frequented by Saint-Saëns, Romain Bussine, André Messager, and the critic Camille Bellaigue, and Fauré was also welcomed at the Clercs' summer residences at Villerville and Sainte-Adresse on the fashionable Normandy coast. They provided everything Fauré's parents could not: spiritual understanding, emotional warmth and an artistically enlightened milieu. Here in Normandy Fauré wrote his First Violin Sonata and Piano Quartet, and his *Ballade* (op. 19), and M. Clerc helped him to get his Violin Sonata published by Breitkopf und Härtel in 1877, shortly before his early death. Fauré dedicated the sonata to Paul Viardot, himself a violinist, and only the *Chant d'automne* (op. 5/1) and the 1906 version of the *Messe basse* are dedicated to Mme Clerc.

Fauré's attraction to Marianne Viardot in the years 1872–7 is a story of unrequited love. His letters during the crucial summer of 1877 were published in the *Revue des Deux Mondes* (Fauré, 1928, pp. 911–43), though it is still not clear quite why Marianne broke off their short engagement in October 1877. Certainly it was not through lack of physical appeal on Fauré's part: women found his slightly Arabic appearance irresistible. As Camille Bellaigue puts it (1928, p. 912) in his introduction to the letters:

> No one possessed to the same degree as Fauré the mysterious gift that no other can replace or surpass: charm. In and around him, all was seductive. Very tanned of face, with dark eyes and hair, he had a dreamy, melancholy air, illuminated now and then by the youthful twinkle of a street-urchin. The sound of his voice was soft and deep.

Marianne had finally agreed to their engagement in July 1877 just before she left for Luc-sur-Mer on the Normandy coast for the summer. Fauré, to improve the condition of his always delicate throat, had already made arrangements to go to Cauterets in the High Pyrenees near the Spanish border, and his affectionate, sometimes twice-daily letters to his fiancée show how upset he was by their inopportune parting. Two hours after arriving at Tarbes on 20 August, en route to Cauterets, he wrote: '*I am anxious to be reassured that you have forgotten the turbulent and suspicious element in my tenderness towards you during these last few days. . .* Your *far-off* fiancé!' As usual he underlined all his important thoughts 'à la Massenet'.

In general the letters are surprisingly innocent for a man of 32. They are modest, often picturesque, and are written in a rather wayward, distracted style. Their affectionate phrases seem always to be concealing a passionate undercurrent, and 1877 represents the major emotional crisis in Fauré's life. It seems that the timid and fragile Marianne was a bit afraid of Fauré, and M. Nectoux quotes a letter from Turgenev to Marianne's sister Claudie Chamerot (N, p. 25) which suggests that

Marianne was not the marrying kind, though in this instance the otherwise perceptive judge of character was wrong, for Marianne later married the minor composer Alphonse Duvernoy (1854–1919). There was also the question of Fauré's career. Pauline Viardot wished her future son-in-law to achieve some sort of operatic success, and M. Nectoux has shown that Fauré tried hard to do this[5], being introduced by Saint-Saëns to his librettist Louis Gallet in 1875 or 1876. Even though Fauré seems to have had a genuine interest in the theatre[6] which continued after the break with Marianne, his son Philippe tells us (FF, p. 59) that he later considered that 'the rupture was perhaps not a bad thing for me, for the Viardot family might have succeeded in deflecting me from my proper musical path'.

Since January 1874 Fauré had been officially deputizing for Saint-Saëns at the Madeleine organ whilst he was away on tours of the provinces or abroad. In 1877, when Saint-Saëns finally resigned his post, Théodore Dubois (1837–1924) became organist and Fauré choirmaster. Although an excellent organist when he chose to be, preferring the works of Bach and Mendelssohn's sonatas, Fauré regarded this work, like teaching, simply as a means of financial survival.

1877 also saw the first of Fauré's German trips. He accompanied Saint-Saëns to Weimar for the première of *Samson et Dalila* on 2 December. Here Saint-Saëns introduced him to Liszt and Fauré told Mme Clerc that Liszt played them the 'Canticle of St Francis of Assisi', one of his latest works, from its original manuscript.[7] In April 1879 Fauré travelled with Messager to hear *Das Rheingold* and *Die Walküre* at Cologne, and in September 1879 the two Wagnerites travelled to Munich to hear the complete Ring cycle. In July 1880 Fauré and Dubois heard *Die Meistersinger von Nürnberg* and *Tannhäuser* in Munich: Fauré greatly admired the first but was disappointed by the second. Fauré's first visit to England in early May 1882 was also motivated by his desire to hear more Wagner; he and Messager were present at the first performance of the complete Ring cycle in England by Angelo Neumann's Wagnerian Theatre Company at Her Majesty's Theatre, London. In 1888, as the result of a 'weird and wonderful lottery' organized by Mme Baugnies to assist the impecunious Fauré and Messager, the pair were at last able to travel to Bayreuth to hear *Parsifal*. Fauré later wrote to his benefactress (FF, p. 62):

> If one has not heard Wagner at Bayreuth, one *has heard nothing!* Take lots of handkerchiefs because you will cry a great deal! Also take a sedative because you will be exalted to the point of delirium!

He told her that he left *Parsifal* with 'broken bones'! (N, pp. 34–5)

Fauré's Wagner-worship was, however, selective; he was bored by Act 3 of *Lohengrin*, for instance. But it was also durable, as can be seen from his later ecstatic Wagner reviews in *Le Figaro*. Although he put what he saw to be the best general aspects of Wagner into *Pénélope*—leitmotifs and the symphonic argument in the orchestra—he was almost alone in the generation of Chabrier, Chausson, d'Indy and Duparc in not succumbing to the harmonic spell of Bayreuth. Indeed the *Souvenirs de Bayreuth*, a rather indifferent quadrille written in 1888 for piano duet on 'favourite motifs from the Ring', shows that both Fauré and Messager were able to see the ridiculous side to the Wagnerian cult.

In July 1882 Fauré again met Liszt in the company of Saint-Saëns, and presented him with the *Ballade* he had written in 1879. He feared that it was too long, but Liszt replied that this was impossible as one wrote what one felt. 'After five or six pages', Fauré recalls (*Excelsior*, 1922), 'Liszt said to me, "I have no more fingers", and he begged me to continue, which greatly intimidated me.' The explanation usually offered is that Fauré's particular brand of pianism did not correspond with Liszt's technique, though it is just as likely that Liszt wanted to hear Saint-Saëns's pupil play himself.

On 27 March the following year Fauré, aged nearly 38, at last married Marie Fremiet, daughter of the celebrated sculptor Emmanuel Fremiet (1824–1910). Two sons were born, Emmanuel (1883–1971), who became professor of biology at the Collège de France, and Philippe (1889–1954), man of letters and music-lover. Both sons added their grandfather's name to their own legally, becoming Fauré-Fremiet in 1905. Fauré's first married home was at 93 Avenue Niel, Paris 17. Previously he had lived at 7 Rue de Parme, Paris 9 (1874–7), then at 13 Rue Mosnier, Paris 8 (now Rue de Berne) where he shared an apartment with Messager between 1877 and his marriage. In 1886 the Faurés moved to 154 Boulevard Malesherbes, Paris 17, and their final move was to 32 Rue des Vignes, Paris 16, in April 1911.

In 1879 Fauré signed a contract with Hamelle which transferred the rights of his songs published by Choudens to them, and 1878–84 saw the composition of most of the songs published as a collection (vol. 2) by Hamelle in 1897. 1884 also marks the end of Fauré's first period with works like the Third and Fourth Nocturnes and the later disclaimed Symphony in d (op. 40). Fauré was still far from comfortably off; Marie's hand-decorated fans sold well in society circles, but Fauré was still forced to spend about three hours in trains on most days of the week travelling to and from private lessons, as their total income at this time was only about 2,000 francs per annum (FF, p. 63). Fauré told Mme Baugnies that he had a 'real need to see other places than the eternal Gare Saint-Lazare', but now that he was married he was unable to afford the holidays he needed to compose.

Marie seems to have been very much a background figure, 'a faithful wife and devoted mother of her family, absorbed in the care of her children' (K, p. 5) who were often ill. She played no part in Fauré's artistic evolution, her life being overshadowed by her brilliant father and husband. Fauré invariably took his holidays alone to compose in peace, and Marie must often have felt the unfairness of her situation. She occasionally expressed her true feelings in letters, such as the one Fauré painfully answered from Nice on 24 March 1921 (LI, pp. 270–71), and she described herself in a letter to Saint-Saëns, with whom she shared an interest in astronomy, in January 1904 as 'the zero of the family' (Nectoux, *RdM*, 1972, p. 228).

On 25 July 1885 Fauré's father died in Toulouse. Fauré was staying with friends at Taverny in the Val d'Oise when the news came through, and he was worried about his wife's health too, which had forced her to spend the summer at Néris-les-Bains. Contrary to popular belief, Fauré did not begin his commemorative *Requiem* until 1887, and before it was completed in its earliest version his mother had also died on New Year's Eve 1887–8. This event may have spurred him on to complete the *Agnus Dei*, *Sanctus*, and *In Paradisum* in the early days of 1888 for the first performance on 16 January.

Although he was awarded the Prix Chartier by the Academy of Fine Arts for his chamber music in 1885, and developed a strong friendship with Tchaikovsky in 1886–89, this was a bleak period in Fauré's life. His deep depressions brought back neuralgic head-pains and feelings of dizziness that he had not experienced since adolescence, and he was often on the point of nervous collapse. Nonetheless he forced himself to continue, turning unexpectedly towards incidental music for the theatre with scores for Alexandre Dumas père's *Caligula* in 1888, Edmond Haraucourt's adaptation of *The Merchant of Venice* entitled *Shylock* in 1889, and Molière's *Le Bourgeois Gentilhomme* in 1893.

Fortunately, the vicious circle of depression was broken by the intervention of the Princesse de Scey-Montbéliard (later the Princesse Edmond de Polignac), the wealthy and astute American patroness of the arts and the daughter of Isaac Merritt Singer of sewing-machine fame. She invited Fauré on a holiday to Venice and Florence in May-June 1891, during which he began his first true song-cycle, the *Cinq mélodies 'de Venise'* (op. 58) to poems by Verlaine, whose 'discovery' in 1887 had been another landmark in Fauré's career.

Fauré and a group of his friends were received at the fifteenth-century palazzo in Venice that the princess had rented from a Russian friend of Wagner, M. Wolkoff. Fauré preferred to work at a table in the Café Florian in the busy piazza rather than in the quiet room the princess had put at his disposal (Polignac, 1945, p. 120), and it is perhaps not surprising that the only tangible product of the idyllic six-week holiday, which restored Fauré's health and spirits, was the song *Mandoline*. But doubtless he did a great deal of planning. In her memoirs the princess is rather shaky over precise dates and details, but it seems that Mme Ernest Duez of the Parisian party had a beautiful voice, and some of Fauré's songs were performed each evening on a large boat in the lagoon, with an orchestra of five or six musicians and 'Fauré playing a little portable yacht piano'. The princess justly observed that 'no one admired and understood Verlaine better than Gabriel Fauré' and suggested that the two collaborate on a joint theatrical project, although this never materialized. She also provides us with an interesting description of Fauré at this period (Polignac, 1945, p. 121):

> He had a keen sense of humour and was intensely alive to the absurdity of the pretentious; but although he was sensitive and sentimental, he was easily carried away by new affections, and was not always a faithful and perfect friend, being too much interested in new ties to trouble much about his old ones. No one could resist his charm of manner, his gaiety, his tenderness, above all his utter sincerity when a new fancy took his heart and mind, as it too often did.

Fauré's attraction towards Emma Bardac was more than just a 'new fancy' and *La Bonne Chanson* (op. 61), mostly written at Bougival in a house on the Bardac estate loaned to Fauré and his family during the summers of 1892 and 1893, is the artistic expression of his passion for her. The second Verlaine cycle is the closest Fauré comes to a completely optimistic and extrovert work, and as such it invites direct comparison with Debussy's *L'Isle joyeuse* inspired by his 'honeymoon' with Emma in Jersey in July 1904. As Fauré told Roger-Ducasse:[8]

> I never wrote anything more spontaneously than *La Bonne Chanson*, and I was aided by the spontaneity of the singer who remained its most moving interpreter—a spontaneity at least the equal of my own. I have never known any pleasure to equal that which I felt as I heard these pages coming to life, one after the other, as I brought them to her.

Each evening Emma tried out the songs Fauré wrote during the day, and Roger-Ducasse also tells us that Emma caused changes to be made in *La Lune blanche* (op. 61/3; see Pitrou, 1957, p. 96). Madame de Tinan (Dolly Bardac) claims that her mother also introduced Fauré to Albert Samain's poem *Soir*[9] which he set to music in December 1894.

Fauré's change of fortune continued with his appointment on 1 June 1892 as successor to Ernest Guiraud as inspector of music in the provincial Conservatoires, a post he held till 1905. This proved something of a mixed blessing, for although it meant he could give up the private teaching that he loathed, he had hoped to be elected professor of composition at the Conservatoire, which would have eliminated the travelling he found so irksome. His hopes were dashed by Ambroise Thomas, and in 1894 he also saw Dubois elected to the Institute in his stead. Only in 1896 with the death of Thomas was the Parisian promotion-blockage eased a little. With the support of André Gédalge, Fauré succeeded Massenet as professor of composition, counterpoint and fugue when the latter resigned on the appointment of Théodore Dubois as director of the Conservatoire. Earlier that same year, on 2 June, Fauré finally became the titular organist at the Madeleine, though his application to the Institute was again rejected in favour of that of Charles Lenepveu, and in 1895 the post of musical critic of *Le Figaro* that Fauré had hoped for had gone to Alfred Bruneau, who had the novelist Émile Zola's influential support.

Like the early 1880s, the last few years of the nineteenth century are biographically rather blank; we know more about his activities abroad than in Paris. They were extremely productive years musically, with a wealth of fine pieces like the Sixth Nocturne and the Fifth Barcarolle completed in the summer of 1894 at the Fremiet home at Prunay near Port-Marly, with its distant views of the forest of Saint-Germain. Finally, as a crown to the 1890s, came the incidental music for *Pelléas et Mélisande* and *Prométhée*.

These were the years during which Fauré attempted to gain a wider audience for his music through performances in England. His first visit to London since 1882 was for a concert in St James's Hall on 22 November 1894 which he shared with the composer Francis Thomé (1850–1909). Fauré's introduction to English society almost certainly came through the famous portrait painter John Singer Sargent (1856–1925), who first captured Fauré's likeness in oils during a visit to the Paris Exhibition of 1889. In 1894 Fauré must have met Frederick and Adela Maddison, for he signed a contract with Metzler and Co (now J. B. Cramer) on 15 January 1896 giving them exclusive rights to publish his compositions in Britain, its Colonies and the USA, and Frederick Brunning Maddison was a director of this firm. Metzler were the first to publish Fauré's Sixth Barcarolle in February 1896, three months before Hamelle, and they published over twenty of his best works between then and 1899, including *Pleurs d'or*, the *Thème et variations* and some songs with uninspired English translations by Adela Maddison. Metzler's unbusinesslike methods led to a running battle with Hamelle and their contract was not renewed in 1901.[10]

Fauré spent a fortnight with the Maddisons at their French villa in Saint-Lunaire in September 1896 and he told his wife that they were planning a concert of his works in London the following year, and each year after that, which would bring him at least 3,000 francs (LI, pp. 21–2). His hosts, he said, were 'charming, never tired, and enthusiasts of his music almost to the point of *stupidity*!' (LI, p. 23). In fact, Adela Maddison was herself a talented composer whose settings of Albert Samain's poems *Hiver* and *Silence* Fauré praised in a letter to Samain on 13 March 1900 (Jean-Aubry, *ReM*, 1945, pp. 57–8). He told his friend Mrs Swinton that Adela was 'extraordinarily gifted. I wish she could be encouraged as much as she deserves.'[11] She translated Paul Collin's text of *La Naissance de Vénus* so that it could be performed at the Leeds Festival in October 1898, and Fauré dedicated his Seventh Nocturne to her. Adela Maddison was almost certainly one of the great loves of Fauré's life, and I have it on good authority that she left her wealthy solicitor husband late in 1898 to live in Paris and be nearer to Fauré. Here she also became a friend of Delius and other Parisian exiles[12].

Fauré was also much attracted to Mrs George Campbell-Swinton, a talented singer of Russian origins who often performed his songs, and with whom he stayed at Llandough Castle at Cowbridge in South Wales in August 1898. His letters to her reflect the extent to which his visits to England were an escape from the reality of everyday life. 'I found here on my return [to Paris]', he wrote[13], 'all the problems of real life! In London all is dreams and poetry: here, alas, all is work and prose!' Elsewhere in his letters to Mrs Swinton, Fauré's wit comes bubbling to the surface in drawings and observations on his society hosts, like Lady Charles Beresford: 'Teagown de rêve, rêves de Teagown!', or Lady de Grey[14]: 'Oh! much changed, except for her teeth!'

But his principal English host was Leo Francis (Frank) Schuster, the wealthy son of a Frankfurt Jewish banking family who chose to devote his life to the advancement of the arts rather than business. Fauré referred to him affectionately as 'my nurse', and a letter referring to his Westminster home in Fauré's schoolboy English is included as plate VIII. Schuster loved sponsoring premières, like that of *La Bonne Chanson* for tenor solo (Maurice Bagès), string quintet and piano given at his home on 1 August 1898; he also helped to put Elgar on the musical map in the 1890s.

Fauré came to England again with his Conservatoire pupil Charles Koechlin (1867–1950) in June-July 1898 to conduct his score for the first stage production with music of Maeterlinck's *Pelléas et Mélisande*. The celebrated actress Mrs Patrick Campbell was Fauré's Mélisande, and she and Fauré were part of a house party on 26 June at Schuster's country residence, curiously named 'The Hut', at Bray-on-Thames, three miles from Maidenhead, where Sargent made the charcoal drawings reproduced in plates IX and X.

By the 1890s Fauré was very much an established figure in the Parisian social scene. The lasting myth of Fauré the salon musician and composer of charming but lightweight songs was formed during this period; Marcel Proust had yet to redeem and immortalise the salons and their artistic products in *A la Recherche du temps perdu*. At the salons of Marguerite Baugnies (later Mme de Saint-Marceaux), Fauré would meet friends like Messager and Ravel, and important artistic figures like Debussy, Ricardo Viñes, Anatole France and Colette, who describes these Wednesday evening gatherings around 1900 in her *Journal à rebours* as[15]

> not merely a diversion for the worldly and the curious, but. . .the bastion of an intimate artistic world. . . .A dinner, invariably excellent, always preceded these musical evenings, during which the mistress of the house achieved an atmosphere of 'supervised freedom'. She never forced anyone to listen to the music, but she would immediately suppress the slightest hint of whispering. Everyone was at liberty to arrive at whatever time best suited him, provided only that the men were dressed in jackets and the women in day-dresses. . .If Fauré were to come on from his duchesses in evening dress and play the dandy. . .then Messager, who is coquetry itself, would feel humiliated and start wearing that dismal, put-upon look of his.

Colette also describes how Fauré and Messager[16]

> improvised piano duets, rivalling each other in their sudden modulations and evasions of the tonic. They both loved these games during which they exchanged attacks like duellists: 'Pull up there! Why are you waiting? Go on, I will catch you up!' Fauré, like a dark-skinned emir, nodded his tuft of silvery hair when giving the signal to use leitmotifs from the Ring.

Fauré frequented the gatherings of Madeleine Lemaire and the Comtesse Greffulhe, as well as those of the Princesse de Polignac. These last in the Rue Cortambert, Paris 16, were a rendezvous for the avant-garde where Fauré met composers like Chabrier, Manuel de Falla, Satie and Stravinsky. Here private premières of Fauré's music took place and Fauré dedicated *Larmes* (op. 51/1), the *Cinq mélodies 'de Venise'* and his *Pelléas et Mélisande* music to the Princess 'Winnie'—more pieces than to any other person except Emma Bardac.

Fauré's next important commission, the powerful lyric tragedy *Prométhée*, again came through Saint-Saëns. The town of Béziers in Languedoc, just east of Fauré's native district of Ariège, had an amphitheatre constructed on ancient Greek lines in 1896, and a wealthy patron in M. Castelbon de Beauxhostes who, with Saint-Saëns's *Déjanire* in 1898, inaugurated a series of highly successful open-air festivals there. The works were modelled on classical Greek tragedies with spoken dialogue and musical interludes. *Prométhée* has a text by Jean Lorrain and Ferdinand Hérold after Aeschylus which describes Prométhée stealing the fire from heaven and the Gods' revenge in the form of Pandore's box filled with human sufferings.

The forces used were enormous: the choruses of Prométhée's companions and the Ocean Nymphs (his sympathizers in misfortune) totalled some 200 singers, together with 400 musicians in three groups. First, 'La Lyre bitteroise'—a local orchestral society. Second, the bands of the 17th Regiment of Infantry at Béziers and the 2nd Regiment of Engineers from Montpellier. To these were added 100 string players from Paris, 18 harps, 30 trumpets, 50 dancers, and the soloists: M. de Max (Prométhée); Cora Laparcerie (Pandore); Odette de Fehl (Hermès); from the Paris Opéra, Rose Feldy (Gaïa), M. Fonteix (Kratos), Mme Fierens-Peters (Bia), Charles Rousselière (Andros—and later Ulysse in *Pénélope*); and from the Théâtre de la Monnaie, Brussels, M. Vallier (Héphaïstos). Altogether Fauré had nearly 800 performers to deal with, some of whom thought that their parts should be more spectacularly operatic, and Fauré was no doubt glad he had left the wind band orchestration to the conductor of the Montpellier contingent, Charles Eustace.

The events surrounding the final rehearsals are well known; a terrific thunderstorm virtually destroyed the set on 26 August 1900, the day before the delayed première. Coincidentally the lightning struck the exact spot where Prométhée was to steal the fire, and Pierre Lalo in *Le Temps* drew the obvious parallel. After a superhuman round-the-clock effort by all concerned, the première before some 10,000 people was a triumphant success, Fauré's music being especially praised. Many considered that it saved the day and found the spoken parts for Prométhée and Pandore feeble and overlong. Saint-Saëns told Fauré: 'With your *Prométhée* you have astounded your colleagues, including me' (LI, p. 50). 'The wind dispersed the sounds a bit', Fauré added in his report to his wife, 'but the performance was as good as it could possibly be.' The Béziers festival never again quite reached the zenith of 1900, and Fauré found that re-creating *Prométhée* the following summer was by no means a straightforward task, despite the assistance of Saint-Saëns and Roger-Ducasse. Indoor revivals, such as that of 5 December 1907 at the Ancien Hippodrome in Paris for the flood victims of the Hérault, met with little artistic success, though transference of this production to the Paris Opéra, using the sets designed for *Die Walküre*, improved matters somewhat. This hybrid work has, however, succeeded rather better in a concert version with a reduced arrangement for symphony orchestra by Roger-Ducasse and Fauré, though when Guy Ropartz wanted to perform it in Strasbourg in November 1922 there was still only one full score available, and Hamelle were reluctant to send the manuscript through the post! (BN, La 92).

About the time of *Prométhée*, Fauré met the young pianist Marguerite Hasselmans who was to become his artistic companion and favourite interpreter in later life. Her father Adolphe Hasselmans was professor of the harp at the Conservatoire and Fauré dedicated the Impromptu for harp (op. 86) to him in 1904.

After 1900 official recognition came more quickly to Fauré. He was appointed professor of composition at the École Niedermeyer in 1901 and Gaston Calmette invited him to be music critic of *Le Figaro* in March 1903. Each article he wrote was for Fauré a 'forced labour, sometimes a torment' (FF, p. 87), as he had no solid literary background. The help of his friend André Beaunier was invaluable in his early days in this field. Fauré's *Figaro* appointment coincided with the serious development of the deafness that was to plague him for the rest of his life. The first mention Fauré makes of deafness comes in a letter to his wife, written whilst recuperating after the revival of *Prométhée* with his brother Fernand and his brother-in-law Casimir Fontes at Bagnères-de-Bigorre in 1901. Fontes had suddenly become extremely deaf and Fauré was sufficiently frightened to consider regular visits to an aural surgeon on his return to Paris. 'I understand fully the anguish of this affliction', he told his wife on 1 September (LI, p. 63), 'which for me would be the worst thing possible!' Whilst helping Saint-Saëns with *Parysatis* at Béziers in August 1902, Fauré complained that 'his ears had been behaving poorly all the while here' (LI, p. 69), and in the summer of 1903 the first positive signs of deafness emerged. This worried Fauré throughout August 1903, and he drew the inevitable comparison with Beethoven on 12 August. 'There are certain phrases of music of which I hear nothing whatsoever, whether it is my own music or not', he lamented to Marie (LI, p. 73). Hopes of an improvement on 1 September, when Fauré wrote that he had 'had less trouble with my piano over the last few days' and had not 'heard those double sounds' which were driving him mad, proved ill-founded. Whilst he complained little in later life, he only heard his opera *Pénélope* and other later works in his head.

Fauré described his particularly cruel form of deafness most fully on 1 April 1919 after attending a Verdi opera in Monte Carlo (LI, p. 254). In this the sounds were

> so wildly distorted that I thought I was going mad. With the spoken word, to be deaf is to hear very feebly and indistinctly; but when it comes to music, my deafness produces an extraordinary phenomenon. The lower-pitched intervals are distorted in proportion to the amount they descend, and the high-pitched intervals are distorted in proportion to the amount they ascend. Can you imagine the result of this divergence? It is infernal. . .it was thus that I heard *Pénélope*. Singing is the least painful music for me to listen to, but instrumental music is all chaos and suffering.

His son Philippe tells us (FF, p. 96) that Fauré actually heard the low notes as much as a third *sharp* and the high notes a third *flat*. Only the middle register was accurate, but faint.

Fauré's deafness was undoubtedly linked with the arterio-sclerosis that affected him progressively in his later life, but this convergence of pitch is excessively rare, if not unique. The opinion of Mr John Ballantyne, a leading Harley Street otologist, is that Fauré's sensori-neural deafness was connected with the recruitment phenomenon in the cochlea and was consistent with the effects of ageing (presbyacusis). Fauré's deafness was not due to obstruction or lack of conduction in the middle ear like Beethoven's, but to increasingly poor function of the sensory nerves from the inner ear to the hearing centres and auditory cortex.[17] It seems unlikely that there was anything hereditary in Fauré's affliction, or that syphilis played any part in it, as it did with Smetana. Another specialist, Mr Andrew Morrison, suggests that Fauré possibly also had hydrops of the inner ear, and his attacks of dizziness in the 1880s may be connected with his later problem. The reason why instrumental music affected him so much more than vocal music is surely due to the far greater range of harmonics produced in the former, and Professor Trethowan of Birmingham University suggests that, if the various instruments were deprived of their harmonics or had their harmonics distorted by Fauré's hearing mechanism, then their pitch might become increasingly difficult to identify, especially in those instruments having a higher range of harmonics. The only suffering which the deafness caused was musical, and speech seems to have been unaffected. The deepening and interiorization of Fauré's musical thought in his final period has often been compared with that of Beethoven, though the changes of style that took place within Fauré's final period suggest that the direct effects of deafness on his music have perhaps been overestimated.

The repercussions of Ravel's repeated failure to win the Prix de Rome in the early years of this century, despite masterpieces like *Jeux d'eau* and the String Quartet, proved as significant for Fauré as they did for his pupil. Quite why Ravel persisted in his quest is another matter, but Théodore Dubois' and the committee's refusal to allow him to proceed to the final part of the *concours* in 1905 caused a sort of musical Dreyfus affair, even though his virtually illegible fugue and his chorus *L'Aurore* were full of harmonic 'errors'. Dubois was obliged to resign and, to the amazement of all concerned, Fauré, who had championed his pupil's cause throughout, was appointed in his place on 1 June. Fauré's nomination by Dujardin-Beaumetz, the Under-Secretary for Fine Arts, was perhaps the deliberate expression of a fresh approach to the sterile institution that the Conservatoire was generally thought to have become. For Fauré had no Prix de Rome and had never even attended the 'holy of holies'. He was still, in effect, the junior professor of composition at the Conservatoire too, having been appointed after Widor and Lenepveu. The gentle Fauré proved a surprisingly positive director, living up to Dujardin-Beaumetz's expectations with a plan of reforms whose ensuing resignations earned him the nickname of 'Robespierre'.

Fauré's seven-point reform plan was formulated with Dujardin-Beaumetz and Jean d'Estournelles de Constant, head of the French Theatre Board, and published in *Musica* in November 1905. First, there were to be separate professors of counterpoint and fugue, and separate classes for each subject. Secondly, the vocal classes were to be reorganized, with first-year students studying exercises and *vocalises* only. Thirdly, Fauré removed the obligation of those studying dramatic and lyrical singing to choose only scenes from the current theatrical repertoire. Fourthly, increasing emphasis was to be placed on ensemble classes in vocal, orchestral and chamber music, and they were to start much earlier in the year, by mid-November at the latest. Fifthly, the renowned history course of Bourgault-Ducoudray was to be attended by all students of composition and harmony and was to assume a more experimental and technical approach to give young musicians a more complete musical education. Pupils in the instrumental and vocal classes were to be enlisted to provide music examples for the lectures. Sixthly, the Government agreed to officially engage the two students gaining first prizes in the *opéra-comique* class, if their artistry justified this. The Paris Opéra was no longer to have precedence over the Opéra-Comique in choosing the best singers and, in cases of dispute, the Ministry of Fine Arts would act as arbitrator. Lastly, the January term-time exams were to be abolished for instrumental candidates, to give them more time to participate in the extra ensemble classes that Fauré had created. Further, Fauré made sure that he was to be artistic director of the Conservatoire only. Although Fernand Bourgeat was appointed to deal with the administrative and economic problems, Fauré still found himself faced with more insignificant matters than he had wished for in time set aside for composition.

Revolt began less than three months after Fauré's appointment, though it was due less to the reforms outlined above than to the formation of selection committees for student admission. This reduced the influence professors had in securing the entry of their own private pupils to the Conservatoire, and they saw their prestige and a necessary supplement to their low Conservatoire pay threatened. Fortunately, Fauré received full support from above in his firm stand against petty corruption and he solved the problem of the malcontents by appointing alongside them people with whom they would find it impossible to coexist! This invariably led to resignations, and even Dubois resigned from the Superior Council (where he had remained as emeritus professor) in November 1905, when Pierre Lalo was appointed there too. It ironically fell to Lalo as critic of *Le Temps* to comment publicly on Dubois' resignation. Officially this had been because 'Fauré was transforming the Conservatoire into a temple for music of the future', but Lalo sagely observed that Fauré's widening of both the scope and audience for Bourgault-Ducoudray's history lectures introduced Palestrina, Monteverdi, Schütz and Rameau to students who were blissfully ignorant of their existence under Dubois' directorship (*Le Temps*, 21 November 1905)! Fauré understood better than anyone that the 'wider one's knowledge of old music, the keener will be one's perception of the new' (Su, p. 31), and he more than compensated for Dubois' departure by the appointment of Debussy and d'Indy to the Superior Council, a move wholly in line with his declared policies. He also made Ravel a member of the counterpoint jury in 1906 as a final blow to Dubois.

On 13 March 1909, Fauré was finally elected a member of the Institute when the death of the composer Ernest Reyer left a vacant seat in the Academy of Fine Arts, one of its four constituent academies. Membership was normally an automatic adjunct to the directorship of the Conservatoire, but Fauré only narrowly defeated his old rival Widor by 18 votes to 16. His success was due largely to an active campaign on his behalf by Saint-Saëns, who returned from Algeria specially, and by his father-in-law Fremiet. Fauré was in Barcelona when the decision was reached, performing in a series of concerts arranged by his friend Isaac Albéniz (1860–1909), with whom he stayed (see plate XX). Fauré had attempted to interest Albert Carré, the director of the Opéra-Comique, in Albéniz's two-act opera *Pépita Jimenez* in August 1905 because Albéniz was 'a Spanish composer who was authentically Spanish', and because he was a 'timid man who needed someone to intervene for him'.[18] Perhaps Fauré himself was too timid in his approaches to Carré, for *Pépita Jimenez* was not performed at the Opéra-Comique until June 1923.

The other significant event of 1909 was the foundation of the SMI, a breakaway group from the old SN. The initiative came from Ravel, as a letter to Charles Koechlin on 16 January shows.[19] Fauré accepted the presidentship even though he had been, and still remained, a founder member of the SN. He knew he would appear to be a conspirator and he did not actively participate in the SMI committee meetings, which involved Ravel, Louis Aubert, André Caplet, Paul Dukas, Jean Huré, Koechlin, A. Z. Mathot, Florent Schmitt and Louis Vuillemin, some of whom can be seen in plate XXI. The aims of the

SMI were to 'make known through performance French or foreign modern music, published or unpublished, without exceptions of genre or style', and the troublesome new society can be seen as a reaction against the pro-Schola Cantorum bias of the SN under Vincent d'Indy.

Ravel had had a series of difficulties with the SN: his overture *Shéhérazade* was accepted for performance only in May 1899 after strenuous efforts by Fauré on his behalf; the première of his *Histoires naturelles* song-cycle by Jane Bathori on 12 January 1907 created yet another scandal. Ravel sensed that he and new music generally were being ostracised by the reactionary SN committee, and that he, Schmitt and Roussel were only insignificant members of it. The final straw came when a symphonic poem by Ravel's pupil Maurice Delage (*Conté par la mer*) was rejected by the committee, d'Indy claiming erroneously[20] that it contained an unplayable low C for the horn! Charles Koechlin's orchestral work *Les Temples* (*Études antiques*, op. 46/1) was also played to the SN committee on 14 January 1909 and rejected the following day; it was perhaps for this reason that Ravel wrote to Koechlin first with his proposal to form a 'new and more independent society'.

At the first SMI concert on 20 April 1910, Fauré accompanied Jeanne Raunay in the première of his complete song cycle *La Chanson d'Ève,* and the concert also included the first performance of Debussy's *D'un cahier d'esquisses* played by Ravel, and Ravel's own *Ma Mère l'Oye.* Fauré defended the SMI against attack from d'Indy, stressing that his reasons in so doing were purely musical. He had 'complete confidence' in the new society, where he was happy to discover men who were both 'old pupils and faithful friends' (*Comoedia*, 20 April 1910).

Being head of the Conservatoire forced Fauré to take the most positive and controversial decisions of his life, and controversial decisions were things he avoided like the plague. His new position brought him welcome financial independence from organ playing, teaching and provincial inspections; miraculously he found time to write a great deal of superb music too, including *Pénélope* in the summers of 1907–12, the composition of which is traced in detail in chapter 6.

Fauré could now travel when and because he chose to, to propagate his music. 1908 saw him back in England again on two occasions. On the first he accompanied a 'young American singer [Miss Susan Metcalfe] whose father and mother were American and Swiss and who was born in Florence and looked Japanese!' (LI, p. 160) in a private song recital before Queen Alexandra and the Russian Empress Marie Feodorovna at Buckingham Palace on the afternoon of 23 March. *Les Berceaux*, *Le Secret*, *La Sérénade toscane*, *Après un rêve*, *Les Roses d'Ispahan* and *Nell* evidently went down so well that the Queen wished 'to visit *our* Conservatoire and come into some of the *classes*! I know she is deaf, but she isn't blind, and she will no doubt be disconcerted by our miserable conditions!', Fauré told his wife. Needless to say, his fears proved groundless for Queen Alexandra never found the time to carry out her threat.

Fauré's second English visit came as a result of the Entente Cordiale between Britain and France declared in 1904. By 1908 the French Concerts Society in Manchester, run by the enterprising Mme Barbier with lectures and visiting celebrity concerts, was in full battle against the pro-Germanic programmes of the resident Hallé Orchestra (see Stonequist, 1972, p. 24f.). On 30 November 1908, Fauré accompanied Mrs George Swinton in various songs, the faithful Lady Speyer in his Violin Sonata and Louis Fleury in the *Fantaisie* for flute (op. 79) in a concert shared with Ethel Smyth. Fauré found Manchester 'black, smoky, foggy and altogether terrible!'; London seemed an 'Eden' in comparison (LI, p. 174). This was not pure French chauvinism on Fauré's part, as a *Manchester Guardian* editorial of 28 March 1910 explained that opera would never be as successful as orchestral music in Manchester because its grey skies and murky atmosphere were 'unfavourable to a refined sense of visual form and colour'!

In September 1908 Fauré attended the concerts at the French Festival in Munich, and in November that year he stayed with Dr Frenkel in Berlin where his music was well received. In 1910, like Berlioz in 1867 and Debussy in 1913, he scored an enormous success in Russia, visiting St Petersburg and Moscow as well as Helsinki. 'What a pity that Dubois and Widor are not able to see this for themselves', he told his wife from Finland on 14 November (LI, p. 192); 'the younger members of the audience shouted, "Fauré! Fauré!" as if to bring the house down!' Plate XXII shows Fauré in Moscow with the pianist Raoul Pugno and the violinist Eugène Ysaÿe, all fascinated by performing toy animals. Evidently this was a welcome relaxation from their concert perform- ances which included the First Quintet (op. 89) and the Violin Sonata. The enthusiastic audiences in Russia were especially encouraging, for the summer had been an anguished and unproductive one for Fauré. Whilst at Bad-Ems in August in the hope of finding a cure for his increasing deafness, he was worried by the developments of what turned out to be his father-in-law Emmanuel Fremiet's final illness.

Fauré had left Hamelle for the publisher Heugel in 1906; he made his final change to Durand in 1913. In the same year on 4 March, *Pénélope* received its first performance at Monte Carlo with Lucienne Bréval as Pénélope and Charles Rousselière as Ulysse. Léon Jéhin was the conductor and musical director and the scenery was by Visconti. Although the director Raoul Gunsbourg had been in on the project from the start, he never understood the significance of the opera and

25

devoted most of his attention to production details. Fauré was frustrated once the responsibility for *Pénélope* had passed out of his hands, and he lamented to his wife on 21 February (LI, p. 215) that, 'except for Jéhin and Rousselière, no one seems interested in my work'. Saint-Saëns wrote to Durand on 5 March after the première that 'Gunsbourg's conduct had been infamous; he did all he could to thwart *Pénélope* for the benefit of his own opera *Venise*' (Nectoux, *RdM*, 1973, p. 62 nl) which was in production at the same time. Saint-Saëns told Fauré on 12 March (id. pp. 62–3) that the singers could not be heard, the brass were too noisy, and the 'suitors lacked youth and distinction'! He also criticised René Fauchois' inaccuracy in the bow scene in Act 3: bending the bow and stringing it for shooting were two different things. Fauchois had also misinterpreted Homer in his libretto by allowing the suitors to flirt with the servants in front of Pénélope, though these points probably did not occur to Fauré, who was less literary-minded and certainly no purist.

Fauré's letter to his wife after the première (LI, p. 217) shows that he considered Monte Carlo as a rehearsal for the Paris gala performance on 9 May, organised by Gabriel Astruc for his new Théâtre des Champs-Élysées. His letters to the singers show how concerned he was that his opera should be a success in Paris. Here Rousselière was replaced by Lucien Muratore as Ulysse and Louis Hasselmans conducted the orchestra. Improved direction by Durec and scenery by Ker-Xavier Roussel (see plate XXIV) resulted in an overwhelming artistic success, though both *Pénélope* and Debussy's ballet *Jeux*, which opened in the same theatre with Diaghilev's Ballets Russes six days later, were overshadowed by the *succès de scandale* of Stravinsky's *Rite of Spring* on 29 May. *Pénélope* received only six performances that season. As the pianist Édouard Risler prophetically told Fauré during the Monte Carlo rehearsals: 'Your opera will last, but it will take a long time to establish itself' (LI, p. 217). Astruc's Paris revival in October 1913 was less carefully prepared than the May performances because of his impending bankruptcy, and October was the worst month of the new season, as Fauré realised. *Pénélope* was more enthusiastically received at the Théâtre de la Monnaie in Brussels in December 1913, but the war prevented Gheusi's proposed production at the Opéra-Comique. By the time *Pénélope* finally reached the Opéra-Comique stage on 20 January 1919 the initial enthusiasm for the opera had evaporated. Although the libretto has its weaknesses, it is no worse than those of many other successful operas, and there is no real reason why *Pénélope* should exist more in theory than in practice in the French opera repertory. There were no performances at the Opéra-Comique after 1931; it was revived in the more suitable Paris Opéra on 14 March

1943 with Germaine Lubin in the title role, but has only enjoyed about 100 performances to this day. In comparison, an opera like Charpentier's *Louise* achieved 940 performances in the 50 years following its première in 1900.

In June 1914 Fauré made his last visit to England to hear his complete piano works performed by Robert Lortat in three concerts in the Aeolian Hall, London. He dedicated the Twelfth Nocturne to Lortat the following year and spent a second idyllic holiday in Venice with Lortat and his wife in September 1920, referring as always to the city in terms of its enchantment and seductive charm.

When Germany declared war on France on 3 August 1914, Fauré was again at Ems in Germany, where he had gone to convalesce and compose the first songs of his cycle *Le Jardin clos*. By the time he came to leave, the French border was closed and Fauré had to travel by train to Saint-Louis, then on via Basle to Geneva, partly on foot and partly by car. Only with great difficulty did he finally regain the safety of Paris. He remained in France throughout the war, mainly in Paris during the academic year, and he spent the summers of 1915 and 1917 in small hotels at Saint-Raphaël, and those of 1916 and 1918 at Évian on the shore of Lake Geneva. He was also forced to take a two-month holiday in Nice in February to April 1918 as his bronchitis that winter had been particularly severe. These were the years of the powerful, energetic and often violent compositions like the Second Violin Sonata (op. 108), the First Cello Sonata (op. 109) and the *Fantaisie* for piano and orchestra (op. 111). He was no doubt very worried about his son Philippe who was on active service, and the pieces he wrote at this time contrast markedly with the more spiritual and confident works of the post-war years.

One positive result of the war years which came about mainly for economic reasons was the proposed fusion of the SN and the SMI late in 1916. On being told that Fauré would be president of the amalgamated society and d'Indy only a committee member, Ravel agreed to the idea. But determined opposition from Charles Koechlin, who pointed out that the two societies were still radically opposed, and objections from d'Indy, who agreed with Koechlin from the other side of the fence, kept the societies apart. It again fell to the lot of the diplomatic and tactful Fauré as president of both societies to maintain the balance. Whilst he gave all his later premières to the SN and made a determined appeal for the burial of hatchets in the *Courrier Musical* in March 1917[21], an act of union did not take place, and it was the SMI who mounted the concert in Fauré's honour on 13 December 1922 to perform the pieces written by his ex-pupils for the special commemorative edition of *La Revue Musicale* of October 1922.

This tribute to Fauré was also a fund-raising activity, for Fauré's increasing deafness and infirmity had led to his being tactfully asked to resign his Conservatoire directorship in 1919 by the Ministry of Fine Arts. The small pension eventually awarded him when he left on 1 October 1920 meant that once again his financial position was insecure. The problem was that Fauré had only been in official Government service for 24 years, and it took a considerable effort by Paul Léon, the Minister for Fine Arts, to secure him a pension at all; making him a Grand Officer of the Légion d'Honneur helped only his pride.

Financial considerations compelled both Fauré and Debussy to turn their hands to editing during the war. The cutting of supplies from Germany led Durand to commission new editions of the classics and Fauré was asked to study and revise Schumann's piano music in 1915 (see LI, pp. 227–8). He also collaborated with Joseph Bonnet (1884–1944) between 1916 and 1920 on a new edition of the organ works of J. S. Bach, though neither his nor Debussy's methods were what we would today call scholarly, having little recourse to original manuscripts or early editions. In September 1918, Fauré accepted a commission from Prince Albert I of Monaco for a one-act choreographic diversion *Masques et Bergamasques*, a suggestion that Fauré was certain had come from Saint-Saëns (LI, p. 245). The spectacle was to include several earlier works (see Appendix B) and was in fact 'a more complete realization of a musical event that took place in the home of Madeleine Lemaire ten or twelve years ago [actually in June 1902]. This will not cost me a great deal of trouble', Fauré told his wife on 13 September (LI, p. 245), 'and will guarantee that I can stay in the south of France in February and March' 1919. The feather-light overture, which Reynaldo Hahn astutely described as 'Mozart imitating Fauré', shows the composer unashamedly enjoying himself for the last time, though this too is based on an earlier composition of 1867–8.

In the summer of 1919 Fauré stayed with M. and Mme Fernand Maillot at their lakeside home in Annecy-le-Vieux in Haute Savoie, the first of several visits which considerably brightened Fauré's last years. Staying with friends perhaps recaptured the happy summers of his youth and was infinitely preferable to small Riviera hotels. Fauré's creative vigour far outstripped his physical capabilities though he remained active to the last. His final concert at Tours took place as late as 1921 at the age of 76.

Fauré was at last able to devote himself to full-time composition, and his final years produced an unexpected wealth of fine works: the song cycle *Mirages* written at Annecy in the summer of 1919 and the Second Quintet completed slowly between 1919 and 1921, to cite but two. The middle movements of the Quintet were begun at Monte Carlo and Nice in the winter of 1919–20 and completed at Veyrier-du-Lac near Annecy in the summer of 1920. The first movement was added in the autumn of 1920 after Fauré returned from Venice, and the finale was completed in Nice in February 1921.

After the Thirteenth Nocturne, his last work for the piano written in only 10 days at the end of 1921 in Nice, Fauré composed nothing for several months and even feared that his abundant invention had dried up. He did, however, write two articles in 1922 for *La Revue Musicale*. The first, a moving obituary for his lifelong friend Saint-Saëns, appeared in February; the second took him back to the days of his youth as he recalled his years at the École Niedermeyer for the special Fauré edition in October.

The success of a Festival organized in his honour by Fernand Maillot at the amphitheatre at the Sorbonne on 20 June 1922 gave Fauré enormous pleasure. All his best interpreters were anxious to be present. The Société des Concerts du Conservatoire provided an orchestra and choir, performing the early *Cantique de Jean Racine* and selections from his theatre music. Pablo Casals played the *Élégie* for cello (op. 24) and Alfred Cortot the *Ballade*; the orchestra was conducted variously by Henri Rabaud, Vincent d'Indy, Philippe Gaubert, Henri Büsser and André Messager. Claire Croiza was accompanied by Cortot, Jeanne Raunay by Robert Lortat, and the baritone Charles Panzéra by his wife Magdeleine Panzéra-Baillot. In his tribute, Panzéra included the cycle *L'Horizon chimérique* which Fauré had dedicated to him the previous year. The concert culminated in the Second Quintet and lasted till 1 o'clock the following morning, and the presence of the President of the Republic Alexandre Millerand turned the event into a national tribute.

Fauré spent his last three summers at Annecy-le-Vieux, writing the slow movement of his Piano Trio there in 1922 and completing the work in Paris by the spring of 1923. In his last two years Fauré grew increasingly feeble and easily exhausted, being unable even to walk for much of the winter of 1923. That summer he had embarked in absolute secrecy on his String Quartet with the difficulty of the medium and Beethoven's overshadowing example ever in mind. Fernand Maillot organized a performance of his *Requiem* together with extracts from Honegger's *King David* in the little church at Annecy on 25 August. His son Philippe attended the performance, and Fauré told his wife in delight that 'he had received a small ovation outside the church, including a little country girl who offered me a bouquet, just as they do for M. Poincaré' (LI, p. 288). By 12 September he had finished the slow movement of his Quartet, to which the first was added in Paris in the autumn.

In June-July 1924 Fauré spent a month at Divonne-les-Bains, mostly confined to his room contemplating the beautiful view and working on the finale of the Quartet. Fernand Maillot took him by car to Annecy on 24 July where, contrary to all expectation, he finished the Quartet in one last tremendous effort by 11 September. The last movement brought him great inner joy and satisfaction but it was a 'discreet and veiled joy, a sort of dance of happy souls which blended with the other parts of the work' (LI, p. 290).

On 19 September Fauré took to his bed with double pneumonia, confiding to Marguerite Hasselmans his last wishes for the Quartet which are recalled by his son Philippe (FF, p. 127). Roger-Ducasse was to add the nuances and performance details that he had not had time to write in, as he knew Fauré's music better than anyone. This done, the Quartet was not to be

> published and played until it had been tried out before the small group of friends who always hear my works first: Dukas, Poujaud, Lalo, Bellaigue, Lallemand, etc. I have confidence in their judgment and it is to them that I give the responsibility of deciding whether the Quartet should be published or destroyed. If it is performed, I should like the proceeds of the première to be given to the Société des Anciens Élèves du Conservatoire.

Fauré seemed to rally a little in October, although he was less well than he maintained. His last letter to his wife of 14 October (LI, pp. 294–5) is extremely touching and philosophical, recalling the inauguration of a statue by his father-in-law in the Jardin des Plantes and ordering all his musical sketches to be destroyed. The mood is one of calm resignation and reflection; he sympathises with Marie's unhappy life and her inability to realize her own ambitions. But successfully bringing up their sons in these troubled times should have given her satisfaction and happiness, and he asks her to tell him where there has been another wife who has been 'so proud of the pure beauty of her father's creations and at the same time so proud of the similarly beautiful and disinterested works and career of her husband'.

On 18 October Fauré returned by train to Paris to spend his last days with his family. He died quietly at 1.50 am on 4 November 1924; his faithful wife died less than a year later. Fauré's last words to his sons on 3 November were (FF, pp. 129–30):

> When I am no longer here you will hear it said of my works: 'After all, that was nothing much to write home about!' You must not let that hurt or depress you. It is the way of the world; it happened with Saint-Saëns and with others. There is always a moment of oblivion. But all that is of no importance. I did what I could . . . now . . . let God judge!

Fauré, the composer so lacking in ambition and 'arrivisme', was given a State funeral at the Madeleine attended by the President of the Republic and the Archbishop of Paris. His own music appropriately accompanied the proceedings: the Nocturne from *Shylock* and excerpts from the *Requiem* sung by Charles Panzéra and Jeanne Laval. The coffin left for the cemetery at Passy to the poignant adagio that Fauré had written for the death of Mélisande in 1898. Speeches were made by various notables, including the Minister of Public Instruction, François Albert, who is supposed to have replied 'Fauré? Who's he?' when first asked to arrange the ceremony! Doubtless he was not the only one present hearing Fauré's music for the first time; Fauré's English host Frank Schuster rushed to Paris to hear the *Requiem* that was not performed in his own country until 1936, as well as to pay his last respects to a dear friend.

Many tributes were published after Fauré's death, but perhaps the most touching is that of Albert Roussel (*Comoedia*, 6 November 1924):

> An essentially French genius, he occupied a place apart in the history of music and, without noise or fuss or meaningless gestures, he pointed the way towards marvellous horizons overflowing with freshness and light where our musicians, for many years to come, will hear re-echoing the harmonious sounds of his voice.

As Leslie Orrey says in *Musical Opinion* (1945, p. 197), Fauré's life 'offers little scope for the romantic biographer, there is no scandal to whip up the interest; no multifarious love affairs; no eccentricities, even in appearance; and the erratic "temperament" associated in the popular mind with the artistic life is conspicuously absent'. The definitive biography of Fauré has yet to be written and all-inclusiveness is not the aim of the present study. Perhaps when a fuller study is published the 'multifarious love affairs' that one suspects the discreet Fauré to have indulged in will form a central panel. I hope not, for there are far more worthwhile avenues to explore than Fauré's undoubted attraction for women. Nonetheless, as Saint-Saëns told him in 1909 (Nectoux, *RdM*, 1972, p. 242), 'it is above all through women that one gets into the Academy', and women proved indispensable to Fauré's advancement as a composer. 'He lacked the honour and benefit of having enemies', Julien Torchet shrewdly observed in *Musica* in the same year (February 1909, p. 28) and, if Fauré had no real enemies, he had many, many friends. Perhaps the aspect of his character that these friends found most attractive, besides his modesty and his equanimity of temperament, was his strongly developed sense of humour. He was a gifted caricaturist (see plates XXVIII and XXIX) and he also had a talent for light verse. In the depressing Rennes period, Fauré and M. Tannery, a mathematician friend, indulged in sonnets in the style of François Coppée (1842–1908) like (FF, p. 54):

> Je regardais passer l'omnibus sur le pont,
> Avec cet air pensif que les omnibus ont.

31

The cover of his sketchbook for *Pénélope* shows Fauré's love of countering the serious with the ridiculous in its song of the seagulls as yet another boat provides them with a fresh supply of food and fascination:

Et les mouettes
En troupe élevant leur essor,
S'écrient: 'Chouette!
Encore un bateau qui sort du port!'[22]

A far cry indeed from the verses Fauré set for *L'Horizon chimérique*.

An interview with Fauré's son Emmanuel conducted shortly before his death in 1971 by Jean-Michel Nectoux affords us a rare glimpse of Fauré's domestic life (BAF, 1972, pp. 12–18). As Fauré did so much teaching himself in his early career, he entrusted his sons' musical education to his pupil Roger-Ducasse. He seems to have been kindly and tolerant as a father, and Emmanuel describes how, when he got angry but could say nothing, as with musical disagreements at the Madeleine, three yellow lines would appear on his face. But what upset him most was the amateur music-making of the Cantegrel family in the flat below him at 154 Boulevard Malesherbes. 'It is as if they were wrenching off the strings' of their instruments he would say, and whenever he could he went out on Tuesday evenings, for it was then that they 'rehearsed'! (Pitrou, 1957, p. 80).

Footnotes to chap. 1

1. Paris, Éditions Rieder, 1929/revised ed., Albin Michel, 1957. Much of the information on Fauré's early life derives from this source.
2. See Fauré's article on Saint-Saëns, *ReM* (1 February 1922).
3. He also came to visit Fauré and his parents at Tarbes in the summer of 1862.
4. Ernest Renan (1823–92) the historian, philologist and critic was then professor of Hebrew at the Collège de France. Louis Blanc (1811–82), left-wing politician and historian, had recently published a *History of the 1848 Revolution* in which he had played a substantial part. Ivan Turgenev (1818–83), the 'gentle barbarian', as the Goncourt brothers described him, had been the most important Russian novelist and interpreter of things Russian in the West since he took up residence in Paris in 1856. His life centred on his love for Pauline Viardot-Garcia who led him on a string for 40 years. Fauré referred to him in correspondence with the Viardots as his 'godfather'.
5. See 'Flaubert, Gallet, Fauré ou Le Démon du Théâtre', *Bulletin du Bibliophile*, no. 1 (1976), pp. 33–47.
6. He left his post as organist at Notre-Dame-de-Clignancourt in 1870 because he had deliberately been to see Meyerbeer's *Les Huguenots* according to *Le Petit Parisien* (28 April 1922), p. 1.
7. Probably the *Cantico del Sol di San Francesco d'Assisi*, originally written for chorus in 1862 and transcribed for piano in 1881. Fauré imagined the

work to be a recent composition because it was still in manuscript. M. Nectoux on pp. 68–9 of his *Gabriel Fauré: Correspondance* (Paris, Flammarion, 1980) suggests that Fauré showed the piano *solo* version of his *Ballade* to Liszt on this visit, when, because of its difficulty, Liszt suggested a version with orchestra, which was duly presented for approval at their second meeting in Zürich in July 1882.

8 and 9. Quoted in 'Memories of Debussy and his Circle' by Mme Gaston de Tinan, *Journal of the British Institute of Recorded Sound*, no. 50–51 (April-July 1973), p. 162.

10. See Orledge, R.: 'Fauré en Angleterre', *BAF*, no. 13 (1976), pp. 10–16 for further details about Metzler and Co, and Fauré's English visits.

11 and 13. Unpublished letter, received 11 July 1898.

12. See Lionel Carley: *Delius. The Paris Years*, Swansea, Triad Press, 1975, pp. 61 and 74.

14. Letter of 29 October [1898]. Fauré stayed with Frederick Oliver Robinson, Earl de Grey, and his wife when he came over for the first English all-Fauré concert given by Léon Delafosse on 10 December 1896. Earl de Grey, like Lord Charles Beresford, had been one of the First Lords of the Admiralty and acted as Secretary of State for the Colonies between 1892 and 1895. The latter became MP for York in 1898. Mrs Swinton (née Elizabeth Ebsworth) married George Sitwell Campbell-Swinton of Kimmerghame, Co Berwick, a captain in the 71st Highland Light Infantry, in October 1895.

15. Quoted in Colette: *Earthly Paradise*. An autobiography drawn from her lifetime writings by Robert Phelps, London, reprinted Penguin Books, 1974, pp. 308–9. Translation by Derek Coltman.

16. From Colette: *Maurice Ravel par quelques-uns de ses familiers*, Paris, Éditions du Tambourinaire, 1939. Quoted in *Journal Musical Français*, no. 131 (10 October 1964), p. 6. The passage probably refers to a performance of their party piece, the *Souvenirs de Bayreuth* (1888) rather than anything specially improvised.

17. I am grateful to Dr Ingle Wright, Senior Lecturer in Otolaryngology at Manchester University for this information.

18. La in the Pierpont Morgan Library (Mary Flagler Cary Music Collection), New York.

19. See J.-M. Nectoux: 'Ravel, Fauré et les débuts de la SMI', *RdM*, LXI (1975), pp. 301–11 for more details. The letter in question is quoted on pp. 302–3.

20. According to José Bruyr: *Maurice Ravel*, Paris, Plon, 1950, p. 120.

21. 'Appel aux musiciens français', *Courrier Musical* (15 March 1917). See Nectoux, *RdM*, 1975, p. 309.

22. Fauré probably added this inscription during or after the visit of Paul Dukas to Lausanne (23 August–early September 1907 and the start of a long friendship), as a letter from the Fauré–Dukas correspondence (Catalogue Hôtel Drouot, Paris, 20.6.77, no. 110) shows that Fauré's verse is a variant of a couplet invented by Dukas 'on the banks of the Léman' (Lake Geneva), with accompanying but unfortunately unrecorded 'musical motifs'.

2

FAURÉ'S REPUTATION—THEN AND NOW

You once reproached me with wanting to shine at your expense. I
hoped only that the development of my reputation—something which
leaves me *absolutely indifferent* because it has come *too late*—would
comfort you and compensate a little for my faults as a man.

(Fauré to his wife, 24 March 1921, LI, p. 270)

1. CONTEMPORARY REPUTATION IN FRANCE

From chapter 1 it should be clear that Fauré's reputation in France was
slow in establishing itself, and that such advances as he made before
1900 were largely as a result of the openings created for him by
Saint-Saëns, who paved his way in salon society and at the Madeleine
from the 1870s onwards. Fauré told his wife on 26 August 1907 (LI,
p. 147) that 'when I was young, Saint-Saëns often told me that he
recognised as missing in me a fault which, for an artist, is a positive
quality: ambition'. The older composer, whose music reflects his urbane
success, must at times have despaired of his talented pupil's lack of
'arrivisme'. Fauré makes this clear in his advice to Florent Schmitt, who
had just failed to win the Prix de Rome in 1898.[1] He is really speaking
about his own career and artistic aims when he says:

If I were him, I would be less preoccupied with finding a direction or path.
Artistic conscience alone should guide him—the desire to express his sentiments faithfully and for perfection of form, without concern for immediate
or eventual external success. To express that which is within you with
sincerity, in the clearest and most *perfect* manner, would seem to me always
the ultimate goal of art.

The salons were both a help and a hindrance to Fauré. On the positive
side they found him generous patrons like the Princesse de Polignac,
a cultured audience for his chamber music and songs, and provided an
artistic milieu into which he could escape from the dreary routine of
earning a living from music. Although it was only a small audience, it
was one in which new music was fashionable and thus enthusiastically
encouraged. But against this there arose the myth that one still encoun-

ters today, of Fauré as the lightweight composer of elegant trifles. *Après un rêve* and the other first-period songs still remain his best known compositions by and large, although the audience that enjoyed Fauré's early songs were shocked by *La Bonne Chanson* in 1895. The *Requiem* and the suite Fauré arranged from his *Pelléas et Mélisande* music enhanced his reputation as a 'serious' composer, although the published orchestral parts of the enlarged *Requiem* were not available till 1901. Such esteem as Fauré enjoyed in the early years of the present century came largely from his individual songs, which were more often performed than relatively popular works like the Violin Sonata and the Piano Quartets. It came as a shock to many people when Fauré was put on the official musical map as director of the Conservatoire in 1905: he was then 60, five years older than Debussy was when he died, and Debussy was himself a late developer.

But as Fauré's official reputation grew and his Conservatoire reforms and championship of the SMI brought him headline publicity, so his music developed beyond the comprehension of even his more intelligent earlier enthusiasts. Saint-Saëns, for instance, could not keep pace with Fauré after *Prométhée,* and even thought he had 'gone completely mad' with *La Bonne Chanson*. He found Van Lerberghe's texts for *Le Jardin clos* as forbidding as Fauré's music in 1915, still preferring the earlier songs like *Les Roses d'Ispahan* (Nectoux, *RdM,* 1973, p. 72). As Nectoux says (*RdM*, 1972, p. 79): '*Pénélope* displeased Saint-Saëns through its general conception, but even more through its musical language'. Opera for the reactionary Saint-Saëns meant arias and ensembles in the classical tradition and, expressing himself honestly to his friend Charles Lecocq in a way he never did to Fauré, he wrote of *Pénélope* on 12 March 1913 (Nectoux, *RdM,* 1972, pp. 80–81):

> In travelling through all the keys without stopping, one experiences an insuperable fatigue. Just as Grétry would have given a louis to hear a chanterelle,[2] so I would give two just to be able to rest for a moment on the tonic! I greatly regret that Fauré did not write an opera twelve years ago when he composed *Prométhée*; now, *there* was a masterpiece.

The sad thing was that, as Saint-Saëns and Fauré parted musical company, it was Saint-Saëns who took popular opinion with him. Whilst both achieved public recognition as academics, only Saint-Saëns achieved equivalent musical recognition. His conservatism and nineteenth-century-orientated Germanic music earned him increasing flattery in his final years, just as Fauré's music encountered growing incomprehension as he faced up to the challenge of the twentieth century.

But Fauré's prospects were not altogether bleak. His band of devoted admirers like the Maillots and the Hasselmans were extremely active on his behalf. Whatever Saint-Saëns may have thought, the press reviews for *Pénélope* were almost all favourable and many were ecstatic. Pierre Lalo in *Le Temps* (15 April 1913) considered that since Gluck's time 'no music has given the same impression of that purity of art and sentiment, that harmony of line and expression, which are to our minds the life and soul of Greek beauty'. Jean Darnaudat, in *L'Action Française* (10 May 1913) after the Paris première, preferred it to the last great summit of French musical history, Debussy's *Pelléas et Mélisande*, because it contained 'equally subtle delights, but spoke in a more general, comprehensible and human language'. The critics however restricted themselves to making general points or simple comparisons, and it is doubtful if even many musicians at the time really appreciated or understood what Fauré was trying to achieve in his final period.

Fauré's reputation was greatly enhanced by a devoted group of amateur and professional performers. Although he told his patroness the Comtesse Greffulhe in a letter of November 1902 that 'it is the amateurs who understand and interpret my music best', it was violinists like Ysaÿe, pianists like Risler, Cortot and Lortat, and singers like Jeanne Raunay, Clare Croiza, Madeleine Grey and Charles Panzéra after the turn of the century whose excellent performances contributed most to such acclaim as Fauré received. Prior to 1900 it was often his friends or patrons themselves who interpreted the songs written for them—Marguerite Baugnies, Emma Bardac, or gifted amateurs like Henriette Fuchs or the tenor Maurice Bagès. Operatic celebrities never had much success with Fauré's intimate creations. As composers go, Fauré suffers more than most from being performed rather than interpreted. It requires total commitment and complete concentration from performer and audience alike for his music to stand a chance of being fully appreciated: the problem intensifies with works written after *Pénélope*. The sensitive music of Fauré and Debussy has not the resilience to indifferent performance that Bach's has; too often a substandard or mechanical performance will leave the listener with an erroneous impression of the author's capabilities and intentions.

Fauré was himself quite an accomplished pianist, as the Steinway piano rolls recorded in 1913 on the Welte-Mignon system show.[3] His performances of the Prelude in g (op. 103/3) and the First Barcarolle (op. 26) prove him to be a far more accurate and competent pianist than Debussy or Ravel at this period. Remembering his age and deafness, these calm and sober performances are quite remarkable, and it is to be hoped that the recording he is known to have made of the more substantial and difficult Theme and Variations (op. 73) will one day emerge. Fauré overpedals the starts of both the Prelude and the Barcarolle in his nervousness at this unaccustomed venture, but this defect soon clears up, and his interpretation of the Prelude in particular reveals a powerful, even passionate personality, with a strong sense of continuity, full tone, and carefully graded crescendos and diminuendos. The polarity of treble and bass lines, so much a feature of Fauré's mature music, is clearly maintained throughout. Both performances are faithful to the printed text in notes and metronome markings; he does not rush the First Barcarolle as so many later pianists have done. He only occasionally succumbs to the contemporary fashion of putting the left hand down slightly ahead of the right, but in another recording of the third of the *Romances sans paroles* (op. 17) his left hand tends to be overheavy. There is little evidence of the romantic *rubato* that spoils Debussy's 1912 recording of *La Plus que lente*, although the inner semiquavers in the First Barcarolle show a certain flexibility when they are decorative adjuncts to the main melody line, as in bars 16–22. This aspect is always sensitively controlled, however, and is really nothing more than the realization of Fauré's frequent marking 'espressivo' in the first two periods. Fauré's playing is, by contemporary standards, of almost classical regularity, with a brilliance and clarity to rival that of Lhévine or Godowsky in the brief treble cadenza leading into the recapitulation in the Barcarolle.

Fauré's son Emmanuel tells us that his father had a horror of deliberately 'pretty' effects (*BAF*, 1972, p. 17) or 'swooning' performances of his music. 'Some reproached him with the sobriety of his interpretation. He was actually very modest and did not like to display his emotion . . . He did not have Saint-Saëns's virtuosity, but he had a very personal touch: an iron hand in a velvet glove, and what velvet!' Fauré's hands were large and powerful and it was here that his technique was concentrated, rather than in arm or shoulder weight. He was completely ambidextrous and this is reflected in the difficulty of some of his pieces, which are technically challenging as well as more fluid. Only a few, like the Fourth Barcarolle, fall within the capabilities of the average 'salon' pianist, to whose domain his music is all too often relegated.

Fauré usually accompanied his own songs in private and public concerts. Whereas he surrendered his role as pianist in the chamber works in later life to Cortot and Lortat, he continued to accompany his songs up to the first performances of *Mirages* with Madeleine Grey in December 1919. By then he was completely deaf, and was only assisted by his inner ear and what he knew to be the general intentions of his interpreters. All this, together with his inflexible tempos, caused singers to despair; if anything went wrong it was up to them to adjust and save the performance. 'With Fauré', Madeleine Grey recalled, 'one often reached the end with a discrepancy of several bars!' Pictures of Fauré show him sitting bolt upright at the piano on a high-backed chair rather than a piano stool, his eyes half-closed in an air of apparent unconcern. Like Ravel and Debussy, he invariably had a cigarette in his mouth or near at hand.

Fauré infinitely preferred the piano to the organ, but one technique he did adopt was the organist's change of fingers on the same note for smoothness of line. This can be seen on numerous occasions like the Third Barcarolle (bar 18) or the Fourth Barcarolle (bars 25 and 29). Fauré's sparing use of the pedal also reflects his organ technique; he even uses the deliberate indication 'without pedal' in the Third Nocturne (bar 28f). The 'romantic' organ with its Franckian orchestral imitation had no interest for Fauré, who preferred the purity of Bach and Mendelssohn. He excelled above all at harmonically ingenious improvisations, as A. M. Henderson attests (1956, pp. 39–40). It is a pity that the only organ piece that survives in Fauré's hand, an Andante mosso in E, is so inferior (BN ms 418). If this is an improvisation, it has lost a lot in the process of notation. The bombastic Andante mosso looks more like a transcription of an operatic overture by a very minor composer and was perhaps an Album-leaf for a friend's collection: there is nothing at all Fauréan about it.

Fauré's reputation as a teacher rests mainly on the important composers that emerged from his Conservatoire class around the turn of the century—Ravel, Enesco, Caplet, Schmitt, Roger-Ducasse and Koechlin, to name just a few. Fauré seems to have done little actual teaching, invariably arriving late or leaving early, or both. Ravel in his autobiographical sketch[4] says: 'I am pleased to acknowledge that I owe the most valuable elements of my technique to André Gédalge. As for Fauré, his advice as an *artist* gave me no less valuable encouragement'. Koechlin too refers to Fauré's artistic 'presence' (K, pp. 7–8), in which his pupils 'all felt both a little shy and immensely stimulated'. Georges Enesco (1881–1955), who was in Fauré's class between 1896 and 1899, recalls that he was[5]

> the absolute opposite to Massenet, as dreamy and taciturn as Massenet was expansive. Psychology bored him, and he never liked analysing the finer points of anyone's character. On the purely technical side his teaching was brief. He was not in the strict sense of the word a teacher, but from him came an aura: he was inspiring, and this inspiration was contagious. We adored him!

Fauré cannot have done any preparation for his classes or any analysis during them, and he refused to encourage his pupils to compete for the Prix de Rome as his more academic counterpart Lenepveu did. Gédalge filled in the multitude of technical gaps that Fauré left, the main one being orchestration, which hardly interested Fauré at all as a subject.

His example as a composer provided all the inspiration that the serious students needed. To those who tried to taunt him with inferior or pompous compositions, his reaction was simply: 'Was there nothing else?' (K, p. 8).

Fauré's reputation as a critic and his views of his contemporaries are discussed in chapter 6. Suffice it to say here that, like the best critics, Fauré could always face the composers he criticized with equanimity on the following day. He found life too short to waste time demolishing music he disliked, preferring to concentrate on the points he admired in a work, even if the composer were Mascagni or Richard Strauss. That is not to say that Fauré was harmless or unduly flattering as a critic: he gave credit only where it was due, and the self-critical high standards he applied to his own compositions led to some astute comments on the music of others.

2. CONTEMPORARY REPUTATION ABROAD

Fauré enjoyed getting away from Paris to compose and perform as much as Debussy hated it, and he made a determined attempt to establish his reputation in England in 1896–98. In this, the escapist element and the prospect of much-needed financial gain should not be overstressed. The works that were most popular across the channel were the songs, the Violin Sonata and the Piano Quartets, but Fauré never attained the popularity of the more eminent-sounding 'Doctor' Grieg in this period or in the ensuing decade. The problem seems to have been the unwise policy, first suggested by the Maddisons, of all-Fauré concerts. Contemporary criticisms, whilst concentrating mainly on the performers, contain remarks like 'it must be confessed that the effect of an entire programme by a composer possessed of great talent, but not of genius, was rather monotonous'[6]. After a concert in the Bechstein (now the Wigmore) Hall which included the first performance of three of the *Chanson d'Ève* cycle (op. 95/1, 2 and 9) by Jeanne Raunay and Fauré, the unnamed critic of *The Times* (20 March 1908) wrote: 'The wisdom of devoting a whole programme to the works of one man is always a little doubtful, and it may be held that the success of the experiment varies inversely as the number of separate compositions performed.'

This last review voices the opinion that 'there is so little difference in the extent and character of the music that a feeling of monotony cannot be quite avoided', and the same misgivings were expressed about Robert Lortat's 1914 London recitals. The *Times* critic on 17 June again wondered whether this was 'after all, the most politic way of pleading his cause'.

Neither did Fauré's *Pelléas et Mélisande* music go down well in 1898. The *Times* critic wrote on 22 June that:

Judged by the ordinary standards of theatrical music, which are perhaps higher in the present day in England than anywhere else, it is scarcely satisfactory, being wanting alike in charm [*sic*] and in dramatic power. It has, indeed, the vagueness of melodic and harmonic progression which may be held to suit best the character of the play, but its continued absence of tangible form, not to speak of its actual ugliness at many points, is such as to disturb rather than assist the illusion of the scene.

Much of this may be due to the critic remembering Lugné-Poë's shadowy production of the play in London in 1896, but generally English critics judged Fauré's music by Germanic standards and reacted against it through ignorance and incomprehension. The *Musical Times* critic of the Second Quintet in December 1921 considered that it gave 'greater pleasure to the performer than to the listener, and lacked the contrasts that could have been obtained by the judicious use of the opportunities the quintet gives for using the piano as a foil, as an antagonist, instead of as a coadjutor'. The unnamed critic added: 'M. Fauré, it is known, takes his stand half-way between the modernists and the conservatives', and this between-two-stools approach infuriated English critics who like to be able to fit their subjects into accepted niches. Elisabeth Stonequist (1972, p. 176) reaches much the same conclusion about Fauré's reception by the French concert societies during the years of the Entente Cordiale. 'The critics did not so much dislike Fauré's music, as that they simply did not understand what little they heard . . . Even today, Fauré's music is not played as much as Debussy's or Ravel's, and possibly for the same reason, lack of understanding.'

All-French concerts were of course no longer practical after the outbreak of the war in 1914. After the war, the music of Stravinsky and Les Six began to figure increasingly in British programmes, Debussy and Fauré becoming suddenly old-fashioned. Fauré's attempt to establish himself in England left only a few fervent admirers after the war, and Edward Elgar gave the following touching but realistic obituary in a letter to Frank Schuster of 15 November 1924[7]:

He was such a real *gentleman*—the highest type of Frenchman and I admire him greatly. His chamber music never had a chance here in the good old Joachim days I fear; I may be wrong but I feel that it was 'held up' to our loss . . . As far as I resent anything—which is not far—I resent such neglect.

Fauré's success elsewhere in Europe was, as we have seen, immediate rather than durable during his lifetime. He did not make the same repeated attempts to establish his reputation in Germany or Russia that he did in England, nor, curiously enough, in Switzerland or Belgium either, although he had many admirers in both countries. America was simply too far away to consider.

3. POSTHUMOUS REPUTATION AT HOME AND ABROAD

Just before Fauré's death, Aaron Copland published a perceptive tribute with the theme of 'Gabriel Fauré, a neglected master' (*MQ*, 1924, pp. 573–86). 'Perhaps no other composer has ever been so generally ignored outside his own country, while at the same time enjoying an unquestionably eminent reputation at home', Copland begins, perhaps confusing academic and musical reputation a little. He gives as his reasons for Fauré being then unknown in the USA his slow development as a composer, and the quintessentially Gallic nature of his art, which was about as easy to export as Racine. The public is not kind to composers who evolve away from a familiar style: the majority of Ravel's enthusiastic audience for *Jeux d'eau* were unsympathetic to the *Histoires naturelles* and the *Valses nobles et sentimentales*, just as Fauré left his audience behind with *La Bonne Chanson*. Time and again his music is judged difficult to understand or place in its proper perspective. 'Like Valéry', Mellers writes (1947, p. 70), 'he disdains facility, and the surface effect. His idiom, so consummately constructed, yields its full flavour only with familiarity, and it is so subtle and reticent an idiom that it is likely to repel those who have not a certain measure of general cultivation'.

Fauré himself complained that it took 'twenty years for one of his works to be appreciated by the public', and Émile Vuillermoz's persuasive study of Fauré (1960, p. 200) speaks of his 'splendid isolation as an artist', again hinting at an exclusiveness comprehended only by true devotees of his music, 'who are proud to have an internal ear sensitive enough to grasp that which certain of their neighbours could not perceive' (p. 201). Whilst it has always been vital that devoted bands of admirers exist to keep Fauré's image alive, a feeling of exclusiveness can render their efforts to reach a wider audience counterproductive. As a result, it is easy for a vicious circle to begin, which can in the end prove detrimental to a composer's reputation.

The other problem is that French music in the early twentieth century seems to consist almost entirely of the work of unjustly neglected masters. The names of Koechlin, Paul Ladmirault, Roger-Ducasse, Maurice Emmanuel spring easily to mind, to name only a few, but there is a very strong case for putting Fauré at the head of the list for reassessment. The call for a reappraisal has come time and again: first from Copland, now that the 'mists of impressionism have drifted away'; then, immediately after Fauré's death, from Paul Dukas, who prophesied (*ReM*, 1924, p. 98) that 'the enthusiasm his music has aroused during his lifetime must of necessity fall short of the importance that posterity will attach to it'. The hope was, as André Gide said of Dostoevsky, that 'the same reasons which have retarded his recognition during his lifetime will be those to ensure his future fame': that is, the advanced nature of his art and its profound interior depth.

The hope for future justice was continued by Koechlin's 1927 biography (K, p. 86):

> Already some of his qualities have ceased to be misunderstood by the younger generation; their successors, if they will reject the influence of operetta and the clamour of the market-place, will be able to comprehend him to the full as a 'gloire classique' of France.

But in 1938 Mellers was still able to write that 'unrecognized for so long, his work should today be studied by any conscientious musician, and his relevance, his importance, is likely to increase in the near future'. This statement was unfortunately just as true when Mellers's article was revised and republished in 1947. He qualified the above opinion, however, by saying that 'the values Fauré stood for, immensely important in themselves, have no longer quite the same significance or the same urgency, "civilisation" becomes at once a more complicated and a less subtle ideal'.

Hope sprang eternal during the post-war centenary tributes. René Dumesnil began with the words (*ReM*, 1945, p. 29): 'The hour seems to have finally arrived when Gabriel Fauré will find recognition with all capable of appreciating beauty', and this was eclipsed by Leslie Orrey in the introduction to his translation of Koechlin's book on Fauré (K, p. vii) where he claimed that there were 'signs in this country that Fauré is at last about to receive some of the recognition due to him'. And by the time of the Second War, composers like Honegger, Auric and Milhaud had in fact rejoined the faithful like Koechlin and Schmitt in recognizing Fauré's importance and timeless musical influence.

But insensitive articles like that by Edward Lockspeiser on the songs in the *Monthly Musical Record* (1945, pp. 79–84) did not help the situation. Lockspeiser shows no evidence of having studied the great third-period song cycles at all, if indeed he had been able to obtain copies of them. To assert (p. 81) that Fauré was 'less concerned with the ultimate union of words and music than with an opportunity for displaying his lyrical gifts, for endowing the singer with a grateful line regardless of the details of inflection and emphasis demanded by the prosody' shows an alarming lack of awareness of Fauré's artistry, and is only true for a small minority of the earlier songs.

Neither does a stream of uncritical panegyric help Fauré's case much, whether it be Norman Demuth's 'there is not an ugly or crude bar to be found anywhere' (1959, p. 84), or Roger-Ducasse's chauvinistic assertion (*ReM*, 1922, pp. 78–9) that 'French music reigns supreme in the world . . . and Gabriel Fauré is the maître par excellence of French music'. He adds that 'the precise and practical English realise that it is useless to go on searching [for greatness in music] since they have never yet found it'!

The real state of Fauré's reputation was in fact little changed by the varied obituary or centenary tributes for, in David Drew's 1957 survey of 'Modern French Music'[8], Fauré is only referred to in passing in a substantial section on Charles Koechlin, although Satie, Roussel et al. merit quite lengthy discussion. The error lies in not recognizing Fauré as a twentieth-century composer, and Bayan Northcott in his masterly article 'Fauré our Contemporary' (*MM*, 1970) stresses that his music has a considerable relevance for the present century that is all too often ignored. He can however still say without fear of contradiction that 'no composer of similar stature in the last 100 years is so neglected' (p. 36). As he points out, Fauré's death in 1924 'could not have come at a worse time for his reputation or the continuance of his musical explorations' and, if his *Masques et Bergamasques* 'showed potential of neo-classical style enough to compose the mock-galanterie of Les Six into the ground', Fauré nevertheless appeared to most people as a nineteenth-century throwback, whose serious style had little influence beyond minor works like Duruflé's *Requiem*.

Perhaps Fauré's genuine neo-classicism was the reason why he was one of the few composers that Poulenc actively disliked. In an unrepentant interview with Claude Rostand[9], he frankly maintains that he has 'always been allergic' to Fauré's music, and that his overexposed Violin Sonata and Piano Quartets were the '*bêtes noires* of my childhood concerts. Evidently, with age I must admit that Fauré is a very great musician, but his *Requiem* makes me lose faith, and it is a real penance for me to hear it. It is one of the few things I hate in music'.

In 1964, on the fortieth anniversary of Fauré's death, Bernard Gavoty repeated the vague-dismissal theory of Fauré[10]. His philosophy could be 'summarized in four words . . . Desire for the non-existent. There is no one less of a realist than Fauré.' Émile Vuillermoz in the same edition of the *Journal Musical Français* (p. 2) reiterated the exclusivist angle: 'Foreigners cannot begin to understand the subtle meaning of these phrases which appear so straightforward, of these discreet melodic inflections, and of this harmonic writing of such surprising fluidity . . . Our age is not conducive to the development of the inner life.' If you believe this negative sort of philosophy, you can believe anything.

Bayan Northcott claimed with justification in 1970 that Fauré, in comparison with Bach, 'still awaited his Mendelssohn', and it is only very recently that signs of an enthusiastic and scholarly rediscovery have begun to emerge. Philippe Fauré-Fremiet began the process with the publication of the *Lettres intimes* in 1951 which gave a fresh insight into the life, mind and music of his secretive but fascinating father. Both this and his revised 1957 biography of Fauré still await English translation. A complete scholarly edition of his works is in progress by Peters of Leipzig, and interest in the recording of his music has recently increased amongst artists worldwide with, at last, the issue of two versions of the complete *Pénélope* in 1981. The prejudice for German music at the expense of French, from which Fauré suffered during his lifetime, and against which Norman Suckling campaigned so vigorously in his 1946 study, at last shows signs of diminishing as interest in the music of Debussy and Ravel increases on both sides of the Atlantic and in Japan. There is hope that Fauré will play an equal part in this renaissance, and it is particularly appropriate that Fauré's Mendelssohn in the 1970s should be the practical and scholarly Frenchman, Jean-Michel Nectoux.

Footnotes to Chap. 2
1. Letter to Mme de Chaumont-Quitry, friend and patroness of Schmitt, c.1 July 1898, reproduced in Jean Vuaillat: *Gabriel Fauré*, Lyon, Emmanuel Vitte, 1973, pp. 48–9.
2. 'Chanterelle' is the French nickname for the top (E) string on the violin. The remark, attributed to Grétry (1741–1813), refers to the overture to Méhul's *Uthal*, produced at the Opéra-Comique in 1806, which, like the first version of Fauré's *Requiem*, had no orchestral violins. Grétry's comment implied that he would give a lot to hear a recognizable melody-line, Saint-Saëns's that he would give even more for a passage of tonal stability in *Pénélope*. I am grateful to Dr David Charlton for the above information on Grétry and Méhul.
3. The Third Prelude (op. 103) and the First Barcarolle (op. 26) are included on the *Album du Cinquanténaire* (side 1) prepared in November 1974 by J-M. Nectoux (EMI 2C 153—12845/6), an indispensable addition to the collection of any Fauré enthusiast.
4. Roland Manuel: 'Une Esquisse autobiographique de Maurice Ravel', *ReM* (December 1938), p. 20.
5. *Les Souvenirs de Georges Enesco*, Paris, Flammarion, 1955, p. 69.
6. *MT*, xxxviii, no. 647 (1897), p. 45 after Léon Delafosse's concert on 10 December 1896.
7. Quoted in Michael Kennedy: *Portrait of Elgar*, London, Oxford University Press, 1968, p. 252.
8. In *European Music in the Twentieth Century*, ed. Hartog, London, Routledge and Kegan Paul, 1957, pp. 252–310.
9. Paris, Julliard, 1954. 16e entretien, pp. 186–7.
10. *Journal Musical Français*, no. 131 (10 October 1964). Edition entitled 'Fauré, qui est-ce?', p. 3.

3
THE FIRST PERIOD: 1860–85

The difficulty with Fauré's first period is dating his compositions. Fauré was indifferent to the fate of his manuscripts once the works concerned were published. Only about half his manuscripts have survived; few of those that have are precisely dated, and he rarely dated his letters before he became director of the Conservatoire in 1905. Matters are further complicated because, as Fauré pointed out in his 1922 *Excelsior* interview, 'everything of mine that was published before these last fifteen years was published with a delay of seven or eight years'. Fauré's memory was never very accurate and he probably had in mind a work like his first song *Le Papillon et la fleur* written in 1861 but published only in 1869. There are, however, many examples to choose from. Apart from a few songs, Fauré had nothing of significance published until 1876–7 when his *Cantique de Jean Racine* and the Violin Sonata appeared as opp. 11 and 13. This left ten opus numbers for over thirty of his youthful works, mostly songs, to which he evidently did not attach much importance. The distribution of these early opus numbers did not take place until Fauré, applying for membership of the Institute in 1896, asked Hamelle to print a catalogue of his works. The opus numbers do not follow the chronological order of composition or even of publication; they were distributed according to the order of the songs in the first volume as published by Hamelle in 1887.[1] This includes the songs opp. 1–8 which cover the period 1861–78; consecutive songs in volume 1 can be separated by a period of nearly ten years, as in the case of *Rêve d'amour* (c.1862) and *L'Absent* (April 1871) from op. 5. Despite the overcrowding, op. 9 was never used; neither later on were opp. 53, 60, 64 and 100, even though there are over forty works, including *Pénélope,* with no opus numbers. The dating of Fauré's compositions, now radically modified through the systematic research of M. Nectoux from that found in Suckling (1946) or Fauré-Fremiet (1957), derives from contemporary letters, publishers' archives, concert programmes and other original sources. The problem persists right through the first period and as far as the mid-1890s.

1. THE ÉCOLE NIEDERMEYER: FIRST COMPOSITIONS (1861–5)

Of Fauré's eight romances written whilst a pupil at the École Niedermeyer, seven are settings of minor verses by the prolific Victor Hugo: *Le Papillon et la fleur* (op. 1/1, 1861); *Mai* (op. 1/2, 1861?); *Rêve d'amour*; *Dans les ruines d'une abbaye* (op. 2/1, c. 1865–8); and the unpublished *L'Aube naît* (1862?), *Puisque j'ai mis* (December 1862), and *Tristesse d'Olympio* (c. 1865–8). John Weightman in the *Observer Review* (14 November 1976, p. 29) described Hugo as 'a sort of half-conscious Aeolian harp, through which the wind of language blew every morning from 6 am to midday for more than 60 years, producing sometimes superbly poetic lines, sometimes grandiose nonsense, but only very infrequently a concentrated, internally organised, totally memorable poem'. The poems Fauré chose in his youthful inexperience, perhaps on Saint-Saëns's advice, were unsuitable for several reasons which he later realised. He admitted in *Musica* (Feb/March 1911) that he 'never succeeded in setting Victor Hugo properly to music'. First, the wealth of lyric imagery in Victor Hugo's poetry is more the demonstration of outward than inward sensitivity and the overall impression is one of shallow prettiness. Secondly, Hugo was, like many of the Parnassian poets, musically unsympathetic; it was Verlaine's musical sensitivity that made him Fauré's ideal poet in his second period. Lastly, the regularity of phrasing and unself-critical style of Hugo's poems tended to produce an instinctively similar response in Fauré, especially in *Le Papillon et la fleur*, his first and worst song whose only saving grace is that its uncharacteristically long scalar introduction is cut back in the later strophes.

Fauré used scale-based ideas throughout his career, though later compositions like the First and Second Barcarolle, the finale of the First Piano Quartet, or the Theme and Variations all produce far superior results to *Le Papillon et la fleur*. Its prosody is defective too, from the accentuation of the first line: 'Le pau*vre* fleur di*sait*' onwards. But Fauré at least does not repeat lines to make an ecstatic, rhetorical ending as his master Niedermeyer was accused of doing in his setting of Lamartine's *Le Lac* (FF, p. 40). Perhaps the most appropriate comment on Fauré's first song is Saint-Saëns's drawing on the cover of the manuscript of the butterfly making an obscene gesture in the flower's direction!

The other early Hugo settings are strophic and unremarkable, with touches of Gounod in, for example, *Dans les ruines d'une abbaye* or *Rêve d'amour*. Whilst they are light and superficial, these songs have a certain freshness that is lacking in *Le Papillon et la fleur*. In *Tristesse d'Olympio* the strophes are subdivided in mood and tempo, the first part being a rather sombre 'grave' in triple time, and the last twelve bars and the piano postlude an 'allegro moderato' in 2/2 time with more than a touch of Mendelssohn to close the stanza (Ex. 1). This is also Fauré's first setting in the minor mode.

Ex. 1
Tristesse d'Olympio (Victor Hugo)
end of stanza; MS p.5, bar 12f.

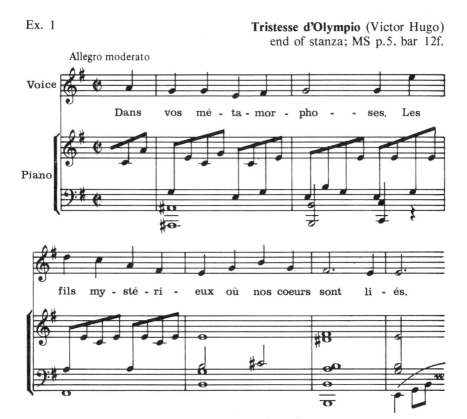

The remaining song from the École Niedermeyer period is a melodically undistinguished setting of Théophile Gautier's *Les Matelots* (op. 2/2, c. 1865–8), whose continuous undulating arpeggios are the first in a long line of piano accompaniments which grow increasingly flexible and poetic as Fauré matures, especially in seascapes from *Les Berceaux* (op. 23/1) to *La Mer est infinie* (op. 118/1).

Also from this period come the three *Romances sans paroles* (op. 17, 1863?), whose title and content recall Mendelssohn. They quickly became popular after their publication in 1880. The first contains an echo of the right-hand melody by the left which creates a gentle harmonic haze around the pristine purity of the theme. The second *Romance* is particularly Mendelssohnian in its arpeggio figuration divided between the hands. In the third we encounter Schumann and Chopin, and the reprise of the opening theme (p. 4) is a canon at the octave at the distance of one crotchet, the first example of a technique to which Fauré returned increasingly in later years in such unacademic creations as *Tendresse* from the *Dolly* suite. Although slight, the *Romances sans paroles* do not deserve to be dismissed as the sort of 'indiscretions every young composer commits' (Copland, 1924, p. 579). Indiscretion of another kind also occurred to Marcel Proust in the context of op. 17, and he joked irreverently to Robert de Montesquiou[2] that, for 'a mixture of lechery and litanies' he knew nothing to beat them: they were the sort of music 'a pederast might hum when raping a choirboy'!

In a higher category are the two École Niedermeyer choral works. The first, a fluid latin setting of Psalm 136 *Super Flumina [Babylonis]*, gained the *proxime accessit* for the composition prize in the summer of 1863. The orchestration by Fauré is light and practical throughout, with some interesting detail in the outer sections. Fauré still shows no signs of melodic or harmonic originality, however, and the central section 'Quomodo cantabimus canticum Domini' is staid and four-square. The *Cantique de Jean Racine*, which gained Fauré the first prize for composition in 1865, is the musical climax of the Niedermeyer years; a concise setting for four-part choir and organ that can take an equal place alongside Fauré's other religious choral works. The mood is one of restrained fervour with the clarity of the vocal writing—the simple imitative entries never get in the way of the harmonic scheme—saving the piece from becoming sentimental or pallid. The pianistic 'organ' part which Fauré orchestrated in 1905 recalls Gounod's sacred style, and in the *Cantique* we get the first signs of the interaction between treble and bass lines, wherein lies the strength of Fauré's mature works. The final, more extended passage prior to the coda, with its faster-moving harmonies and its III—V^7—I Fauréan cadence, lends the piece a measure of distinction.

2. THE RENNES PERIOD (1866–70)

Most previous lists of Fauré's songs have revealed a large and inexplicable gap between op. 8 of 1865 and op. 18 of 1880. In reality, the gap was much smaller and arose for circumstantial rather than artistic reasons. The unhappy Rennes period, as far as is known, produced only a handful of short piano pieces, together with the *Cantique à St-Vincent-de-Paul*, which was first performed at Fauré's church of

Saint-Sauveur in Rennes on 19 July 1868 but has now unfortunately disappeared. 1869 seems to have been the only productive year in Rennes, the inspiration coming either from the de Leyritz sisters, Valentine and Laure, or the signing of Fauré's first contract with Choudens, or both. As Appendix B shows, several of the Leyritz pieces were used again in later works and the two fugues re-used as op. 84/3 and 6 are Fauré's earliest precisely datable fugues. The only other known fugues are a three-part one in manuscript at the Humanities Research Center at the University of Texas at Austin, and BN ms 17752 (see p. 279) that date from the École Niedermeyer period.

Op. 84/3 of June 1869, described by Fauré as a 'little fugue', is contrapuntally undistinguished. Its subject consists mostly of a rhythmicized dominant pedal, and the counter-subject lacks a separate identity, being based on the end of the subject. Fauré does not get round to stretto and is most interested in the episodes, which link easily with the middle entries. The final section in the tonic major (A) begins promisingly with sliding inner harmonies over a dominant pedal, but the end is disappointing, being more like Mendelssohn than Fauré. The second four-part fugue in e (op. 84/6) of November 1869 is altogether subtler. Again the counter-subject is based on the second bar of a subject which itself contains repeated notes, but the construction is tighter with thematic episodes, stretti, and more involved, richer contrapuntal writing throughout. A fine climactic section leading to a dominant pedal on the final page contains some characteristically Fauréan harmonies based on the chord of the augmented fifth.

The Gavotte and the *Intermezzo de symphonie* (1867–8) were both re-used in the *Suite d'orchestre* or Symphony in F (op. 20). The attractive and rhythmic Gavotte found its way into *Masques et Bergamasques* without difficulty half a century later; the *Intermezzo* became the overture. From the Rennes period also comes the cadenza for the opening movement of Beethoven's Third Piano Concerto which remained unpublished during Fauré's lifetime. It is a good deal more Beethovenian than the 1902 cadenza written for Marguerite Hasselmans to use in the first movement of Mozart's Concerto in c (K. 491) is Mozartian. The opening section of the Beethoven cadenza is based on the more lyrical second subject group and tells us more about Fauré than about Beethoven harmonically. But with the entrance of the dynamic opening arpeggio theme (bar 32), the cadenza assumes a Beethovenian power in its rushing semiquavers that is maintained until the trill-based final section, which is not unlike the end of Beethoven's own cadenza for the concerto. Fauré tries the same device with his 1902 Mozart cadenza which is similar in mood. This begins with enormous un-Mozartian thirteen-bar sequences which continually exceed the five-octave range of Mozart's piano. The harmonic language of the central section in particular is far too advanced, and the cadenza fits in less well than its 1869 counterpart into its surrounding concerto. Around 1875, Fauré also wrote a cadenza for Mozart's First Piano Concerto (K. 37) in F, but this remains unpublished.

3. THE REST OF THE FIRST PERIOD (1870–85)

(i) *Songs*

Beginning with another Hugo setting *L'Aurore* (published in Noske, 1954, p. 195) and Baudelaire's *Hymne* around 1870, Fauré produced songs throughout the decade. In 1876–7 he focused his attention more on piano and chamber music in an attempt to broaden his range, but he resumed songwriting in 1878 with *Sylvie* (op. 6/3) and *Poème d'un jour* (op. 21) and continued writing *mélodies* till the end of the first period, though the lean years 1880–81, 1883 and 1885 reflect his developing interest in the piano.

L'Aurore is the subtlest of the Hugo songs and for the first time Fauré uses an ABA form. The part-writing, heavily reliant on sliding parallel thirds, is immaculate, and the brief piano postlude caps the song perfectly, rising swiftly to the higher notes that Fauré has deliberately reserved for this purpose. The introduction too is cut back to the absolute minimum.

L'Absent ('Sentiers où l'herbe se balance') has assymetrical strophes and, as in *Tristesse d'Olympio*, there are two tempos in this dramatic dialogue. The faster second section leads to a vocal climax which is intensified in a brief piano interlude that also gradually returns to the mood and material of the start, in a manner prophetic of the Thirteenth Nocturne (op. 119, p. 10).

The breakthrough in Fauré's career as a songwriter came with the creation of *Lydia* (op. 4/2) around 1870, which embraces many of the features we have come to regard as typically Fauréan. The smooth vocal line consists of narrow intervals up to a perfect fourth and is exquisitely phrased. The sparse choral four-part accompaniment has a feeling of almost Hellenic restraint. The form is still strophic, but the inspired simplicity of its unexpected coda recalls that of *L'Aurore* with its sliding thirds, its use of the specially saved upper register, and its perfect timing. As the pianist's hands cross in the final bars, the rising thirds prove themselves to have been the most important aspect of the coda after all, with the right-hand part only a rhythmic counter-subject. In *Lydia* Fauré strikes the happy balance between tonality and modality which characterizes his best music; in his subtle mixture of F major and the Lydian mode, with its raised fourth degree and tritonal suggestions, he may be making a gentle pun on the subject of Leconte de Lisle's poem. Leslie Orrey (*Music Review*, 1945, p. 76) also points out the interesting affinity between the Lydian fourth and the nasal quality of spoken or sung French.

The Lydia theme (Ex. 2) which enters after repeated tonic chords have wooed the audience's attention away from any external distractions, was a fortunate discovery which re-emerged from Fauré's subconscious on numerous occasions and in numerous guises throughout his career.

Seule! (Théophile Gautier), the unequal Baudelaire settings *Chant d'automne* and *La Rançon* (1871?), together with *L'Absent* and *Tristesse* have a common feeling of melancholy and are amongst the few first-period works to foreshadow the graver side of Fauré's genius.

Ex. 2   **Lydia** (op. 4/2, c.1870)
Bars 3–6   Leconte de Lisle

Seule! is closer in mood and key to the early *Tristesse d'Olympio* but is a good deal more chromatic. A musical dialogue between the treble and a motivic bass line, and a recurrent tonic pedal, contribute towards the feeling of desolation. *Chant d'automne* is an extended motivic song with an unusually long introduction that sets the mood of powerful, restless undulation over which the sustained vocal line calmly pursues its course. Fauré's closing bars, with the straightforward perfect cadences he would have altered in maturity, cannot quite match Baudelaire's magnificent text. There is an even more noticeable discrepancy in the quality of words and music in *La Rançon* (op. 8/2), where the bleak measured tread of the opening, which recalls temporarily the chorale of the armed men in Mozart's *Magic Flute*, is followed by a weak section in the inevitable tonic major ('L'un est l'Art'): the final impression is of a sentimental short cantata that is unbalanced both formally and stylistically.

Quite different and far more successful are the group of early Italianate songs: *La Chanson du pêcheur* subtitled *Lamento* (Th. Gautier, 1872?), *Barcarolle* (Marc Monnier, 1873?) and the two fine adaptations of anonymous Italian poetry by Romain Bussine, *Sérénade toscane* and *Après un rêve*, set around 1878. Here there are freer and more virtuoso vocal lines which perhaps reflect the encouragement and inspiration of Pauline Viardot. The *Sérénade toscane* and *Barcarolle* have rather similar descending scalar starts, stressing the flattened leading-note of the home key in the vocal part. But the crowning song of the group is *Après un rêve*, an emotional though restrained masterpiece which maintains its high level of inspiration to the end. The restless harmonies in repeated quaver chords recall Schumann's *Ich grolle nicht* and the tension is never allowed to flag from the unexpected series of major ninths based on the circle of fifths (bars 3–5) onwards, despite frequent returns to the tonic. Fauré begins to show his mastery of harmonic phrasing here. Four bars from the end he shifts the emphasis within the recurring cadence progression to the tonic, by placing the tonic resolution over a dominant pedal on the weak third beat of the bar. At the same time the tonic chord in the accompaniment clashes with the vocal line, and tension is thus sustained till the very last note of the last vocal phrase when both harmony and melody resolve together on a strong beat. The phrasing of the vocal line in this song is extremely flexible throughout, beginning with seven-bar units (3 plus 4) and growing subtler in the second stanza as the phrases also cross the barlines.

Après un rêve has clear affinities with the cello *Élégie* (op. 24), although this piece is not thought of as Italianate. Also in the Italian group of songs must come the irresistible and brilliant duet for two sopranos, *Tarentelle* (Marc Monnier, 1873?), an example of Fauré's natural humour at work. The less interesting and repetitive companion duet *Puisqu'ici-bas toute âme* is another Victor Hugo setting that is probably based on an earlier composition of around 1863–4.

Amongst the other songs in Hamelle's first volume, both *Sylvie* (Paul de Choudens, 1878) and the charming and unpretentious *Ici-bas!* (Sully-Prudhomme, 1874?) have recomposed third strophes which show Fauré breaking away from the couplet technique. Bar-form (AAB) is also evident in *Sérénade toscane*, *Chanson du pêcheur* and *Après un rêve*, whereas the circular ABA form, which predominates in volume 2, is only found in *L'Absent*. The idea of the through-composed song, like *Chant d'automne* and *La Rançon*, does not seem to have interested Fauré greatly in his first period and is only followed up in the second volume in *Toujours* (op. 21/2).

In volume 2, the opp. 18 and 39 songs and the outer songs of op. 23 (*Les Berceaux* and *Le Secret*) reflect the deepening experience of the Violin Sonata and the First Piano Quartet. Fauré's developing maturity is evident in the greater variety, continuity and assurance of these songs and in their broader harmonic and formal conceptions. Several distinct traits are worth noting. First, there are the sentimental songs which hark back to the romances of volume 1: the strophic *Rencontre*, the first of the *Poèmes d'un jour* (1878); *Notre amour* (op. 23/2, 1879?); *Chanson d'amour* (op. 27/1, 1882), and *Le Pays des rêves* (op. 39/3, 1884). Much of the blame for these pieces must be placed on Fauré's choice of the inferior poetry of Armand Silvestre (1838–1901), and it is all too easy for these songs to sound insipid in performance. The second category consists of the songs of restrained intimacy and beauty: in *Le Secret* (op. 23/3, 1880–81), Fauré is able to transcend Silvestre's mediocre verses to produce a masterpiece in miniature in which the arpeggios disappear and there is room to think without distraction. If it were not for the slow regular procession of chords which characterize Fauré's most personal creations and are 'reborn on each occasion' (N, p. 43), the song would be virtually a recitative.

Adieu (op. 21/3) and, on a higher plane, *Aurore* (op. 39/1) come somewhere between the two categories. The latter is often underestimated; the harmonic originality and sparseness of its central minor section look forward to the songs of the third collection and to *Dans la forêt de septembre* (op. 85/1) in particular. The phrasing and melody of the outer major sections are subtler than the scalar repetitions of *Notre amour*, or even the voluptuous *Les Roses d'Ispahan* (op. 39/4). This last song also belongs to the sentimental category, but is saved by what amounts to a development section in the third stanza ('O Leïlah!'). As elsewhere, Fauré omits stanzas, here the third and fifth, to bring the original poem within a manageable length.

The other song on the same level as *Le Secret*, if less difficult to interpret, is the justly famous setting of Sully-Prudhomme's *Les Berceaux* (op. 23/1, 1879). Here Fauré invents an undulating and unifying accompaniment that suggests both the cradles ('berceaux') rocked by the sailors' wives, and the boats ('vaisseaux') taking their menfolk over the sea towards the unknown and possibly to their death. The unexpected harmonies at the climax of the second stanza ('Tentent les horizons qui leurent!') and the gradual return to the tonic for the third lend this song distinction, though Fauré's deliberate stressing of the vocal part is very different from that intended by Sully-Prudhomme.

The third and final category of songs are more expansive and dramatic: romantic in the true sense of the word, like *Le Voyageur* and *Automne* (op. 18, 1878), *Fleur jetée* (op. 39/2) and, to a lesser extent, *Toujours* (op. 21/2), although this greatly over-uses the chord of the augmented fifth in its quest for drama. Both *Le Voyageur* and *Fleur jetée* are explosions of force rare in Fauré, the former having a relentless marching chordal accompaniment and a decisive rhythmic vocal line in its outer sections, whose first five-bar phrase seems deliberately mis-stressed for dramatic reasons, as in *Les Berceaux*. The central section of *Le Voyageur* has a rising idea in the piano part which, like that of *Au Bord de l'eau* (op. 8/1) three years earlier, is subtly interwoven with the vocal line. The harmonic tension and the dynamics build gradually into a return of the opening material that is even more powerful than before, and it is a pity that the tension is reduced in the quieter coda.

In *Fleur jetée*, the vocal line is no less vehement, but the furious Erlkönig-type hammered octaves and chords with their rapid changes of register are something quite new, and far outside the scope of the salon romance. Both these songs and the Germanic *Automne*, with its sinister syncopated bass figure, diminished seventh chords, and its neapolitan modulation at the end, show Fauré again transcending the verses of Silvestre.

It has been claimed that the three *Poème d'un jour* songs are Fauré's first song-cycle. But beyond the fact that the songs tell of the poet Charles Grandmougin's meeting his beloved, declaring his faithfulness to her, and then sadly bidding her farewell, and the fact that there is a link between the original keys (D flat/f sharp/G flat), there is no real justification for this hypothesis. None of Fauré's later cycles are unified by key relationships, and there is nothing motivic to bind op. 21 together. The two songs of op. 27 being by Silvestre makes them just as much a cycle as *Poème d'un jour*, and the descending scales which characterize the vocal lines of *Rencontre* and *Adieu* are as much an integral part of *Le Voyageur* or *Fleur jetée*, or the *Sérénade toscane* or *Barcarolle*. Really, the only common factor of the three op. 21 songs is their relative mediocrity. Whereas Jankélévitch (1974, p. 66) aptly compares Fauré's skill at balancing tonalities and enharmonic modulations with a cat 'which always falls on its feet', Fauré comes close to disaster near the end of *Adieu*, as he does near the end of *Chanson d'amour*, and these songs lack the finesse of the unexpected harmonic sidesteps found in bars 19 and 27–8 of *Nell* (op. 18/1). *Nell*, with its fluid and continuously evolving harmonies and its stepwise implied part-movement, is one of Fauré's finest creations. He only set Leconte de Lisle's formally perfect and objective poetry on five occasions: *Lydia*, *Nell*, *Les Roses d'Ispahan*, *La Rose* and *Le Parfum impérissable*, but each one is a masterpiece in its own way. After the Symbolists Van Lerberghe and Verlaine, de Lisle was the poet with whom Fauré 'collaborated' most successfully.

(ii) *Piano Music*

There seems to have been a gap in Fauré's piano music between 1870 and 1875 and again between 1876 and 1878, and the most important piano compositions of the first period come from the years 1880–86 when Fauré was building his reputation as a writer for the instrument. During the first period Fauré adopted from Chopin the impersonal but 'romantic' formats of the Nocturne, Impromptu and Barcarolle which were to dominate his career. He used the Mazurka and Ballade once only, probably finding the first too slight and un-French and the latter too massive and Germanic for his taste. Fauré's main musical influences in this period, which is extended slightly to include Barcarolles nos. 2–4 of 1885–6, are Chopin and, to a lesser extent, Liszt. The other form Fauré used, the Valse-Caprice, owes a debt to Chopin's more extended Valses and to the brilliant salon style of Saint-Saëns. The piano works are less important than the songs in the first period and their virtuosity reflects the influence of the fashionable soirées in which Fauré's career developed. The first period is largely one of sensual and sonorous seduction; it is only with the Fifth Barcarolle and the Sixth Nocturne in the second period that we penetrate beneath the surface of Fauré's genius to more profound and personal statements.

The *Mazurka* (op. 32, c.1875), despite its title, sounds more French than Polish, and Fauré's unease is reflected in the length and virtuosity of this piece in comparison with the Mazurkas of Chopin. It is one of Fauré's least characteristic creations, with an overloaded ternary structure that belongs rather to the genre of the Valse-Caprice:

$$\underbrace{ABA_1}_{A} - \underbrace{CCD}_{B} - \underbrace{A_1B_1}_{A}$$

In the A section only the dotted rhythms recall Chopin, though the B section has some of the haunting sadness of Chopin's *Mazurka* in g (op. 24/1), especially when B returns modified at the close (p. 14).

The first five Nocturnes are in ternary form with modified reprises and quiet, pianistic codas, apart from no. 4 which has a more extended $ABA_1B_1A_2B_2$-coda format. Of the five, only the last has its coda based on the A section. The plan: calm—more anguished—calm, varied reprise of the opening was one of Fauré's favourites and is the reverse of the plan normally found in Liszt or Schumann. The influence of Chopin is clear, especially in the Second Nocturne which has close affinities with Chopin's 17th Nocturne (op. 62/1) in the same key, down to the trills which usher in the reprise. The B section of this Nocturne, with its theme disguised in brilliant cross-hand figuration, could easily be by Saint-Saëns, as could the B section of the Fifth Nocturne. It is not surprising that Saint-Saëns was 'delighted to the nth degree' by the Second Nocturne (Nectoux, *RdM*, 1972, p. 206) in 1887.

Liszt's influence is most evident in the 'three-hand' effects in the Fifth Nocturne and in the recitative-like single-note passage immediately before the return of A (pp. 41–2). The most Fauréan moments in the Nocturnes which look forward to the second period are the chromatic sidesteps in the Third Nocturne (bars 11–12) and the limpid bell-like theme in falling fourths which opens the Fourth Nocturne. This could come straight out of the *Dolly* suite (op. 56) a decade later; sadly it loses its appeal and freshness as it is developed during the course of the Nocturne and only temporarily regains its composure on its final re-statement (p. 32). Just prior to this is an impassioned climax which, as Suckling points out (Su, p. 129), could have been transferred direct from the *Ballade* written five years earlier (cf. bars 56–9 with the *Ballade* bars 53f).

The first five Nocturnes are all complex chromatically, and their self-contained opening sections are characterized by a mood of expressive sadness. That of the First Nocturne recalls the elegiac repeated quavers of Chopin's Prelude in e; it also contains some original pianistic textures, notably the doubling of the right-hand melody in a more complete and rhythmically different manner an octave *higher* in the left hand (p. 5), and the clever repeated note effects in the decorated return of A (p. 9) in which four different pianistic touches occur simultaneously (Ex. 96).

The *Ballade* (op. 19), dedicated to Saint-Saëns, was originally written for piano solo in 1879; the light and skilful version for piano and orchestra by the composer dates from 1881. In its three-in-one formal concept, the *Ballade* is a direct descendant of Liszt's Sonata in b of 1852, although Fauré reverses Liszt's scheme by having a central section framed by two calmer sections—an extension of the plan adopted in the Nocturnes. What appears at first to be a sectional rhapsody turns out to be an original experiment in the creation of unity from diversity, involving Lisztian thematic metamorphosis in the process (N, p. 37).

The initial theme A (Ex. 3) is one of the models for the 'little phrase of Vinteuil' in Marcel Proust's *A la Recherche du temps perdu*, though George Painter in his biography of Proust[3] tells us that the author

> took a sly pleasure in multiplying the minor origins of the [Vinteuil] Sonata; he mentioned to Antoine Bibesco in 1913 the prelude to Act 1 of *Lohengrin*, and Fauré's *Ballade*, to Jacques de Lacretelje in 1918 both these and the Good Friday Spell from *Parsifal*, and 'something by Schubert'. But to each of these confidants he also revealed the profounder models for the 'little phrase' in Saint-Saëns's [Violin] Sonata in d [op. 75, 1885, which he first heard played by Ysaÿe at the soirées of Madeleine Lemaire], and for the Sonata as a whole in César Franck's Sonata in A.

Ex. 3   **Ballade** (op. 19)

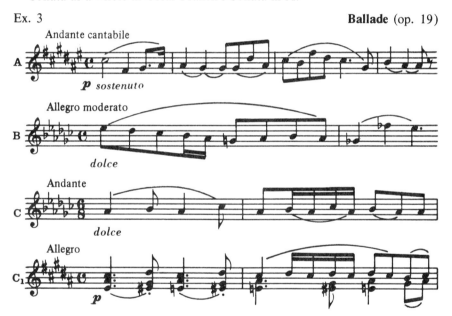

Nonetheless, theme A and its extension at the start of the *Ballade* fit closely with the description of Vinteuil's little phrase in *Du côté de chez Swann*[4]:

> With a slow and rhythmical movement, it led him here, there and everywhere, towards a state of happiness, noble, unintelligible, yet clearly indicated. Suddenly, it changed direction and, with a fresh movement, more rapid, slender, melancholy, incessant and sweet, bore him off with it towards unknown horizons. Then it vanished.

During the self-contained opening section of the *Ballade*, A is extended and later restated in canon at the octave at a crotchet's distance (bar 21f). In the orchestral version a sensitive, atmospheric dialogue develops at this point between piano and flute over a bed of sustained strings (OS, pp. 6–7). In the complex Allegro moderato based on B (p. 4f), the thematic imitation is shared equally between the hands, which is what may have put Liszt off as he tried to sight-read the *Ballade*. B and A (Ex. 3) are developed side by side before C appears (p. 7), though this is only an introduction to C_1 (p. 8), a metamorphosis of C. Fauré told Mme Clerc (N, p. 40) that he intended this section (pp. 8–12) 'to be a sort of intermezzo' with B and C_1 developed alongside each other, before C_1 received its true exposition as the third theme proper (C) at the start of the final section (p. 13).[5] Thus, Fauré pointed out, the 'three movements are in reality only one'. This does not, however, quite work in performance; the short *andante* sections on pp. 7 and 12 anticipating the final section (p. 13) give the piece the appearance of an organized *fantaisie* rather than a fully integrated three-in-one structure. C is rather overstated in the process, and does not come as any sort of revelation as the final section begins. This last part, replete with bird-like double trills (pp. 13–19), is the passage which Fauré claimed was inspired by an 'impression of nature' similar to that which caused Wagner to write his *Forest murmurs* in *Siegfried*. Elements of B return in this, but the final coda over a tonic pedal and the preceding cadenza are both feather-light and Lisztian in inspiration.

The five Impromptus belong together as a group through their lightness and virtuosity and their use of duple or compound duple time, even though twenty-two years separate the third and fourth. The Sixth Impromptu, the fourth in chronological sequence, is a transcription of the Impromptu for harp (op. 86) and is the odd man out, both in its chordal style and its triple metre. Being less complex than the Nocturnes does not mean that the Impromptus are more improvisational or less tightly constructed. The first three Impromptus (opp. 25/31/34) of 1881–3 reverse the general ternary plan of the Nocturnes with a more dynamic opening section and a slower, more reflective B section. The A sections are again self-contained and, in the Impromptus, are repeated exactly after a smooth transition from B. It is the final pages of the Impromptus that are the most important; only in the First is there a straightforward coda simply tacked on the end. In the Second Impromptu, the return of the tarantella A leads to a varied reprise of B, with its rhythmically involved chorale theme that looks like precisely notated *rubato*. The delightfully fresh Third Impromptu, after the usual ABA, adds an extra section which juxtaposes the slower, haunting B

58

with the scherzo material of A. This receives further harmonic development before four brusque chords in contrary motion make a dramatic finish in the manner of Chopin's Third Ballade.

Martin Cooper sees the Third Impromptu as lacking in strong contrasts of mood (1945, p. 77). That may be partly true in this particular case, but it is wrong to assume that the Third Impromptu is therefore 'typical of Fauré's genius, which always tended to fight shy of extremes of mood or violent contrasts, preferring to create diversity from unity rather than unity from diversity in the more classical manner'. Fauré's best works, like the Sixth, Seventh and Thirteenth Nocturnes, and the wartime works in particular, point to an opposite view of his genius. It is difficult to think of a better example of the creation of unity from diversity than the *Fantaisie* for piano and orchestra (op. 111) or the song cycle *La Chanson d'Ève*; only isolated, mostly early examples can be summoned in support of Mr Cooper's case.

The first three Impromptus reveal the influence of Chopin rather than Liszt, and it is hard to believe that Fauré did not once think of Chopin's Prelude in G when beginning the Third.

Fauré's thirteen Barcarolles are the largest contribution by any composer to the genre. Apart from Chopin's isolated example (op. 60) and Mendelssohn's three rather simple Venetian Gondola Songs (opp. 19/6, 30/6, 62/5), Fauré had little to go on pianistically. Neither did he visit Venice until after the first period Barcarolles (nos. 1–4) had been composed. Whether it was a motive or not in Fauré's choice of the title, the Barcarolle had become increasingly popular during the Second Empire, as in Offenbach's *Tales of Hoffmann*, first produced in the year Fauré composed his First Barcarolle (1881). Its use on the stage dates back to Auber's *Fra Diavolo* (1830) and Rossini's *Otello* (1816).

Only Barcarolles nos. 1 and 4 come close to the lilting sentimental model one expects. The first (op. 26), with its gentle falling and rising scales, recalls Fauré's setting of Marc Monnier's poem *Gondolier du Rialto* (*Barcarolle*) some eight years earlier, but is spoilt by its second section in the relative (C) major with its repetitive and rhythmically unvaried scalar theme and its falling accompaniment forever covering the same small pitch area. The short Fourth Barcarolle (op. 44, 1886) is not a strong piece either, with some unconvincing modulations in its B section (e.g. p. 5 bars 6–9). The over-use of the chord of the augmented fifth, and a first section that feels as if it never leaves the tonic but only takes short cadential sidesteps away from it, place this piece firmly within Fauré's first period.

Barcarolles nos. 2 and 3 (opp. 41–2, 1885) are longer and more complex. In the Second Barcarolle, Alfred Cortot (trans. Andrews, 1932, p. 124) considers that 'the ornamentation seems to weigh it down without enriching it, and almost to impede the blossoming of a melodic phrase which recalls the curves of his earlier manner'. To my mind, the Second Barcarolle too belongs within the first period, and it is difficult to find much evidence of the Barcarolle spirit at all in this extrovert, Lisztian piece. The offbeat rhythms and ties in the opening melody quickly cause metric ambiguity, and the impassioned third theme in the opening section is cast in the romantic grand manner and threatens to overbalance the piece.

The format of the early Barcarolles is basically ABA plus coda, with exact repeats of sections as in the Impromptus, but in Barcarolles nos. 1 and 2 the various contrasted ideas which make up the A section are recapitulated in a different order. The Third Barcarolle is more restrained and subtle than the second, bearing the imprint of Chopin rather than Liszt. Perhaps the extended decorative augmented sixth chord which joins A so perfectly to the three-stave filigree writing of A_1 (bars 24–6) gave Granados the idea for the final cadenzas of the *Maiden and the Nightingale* in *Goyescas* (I, no. 4).

The two spirited Valse-Caprices (opp. 30 and 38, 1882–4) that Saint-Saëns so much enjoyed (see Nectoux, *RdM*, 1973, pp. 72–89) also owe a debt to Chopin. The right-hand figuration at the end of the First Valse-Caprice (p. 15, lines 3–5) is remarkably similar to that at the end of Chopin's Waltz in e (op. posth.); the last two lines of p. 5 of the more successful Second Valse-Caprice bring to mind the end of Chopin's *Grande Valse Brillante* (op. 18), and so on. The closing bars of the Valse-Caprices are repetitive and ineffective, and the impression given is that Fauré was not altogether happy in these sparkling sectional marathons, although he wrote two more a decade later. As Copland says (1924, p. 579), the 'Brahms of France' had 'too orderly, too logical a mind to be really capricious'. Fauré the sensitive introvert only occasionally comes to the fore in quieter moments like the start of the coda of the First Valse-Caprice (p. 14), so unexpected after the brilliant passage that leads into it, or the c sharp theme in the Second Valse-Caprice (pp. 7–8). The Valse-Caprice themes are in general, however, undistinguished and foursquare; sequence is over-used, and the joins between the sections are rather too obvious.

(iii) *Chamber Music*

Fauré's most important creations in the first period were the Violin Sonata of 1875–6 and the First Piano Quartet of 1876–9, whose finale he rewrote 'new from top to toe' in 1883. The four minor chamber works of the early years reveal Hamelle's haphazard publishing activities in their opus numbers: the *Romance* for violin and piano (op. 28) and the *Berceuse* (op. 16) are both contemporary with the First Piano Quartet; the two works for cello and piano, the *Élégie* of 1880 and *Papillon* of 1884 were given the respective opus numbers 24 and 77.

In writing the Violin Sonata in the summer of 1875, Fauré was fortunate to have the young Belgian violinist Hubert Léonard on hand to try through passages as he wrote them. This four-movement sonata is one of the first landmarks in the renaissance of French chamber music which the SN helped to promote, and was written ten years before Franck's celebrated Sonata in the same key (A) (N, pp. 21–2). Koechlin comments (K, p. 41) that 'the vehemence of the [opening] Allegro does show some affinity at times with Franck's second movement', but he adds humorously: 'render unto Gabriel, and not unto "César", that which is Gabriel's.'

The Violin Sonata, like the Piano Quartet, is constructed upon the classical plan. Its opening theme (Ex. 4A) tells us quite a lot about Fauré. There is no introduction and, like many of Fauré's early themes,

Ex. 4   **Violin Sonata** (op. 13)
(1st movement)

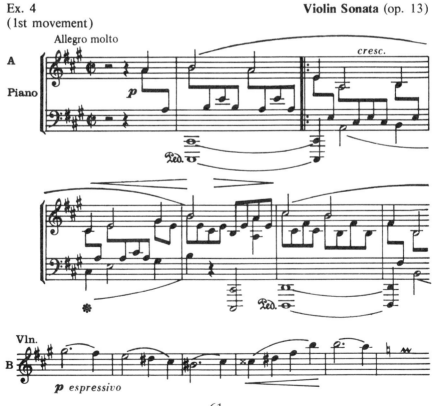

Ex. 4 (contd.)
(2nd movement)

it begins on an upbeat. It is long, expansive and fluid, extending through sequence to a Berliozian twenty-one bars. Besides being expressive and well contoured, the theme has a great deal of energy which drives the sonata along, continuity being one of Fauré's chief concerns. Theme A also contains the motifs which the sonata needs for its development, in particular that of the syncopated third bar. The piano and violin writing throughout is sonorous and positive with more than a touch of Schumann in both melody and harmony; Fauré makes certain that we know exactly what the situation is within the first four bars. When the violin takes over in bar 23 at the end of the first paragraph, A is developed rather than repeated and Fauré makes full use of the harmonic restlessness that it implies. A long crescendo leads to another favourite device: the entry of B *subito piano*. This is our familiar descending and ascending minor scale, but with a rhythm that is carefully contrasted to that of A. Again B extends itself through sequence and its rising four crotchets in the last bar fuse it with the similar last section of A (bars 15–19).

The development is based entirely on the themes already announced; and the reprise is literal but differently scored, with A on the violin. To round the movement off, Fauré constructs one of the expansive codas of which he grew so fond, here over a tonic pedal (p. 15 line 2) and, for once in his career, the classical plan even extends to a repeat of the exposition with first and second time bars.

The slow movement in the subdominant minor is dominated by the plodding iambic rhythm of its opening bar, a rhythm to which Fauré returned time and again in later life (Seventh Nocturne, Barcarolles nos. 11–13 etc). Over this rises a diminished seventh chord, something that Fauré conversely avoided in later years, and this is answered by a tender overlapping cadential figure on the violin (see Ex. 4C). With the second theme D, the accompaniment becomes more continuous, and D quickly passes to the piano in passionate octaves. These roles are maintained during the development, C being quieter and more interiorized, and D more passionate, though it is a lyrical episode based on the violin answer in C that leads to the main climax of the central section based on D. This time the recapitulation is not exact, setting the usual pattern for Fauré's chamber music with development beginning immediately after the exposition of the themes and being carried over into the varied reprise and coda.

The scherzo in A trips the light fantastic with flying pizzicati which are nowhere paralleled in Franck's less varied sonata. The opening scale idea (E) later passes into D flat, and from 2/8 into 3/4 with some interesting cross-rhythm between violin and piano (p. 27). The trio in f sharp minor in contrast sings calmly and reassuringly, and manages to lead back to the scherzo reprise without a break.

In the finale the mood is again energetic, restrained at first, but soon becoming more expansive and impassioned with a second more syncopated theme (H), which has a smoother violin counter-subject. Against H we also hear another idea in octaves on the violin, though this is only of secondary importance and there are many 'red herrings' of this sort in Fauré's chamber music. The reprise (p. 38) is again a further development section and the coda, again over a tonic pedal, dips suddenly to *pianissimo* for a final build-up in continuous *spiccato* violin quavers to a spectacular finish. The first performance of the Violin Sonata in 1877 was a success 'beyond my wildest dreams' (N, p. 24), Fauré told Mme Clerc, especially the scherzo, which was 'energetically encored'.

In the First Piano Quartet Fauré places his scherzo before the slow movement. The dominant and energetic modal theme (Ex. 5A), which begins the Quartet, again provides Fauré with a rhythmic motif that dominates the movement, and bar 2 of A is fused with the more feminine second subject B in later development (p. 13). The surprise in the development section is that A becomes a gentle and lyrical melody, with a new continuation which first appears beneath a hushed, sustained chord on the strings (p. 10). From then on it appears in both guises, the layout of the ubiquitous piano arpeggios making it clear which is which, and texture has a lot to do with thematic identification in Fauré. The stabbing off-beat chords in the piano from the first appearance of A are, however, reserved for the recapitulation (p. 16). This is literal, as in the first movement of the Violin Sonata, with B in the tonic major. In the brief coda, A for once appears quietly in its original form on the viola over off-beat chords.

The scherzo is of entrancing lightness with pizzicato string chords forming a background for the breathless and aerial theme C. This is announced in single notes on the piano and cannot make its mind up whether it is in E flat or c minor. After various developments, in which a duple time version of C is juxtaposed with the original version in 6/8, the scherzo comes to an apparent halt. But a rather irreverent

Ex. 5   **First Piano Quartet** (op. 15)
(1st movement)

(2nd movement: Scherzo)

64

Ex. 5 (contd.)
(3rd movement: Adagio)

(4th movement: Finale)

piano introduction in B flat leads to a lyrical chorale on muted strings (D) for a sort of mock-serious trio. The piano, however, continues to add its flippant comments, and so maintains the lightness of the scherzo throughout.

The Adagio is perhaps the zenith of Fauré's first period. Contemplative and beautiful, alternately serene and powerful, it demands the maximum of concentration from performer and audience alike. The short first idea (E) belongs with the chordal accompaniment that introduces it; this shows, incidentally, that Fauré was capable of stretching filled tenth chords in his left hand without arpeggiating them. A swift modulation at the end of the first musical paragraph leads straight into F, a longer and more pliant theme over a rocking piano accompaniment.

In the return of E (pp. 52–3), there is a feeling of restrained passion, of suppressed resistance to an overwhelming grief for which the serene coda acts as an appeasement, with the piano taking the tender theme F ever higher against sustained string chords until it dissolves in a shower of falling arpeggios, like a cascade of stars.

The finale is full of power and energy. Again a rising scale idea (G) appears immediately over a surging, but temporarily restrained arpeggio accompaniment. The explosive and syncopated H suddenly erupts from G with its own rising bass counter-subject on the strings, but the real second subject (J) does not appear for some pages and is announced on the viola. It too has its own rising bass line, together with the inevitable arpeggio accompaniment on the piano. The development is rather weak in comparison with the rest of the movement: the chorale-like passages on pp. 66–7 invariably slow up despite the use of the rhythmic bass of H on the strings. The recapitulation makes much use of H, with plenty of virtuoso work on the piano in Fauré's favourite double-handed parallel sixths. But J is accompanied by some curious *pianissimo* double trills on the piano (pp. 78–9) which recall the final *Forest murmurs* section of the *Ballade*. Fauré's concern to create unity from diversity can be seen in the Piano Quartet by comparing themes E, F, G and J (Ex. 5), or B and C. The themes preserve their identities in development, yet are capable of being fused together (A and B), and the unity stretches across the entire work without recourse to cyclic principles. The idea of having more than one theme in a section (H and J) has already been seen in the Barcarolles, and it was a device Fauré was to use increasingly in his later chamber music (N, pp. 29–31).

Fauré had considerable trouble finding a publisher for his First Piano Quartet. After Durand and Choudens had refused it, Fauré broke with the latter house and concentrated his efforts on Hamelle, who agreed to publish it, but only on condition that Fauré surrendered all his rights as author, as he had done with the Violin Sonata.

The remaining chamber works of the first period are relatively slight. The *Berceuse*, perhaps Fauré's most transcribed piece, was written in 1878–9 and was first performed at the same concert as the Piano Quartet by Ovide Musin and Fauré in 1880. It is simply a soothing melody with piano accompaniment which recalls Chopin's *Berceuse* (op. 57) at the start. The *Romance* is a slightly superior though much more pretentious piece. Its central section in g is quite passionate, if repetitive. The main theme is disappointing, consisting almost entirely of scales in even quavers; it over-uses the tonic pedal in its harmony too.

The *Élégie* seems to have been conceived as the slow movement for a cello sonata that was left unfinished. Like the *Romance*, it is dedicated to its first interpreter, in this case Jules Loëb, who performed it at the

SN in the same year (1883). It is a powerful emotional work of great beauty, its first theme having a poignant, funereal sadness to it. The second theme is more sinuous and syncopated, a sort of arabesque and the equivalent of *art nouveau* in music. An impassioned cello cadenza leads to a return of theme A an octave higher than at the start, with three-octave Lisztian arpeggios making an overwhelming romantic noise on the piano that is unusual for Fauré. Curiously, when Fauré came to orchestrate the *Élégie*, probably in 1895, he put this accompaniment almost entirely on the strings, using the full orchestra only in the emphatic chords of the previous cello cadenza (OS, letters F to G). The remainder of the piece is a gradual diminuendo, with B making a reappearance in the extended coda, which is a less transcendental equivalent of that of the Adagio of the First Piano Quartet.

Papillon, like the *Fantaisie* for flute and piano (op. 79), is a circumstantial piece, written at Hamelle's request as a companion for the *Élégie*, though not published till 1898. In ABAB$_1$ plus coda form, its opening is a will-o'-the-wisp perpetuum mobile, a latter-day recreation of Mendelssohn's fairy music. The more expansive B is uninspired and repetitive. Thankfully, A returns in the coda which vanishes into thin air.

(iv) *Secular Choral Music*

Why Fauré chose Victor Hugo's Gothic text for his extended chorus for mixed choir and orchestra *Les Djinns* around 1875 remains a mystery. Perhaps he considered the graphic 'Screams from Hell! Voices that yell and cry! The dreadful host driven by the gale!' etc, would result in powerful, dramatic music appealing to amateur choral societies, or that the unusual poetic form, with its lines of two syllables increasing to ten and returning to two again, would provide him with a useful technical challenge at an early stage in his career. But, as with the other Hugo settings, the result was not a success, and the original piano accompaniment falls mostly within the silent film 'villain' category. As Koechlin rightly observed (K, p. 26), the sudden crescendo and change to the major at 'Prophet, if your hand saves me' (pp. 11–12) is pompous and inflated; 'the excuse of juvenility cannot be put forward, since the *Cantique de Racine*, as well as some of the songs of the first collection . . . preserve a character infinitely more in conformity with the master's personality'. Perhaps the most successful passage comes at the end, when the breathy alto staccato line from the start returns and the music is imperceptibly altered to vanish into the distance.

Le Ruisseau (op. 22, c.1881), for female chorus and piano on an anonymous text, is a far subtler piece. Short, sensitive, and with harmonic inversions that foreshadow the beautiful later duet in the same key *Pleurs d'or* (op. 72), it is only the rather obvious perfect cadence in the dominant in bars 6–7 that indicates first-period Fauré. The passages separating the more expansive central section could be shorter, and the link between G flat and the tonic (E flat) is overstressed. But the coda, in which the melodic interest passes into the accompaniment as the voices fade away, fits the chorus perfectly with some unexpected

Ex. 6   **La Naissance de Vénus** (op. 29)
VS p.21, lines 3–5

parallel dominant seventh chords to tell us this is Fauré right to the end.

The long orchestral introduction should be sufficient warning that *La Naissance de Vénus* (op. 29, 1882), a mythological cantata for soloists, chorus and orchestra to words by Paul Collin, is unlikely to represent Fauré at his best. The undulating introduction in fact acquaints us with the music of the opening chorus (pp. 8–16), and is one of the more poetic passages in this over-inflated pagan creation. As Koechlin says (K, p. 27), 'One page of *La Rose* [op. 51/4] tells us more, and suggests more of the life and beauty of Aphrodite emerging from the briny wave, than all the musical commentaries accompanying the poem of Paul Collin'. Another huge orchestral interlude separates the opening choruses, in which the miracle of the birth of Venus presumably takes place (pp. 17–21). Fauré may have had some sort of theatrical performance in the back of his mind, although he made no indications of staging on the score. He wrote jokingly to Mrs Swinton after the 10th Leeds Festival performance on 8 October 1898[6] that he had told Collin that his

> little work had been marvellously performed. I was able to hear 400 voices singing . . . Collin appeared worried and suddenly said to me: 'I am afraid that this performance did not present the poetic truth, for Venus was certainly not born in front of so many people gathered together'. His concern for poetic truth prevented me telling him of the orchestra, since that had added over 100 extra witnesses!

1878 to 1884 were the great Wagner years for Fauré, and the small influence he exerted in Fauré's music is most evident in *La Naissance de Vénus*. The Wagnerian nature of Ex. 6 from the end of the Venus interlude (p. 21) is obvious and the more diatonic style of *Die Meistersinger von Nürnberg* can be seen in Jupiter's ensuing recitative and monologue in which he promises Venus heaven, earth and immortality in return for her 'services' (pp. 28–30).

The vast and over-repetitive final chorus 'Salut à toi, déesse blonde' (pp. 36–70) goes into eight antiphonal parts in double choir formation in places. Although the quieter moments of the A flat section (pp. 42–57) have some appeal, the closing section in the tonic (D) is banal and overblown. The final impression given by *La Naissance de Vénus* is of much ado about nothing; the moments when it becomes musically alive are far outweighed by the pages of routine response to an uninspired and pedestrian text. The first performance of *La Naissance* with orchestra was not given until 1886; the Paris première of 8 March 1883 by the Amateur Choral Society under the baton of Guillot de Sainbris involved Fauré, César Franck and a M. Maton accompanying on three pianos!

Fauré's setting of Armand Silvestre's *Madrigal* late in 1883 for vocal quartet or chorus with piano or orchestra tries hard at the outset to create an antique mood, with its lute-like accompanying chords and two-part vocal imitation. The main melodic idea is surprisingly the liturgical chorale from Bach's Cantata no. 38: *Aus tiefer Not*, and Fauré had no qualms about allying this with a secular text. Any ideas of sixteenth-century style are, however, firmly crushed by the interlude separating the stanzas; its anachronistic chain of descending chromatic chords is pure nineteenth-century Fauré. *Madrigal* is much lighter and more concise than *La Naissance de Vénus* and the choral writing throughout is clear and effective.

(v) *Religious Vocal Music*

Apart from the *Requiem*, Fauré's religious music forms his least inspired genre; he regarded being organist and choirmaster as a financially necessary chore, and this is reflected in his music which is technically undemanding and can succeed on a minimum of rehearsal. This was certainly Fauré's aim when he arranged the Christmas carol *Il est né, le divin enfant* for the Madeleine as late as 23 December 1888!

The *Ave Maria* for male voices and organ was written in 1871 whilst Fauré was teaching at the exiled École Niedermeyer in Switzerland, and was first performed on 20 August that year on the occasion when the pupils climbed up to the Hospice on the Mont Saint-Bernard. The *Ave Maria* is a graceless piece, undistinguished apart from the inappropriate stressing of its final amens which are accompanied by an over-obvious return to the tonic by means of an augmented sixth chord.

Tu es Petrus (c.1872) for baritone solo, mixed chorus and organ is better ignored, with the chorus lamely anticipating or accompanying the foursquare phrases of the soloist after the customary organ chord has established the tonality of C.

Material for the second *Ave Maria* for two sopranos and organ, first performed by the Viardot daughters Claudie and Marianne at the Madeleine on 30 May 1877, later found its way into the far superior *Ave Maria* of 1906. The famous *Libera me* from the *Requiem* was actually written as a separate item for baritone and organ as early as the autumn of 1877, and the *O Salutaris* of 1878 is probably the same as that published by Hamelle as op. 47/1 in 1888. This was first performed by Fauré's namesake, the celebrated baritone Jean-Baptiste Faure (1830–1914). Unfortunately, Faure was also a composer with a number of well-known religious compositions to his credit, as well as a setting of Hugo's *Puisqu'ici-bas* published five years before Fauré's, and confusion between the two composers has been long in dying. The *O*

Salutaris has a quiet, undulating introduction that also introduces the second section 'Bella premunt hostilia' when transposed up a fifth.

The most important religious composition of the first period is the *Low Mass (Messe basse)*, wrongly named because it is sung. Fauré referred to it as his 'little mass', and M. Nectoux has discovered (N, p. 48) that there are no less than three distinct versions of the work covering a quarter of a century. The first version dates from 1881 and was performed for the benefit of the fishermen of Villerville, where the Clerc family had a summer residence, on 4 September 1881. The Mass was a collaboration between Fauré, who wrote the *Gloria, Sanctus* and *Agnus Dei*, and Messager, who wrote the *Kyrie* and *O Salutaris*. The first version for three-part female choir with soloist, harmonium and violin solo was repeated in September 1882 in an orchestrated version mainly by Messager, though Fauré orchestrated the final *Agnus Dei* himself. In the third version of December 1906, which is entirely by Fauré, the *Gloria* was omitted as a whole, but its 'Qui tollis' section was adapted to the words of the *Benedictus*. Messager's *Kyrie* and *O Salutaris* were left out, and Fauré added a new *Kyrie* of his own, probably around 1906, though its gently chromatic chorale-like accompaniment is closely akin to that of *Une Sainte en son auréole* (op. 61/ 1) of 1892. The final order of the *Low Mass* was thus: *Kyrie— Sanctus—Benedictus—Agnus Dei,* and it is certainly within the grasp of small choirs anywhere, unlike most contemporary French Mass settings.

Designed for amateurs, the *Low Mass* still possesses a certain charm and freshness, with carefully modulated climaxes near the ends of the *Kyrie* and *Sanctus*. The final *Agnus Dei* is the weakest of the movements with an all-pervading palindromic quaver figure (bar 1) and a rather long coda on a tonic pedal, which causes the otherwise harmonically supple Mass to stagnate a little. But there is a good deal of harmonic interest in the other movements with some typically Fauréan cadences, such as the one with a falling sixth in the bass in the *Kyrie* (bars 11–12), and superb rising passages in both the *Kyrie* (bars 19–22) and the gently rocking *Benedictus* (bars 1–6).

(vi) *Orchestral Music*

The apparently unsuccessful performances of the Symphony in d (op. 40; see Appendix A) mark the end of Fauré's first period. After his three essays in the grand orchestral style: the *Suite d'orchestre* or Symphony in F (op. 20) of 1867–73; the Violin Concerto (op. 14) of 1878–9; and the Symphony in d of 1884, Fauré gradually came to realize that his talents lay elsewhere and concentrated on chamber music and songs. He did begin a Third Symphony in the late 1880s apparently, but a letter to the Vicomtesse Greffulhe in September 1887[7] shows how uncongenial this was in comparison with writing the lighter *Pavane*. 'This is the amusing aspect of my work', he told her. 'The grave part consists of an austere symphony that causes me great anxiety, because the manner in which I work too much resembles an incoherent parody ('coq-à-l'âne'). Unfortunately it cannot be otherwise'. Nothing remains of this symphony, if indeed the project ever got properly under way, and all that remains of the three earlier works as such are the opening Allegros of the Symphony in F and the Violin Concerto, and two first violin parts of the destroyed Symphony in d now in the BN (mss 17780, 17749 and Rés. Vma. ms 954).

The first movement of the *Suite d'orchestre*, published later by Hamelle as the *Allegro symphonique* (op. 68) in a piano duet transcription by Léon Boëllmann, shows Fauré struggling a bit as an orchestrator, the manuscript disclosing his uncertainty over balance and some unnecessary doublings. The Allegro is in conventional sonata form, plunging straight into its irregularly phrased first subject (Ex. 7A), again a syncopated rising scale. B is another rising theme, but more lyrical and expansive. The problem with the *Allegro symphonique* is that the level of musical interest is not maintained. Theme A tends to be mechanically over-used in short, regular sequences, and Fauré finds it difficult to build up tension with B, even when using the triplet aspect of it in sequence. In short, the ideas he invents are not ideally suited to symphonic development, and Fauré probably sensed that his First Symphony fell short of perfection when it was performed at the SN on 16 May 1874. I suspect that the first movement would work better in

Ex. 7   **Allegro symphonique** (op. 20/1, 68/1)

the original two-piano form in which it was premièred by Fauré and Saint-Saëns on 8 February 1873 than as a piano duet, but this version has not been recovered.

The Violin Concerto was intended to be a three-movement work, but only the first two movements, Allegro and Andante, were performed by Ovide Musin at the SN on 12 April 1880. Fauré began a finale in 1879, but never completed it, and the Andante has since disappeared too, though Fauré may have used parts of it in his Andante for violin and piano (op. 75) in 1897.

Ex. 8   **Violin Concerto** (op. 14) 1st movt. A–C
cf. **String Quartet** (op. 121) 1st movt. A_1–C_1

The two themes of the surviving Allegro of the Violin Concerto (Exx. 8A and B) again show Fauré grappling with unsuitable material, only here the ideas, as well as being scale-based, are both lyrical and long-breathed. B in particular has a tendency to languish romantically. A proved far better suited to the more intimate medium of the String Quartet when Fauré used it again (A_1) in the light of a lifetime's experience in 1923. He wisely removed the triplets and gave B a better shape (B_1) too, putting the ties across the barline earlier, to give the theme extra impetus where it needed it most. The subsidiary idea (C_1), which begins the String Quartet and assumes almost equal importance with A_1 in the opening paragraph, is missing in the Violin Concerto as a counter-subject to A, although C_1 may well have derived from a subsidiary idea C, which makes its separate appearance on p. 6 of the manuscript score, and bears a certain resemblance to the violin echo in the slow movement of the Violin Sonata (cf. Ex. 4C). The first movement of the String Quartet is much more compact and closely worked; the exposition alone of the Violin Concerto is almost as long as the Quartet's whole opening movement. The Violin Concerto is more extrovert, though Fauré only added one cadenza passage later in pencil at the point where the violin first enters (pp. 7–8), presumably after consultation with Musin.

(vii) *Fauré and the Theatre*

Fauré's interest in the theatre in relation to the Viardot family, and his introduction by Saint-Saëns to his librettist Louis Gallet (1835–98) were briefly mentioned in chapter 1. But Gallet, the librettist of *La Princesse jaune* and *Le Déluge*, was much in demand, writing libretti in this period for Bizet, Gounod and Massenet amongst others, and he must have had many similar demands to Fauré's, all on recommendations by friends. In addition, Fauré, although a regular theatre-goer since the 1860s, was naturally inexperienced in composing for the medium and wanted a one-act libretto for his first attempt, which Gallet was too busy to devote time to.[8] Even if Gallet had produced a libretto for Fauré, it is by no means certain that it would have led to a successful lyric work, for Fauré in the period 1879–95 seems to have toyed with as many theatrical projects as the indecisive Debussy.

Fauré's main concern in 1879–80 was a drama by Louis Bouilhet, *Faustine* (1864). As Bouilhet had died in 1869, Fauré wrote to Gustave Flaubert for permission to transform his friend's work into a libretto. He obtained this in March 1879, though Gallet initially thought that another Spanish play by Bouilhet, *Dolorès* (1862), would make a better subject as it needed less modification. Fauré finally persuaded Gallet

to work on *Faustine* but the situation was complicated by his editor's
son Paul de Choudens wanting to collaborate with Gallet on the same
subject! The difficulties persisted after Gallet at last got round to
drawing up a scenario in four acts and five tableaux for Fauré in April
1880, because this did not coincide with the modifications required by
Flaubert. Nevertheless Fauré began work and, as was the custom then,
drew up a musical plan for Act 1 in six sections. Then Flaubert died
in May 1880! Fauré, despite much entreating and flattery, never
obtained a single scene of his libretto from Gallet, who was at the time
fully occupied with the five-act libretto of *Les Guelfes* for the then-
successful Benjamin Godard.

In 1883 Fauré was still trying without any luck to provoke Gallet into
action by telling him of his recent talks with a rival librettist Philippe

Ex. 9   Start of the Sextet from **Barnabé** (1879)

Gille, and he even turned down a collaboration with the poet he then admired, Armand Silvestre, simply in the hope of working with the renowned Gallet.

The only theatre music that came out of the first period was for a one-act comic opera, probably entitled *Barnabé*, on a libretto by Jules Moineaux, author of vaudevilles and operettas and the father of Georges Courteline (1861–1929). The libretto, which dates from the autumn of 1879, seems to have been of mind-bending stupidity, if we can judge from the final sextet, Fauré's incomplete setting of which survives in the BN (ms 17744). In this three girls, Georgette, Margot and Simone, and a boy Gervais for no apparent reason enter the house of Barnabé and his wife Jeanne. They plague them and squabble amongst themselves, first waking Barnabé and eventually causing him to evict them from the house. The dialogue Fauré was required to set was long, superficial and fast-moving, and he may have gone straight to this final sextet as it was the most interesting part of the opera. He seems to have got quite a long way with it, producing nine pages in short score in a light musical style closest to that of the Valse-Caprices, which presents the various voices to their best advantage with a minimum of linking instrumental material. There is nothing original about the opening (Ex. 9) or Georgette's sentimental arietta à la Massenet: 'Nous venions simplement vous faire notre compliment' (p. 7), but this fragment shows that Fauré was not utterly impractical as far as composing for the conventional theatre went. There have been plenty of worse sextets in comic operas and many operas do not even aspire to six soloists singing together. It is simply fortunate for music that Fauré realised in time that his talents were unsuited for symphonic writing, and that he was also thwarted in his search for a viable libretto in a period that otherwise produced the Piano Quartets, the Verlaine settings and the *Requiem*.

Footnotes to Chap. 3
1. The borrowing of *Barcarolle* (op. 7/3) for volume 2 and the substitution of *Noël* (op. 43/1) took place during Hamelle's reordering of the three collections of songs in 1908 (see the introduction to Appendix A).
2. *Correspondance générale*, vol. 1, Paris, Plon, 1930, p. 229. Letter c.1912.
3. Vol. 2, London, Chatto and Windus, 1965, p. 245.
4. Vol. 1, Paris, Gallimard, 1927, p. 301. See J-M. Nectoux: *Gabriel Fauré: Correspondance* (Paris, Flammarion, 1980), pp. 203–19 for a full account of the links between the composer and Proust, and about the *Ballade* in particular.
5. The confusion is increased by the fact that Fauré changed his original Allegro moderato at this point (p. 13) to Allegro molto moderato in the orchestral version (OS, p. 41), and reduced the speed so that it exactly matched that of the Andante (dotted crotchet = 66) which led into it (OS, p. 39; piano

score, p. 12). Presumably this was an attempt to enhance the feeling of overall unity.

6. Letter of 29 October 1898 sent to Llandough Castle, Cowbridge, Wales, pp. 3–4.

7. La in the Pierpont Morgan Library, New York (Mary Flagler Cary Music Collection). The Comtesse Élisabeth de Caraman-Chimay (b. 1860) became Vicomtesse Greffulhe on her marriage in 1878 to the Dutch banker Henri Greffulhe. She became Comtesse again with her husband's elevation to Comte in 1898.

8. For fuller details on Fauré's theatrical aspirations see J-M. Nectoux: 'Flaubert, Gallet, Fauré ou Le Démon de Théâtre', *Bulletin du Bibliophile*, no. 1 (1976), pp. 33–47.

4

MATURITY AND THE SECOND PERIOD: 1885–1906

De la musique avant toute chose, . . .
De la musique encore et toujours!

(Verlaine: *Art poétique*)

The first years of the second period were 'sombre' ones (N, p. 56) in Fauré's life and art. Financial difficulties, teaching commitments and the death of his parents resulted in periods of acute depression. This was only relieved artistically by the discovery of Verlaine's poetry in 1887, thanks to Comte Robert de Montesquiou, and practically through the Venetian holiday arranged in 1891 by the Princesse de Polignac. This is not to say that sad or reflective compositions do not exist in the first period—the *Élégie* and the slow movement of the First Piano Quartet spring readily to mind—but at the beginning of the second period this becomes the rule rather than the exception. In these years, Fauré also turned to incidental music for the stage, perhaps as a substitute for symphonic composition, or perhaps as a substitute for the ideal opera libretto he never found, though he kept on searching. *Prométhée* to some extent provided Fauré with an outlet for his undoubted dramatic talents, but he retained his salon image despite his efforts, and Debussy reflected the popular view when he described Fauré as the 'master of charms' in *Gil Blas* in 1903. In comparison with the late 1880s, the post-Venice years were happy and productive with creative peaks like *La Bonne Chanson,* the Sixth and Seventh Nocturnes, and *Pelléas et Mélisande.* As Fauré faced up to the twentieth century his style began to change. Some works in the period 1897–1906 remain firmly within the second period, like the song *Arpège* or *Pelléas et Mélisande,* whilst others, like *Le Don silencieux* and parts of *Prométhée* Act 1, anticipate the third period. Each genre reflects, to a varying degree, Fauré's developing maturity as a composer, which is most evident in the subtler cadences, the sectional links and the increasing use of modality. More important are the developments beneath the

78

surface: the increasing poetic awareness, self-criticism and emotional depth.

(i) *Songs*

The second period songs are dominated by the first of Fauré's six song cycles: the *Cinq mélodies 'de Venise'* (June-Sept 1891) and *La Bonne Chanson* (1892–4). Both are settings of the poetry of Verlaine, and both can claim to be deliberately cyclic through recurring motifs and stylistic similarities.

Of the five op. 58 songs—*Mandoline, En Sourdine, Green, A Clymène* and *C'est l'extase*—only the first justifies the epithet 'de Venise'. The remainder were either composed—or finished (*En Sourdine*)—in Paris. *Mandoline*, like Fauré's first Verlaine setting *Clair de lune* (op. 46/2, 1887) with its unusually long introduction and its modal nostalgia, relates to the Italian *commedia dell' arte*, continuing (Su, p. 70) 'to translate into musical form that rarefied and yet voluptuous civilization of which the *fête galante* was the symbol, Watteau the prophet and Verlaine the later rhapsodist'. Venice was the home of both the Barcarolle (*A Clymène*) and the carnival, but both become translated in the French imagination into idealized backgrounds for moonlit meetings and refined passions. All is restrained, veiled and subtle in the 'quasi tristes' masques and bergamasques of Verlaine and Fauré, which retain no traces of the courtly theatrical spectacle or the clumsy peasant dance from Bergamo in their evocative appeal.

There is no overall tonal plan to op. 58, but there is a recurrent figure which incorporates either falling thirds or modal cadences with flattened leading notes, or both (Exx. 10 a-f). This recurs in various guises, though in its most concentrated form at the start of *Green* (Ex. 10c) and *A Clymène* (Ex. 10d). The accompaniment motif (Ex. 10f) from *Green* (bar 20f.) also recurs in *C'est l'extase* (bar 16f.), and the second motif of *C'est l'extase* (Ex. 10g) is none other than the second motif of *En Sourdine* (cf. Hamelle vol. 3, pp. 36 and 51). In both cases this motif appears in vocal line and accompaniment.

From a letter to the Princesse de Polignac we know that this unity was deliberate on Fauré's part, and that he was aware that he was achieving something new in the process. Whilst finishing *C'est l'extase* in September 1891, he wrote[1]:

You will see that as in *Clymène,* I have tried out a *form* that I believe to be new, at least I do not know of anything similar; it is appropriate that I try to create something *new* when I write for you, the one person in the world who least resembles any other! After an initial theme which does not reappear, I introduce for the second strophe ['Ô le frêle et frais murmure']

Ex. 10 **Cinq mélodies 'de Venise'** (op. 58)

Mandoline bar 14f.

a Et c'est Da - mis qui, pour main - te cru - el - le, fit maint vers ten-(dre)

En Sourdine bar 27f.

Piano

b Souf- fle ber-ceur et doux _____

Green bar 1f.

c Voi- ci des fruits, des fleurs, des feuilles et des bran - ches __

A Clymène (piano introduction)

d *dolce espressivo*

C'est l'extase bars 8ff.

e C'est tous les fris- sons des bois, Par- mi l'é-treinte des

bri - ses, C'est vers les ra-mu - res gri - ses

C'est l'extase accompaniment motif bar 16f. (cf. **Green** bar 20f.)

f *dolce espressivo*

C'est l'extase bar 32f. (cf. **En Sourdine** bar 17f.)

g Cette â - - - me qui se la - men - te___

a calm and mitigating return of *Green* [Ex. 10f], and for the third ['Cette âme qui se lamente', Ex. 10g], a return of *En Sourdine* which is, on the contrary, inflamed, becoming still more intense and profound right through to the end. This forms a sort of conclusion and makes the five songs into a sort of *suite*.

Apart from *A Clymène,* Debussy set all the texts of op. 58 before Fauré: *Mandoline* in 1882; *En Sourdine* in September 1882 and again in *Fêtes galantes* in 1891; *Green* in January 1886; and *C'est l'extase* in 1887, the last two songs belonging to the *Ariettes oubliées.* Whilst there are no direct musical links in *Mandoline,* both composers chose to retain the same mood throughout instead of following the changing perspectives of the poem. Fauré's setting is most in sympathy with the pastoral charm of Verlaine, whilst Debussy pokes fun at his amateur serenaders. As Arthur Wenk points out (1976, pp. 33, 289), both alter the texts of the poems; Fauré repeats the first stanza at the end, implying an endless serenade, though he does not go as far as Debussy, with his twenty-bar 'la, la, la' refrain. In Fauré's setting the mood is joyous and dance-like, with a repressed exhilaration that is always threatening to break its bonds.

In the case of *En Sourdine* it is more profitable to compare Fauré's version with Debussy's *Fêtes galantes* setting of the same year. Fauré's is both the more continuous setting and the one which reveals the clearest understanding of the poem. This continually builds towards the final line 'Le rossignol *chant*era', and for this accented syllable Fauré saves his highest note, aptly the tonic, so that there is a natural feeling of culmination, but one that is all the more effective for its deliberate dynamic restraint (*pianissimo sempre*). Fauré does not use a specific musical idea to represent the nightingale as Debussy does; his motif in the second part of *En Sourdine* (p. 36) belongs to the cycle as a whole. Fauré's nightingale sings throughout in one of the composer's most serene nocturnal evocations; there is no need for a monotone setting of the opening line 'Calmes dans le demi-jour', for the short introduction of lulling arpeggios establishes the mood perfectly.

The two settings of *Green* are as different as chalk and cheese on the surface. Debussy's setting is full of the youthful joy of a new love, whereas Fauré's more accurately represents the quickly changing emotions of the lover who is ready to give away his heart in the anxious opening bars just as readily as the fruit and flowers he has brought. Both composers, as Wenk demonstrates (1976, pp. 52–7), use harmonic devices to reflect the mood of the poem: Debussy's strong fifth-based progressions and postponement of the tonic suggest the earnestness of the lover and his simultaneous uncertainty, whilst Fauré's frequent returns to the tonic amid faster but less decisive harmonic progressions suggest underlying timidity, as well as a confused eagerness. 'In the case of *Green*', Fauré wrote to Mme Baugnies (FF, pp. 71–2), 'I cannot too strongly recommend to you not to sing it *slowly*: its nature is *lively*, moving, almost *breathless*. *Above all*, sing it for yourself alone'.

In *C'est l'extase*, Debussy's setting is the more languorous. A descending figure based on the chord of the dominant ninth instantly creates the required mood, and his use of vocal phrases on a monotone throws the more lyrical moments into sharp relief. Fauré, on the other hand, suggests languor by musical sighs in the introduction, and covert ecstasy through his syncopated accompaniment, which becomes more continuous later on to reflect the rustling grass and the water on the pebbles. His two melodic motifs (Exx. 10 f and g) and the continuity of his piano part complement the rhythmic scheme and indicate the underlying links between Verlaine's stanzas in a way Debussy's setting does not.

A Clymène, though characteristically modal with implied or actual tritonal effects between the outer parts, is rather weak in comparison with the other Venetian songs; perhaps Debussy was wise not to set this poem.

In *La Bonne Chanson*, Fauré set nine of the twenty-one poems Verlaine wrote for his fiancée Mathilde Mauté de Fleurville in 1870, in the order: VIII: *Une Sainte en son auréole*; IV: *Puisque l'aube grandit*; VI: *La Lune blanche luit dans les bois*; XX: *J'allais par des chemins perfides*; XV: *J'ai presque peur, en vérité*; V: *Avant que tu ne t'en ailles*; XIX: *Donc, ce sera par un clair jour d'été*; XVII: *N'est-ce pas?*; and XXI: *L'Hiver a cessé*. Fauré wrote the first eight songs in 1892–3, but spent a great deal of time considering the last song which was not completed until February 1894. The poems are the powerful expression of Verlaine's love for a young girl too timid and immature for their marriage that same year. It is likely that the predominantly homosexual Verlaine put more genuine passion into *La Bonne Chanson* than he ever found for Mathilde. His increasing drunkenness, coupled with the emotional events of 1870–71 and the appearance on the scene of the boy-poet Arthur Rimbaud, led to disaster and desertion in 1872: the poet of *La Lune blanche* became 'the infernal husband'. But only the poetry concerned Fauré as he carefully arranged his chosen texts into a cycle, both through poetic content and mood and through recurring themes. The ordering of op. 61 is not chronological, as Appendix A shows.

Again there is no overall tonal plan but, whereas there are two main ideas in op. 58, there are five in *La Bonne Chanson* (Ex. 11 A–E). These occur most often in the piano part, which is as important as the voice throughout. The function of the themes is purely musical, for they are not linked with recurring poetic images or ideas, and thus have no similarity with Wagnerian leitmotifs. As Jankélévitch says (1974, p. 132), *La Bonne Chanson* is 'a veritable symphony', and whilst some thematic references are more obvious than others, there is again no doubt that most are deliberate.

In the same interview in July 1902 in which Fauré spoke of his *Requiem* to Louis Aguettant (*Comoedia*, 1954, p. 6), he began by saying that there was only one 'Lydia' theme (B) in *La Bonne Chanson* and that 'it related to an interpreter' (almost certainly Emma Bardac). Then, little by little, Fauré admitted that there were other themes. First, the 'carlovingien' theme recalled in the tonic major epilogue of no. 4: *J'allais par des chemins perfides* (A). Secondly, the theme 'à la caille' (quail) in *Avant que tu ne t'en ailles* (D). Thirdly, the accompaniment idea in no. 7, *Donc, ce sera par un clair jour d'été*, borrowed from the end of the previous song (E). Fourthly, the formula 'Que je

Ex. 11   **La Bonne Chanson** (op. 61)

'Carlovingien' theme, 1, bars 15–16/79–80

'Lydia' theme (cf. Ex. 2), 3, bars 9–12

'Que je vous aime' theme, 5, bars 65–9

Theme 'A la caille', 6, bars 8–9

6, coda, bars 72–3

vous aime' at the end of *J'ai presque peur, en vérité* (C). Finally, Fauré admitted that all the themes were 'clustered together' in the final song *L'Hiver a cessé*. 'But', added Aguettant, 'it was necessary to put one's finger on each of these analogies, to force him to identify, one by one, all these recurring ideas whose identities he seemed to have forgotten.' Indeed, Fauré significantly said before being asked about the thematic links in *La Bonne Chanson*: 'One frequently attributes to composers intentions they never dreamed of. I seek above all to extricate the general feeling of a poem, rather than to concentrate on its details.'

The themes in Ex. 11 are listed in the order in which they occur in *La Bonne Chanson*. The recurrences are rather more numerous than Fauré claimed: some may have been subconscious, evidence of Fauré's consummate craftsmanship in large-scale as well as smaller works, and some themes are transformed or developed in the process of composition. The most important thematic cross-references are as follows:

Ex.11 A Songs nos. 1: bar 15f and coda (p. 5); 3: p. 14 lines 3–4; 4: final section 'un poco più mosso' pp. 18–19; 5: first motif bars 10–12 based on bar 2 of A; 6: p. 27 lines 1–3; 9: final section p. 45 bars 6–7.

B Songs nos. 1: bars 34–7?; 2: bars 3–4; 3: main statement in the cycle bars 9–11 and p. 15; 4: bar 13f; 5: bars 19–22, second main statement; 8: p. 36 lines 3–4; 9: p. 44 last bar—p. 45 bar 2. The rising scale in bar 3 of B is its most used feature, which occurs more often than listed here.

C Songs nos. 5: p. 23 line 3; 7: final section 'molto più lento' pp. 32–3; 8: p. 36 line 2 and p. 38 lines 3–4; 9: vocal line bars 15–16?

D Songs nos. 6: theme of 'allegro moderato' sections pp. 24–5; 9: pp. 39–40 and 44–5.

E Songs nos. 6: last 8 bars (p. 28); 8: main idea bar 4f; 9: bars 6–7 and 21 (p. 41).

Une Sainte en son auréole carries 'grace and love' on to a higher level, and its measured religious tread is made flexible by three-bar phrases which often overlap between voice and piano. In stanza 2, Fauré indulges in some rare word-painting, but one would never guess that the 'golden horn note from the distant woods' could be F flat from the vocal line alone, or that in 1892 it would be enharmonically repeated over changing minor ninth chords on E flat and C. Expansive joy is the theme of *Puisque l'aube grandit, Avant que tu ne t'en ailles, Donc, ce sera par un clair jour d'été* and *L'Hiver a cessé*, with wide-ranging sonorous arpeggios and triumphant vocal lines in all four songs. This is the exuberant Fauré that burst forth all too rarely in the previous decade, and which forms a perfect contrast with the tender calm of *La*

Lune blanche or the placid intimacy of *N'est-ce pas*?

In *J'allais par des chemins perfides* the mood is one of anguished uncertainty, with sudden accents and tortured harmonies from bar 2 onwards, which only soften in the final section when 'love' reunites the pair in joy. The smooth rising scales here are a logical extension of the Lydia theme which, with its whole-tone implications, had enabled *La Lune blanche* to modulate so freely. *J'ai presque peur, en vérité* is all breathless uncertainty, the Lydia theme this time contributing to the tension. Only at the end does the lover loose his restrained passion in a long, ecstatic 'Je vous aime . . . je t'aime' which feels all the more expansive after the melodically repetitive passage that precedes it.

Avant que tu ne t'en ailles is one of the highspots of the second period with mercurial changes of mood at the start as the excited awakening of nature is balanced against the uneasy passion of the poet, his 'eyes full of love', dreaming, if the music is a guide, of 'a saint in his glory, a lady in her tower' (song no. 1). Fauré's talent is able to make a unified song from all this restless diversity; he never loses hold of the continuity, and the result is an elevating experience which looks forward at times to Fauré's final song-cycle *L'Horizon chimérique*.

The natural artistic summit of *La Bonne Chanson* is its final song *L'Hiver a cessé*, which rounds off the cycle with enviable precision. The unusually long introduction depicts the coming of spring with irresistible élan, and the song deals in long musical paragraphs that avoid the tonic. The first such chord is reached in bar 11, and only Fauré would mark this culminating point *pianissimo*. All the songs of the second period end quietly too, however radiant or intense they have been en route.

La Bonne Chanson can stand as an equal beside any nineteenth-century song-cycle, German or French: in a sense it is Fauré's *Dichterliebe* or *Die schöne Müllerin*. It still sounds fresh and original today, and it is hard to believe that Fauré, aged nearly 50, could so perfectly match the youthful lyricism and ardour of a poet only half his age. When the work was first performed in public on 20 April 1895 by Jeanne Remacle and Fauré, the SN audience were not ready for its audacities: Fauré, who never set out deliberately to shock, must have been taken aback. Marcel Proust wrote to his friend Pierre Lavallée after a private performance at the house of Madeleine Lemaire almost a year earlier that[2]

the young musicians are virtually unanimous in disliking *La Bonne Chanson*. It appears that it is needlessly complex, very inferior to the rest of his output. Bréville and Debussy (who is generally regarded as a great genius, superior to Fauré) think the same. But I don't care, I adore it.

Proust was almost alone in preferring *La Bonne Chanson* to Fauré's earlier songs ('*Au Cimetière* is really dreadful, and *Après un rêve* worthless'). Camille Bellaigue complained in *La Revue des Deux Mondes* (15 October 1897, pp. 934–6), the bastion of artistic respectability, of the

> incessant modulations . . . The prime character of these songs is to be terribly difficult . . . all the sonorous elements appear in contradiction: the voice with the accompaniment . . . the chords with each other, and the notes of the vocal part amongst themselves. The songs give the impression of following each other without order or logic, tracing haphazard lines without grace or certainty; above all without direction.

For the misguided Bellaigue, as for many others, Fauré's 'bonnes chansons' were his old chansons!

Fauré regretted the arrangement of *La Bonne Chanson* he made with string quintet accompaniment for a concert at Frank Schuster's London home in 1898. He told his wife on 2 April after the performance (LI, p. 28) that the extra 'accompaniment was redundant; I prefer the simple piano accompaniment'. The 'simple' must refer to the texture and not to the technique involved.

Prior to the two cycles comes a collection of varied songs in which several distinct traits are again visible. *Larmes* (op. 51/1, 1888) is a direct descendant of the powerful *Fleur jetée* and *Le Voyageur*, though its construction is subtler with three rising statements of the ferociously accented opening maintaining the intensity of the bitter grief that Fauré sets out to portray. The other op. 51 setting from Jean Richepin's *La Mer*, *Au Cimetière*, has an equally anguished central climax in whose slow ascent every doggèd footstep hurts. The restrained funereal plodding of the outer parts makes the climax all the more overwhelming. On a different level, the swift return to the texture of the opening in contrary motion finds a direct parallel in *Soir* (bars 21–3).

The songs that most look back to the first period are those with a religious flavour: the sentimental and rather nondescript 'cantique' *En Prière* (1889), and the slightly superior *Noël* (1886) to words by Victor Wilder, in which an attractive vocal line is burdened by a rather heavy and inept accompaniment. The companion song in op. 43, *Nocturne* (Villiers de l'Isle-Adam, 1886) belongs more with *Les Présents* (op. 46/1, 1887), both in mood and in its fascination with a simple repeated motif. *Nocturne* has an ascending piano figure of a type encountered elsewhere in the second period, in *La Rose* and *Mandoline* for example. This is the direct opposite of Debussy's geotropic arabesques. In *Nocturne* the rising line perhaps suggests twinkling stars; on its final occurrence the chord of resolution is g minor instead of the expected tonic E flat ('Mon amour et ta beau*té*') and the whole song receives a poetic lift, just as it does when the tonic pedal which dominates it first gives way to the subdominant at 'Moi, ma *nuit* au sombre voile'. *Les Présents* has the same nocturnal atmosphere, but its overlong introduction establishes a pattern of foursquare phrasing, and suggests that what appear to be complex harmonies are really only tonal sidesteps from an ubiquitous tonic.

The two Verlaine settings, *Clair de lune* and *Spleen* (op. 51/3), both have a guitar-like feel to their accompaniments. Both were again set earlier by Debussy: *Clair de lune* in 1882 and 1891 (*Fêtes galantes*), and *Spleen* around 1885. This last song was wrongly titled by Fauré, *Spleen* being the second of Verlaine's *Aquarelles* ('Les roses étaient toutes rouges') rather than the third of his *Ariettes oubliées*. There is some similarity with *Mandoline* in Fauré's *Clair de lune* and his setting is dominated by the minuet of the masqueraders in the accompaniment which begins in the long introduction. This is one of the first of Fauré's great compositions bound together by an 'endless melody' (cf. *En Sourdine*, *Soir*, the *Nocturne* from *Shylock*), though his conception of the term is on a very different level from that of Wagner. The vocal line is really an expressive adjunct to the piano part, but the two mingle briefly with each other at the point where the song of the masqueraders 'blends with the moonlight' ('Au calme clair de lune', see bars 35–41). Fauré whimsically sets the masqueraders' song in the 'mode mineur' in a modal B flat major at the point in the text which refers to this (bars 26–7). In Debussy's *Fêtes galantes* setting, the piano part for once has a continuity comparable to that of Fauré, but it rather represents the voice of nature as a background to the masquers.

In *Il pleure dans mon coeur*, both Fauré and Debussy use the minor mode to express the feeling of languor in Verlaine, and both use harmonic prolongations 'to convey the monotony of pain without cause and to set off sections of the text without interrupting the accompaniment of the rain' (Wenk, 1976, pp. 62–3). Both Debussy and Fauré double the vocal line in the left hand of the piano an octave lower in places, but Fauré obtains effects out of proportion to the means he employs in his final section, with a modified reprise and a sudden leap downwards in the bass to give unexpected weight to the final line 'mon *coeur* a tant de peine!'. This is made all the more effective by the previous bars in which the bass line doubles the voice, and by the fact that the earlier sudden descent of the bass was used for a different purpose, that of announcing a change of mood for the second stanza: 'O bruit doux de la pluie'.

La Rose is a supple setting of an anacreontic ode by Leconte de Lisle, full of light and Mediterranean charm. The rising phrase in its accompaniment provides a natural springboard for the sudden upward leaps in the piano part: first, at the start of a sparkling central seascape of the sort from which Aphrodite appeared, and secondly, to point the climax of the final part, when Fauré begins the last phrase '*sa*lua la fleur' on a high g″ specially reserved for the occasion.

The marvellously productive year 1894 saw the appearance of the very different but complementary songs *Prison* and *Soir* (op. 83). *Prison,* the last Verlaine setting, is the ultimate in powerful compression with introduction and postlude cut to an absolute minimum and only just room for the singer to snatch the tremendous breaths necessary for the angry central phrases. The fourth bar with the sudden change of piano register at the end, an effect used again in *Pleurs d'or* two years later, provides a recurring motif for the first part of the song. The non-repeating AB form follows the poem closely and the mood is suitably claustrophobic, a perfect contrast with the soft beauty of *Soir*. *Soir* is the first of the great Samain songs that dominate the transitional years to the third period. The rather weak text is outclassed in inspiration by Fauré's setting, in which the form and mood are controlled by the harmony, which is the distilled essence of Chopin. The returns to the tonic chord D flat lend reassurance at strategic moments (bars 4, 7, 12, 35–7). Bar 12 marks the start of the more chromatic middle section, with a right-hand piano melody that the singer joins and to which he finally forms a counter-subject. Bar 25 marks the end of the first phrase of the varied reprise which, as in other second period songs like *Green*, *N'est-ce pas?* and *Dans la forêt de septembre*, contains the vocal climax of the song. *Prison* and *Soir* together make up less than 70 bars of music in which every note counts: the return to the single-note texture of the opening in *Soir* from the complexity of the middle section is achieved with breathtaking skill.

Pleurs d'or (op. 72) was written in London for Camille Landi (mezzo-soprano) and the celebrated baritone David Bispham, for a concert in St James's Hall on 1 May 1896 which also included settings by Adela Maddison of *Ob ich dich liebe* and *Im Traum*. The *Times* announcement of this special extra concert mentions that *Pleurs d'or* had a violin obbligato, though this has not survived. In London, the duet was performed with its original title *Larmes*, but a letter from Fauré to Albert Samain of 13 April 1896 (Jean-Aubry, *ReM*, 1945, p. 54) shows that he was worried about confusion with his earlier Richepin setting (op. 51/1) and asked Samain to supply a new title. *Pleurs d'or*, which does not borrow anything directly from his original poem 'Larmes aux fleurs suspendues' published in *Au Jardin de l'Infante* (1893), was almost certainly supplied by Samain himself. Fauré was always careful to request the permission of the poets whose work he set to music and a letter quoted by Jean-Aubry (1945, p. 56) shows his concern that they should hear his settings of their poetry when this was possible. To this end he invited Samain to hear *Arpège* on 7? October 1897. However, as Jean-Aubry says, it is unlikely that either *Soir* or *Arpège* satisfied Samain, who still had 750 unset verses of the operatic project *Bouddha* to remind him of Fauré's independent will (see section vi). He wrote to his sister on 25 June 1898 after a soirée given by Emma Bardac: 'Why was the music so modern? . . . Ah! these gentlemen of the SN (d'Indy, Chausson, Fauré etc.) punish me severely.'

The beautiful and rewarding *Pleurs d'or* deserves to be far more widely known. It is an exercise both in long descending whole-tone phrases like *Soir*, and in delaying the final tonic through a series of unexpected cadences. The end is made all the more effective by the repetitive nature of the section 'Larmes des cloches latines' (pp. 3–4) in G; and by the long sustained climax in the final pages ('Larmes aux grands cils perlées'), which is really a series of dominant seventh chords with harmonic sidesteps in between, but which arrives on G again instead of the tonic E flat (p. 6, bar 1). The duet is bound together by its triplet arpeggio accompaniment and by its off-beat falling fifth motif, which serves both as falling tears and later as bells: it disappears as the texture becomes more sustained at 'Larmes des nuits étoilées' (p. 4 bar 6).

Apart from the songs in the incidental theatre music, which more properly belong to section vi, one curiosity remains from the early 1890s. This is the *Hymn to Apollo* (op. 63bis), a Greek hymn from the third century BC discovered at Delphi by the École Française d'Athènes in May 1893 and transcribed by Théodore Reinach. This is Fauré's first and closest direct contact with Hellenic civilization, though his accompaniment for harp, two flutes and two clarinets is more like a Niedermeyer modal plainchant realization in 5/4 time. The flutes and clarinets replace the harp in the third section (C) with a characteristic Fauréan sliding accompaniment complete with augmented fifth chords, although this does match the thoroughly un-Grecian chromatic chant. The final section (E) is a repeat of the second (B) for harp and flute, with decorated cadences on the flute that have a distinct sixteenth-century feel to them. The anti-semitic d'Indy[3] called the whole exercise a 'musical imposture, the sort of thing one might expect from Reinach, who was of Jewish origin!' He seems to have been right, but for the wrong reasons.

The two op. 76 songs of 1897 are, like *Prison* and *Soir*, very different in style. *Arpège* has a quintessentially French accompaniment, a sort of interlude for flute and harp recalling the 'bergamasque' manner of *Clair de lune*. The rising and falling scale figure that weaves its graceful way through this aerial sicilienne was probably suggested by the opening line of Samain's rather insipid text: 'L'âme d'une flûte soupire'. The

Ex. 12   **Le Parfum impérissable** (op. 76/1)

Bars 25–7

continuity of the accompaniment and the less interesting central section 'Sylva, Sylvie et Sylvanire' place *Arpège* firmly in the second period, though the more complex section in the tonic major at the end is a sign of change to come. Both the text by de Lisle, and the music of *Le Parfum impérissable* are in a higher class altogether, and the title itself is often applied to Fauré as an epithet. *Le Parfum impérissable* has the conciseness of the op. 83 songs; its opening chords temporarily recall *Prison* and place it in the direct line of descent from Fauré's deeply contemplative chordal *mélodies* from *Le Secret* onwards. The chromatic progressions appear tortuous to the eye but not to the ear and, as Bayan Northcott observes (1970, p. 34): 'had Fauré stopped to dwell on some of these . . . to reiterate them for their innate luxuriousness, he might have gone the same way as Debussy'. He probably had in mind a passage like Ex. 12, the start of the build into the final climax. The reason for the cohesion in *Le Parfum impérissable* lies in its part-writing and its frequent references back to the tonic, as in *Green* or *Soir*. It is a powerful song too, despite the suggestion of its title: the accent is on imperishability rather than perfume (N, pp. 85–6).

Le Parfum impérissable so inspired Proust that he wrote to Fauré in 1897 (see N, p. 173):

> I not only admire, adore and venerate your music, I have been and I still am in love with it. Long before you met me you used to thank me with a smile when, at a concert or an evening party, the clamour of my enthusiasm obliged your disdainful indifference to success to bow a fifth time to your audience!

And love for Proust had been associated with Fauré's music before he met the composer, probably at Comte Henri de Saussine's in 1893.[4] Fernand Gregh recalls[5] that at the time of Proust's early love for Marie Finaly (c.1892):

> The strange colour of Marie's eyes, the season of the year, the seascapes of their clifftop walks, seemed fully expressed by Fauré's setting of Baudelaire's *Chant d'automne* [op. 5/1]. Fifty years later he could still remember his friend ecstatically humming, with half-closed eyes and head thrown back: 'J'aime [de] vos longs yeux, la lumière verdâtre' [Songs vol. 1, pp. 40–41].

Of the three little-known op. 85 songs of autumn 1902, the first, *Dans la forêt de septembre* (Catulle Mendès), is the most successful. This resigned meditation has an autumnal flavour in the music appropriate to the theme of a man confronted by old age in a forest as the first dead leaves fall. It provides us with a rare glimpse of Fauré's thoughts for his future (he was then approaching 60), and the lack of sentimentality in the outer sections is balanced by the warm humanity and hope of the central passage: 'Bonne forêt!' The other two songs: *La Fleur qui va sur l'eau* (Mendès) and *Accompagnement* (Samain) have enormous unwieldy bars that Fauré does not seem altogether at ease in. The restless undercurrent of activity in *La Fleur* peters out rather unconvincingly towards the end and has weak moments (like bar 14) before this. The halting piano part of *Accompagnement* looks forward to the third period and is yet another varied sea-picture with four separate sections in which the first is varied as the last. As a result of the three very different piano textures involved, *Accompagnement* feels, by Fauréan standards, disunified, though it far surpasses Samain's exaggeratedly aesthetic text in its harmonic richness.

Le Plus Doux Chemin and *Le Ramier* (op. 87) represent Fauré's last and rather surprising return to his favourite poet of the second volume of songs, Armand Silvestre, who suited his style of the 1880s better than that which had developed by 1904. Both songs are 'madrigals' and *Le Plus Doux Chemin* is a sort of melancholy *Chanson d'amour* with the air of a poignant farewell. *Le Ramier* has a short motif that develops as the song progresses in the halting manner and key of the *Chanson* of Henri de Régnier (op. 94) of 1906, with which it forms a pair. Both share the idea of a sustained bass-line in duet with the vocal line around a guitar-like accompaniment, and as such inner parts became more fragmented so the transition to the third period gradually took place. 1906 marks the end of a long line of 'madrigal' settings in the 'style galant' stretching right across the second period. There is nothing polyphonic about them, and most are 'quasi triste' in mood like *Clair de lune*.

The most significant song in the transition to the third period is *Le Don silencieux*, originally titled *Offrande* by Fauré. Mostly written at

Vitznau in Switzerland in a burst of creative energy between 17 and 21 August 1906 to a love song from *L'Anémone de mer* by Mme Marie Closset (alias Jean Dominique), Fauré realised its significance straight away. 'It does not in the least resemble any of my previous works', he told his wife on 22 August (LI, p. 121), 'nor anything that I am aware

Ex. 13

Vocalise-étude (1906) 1st version, bars 26–7
(two central bars cut in 2nd version)

of; I am very pleased about this. There is not even a main theme; the song is of a free nature which would strongly upset Théodore Dubois. It translates the words gradually as they unfold themselves; it begins, opens out, and finishes, nothing more, and nevertheless it is unified.' *Le Don silencieux* again derives its strength from the contrapuntal interplay between the vocal part and the bass; the halting rhythms and sparseness of its central supporting chords signify that the final period has begun.

Lastly in the transition period comes the far from insignificant *Vocalise-étude* written for the collection of A.L.Hettich in 1906–7, to which Honegger, Ibert, Ravel and Roussel also contributed. Fauré's *Vocalise* is a calm, sunlit 'song without words' whose slow chain of accompanying chords and unpredictable harmonic sequences look forward to the Fauré of the Piano Trio. The voice weaves in and out of the piano part in a line of great difficulty but devoid of superficial virtuosity. Fauré's first impulse was to allow the climax in bars 25–6 to be fulfilled, going straight to the tonic major and coming back to the tonic minor two bars later, but he wisely cut out these extra climactic bars and saved the tonic major for the last three bars (30–32), adding his extra sharps as accidentals in the process (Ex. 13).

(ii) *Piano Music*

The gap in Fauré's piano music between 1886 and 1893 cannot be explained by his dissatisfaction with his Fourth Barcarolle, for he began again with the lighter Valse-Caprice style and the popular *Berceuse* from the *Dolly* suite. Rather, he turned his attention temporarily to other forms of composition, and it may well have been the desire to provide a musical gift for Dolly (Hélène), the daughter of Emma Bardac who was proving so helpful with *La Bonne Chanson*, that returned Fauré to the piano.

The Third and Fourth Valse-Caprices (opp. 59 and 62) of 1893–4 are more subtle and better integrated than the first two essays in this genre, and are full of the complex rhythmic patterns that are a vital feature of the piano music of the middle period. Cross-rhythms are perhaps over-used in the Fourth Valse-Caprice with its duplets and hemiola effects. Both Valse-Caprices are still sectional in construction, but they contain more moments of quiet contemplation and more thematic development than before. Virtuosity and traces of Liszt are still in evidence, and the Valse-Caprices are the only solo piano pieces in the middle period to end in a loud and spectacular manner.

With the Sixth Nocturne in D flat (op. 63) and the Fifth Barcarolle in f sharp (op. 66), both written in the late summer of 1894 at the

Fremiet country home at Bas-Prunay, we reach the breakthrough point, and for some the zenith, of both genres. Like *Prison* and *Soir*, the two pieces are markedly different but complementary. The Sixth Nocturne is profound, pure and contemplative: the Fifth Barcarolle powerful, agitated and virile. The Nocturne sings forth in long musical paragraphs of timeless serenity, and for the first time in the Nocturnes the music has room to breathe freely as a Nocturne should. This is the apotheosis of the starlit night with no virtuosity for its own sake. In Alfred Cortot's opinion (1932, p. 127): 'Few works in the piano literature can be found to compare with this . . . The emotion in this Nocturne goes far beyond personal sentiments to arrive at a universality which is the mark of a masterpiece'.

The long first theme, lyrical and tender, unfolds gradually towards a powerful climax (p. 46). The theme really begins in the fourth complete bar with the main motif A, the opening bars being a sort of lulling introduction. The second theme (B) in the tonic minor is a mixture of firmness and nonchalance; it has the same sort of evasive precision that characterizes such middle period pieces as the seventh variation of op. 73. This section has the function of an intermezzo and B emerges as A at the second climax (p. 48). Next a fluid semiquaver figuration introduces a long, sequentially-extended theme (C, p. 49) in an A major passage of limpid beauty. B and C develop side by side and the final climax brings back A in the bass (p. 53) and this theme dominates the remainder of the Nocturne. The long climb upwards near the end, with its melting diminuendo as it reaches the summit, recalls the close of the Adagio of the First Piano Quartet.

The rhythmic subtlety of the opening idea of the Fifth Barcarolle (bar 1) and its false relations tell us immediately that this is second-period Fauré. The first two-quaver unit develops into a powerful cadence figure, and the second group of four descending quavers forms the basis of the syncopated scales which appear in the second section in G flat (theme B). B at times recalls the *Ballade* in its passionate intensity. The importance of the Fifth Barcarolle lies in its being the first piano work without any self-contained sections; its changes are in metre not in tempo, and its thematic integration is remarkable. A subsidiary idea (C) in E flat, with falling thirds resembling the *Cinq mélodies 'de Venise'*, does not recur and again has the function of an intermezzo, the diversity within the unity. C is soon absorbed into B, and the real differentiation between A and B in this concise essay in development derives from their contrasting textures rather than anything thematic. That is, from chains of block chords as opposed to semiquavers. 'The whole piece plays on the opposition of tonalities, rhythms and light' (N, p. 79), and is a key work in Fauré's development as a composer.

The Sixth Barcarolle (op. 70) of 1895–6 is more straightforward than the Fifth, extrovert and appealing with familiar, often gapped, scales running up and down in both its main themes. The more brilliant end of the A section with its impulsive triplet semiquavers returns to complete the B section (bar 62f.), a principle adopted from the Fifth Nocturne, though in very different circumstances. Only the occasional harmonic progression or rhythmic complexity indicates that this light and alluring piece is not from the first period.

The Germanic *Thème et Variations* (op. 73) of the same year belongs to a much more serious category and is one of Fauré's most powerful and sustained creations. It stands comparison with the great sets of variations of the nineteenth century, and Fauré must surely have had Schumann's *Études symphoniques* (op. 13) in mind when he wrote his sixth and tenth variations. The theme itself is of almost Brahmsian solidity but with off-beat accents, and is constructed from two alternating four-bar phrases repeated in the pattern ABABA. Fauré allowed this to be shortened to ABA for the Conservatoire piano competition of 1910, also cutting out variations six and eight in the process.

The theme unfolds nobly with a slow marchlike tread. The eleven variations are all in the tonic key of c sharp, except for the last which is in the tonic major; they tend to be melodic rather than motivic variations. Variations one and two, three and four, and eight and nine are continuous; variations one to four and variations five to nine belong together as outward and inward-looking groups respectively. In the first variation the theme sings out clearly (ABA) in the bass against right-hand semiquavers. The second scherzo variation plays on the off-beat accents of the theme and also delays it in a Schumannesque manner in its B section. The third variation in triple as opposed to common time is more fiery and dramatic, following the outline of the theme as in the second variation but in a rhythmic transformation: it also makes even more use of the displaced accents of A. The fourth variation of virtuoso agility carries the theme in the middle of the texture and is unusually spiky for Fauré. The mood of the fifth variation is, in contrast to those preceding it, fluid and expansive. The accents give way to smooth singing lines in both the melody and its accompaniment in parallel thirds and sixths. The next variation is slow and contemplative, with the theme in the bass complemented by a falling counter-subject which begins at the very top of the keyboard and becomes progressively more decorated as the variation proceeds. In the quiet and reflective seventh variation the theme is expressively ornamented with passing notes and is transferred in imitation from one hand to the other in an unforced manner. The serenely peaceful and linear eighth variation pairs perfectly with the seventh, and its inner parts in parallel thirds recall the fifth variation, as do the long scalar phrases of the theme. The off-beat accents are subtly transformed into a smooth pedal bass which binds the texture together, and which M. Nectoux has compared (N, p. 80) to the 'evening bells' of the Adagio of the Second Piano Quartet (see section iii).

The ninth variation takes the tenderness of the eighth a stage further and is more developed harmonically. The descending thirds of variations five and eight flutter down from above as the theme passes from the treble to the middle register of the piano. In complete contrast, the tenth variation is a scherzo of fantastic lightness whose long crescendo to a spectacular finish makes it feel as if it should be the last. But Fauré adds a 'variation-conclusion' that looks forward to his 'pure' post-war music and raises the whole work onto a higher, almost religious plane. The theme, which begins in the bass, is soon absorbed into the wide-ranging four-voiced polyphonic texture. The chorale rises from its serenity to a climax of transcendental intensity, making the flashy excitement of the penultimate variation seem trivial in comparison.

As Mme Dommel-Diény has observed (1974), the note D natural plays an important role in the *Thème et Variations*, producing the neapolitan sixth progressions that Fauré was so fond of in the middle period, and helping to envelop the work in a modal atmosphere. It can be seen at work in the expressive fifth, seventh and final variations in particular, and the source is the theme itself, D natural being prominent in the B part (bars 6 and 8).

The mood of the final 'variation-conclusion' is recaptured in the third period in the sixth, and especially in the ninth of the Preludes (op. 103). It also finds an equivalent in the contemporary *Tendresse* from *Dolly* for piano duet. This charming suite has an appropriate naïve freshness and inspired simplicity throughout. As in so much of Fauré's music, 'art conceals art', and this six-movement suite is deservedly well-known. The *Berceuse* from 1893 was published as a separate piece to which the others were added, with erroneous titles by Hamelle that have persisted to this day. There was nothing feline in Fauré's conception of *Dolly*: no. 2, *Mi-a-ou* was originally *Messieu Aoul!*, a nickname for Monsieur Raoul, the brother of Dolly Bardac; no. 4, *Kitty Valse* should in fact be *Ketty Valse*, Ketty being the name of Raoul's pet dog! These vivacious waltzes were birthday presents for Dolly on 20 June 1894 and 1896 respectively. The beautiful *Le Jardin de Dolly* was composed as a New Year present for 1895 and, with the *Berceuse,* is one of Fauré's most inspired melodies, achieving the seemingly impossible in its com-bination of intimacy and expansiveness. *Le Pas Espagnol* (no. 6) of 1897 is Fauré's answer to Chabrier, a glittering showpiece full of cas-tanets and guitars, with some interesting intertwining of the primo and secondo parts midway through (pp. 42–5). This is one of Fauré's few purely extrovert pieces and his only venture into the Spanish world that so intrigued Debussy and Ravel (N, pp. 81–2).

Tendresse (no. 5) was probably completed during Fauré's stay with the Maddisons at Saint-Lunaire on 25 September 1896 (see LI, p. 22), and his true feelings towards his hostess are poured out in the second great c sharp creation of the second period, the majestic Seventh Nocturne of August 1898. This was probably written, in part at least, whilst Fauré was staying with the Swintons at Llandough Castle in South Wales, though it is dedicated to Adela Maddison.

The Seventh Nocturne is complex in both form and rhythm; a deeply felt piece that is tender and stormily passionate by turns. But the main theme (Ex. 14A), a slightly severe chorale accompanied by iambic rhythms, is continually making its presence felt and exerts a rondo influence over this extensive and very varied piece which is far from rondo-like in appearance. 'An interesting departure', Thomas Wegren points out (1973, p. 57), 'is Fauré's attempt to hide key-centres at the beginning of sections.' A begins on the submediant chord; theme B (Ex. 14) starts on the dominant seventh of its home key D, after a first section ending on the dominant (G sharp); the return to A in bar 19 begins in d; the C section, a central episode in F sharp, begins with an upper dominant pedal, and so on.

As in the Sixth Nocturne, the B section (p. 57) is a sort of intermezzo which culminates in a return of A. Again there is a complete break before a faster, gentler C section of great beauty begins (p. 59). The problem arises as the C section becomes passionate, for is Ex. 14 D (p. 60) a new theme or a variation on A, B or C? Similarly, when the passion of D subsides, is the gently singing E (p. 61) which rises like a phoenix from a long-held dominant pedal note a variant of B or C? Is C itself perhaps a variant of B? Are there just two themes A and B as is often maintained, or is B in fact a variant of A?

The answer is that we shall never know Fauré's intentions for certain, though there is a strong case for saying that everything derives from the bipartite A, and that the subtle thematic links which bind this piece together arose naturally from Fauré's highly developed craftsmanship. Certainly the prominent falling scale that recurs at the main climaxes in Fauré's favourite position near the ends of the sections derives from the falling iambic figure at the start. But Fauré was a self-critical composer who had a genius for making minutely worked-out pieces like the *Thème et Variations* seem spontaneous, and for creating unity from apparent diversity. As in the Fifth Barcarolle, we must take our clue to the form from the changes in mood and texture which are the clearest indications as to where the various sections in this complicated jigsaw puzzle begin and end.

Ex. 14   **Seventh Nocturne** (op. 74)

In the final pages, a rising whole-tone passage in triplets (p. 65, E?) leads to a final return of A, this time beginning on a dominant ninth chord in the submediant key of A. This is the last and most intensely chromatic of the nine powerful crescendos in the Seventh Nocturne which also bind it together, and the tonic is avoided until the magical, dreamy coda in the tonic major begins. The overall form is thus, in terms of Ex. 14:

$$ABA_1—CDEDCE—A_2C(coda)$$

at its most complex, or else variations on a rising and falling scale (A) at its simplest, depending on which way you view this elusive piece. The coda is the most tender and loving music imaginable, the perfect completion of the evocation of a relationship made immortal through music.

The *Huit pièces brèves* (op. 84) were given their descriptive titles by Hamelle when he published them in 1903, against Fauré's wishes. The idea for the collection probably arose from Fauré's not wanting to waste pieces he had written as sight-reading tests for the summer Conservatoire exams of 1899 and 1901 (nos. 1 and 5). These were published in *Le Figaro* (29 July 1899) and in *Le Monde Musical* (30 August 1901) before they appeared in op. 84, and the first was further elaborated in the intervening period to form an ABA_1B_1 + coda structure with an easy diatonic appeal like that of the Sixth Barcarolle. To these pieces, Fauré added the two fugues from the Rennes period (nos. 3 and 6), and four more pieces written in the second part of 1902. It is possible however that the so-called *Fantaisie* (no. 2) is also an earlier composition, though it shares rising sequential patterns with the first 'pièce brève' and frequent neapolitan sixth sidesteps with no. 8, the 'Eighth Nocturne'. This last piece is in one continuous section and is not in the same emotional category as the other Nocturnes of the second period. Fauré in fact described it as a 'Pièce' on the manuscript at the Abbaye de Royaumont (Collection Mme Henry Goüin). It does however have the same peaceful scales and arpeggios floating around a central theme that occur in the codas of the Seventh Nocturne and the Seventh Barcarolle, and an attractive bell-like second idea (p. 70, cf. *Pleurs d'or,* the Adagio of op. 45 etc). Pieces nos. 5 and 7 are the second period equivalent of 'songs without words', no. 7 being a bubbling perpetuum mobile whose surging romantic feelings are only just kept under restraint. The most striking piece of all is no. 4, 'Adagietto', with its stabbing opening chords and its discordant, tortured B section which becomes extremely involved chromatically on its return, with some bitter harmonic clashes over a dominant pedal (p. 14 lines 2–3). The brief coda provides the only relief in this tense, dramatic and questioning piece.

The Sixth Impromptu (op. 86 bis) again began as a Conservatoire examination piece, this time for the harp *concours* on 25 July 1904. The first section of the piano transcription is rather grandiose, with a bell-like chordal opening and flashy cadenza passages. This very positive piece only occasionally approaches the harmonic subtlety of the other solo pieces of the period, as when the strident opening idea returns in E [F flat] major beneath a delicate c''' flat upper pedal (p. 11).

The Fourth Impromptu (op. 91) in the same key (D flat) of 1905 is on a higher musical plane than the earlier Impromptus, but is alike in having an exact repeat of its A section before a final coda. A is a gossamer scherzo based on a two-bar rising chromatic scale with the usual syncopation. B, however, is strange and unexpected; its melody is almost subsumed beneath anguished enharmonic progressions which are a more sustained version of the B part of no. 4 of the *Huit pièces brèves*. B does not return later, but is straight away developed alongside A.

Whole-tone experiments make increasingly regular appearances in the transitional years to the third period (1897–1906), before they culminate in the Fifth Impromptu of 1909. Fauré deliberately did not dwell on whole-tone harmonies, however, and to a large extent they are the logical development of his favourite Lisztian augmented fifth chord. This is certainly how they occur in the return of the B section in the Seventh Barcarolle in d (op. 90, pp. 6–7), whose sequences momentarily recall Madame Butterfly's Act 1 entrance in Puccini's celebrated opera of the previous year (1904). Whole-tone passages appear in the Seventh Nocturne and their origins can be traced back to the tritonal effects of the Lydian mode (see Ex. 2). What the Seventh Nocturne lacks and the Seventh Barcarolle possesses, however, is a short main melodic idea subjected to endless sequential repetition in an ever-changing harmonic context and which characterizes the piano works of the first part of the third period. As Alfred Cortot says (*ReM*, 1922, p. 99), this piece marks the beginning of the second evolution in Fauré's piano writing in which his thoughts 'detach themselves little by little from a musical substance too reliant on exterior grace notes for the emotion it wishes to communicate'. The rigorous development of the Ninth Nocturne (op. 97) is the 'definitive statement' of this new departure.

The upheaval in Fauré's life which came with his Conservatoire directorship seems then to have been reflected in the changes that took place in his music and carried on into the third period. The Seventh Barcarolle is the pianistic equivalent of *Le Don silencieux* and was again written with surprising sureness of inspiration in just four days (11–14 August 1905) at the Pension Sternwarte in Zürich. It first appeared in the Christmas edition of *Le Figaro illustré* and was reprinted in *Le Ménestrel* on 18 February 1906, shortly after its première at the Salle Érard by Arnold Reitlinger.

(iii) *Chamber Music*

With the Second Piano Quartet in g (op. 45) Fauré announces his full artistic maturity and the beginning of his second period. All we know about this work is that its première took place at the SN on 22 January 1887 with Fauré at the piano, which means that it probably dates from 1885–6. It marks a significant advance on the First Quartet in the force of its expression, the greater rhythmic drive and complexity of its themes, and its deliberately unified conception. The Second Quartet and the Second Violin Sonata (op. 108) are Fauré's only instrumental essays in cyclic form, and the Second Quartet is also one of the most successful nineteenth-century chamber works for a number of reasons. First, Fauré always knows exactly where he is going in a movement. He never marks time, and his extended sonata form movements on the classical plan never seem artificially drawn out. Climaxes always lead somewhere, there is nothing redundant or rhetorical, and the dramatic pauses and restarts that mar the works of Liszt and Franck are conspicuously absent. Secondly, Fauré's developments never give the impression that they are there because they are obligatory, as they can do in Dvořák; neither do they feel in the least academic, as they can do in Brahms. In addition to the basic techniques of thematic and motivic development in the classical manner, Fauré has a talent for transforming the mood and implications of a theme, as we have already seen in the First Piano Quartet. Thirdly, his harmonic fluency and his original approach to cadences and modulation allow him to avoid obvious sectional joins without difficulty. There are no laborious transitions and introductions, and he has a Schubertian talent for making the return to the tonic feel the most natural thing in the world, whatever has happened tonally en route. Fourthly, his mature recapitulations are always varied. Those expecting reassuring restatements that allow them to disengage their concentration for a while will not warm towards Fauré's chamber music, where the interest and sense of purpose are maintained throughout unified movements of remarkable internal variety. Fauré often puts his most significant thoughts into his codas. He has carried his audience along with him by persuasion rather than by command with subtle sequential patterns and a sense of unimpeded movement and inner energy; now it is time to reveal to them his most intimate feelings. Always assuming, of course, that they have ears to hear. Lastly, Fauré's feeling for instrumental balance and tone colour is often underestimated. The viola was made for moments like the opening of the Adagio of the Second Piano Quartet, and Fauré's frequent use of strings in unison allows them to maintain their independence as a group above his surging, arpeggiated piano parts: he solves the problem of balance far better than Brahms, for example, in a work like the Piano Quintet (op. 34).

With the second period the traces of romantic indulgence and unevenness disappear, and his firm control over his medium and his material is nowhere more evident than in the long opening theme (Ex. 15A), which begins in the transposed phrygian mode and only with a deliberate struggle attains the home key of g again at the start of bar 11. The piano part is volcanic both in its texture and its harmonies, a very powerful contrast to the Fauré of the contemporary *Nocturne* (op. 43/2) or the Fourth Barcarolle. A degree of appeasement is provided only when the viola announces A_1 which has the position and mood of a second subject; but, as in the Seventh Nocturne, it is really another aspect of the opening theme, and the mood does not settle until the end of the exposition when Fauré springs a Mozartian surprise by introducing a new theme B at the start of the development (p. 10). He confounds us still further by alternating this with development of A in E major. Theme A then takes over until the last part of the development, when a softly singing version of B in f sharp leads to B in diminution and stretto (letter G). This, paradoxically, feels the most natural thing in the world and provides an ideal vehicle for the crescendo which builds into the recapitulation at H (p. 19). This is varied, and its predominant use of A and A_1 means that there is a strong case for saying that A_1 should be B, and B a third theme C, whose activities are essentially confined to the development section. With the return of A_1 (p. 21), the music stays in the tonic major, and this weakens the original dynamic force of A. Perhaps this is deliberate, for the quiet close of the movement is easily achieved, with harmonic sidesteps from the tonic persisting to the last.

The second movement is a scherzo without a trio, with the same sort of flying pizzicatos and restless piano theme as in the First Quartet. The difference is that everything here is *forte* or *fortissimo* with rhythmic accents and a violent streak that are entirely new. The opening theme (Ex. 15 C), a sinuous scale erupting into violence, and the introductory pizzicatos are accompanied by bubbling left-hand arpeggios that persist for most of the first part of the scherzo. Again, what looks like a more lyrical second theme (C_1) is really only A_1 from the first movement, and C_1 also has scalar affinities with C. The second idea proper (D) turns out to be none other than an expressive version of A (pp. 36–7). This section might be considered as a trio, were it not for the continued presence of C, often at rhythmic cross-purposes with D. A ferociously accented three-note descending phrase appears before letter E (p. 39), lest anyone should think Fauré's dramatic inspiration was flagging. This is perhaps a reference to B. In the quiet reprise on p. 41, the piano accompanies C in canon on violin and viola, and C_1 replaces D at letter G, making us believe that this again might be the real second subject after all (N, pp. 62–3).

The origin of the slow movement in the Cadirac bells has already

Ex. 15   **Second Piano Quartet** (op. 45)

been mentioned in chapter 1, and this movement is as serene, meditative and straightforward as the others are violent and complex. The idea of oscillation in the opening figure of E is by no means unique to this movement. There is something naïve and child-like about Fauré's love of rocking movements and accompaniments: most of his Barcarolles are really Berceuses (like nos. 3, 4, 6, 7, 9, 10, 12 and 13), and his love of elliptical chord progressions and harmonic sidestepping is closely

Ex. 15 (contd.)
III

Adagio non troppo

IV: Finale

Allegro molto

(p. 63)

(p. 65)

(p. 66)

(p. 67)

104

associated with this inner need for everything to balance properly. E (Ex. 15), with its melancholy viola complement, provides all the material needed for this extended song, which proceeds by decoration and lyrical extension of the viola phrase rather than by direct contrast. In the beautiful twilight coda, the piano-part once again rises gracefully only to dissolve in warm, caressing arpeggios (pp. 59–60). As Copland says of this movement (1924, p. 583), 'its beauty is a truly classic one if we define classicism as intensity on a background of calm'.

The finale, 'a kind of possessed waltz' (Northcott, 1970, p. 34), returns to g and the tremendous energy of the first movement. As with the First Quartet, the finale is the most routine and protracted of the four movements, though this is judging it by exceptionally high standards. The bounding triplet theme (F) and its surging arpeggio accompaniment are similar in intent to the start of the finale of op. 15, though here the theme is longer, more rhythmically accented and violent. As in the first two movements, what appears to be a second idea (F₁) is really only an extension of F. G, the hammered second subject proper, turns out to be a variant of B from the first movement. F proves to be the better theme for development, G being itself repetitive. What looks like a development of G is in fact a new bipartite theme, H (pp. 66–7), which itself develops and recurs in the recapitulation. H has affinities with D, in the last pages of the Scherzo in particular, and is therefore linked to A too. In the recapitulation, G, after one dynamic statement, is suddenly presented *pianissimo,* and its constituent block chords are replaced by filigree treble decoration on the piano (p. 81). The sparse accompaniment line in octaves on the strings recalls the original presentation of B in the first movement, from which G derives. F and G are welded together in the climax of the final pages, when G regains its strength after an electrifying rising chordal sequence (p. 90) leading to the final *più mosso.*

The cyclic plan of op. 45 is, therefore, in broad terms:

The first movement provides material for both the scherzo and the finale; only the Adagio is absent from the plan and forms an oasis of calm in the midst of passionate turbulence. With Fauré, as will I hope now be evident, the reality is more complex than the above plan suggests, with thematic transformation playing a subtle and natural part in all three outer movements. There is never any question of the cyclic references being forced, as they can be in Franck, or of themes lining up for assimilation in the finale. In the Second Piano Quartet the balance between spontaneity and formal unity is carefully maintained. The struggle Fauré had with composition, and with his concluding sections in particular, precisely reflects his desire to maintain this precarious equilibrium (N, p. 65).

Of the smaller chamber works of the middle period, the *Petite pièce* (op. 49) for cello, possibly of 1888, has been lost, and the famous cello *Sicilienne* (op. 78) more properly belongs to section (vi) with the theatre music. There are also several other short Conservatoire sight-reading pieces which do not merit detailed consideration: for cello (July 1897), with a pizzicato accompaniment added later for second cello; for flute (July 1898); for violin (July 1903); and for harp (July 1904). Only the 1903 violin piece was published, in *Le Monde Musical* on 30 August 1903. With the Conservatoire pieces belongs the *Fantaisie* for flute (op. 79) written for the *concours* of 1898 and first performed by the winner Gaston Blanquart on 28 July that year. The *Fantaisie* is dominated by a long, spectacular but superficial allegro in C of no great musical interest, which is preceded by an attractive, self-contained section in e, cast in the form of a sicilienne with a beautifully shaped soaring flute cantilena. The restrained cadenza at the end evolves easily out of the preceding material and is as natural as the pyrotechnics at the end of the allegro are contrived.

The *Romance* for cello and piano (op. 69) in A of 1894 is a curious piece, for the manuscript from the collection of Mme Fauré-Fremiet shows that it began life as a simple Andante for cello and organ, with the solo part much the same as that of the published *Romance,* but with an accompaniment in simple block chords. The title *Romance* was not Fauré's choice and the piece in its original form could well date from the first period, the inked manuscript being covered with additions in pencil made as Fauré arranged the piece for cello and piano, and transferred it from church to salon. He also added some harmonic subtleties, for bars 36–7 were originally simple extensions of bar 35. Ex. 16a shows the original form; Ex 16b shows the revised form with added seventh chords and a bass pedal, and bar 38 (the start of the recapitulation) is included to show how Fauré decorated his earlier chordal plan. The original ending was also different, with the cello descending in semiquavers through three octaves from the high a″ reached at the beginning of bar 55. The printed version is a bar shorter and here the cello simply holds the high a″ above the repeated tonic chords which end so many of Fauré's slow movements.

The *Romance* is also unusual in having what looks like a rather Brahmsian chordal introduction. But this four-bar passage proves to

Ex. 16   **Romance** for cello and piano (op. 69)

a: 1st version, bars 35–8

b: final version, bars 35–8

be an integral part of the piece, recurring in exactly the same role but in a slightly more spectacular form (Ex. 16b) to herald the recapitulation. It is also used to end the piece after a brief cadenza whose unexpected and unresolved cadences foreshadow those of *Pleurs d'or* (op. 72). Otherwise the *Romance* is one long cello-song in the tenor register, with a more flexible and harmonically interesting second paragraph (bars 16–33) that is replaced by a coda later on. Its main failing is the regularity of the phrasing and the bass quaver figure that endeavours to link the phrases together in the second paragraph (bars 15, 17, 23 and 25). This only draws attention to the gaping holes between the phrases of the melody and emphasizes the rather pedestrian feeling established by the regular tread of the organ pedal bass in the first paragraph.

The Andante for violin and piano in B flat (op. 75) of 1897 is more flexible, with a contrasting, more dramatic section in d. A is again an extended song in two definite paragraphs with a hiccoughing accompaniment; as in the *Romance* the second paragraph (bars 29–44) does not recur. The joins are particularly good in this little piece, and B does not lose any of its accumulated tension as it descends powerfully into a repeat of A with a more dramatic and continuous accompaniment.

107

Far superior to the earlier violin *Romance* (op. 28), the Andante deserves more regular performances than it has received since its première by Armand Parent at the SN on 22 January 1898.

The transition years to the third period are entirely dominated by the rarely heard First Piano Quintet (op. 89) whose long genesis (1887, 1891–94, 1903–5) is outlined in chapter 6. In a sense it dominates the whole of the second period, though it is not certain how much beyond the themes, and possibly the exposition of the first movement, survived into the radical restructuring of 1903–5. The whole of the central movement is without doubt completely new, and the Quintet established

Ex. 17   **First Piano Quintet** (op. 89)

III

Allegretto moderato

(p. 57)

the later pattern of three-movement chamber works without a scherzo proper, that was only broken by the Second Quintet.

The First Piano Quintet stands at a vital midway point in Fauré's chamber music and both renews the powerful message of the Piano Quartets in its outer movements, and looks forward into the third period in the intensity, phrasing and chromaticism of its extended Adagio. The Quintet is Fauré's only work published by Schirmer of New York and the rarity of scores and parts goes some way towards explaining its neglect. The other reason why the Quintet is so little known perhaps lies in the quality of its finale. After the 1906 performance had not proved as successful as Fauré had hoped, Philippe Fauré-Fremiet tells us (FF, p. 85) that his father feared that the finale would appear inspired by Beethoven's *Ode to Joy* from the Ninth Symphony, and its diatonic marching theme does show some similarities and is presented three times at the outset in different instrumental combinations (see Ex. 17E). As Suckling observes (Su, p. 106), this was a theme 'even less calculated to draw the best from Fauré than it was from Beethoven'.

Fauré also feared that Schirmer's haste to publish the Quintet might have led him to hurry the finale more than he should have done in the autumn and winter of 1905, at a time when he was no doubt worried by his new duties at the Conservatoire. His lowering of the tension in the final *un poco più mosso* and the return to the opening tempo were not amongst his happiest inspirations (pp. 70–72).

The opening movement is, however, one of Fauré's best, radiant with life and intensity. The modal first theme (A) sings calmly out of

109

the cascades of high piano arpeggios in quiet confidence. The second theme (Ex. 17B) is, in contrast, more virile and rhythmic, and is announced *fortissimo* by the strings alone, all on their fourth strings. The piano re-enters with A at the end of B, and soon has its own secondary motif (B$_1$), whose similarity to the descending thirds in the *Cinq mélodies 'de Venise'* (cf. Ex. 10) suggests that this may be a survival from the 1890s version of the Quintet. The development begins with a lyrical version of B and is a mine of inventiveness, interweaving all three ideas in a strongly directional section that contains some marvellous slowly-rising sequential climaxes. The skill lies in choosing which phrase to use in these passages, and in having an inexhaustible fund of harmonies to make each passage seem as if the sequential technique had been born anew. The climax at fig. 13 (p. 18) so skilfully leads into the beginning of the recapitulation six bars later that this seems to be the 'inevitable climax of the development' as a whole (Copland, 1924, p. 583). Half the skill lies in the topping of A on the second violin and cello with the start of B on the first violin, on which the rising sequence was based.

As usual, the detail in every sequential unit is worked out with the utmost precision so that each separate part is balanced between the units, however fast the harmonies change. The parts interact constantly with each other to maintain the sense of inner life that is an integral part of Fauré's chamber music, and there are some rewarding first violin lines, surely designed with Ysaÿe in mind, as in the passage after fig. 14 (p. 19). In the coda, Fauré's inexhaustible imagination is still hard at work, and he creates an accompanying figure in light staggered octaves for the piano from A that he uses to accompany phrases based on both A and B, before transforming it smoothly into a version of A in quavers (fig. 23). In the closing bars, the motif 'x' from B that has dominated so much of the opening movement is isolated in the accompaniment in a manner reminiscent of Brahms's Second Symphony.

I cannot agree with Copland (1924, p. 583) that the Adagio in G major is 'one of Fauré's lesser creations'. This unified and forward-looking movement has a timeless quality to it; there is not the same evidence that Fauré is thinking in terms of instrumental timbres, and much of the Adagio is scored simply for full quintet as 'pure' music. Both main ideas (C and D) are long-breathed and, as in the first movement, it is the second idea that is the more clear-cut and rhythmically active. C is like a dreamy siren's song over a lulling barcarolle accompaniment and, as with D, its bass-line is an inseparable part of it. The first of the long slow sequential climbs reaches its summit at fig. 2 (p. 35), and quite extensive development follows before a sudden silence and a hushed dominant minor ninth announce the second sub-

110

ject. The first thing that is evident from D is its close imitation; much of the time this results in a sinewy dialogue between the outer parts which forms the shell that encases so many of Fauré's later masterpieces, from *Le Don silencieux* onwards.

The charming and fluid D is soon transformed into a vehicle for forceful passion (fig. 9), and its restless bass keeps the movement from flagging. At the end of the development (fig. 10), C reappears, also surging and passionate, and the sudden diminuendo at fig. 12 for the varied recapitulation perhaps deliberately brings no feeling of relief. As in the first movement, it grows out of the development and its troubled mood takes a long while to subside. Development persists to the very end with elements from C and D combined at fig. 17; it is only in the last eight bars that the tonic is firmly reached in a most moving coda based on D.

The slow movement of the Piano Quintet has a much more important role to play than its counterparts in the Piano Quartets; its form is more complex and it carries on the intensity and continuous development begun in the opening movement. The finale therefore has a lot to match up to, and Fauré's intention with the buoyant and repetitive E was perhaps to provide an absolute contrast with the slow movement, and to compensate for the missing scherzo. E becomes a lot more substantial when the string pizzicatos behind the first statement give way to a chorale-like counter-subject à 4 on the strings during the second. The third complete statement of the 24-bar theme is on the strings, with a running quaver figure on the piano to add new interest. Some while later, after development of E, F appears (fig. 10). This is a forceful theme, again with an inseparable and virile bass-line, and its leaping octaves foreshadow Ulysse's theme in *Pénélope* (cf. Ex. 32 B). Its sustained but angular nature and its irregular phrasing make it the perfect complement to E; as such it is an early third-period equivalent of H (Ex. 5) from the First Piano Quartet. The form of the finale is rather novel; as it is all development, there is no need for a development section as such. After F has developed, E returns in the tonic (p. 60, after fig. 14), feeling exactly like a recapitulation even though the movement is less than half-way through. This technique, which owes something to rondo form, was one Fauré used increasingly to unify his chamber music during the third period. E does not remain the same for long, however; rising sequences soon appear based first on E, then F. The two themes become fused together as they did in the other movements. The development in the Quintet is so much more integrated than in the Quartets that there is only one subsidiary theme (B_1), instead of several. F never reappears as it did initially, though the rising octave motif from it is employed with ingenuity and forcefulness in the closing pages, where it gradually blends with a triplet version of E, which takes over at *un poco più mosso* (fig. 24), (N, p. 101).

(iv) *Secular Choral Music*

This genre includes only the well-known *Pavane* in f sharp (op. 50) which was originally written for orchestra only for the concerts of Jules Danbé. Its mood is one of light seductiveness and the opening flute melody is one of Fauré's most memorable inventions, on a par with that of the contemporary *Clair de lune*, and in much the same nostalgic style. Fauré added the chorus parts on the suggestion of the Vicomtesse Greffulhe, and Robert de Montesquiou was prevailed upon to produce some trivial verses in the manner of Verlaine as a text. Fauré told the Vicomtesse in late September 1887[6] that he found de Montesquiou's additions 'delightful: the artfulness and coquetries of the female dancers and the great sighs of the male dancers will singularly enliven the music. If all this wonderful combination of attractive dance with handsome costumes, an invisible orchestra and choir comes off, what a treat it should be!' This letter may however be more indicative of Fauré's desire to please his patroness than of his considered artistic opinion.

The chorus parts were included at the first public performance at the SN on 28 April 1888, but are really better omitted as they give the gentle *Pavane* a dramatic, almost theatrical feeling if they are not kept firmly restrained. Fauré wisely makes the choral parts very light, and Sir Adrian Boult has told me that Fauré always performed the *Pavane* faster than is generally done now, absolutely without sentimentality or final rallentando at at least crotchet = 100.

The orchestral scoring of the *Pavane* is delicate and airy, with some practical and inspired woodwind writing and a variety of string textures which, however, tend to double the viola part on either second violins or cellos, perhaps for safety's sake. The more dramatic central section is constructed from a series of four-bar sequences over bass pedals which descend in Fauré's favourite whole tones, and the minute changes that imperceptibly take place in the main theme and its subtle reharmonizations are a miracle of Fauréan ingenuity. As M. Nectoux has pointed out (N, p. 57), Debussy greatly admired Fauré's *Pavane* and modelled a *Pavane* of his own on it in 1890, now known as the *Passepied* from the *Suite Bergamasque*.

(v) *Religious Vocal Music*

Hearing Fauré's *Requiem* as he originally intended it to be performed would be a revelation to most people. The published version used today did not appear till 1901, by which time its intimate conception had been expanded considerably, both in terms of length and orchestration. Hamelle probably thought this would lead to more performances, and Fauré complied with his wishes. He intended his *Requiem* to be intimate, peaceful and loving, with none of the horrors of death he so detested in Berlioz's 1837 *Requiem*. In *Le Figaro* of 25 January 1904 he referred to the latter as a work 'in which a taste for large-scale dramatic effects, and an indifference towards religious music . . . may find equal satisfaction'. He listed with deliberation and evident distaste the colossal orchestra assembled for the 'apocalyptic' *Tuba mirum 'ad majorem Dei gloriam'* (OM, p. 21).

The first version of the *Requiem* (op. 48) performed in the Madeleine in 1888 consisted of the *Introït et Kyrie, Sanctus, Pie Jesu, Agnus Dei,* and *In Paradisum* scored for a small orchestra of violas, cellos, contrabasses, harp, timpani and organ, with an unmuted violin solo in the *Sanctus* an octave higher than in the printed Hamelle score. The rich and sombre string scoring which is one of the *Requiem's* most individual features was deliberate, and makes the ethereal solo in the *Sanctus* all the more effective when it appears. Of the five original movements, only the *Introït et Kyrie* and the *Pie Jesu* were definitely completed when his mother died at the end of 1887. The *Pie Jesu* solo was intended for a boy soprano (Louis Aubert) and the soprano choir line was taken by the children that Fauré trained at the Madeleine. Both factors fitted with the pure and restrained original conception; the *In Paradisum* in particular suffers from the presence in most choirs of what Fauré irreverently described as 'old goats who have never loved' (N, p. 50)!

In June 1889, Fauré told the Vicomtesse Greffulhe that he had completed the *Offertoire,* and this and the *Libera me* of 1877 were included in the first complete performance with added horns, trumpets and trombones at the Madeleine on 21 January 1893. This performance included a baritone as well as a boy soprano soloist. The *Libera me* had already been performed as a separate item in its final orchestrated version at the Church of Saint-Gervais on 28 January 1892, with Louis Ballard as soloist. The third and final version of the *Requiem,* with added woodwind parts and the organ part by now reduced in importance, took place as late as 12 July 1900 at the Trocadéro in Paris, with Mlle Torrès, M. Vallier, Eugène Gigout (organ) and the Lamoureux Orchestra conducted by Paul Taffanel.

The 1887–8 manuscripts of the *Introït et Kyrie, Sanctus, Agnus Dei* and *In Paradisum* (BN mss. 410–13) show that the three stages outlined above do not represent the whole story. They contain later additions, mostly in pencil, by Fauré which do not all correspond with the later enlarged orchestral versions, and it seems that Fauré considered a version adding two trumpets, four horns, two bassoons and violins prior to the 1893 version. It also reveals that some dramatic elements in the original were later discarded by Fauré, like the sudden forte entry of a timpani roll at the first cry of 'Christe eleison' (OS, p. 18). The last six bars of the *Kyrie* were accompanied by a long pianissimo roll too (OS, pp. 21–2). Fauré intended to use bassoons at one stage in both the *Sanctus* and the *In Paradisum* (see N, p. 52), and to use them more extensively in the *Agnus Dei*. Two bassoons and two horns enter in bar 26 of the *Sanctus* (OS, p. 51, one bar before the 'Pleni sunt coeli'), seventeen bars earlier than they enter in the printed orchestral score. The manuscripts show that the role of the organ was later taken over by the added brass, as at the start, leaving it mostly as a harmonic support for the choir and/or the strings. Fauré does not seem to have been too sure about his additional orchestration in some places, which suggests that the BN manuscripts may represent his first attempts at expansion. Some of his ideas were wisely discarded, like doubling the top line of the organ part by trumpets and horns in octaves in bars 11–12 of the Andante moderato in the *Introït et Kyrie* (OS, p. 7).

Apart from a varied reprise of the opening 'Requiem aeternam' near the end of the *Agnus Dei,* with its bass pedals descending in whole tones like the middle section of the *Pavane,* the *Requiem* makes no attempts at obvious cyclic unity. There are five distinct orchestral figures (OS, pp. 5, 31, 46, 70 and 100), not including recurring accompaniment figures like those of the *Introït, Libera me* or *In Paradisum.* The orchestral figures do not appear in the vocal parts, which have 11 themes (A–H, J–L) of their own that fall into several complementary categories. First, straightforward, almost motivic ideas that do not develop much, like A (*Introït et Kyrie*), E (*Sanctus*) and the fanfare-like F ('Hosanna in excelsis', OS, p. 56); or K ('Dies illa', OS, p. 100) which begins with the same rising minor third as A. Secondly, there are the justly famous, long-breathed melodies, like G (*Pie Jesu*), J (*Libera me*), and L (*In Paradisum*). Thirdly, comes an intermediate category of less expansive, more sober themes, like B ('Te decet hymnus', OS, p. 11) or the scalar H (*Agnus Dei*). The short dramatic passages like the 'Hosanna' and 'Dies illa, dies irae' are all the more effective for their brevity. These, together with the powerful musical incisions in the opening movement and the emotional warmth of the *Libera me*, adequately balance the predominantly slow and restrained music of the remainder of the *Requiem* without destroying the sense of mystery and tenderness created by the *Sanctus, Pie Jesu* and *In Paradisum.* Only the *Offertoire* seems to me to be out of place in the final scheme of things, its slow and deliberate canon (C) lacking poetry and its 'Hostias' (D) lacking melodic distinction.

Fauré's choice of texts has often been criticized. He presents us with a Mass for the Dead without a real Last Judgement, and the *Requiem* is primarily suited for liturgical use, as was the *Low Mass,* and has no overtones of the concert-hall or opera-house as so many other nineteenth-century masses do. As Suckling has observed (Su, p. 179), the word 'requiem' is given considerable prominence in five of the seven movements, and is 'thrown into strong relief whenever it occurs'. It is also appropriately the word with which op. 48 begins and ends, and this may have been the reason why Fauré chose the antiphon *In Paradisum* for his conclusion. The last two lines of the Sequence for the Dead (*Pie Jesu*), which replace the *Benedictus,* also centre on the phrase 'dona eis requiem', just as the short 'Dies irae' section focuses on the hushed words 'requiem aeternam' (OS, pp. 102–3). With the responsory *Libera me* and the *In Paradisum,* we switch from the Mass for the Dead to the Order of Burial to conclude what is a selective and personal vision of the Requiem Mass in supremely beautiful pages whose mood is of Elysian calm and resignation rather than fervent hope or drama.

This has led to the accusation that the *Requiem* is pagan rather than Christian in its outlook (Benoît, 1888), and it was Benoît who immediately pointed out the similarities with the neo-Hellenic, non-Christian sympathies of the Parnassian poets, quoting from Anatole France's verse drama *Les Noces corinthiennes* (1876) to support his claim. This view was zealously contested by Philippe Fauré-Fremiet (pp. 65–70), and in doing so in 1928 he faced up to the strong contemporary reaction against French Hellenists like Anatole France and his generation. But his deeply philosophical mind made complex assumptions about the *Requiem* that were as far apart from Fauré's own uncomplicated conception as the 'voluptuous paganism' of Benoît. Fortunately, Fauré described his intentions in an interview, and he makes nonsense also of Camille Bellaigue's suggestion that the *Requiem* was inspired by the memory of his lost love, Marianne Viardot (Fauré, *Revue des Deux Mondes,* 1928, pp. 912–13). Talking to Louis Aguettant on 12 July 1902 (*Comoedia,* 1954, p. 6), Fauré explained:

> It has been said that my *Requiem* does not express the fear of death and someone has called it a lullaby of death. But it is thus that I see death: as a happy deliverance, an aspiration towards happiness above, rather than as a painful experience. The music of Gounod has been criticized for its over-inclination towards human tenderness. But his nature predisposed him to feel this way: religious emotion took this form inside him. Is it not necessary to accept the artist's nature? As to my *Requiem,* perhaps I have also instinctively sought to escape from what is thought right and proper, after all the years of accompanying burial services on the organ! I know it all by heart. I wanted to write something different.

Fauré's *Requiem* comes as near as any work can to expressing the inexpressible, to transcending ordinary reality—as he set out to do. In the face of the purity, mystery and restraint of its original conception, criticism pales into insignificance.

Fauré's other religious works of the second period mostly continue in the sentimental tradition of Gounod with an easy charm and a general lack of profundity. The foursquare phrases and frequent recourse to the tonic chord are saved only by modal harmonies, craftsmanship and the odd through-composed section. Only the late *Ave Maria* of 1906 (op. 93) makes a significant advance on the *Cantique de Jean Racine* of 1865, though the *Maria, Mater gratiae* (op. 47/2), composed in the wake of the *Requiem* in 1888, shares a certain grace and flexibility with the *Ave Maria* (op. 67/2) of 1894–5, which Nadia Boulanger has described (*ReM*, 1922, p. 108) as 'the prayer of the voice which concludes *La Bonne Chanson*'. Most of the pieces however are uneven, like the *Ave Verum* of 1894 (op. 65/1) which begins subtly in f but has a sort of operatic love duet for its second half in the tonic major ('O Jesu dulcis'); or the pedestrian *Ecce fidelis servus* (op. 54, 1889), with its repetitive progression at the start and finish and its impractical new high tenor part for the reprise of the opening. Frequent returns to the tonic spoil the *Salve Regina* (op 67/1) of 1895, and this treads very thin modulatory ice in its second phrase (bars 6–9), especially as it comes so soon after a conventional start in F.

The most saccharine pieces are the three *Tantum ergos:* op. 55 in A (1890), in which the harp arpeggios, organ, optional double-basses and five-part choir cannot conceal its routine inspiration; op. 65/2 in E for three-part female chorus with soloists and organ, which recaptures some

Ex. 18   **Tantum ergo** (op. 65/2)

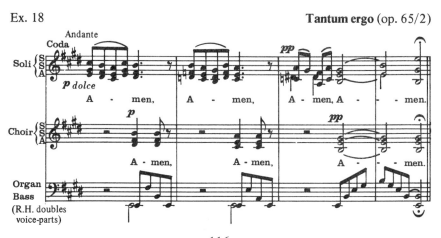

116

of the unconscious charm of the first period, but was surprisingly written between the great Sixth Nocturne and Fifth Barcarolle in the summer of 1894, considering its final 'Victorian' cadences (Ex. 18); and the *Tantum ergo* in G flat, written for the marriage of Mlle Élaine Greffulhe to the Duc de Guiche (later de Gramont) at the Madeleine on 14 November 1904, which is another easily-rehearsed vignette with lingering final Amens for soloist and choir only slightly superior to those in op. 65/2.

Apart from this occasional piece for the daughter of his patroness and the late *Ave Maria*, Fauré's religious composition ceased in 1896, the year he gained relative security as official organist at the Madeleine and became professor of composition at the Conservatoire. One can only suppose that he stopped this branch of activity thankfully.

Fauré's ideals in religious music were those taught by Niedermeyer. In 1904, giving his opinion on recent instructions from Pope Pius X for a return to the primitive purity of Gregorian chant (*Le Monde Musical*, 15 February 1904, p. 35), Fauré commented:

> The truth is that the ruling is not radical enough. One ought not to sing in churches anything but plainchant in unison, considering that it dates from an age when no one foresaw polyphony.

But if sixteenth-century religious music such as that of Palestrina *was* used in church services, it should not be approached from a purist's point of view, or regarded as the only authentic religious music.

> At the time of its composition, this music represented the last word in luxurious art; it only appears to us today to be a simple art because of all that has happened to music in the meantime.

Fauré added that Niedermeyer had rediscovered Palestrina and restored Gregorian chant to its original splendour before those who were now claiming to do this were even born; his teaching had done more for the reform of religious music than all the 'flashy, loud performances of the Saint-Gervaisiens'. Choirmasters, unfortunately, had not had much success in trying to introduce Palestrina into fashionable Parisian churches, and he cited the Abbé Chérion who had tried to do this at the Madeleine after a success at the Maîtrise de Moulins. He was eventually forced to return to the 'repertoire demanded by first-class marriages and burials', and Fauré in his religious music must have been more of a realist than an idealist. But he did have a choice, and his inclination towards the Gounod style must have been, as he pointed out in the same interview, because 'the religious faith of a Gounod is totally different from that of a Franck or a Bach. Gounod is all heart and Franck is all spirit.'

The fact that the religious music of the second period is almost all in major keys should perhaps be sufficient indication that it is not of the highest calibre. But the *Ave Maria* of 1906, which progresses from b to the tonic major, is worthy of more detailed consideration. It was written immediately before *Le Don silencieux* at Vitznau in Switzerland in August 1906, using elements from an unpublished *Ave Maria* of 1877. As Fauré pointed out to his wife on 17 August (LI, p. 121), 'no one is likely to suspect the age' of the borrowed sections in this 'considerably developed' piece. Cast in ABA_1B_1 + coda form, the first noticeable feature is the flexibility of its three-bar opening vocal phrase (see plate XV) with its independent bass in contrary motion. The late *Ave Maria* is more expansive in both its chromatic climaxes and its melodic conception than the other smaller religious works of the period, though Fauré told his publisher Heugel (BN, La 23, 22 August 1906) that it was 'more destined by its character for the chapel than for the salon or for a large church. I believe that its career will, above all, be in the "cours mondains" of young women and girls, and I count on the pretty students of Mme [Marie] Trélat to launch it.'

(vi) *Fauré and the Theatre*

After his problems with the Bouilhet-Gallet opera *Faustine,* Fauré had no more success with his proposals either to Ernest Dupuy in 1885 for an opera after Pushkin entitled *Mazeppa*, or to Catulle Mendès in 1893 for one called *Lavallière*. During the same period Fauré also curiously turned down libretti that were offered to him, or even written specially for his benefit. First, there was an adaptation in the manner of the comedy *Les Uns et les autres* suggested by Verlaine in 1891; secondly, there was *Bouddha* with Albert Samain in 1892; thirdly, *Ondine* adapted from La Motte Fouqué by Jean Thorel in 1895 on the request of Vicomtesse Greffulhe; lastly, Fauré also rejected the early thirteenth-century 'chantefable' *Aucassin et Nicolette* as a possible basis for an opera because it was too 'similar in colour and atmosphere to *Esclaramonde*, *Griselidis* and *Pelléas et Mélisande*'.[7] He added on this occasion that his aim was to 'throw myself into a three-act opera of which I cannot predict the end'.

Fauré was very keen on the *Mazeppa* project, as Philippe Fauré-Fremiet has shown (*ReM*, 1945, pp. 11–14), and it only seems to have fallen through because of Dupuy's reservations and indecisiveness. The project looks forward to *Pénélope* in two ways. First, Fauré explained to his friend Paul Poujaud on 1 July 1885 that the Opéra-Comique was 'gradually closing its doors to all but a certain clique. . . .A lyric theatre is too evident a necessity not to become a reality soon.' His dream of a third Parisian theatre was only realised with Gabriel Astruc's Théâtre des Champs-Élysées in 1913, to which Fauré willingly entrusted

Pénélope. Secondly, commenting to Poujaud in September 1885 on Dupuy's qualms about the nationalistic traits in *Mazeppa,* Fauré looks forward to the spirit in which he composed *Pénélope* nearly a quarter of a century later. 'I assure you it will carry no trace of French or German preoccupation. I shall try to the best of my abilities to translate the human sentiments it contains in accents which, if possible, will transcend the humane.'

The idea for *La Tentation de Bouddha* came from the Princesse de Scey-Montbéliard late in 1891 after Fauré's Venetian holiday, and the letter from Samain that accompanied the first scene in early January 1892 perhaps suggests why Fauré considered the subject only out of deference to his patroness (Jean-Aubry, *ReM*, 1945, p. 41):

> I have tried to vary the funereal impression of the opening, bringing in the voices of young men and women; the wailing of the mothers in the same scene permits different nuances, from sombre tragedy to desolate melancholy.

Fauré's non-co-operation on the Verlaine project is more surprising and again centres around the Princesse de Scey-Montbéliard (later de Polignac). It seems that a short inaugural cantata was planned for the princess's salon at 3 Rue Cortambert, Paris 16 in the spring of 1891, rather along the lines of Chabrier's *Ode à la musique* composed for the same sort of event *chez* Jules Griset the previous winter. When this fell through, the princess, always eager to help struggling artists, suggested another more substantial collaboration, though this was not *Bouddha* as Jean-Aubry suggests (p. 47). As the princess wrote in her memoirs (Polignac, 1945, pp. 120–21):

> Soon after Fauré's visit to Venice, it struck me that I might ask Verlaine to write a libretto in the manner of *Les Uns et les autres,* for which Fauré would write the music. I suggested this to Fauré, and he gladly promised to collaborate; and, as he knew Verlaine very well, he promised to write to him and to make him understand that of course I would remunerate him for his work. . . . Some time having passed before I heard anything more from Verlaine, I asked Fauré to write to him again, and Verlaine replied that he had not forgotten our agreement and had now chosen the subject that he was to submit to Fauré.

> The subject chosen was the end of the *Comédie Italienne* and the scene was a ward in a hospital[8] in which from one bed to another Pierrot, Columbine, Harlequin and others discoursed on the various aspects of life and love. Verlaine's letter to Fauré which I have kept, seemed to me promising, and I am sure his libretto would have been wonderful, but I am sorry to say that Fauré refused to write the music, although it would have been a delightful theme that he could have treated marvellously.

At this time Fauré was in correspondence with Maurice Bouchor,

119

though nothing came of this proposed (untitled) collaboration either, and Bouchor must have spent much of his time in 1891 on a three-act verse drama with incidental music by Ernest Chausson, *La Légende de Sainte Cécile*, which was first produced at the Petit Théâtre des Marionnettes on 25 January 1892[9]. Verlaine seems to have been embarrassed by Fauré's refusal to co-operate on his scenario, due to the extent of the financial assistance the princess had offered him in advance. A letter of 26 September 1891 (Jean-Aubry, p. 50) shows that he did the persuading on this occasion. Relations however remained cordial, especially after the consolation provided by Fauré's two Verlaine song-cycles in the early 1890s, and in 1892 the lot of the suffering poet fell from Verlaine's shoulders on to those of Samain, who was actually unwise enough to produce his libretto of *Bouddha* for Fauré, all 750 high-flown stanzas of which remained untouched.

The real reason behind these abandoned projects was probably that Fauré was frightened to enter into a full-scale theatrical enterprise in the 1890s, both from a musical point of view and because of the time it would involve. Incidental music gave him the opportunity to write for the theatre, towards which he was genuinely attracted, and to continue to use the smaller musical forms with which he knew his musical talents lay. He wrote to Saint-Saëns in October 1893 (Nectoux, *RdM*, 1972, p. 211): 'If by any chance you wake up one morning with a revulsion for *Antigone*.[10] . . .pass it on to me! Incidental music is the only genre which suits my limited abilities!'

Fauré's first venture into this new world was for a revival of Alexandre Dumas père's tragedy *Caligula* (op. 52), at the Théâtre National de l'Odéon on 8 November 1888. The score, for female chorus and an orchestra which Fauré conducted, consisted of three continuous items in the prologue: fanfare-march, chorus of the Hours of Day and Night, and an Andante for orchestra. In addition there were four separate items in the fifth and final act: the chorus 'L'hiver s'en fuit'; an *Air de danse* for flute and orchestra; the melodrama and chorus 'De roses vermeilles'; and a final melodrama and chorus 'César a fermé la paupière'.

The opening fanfare and march are indifferent musically, but the march leads straight to the powerful chorus of the Hours of Day with its menacing bass line, which contrasts theatrically with the seductive and rather decadent chorus of the Hours of Night. In the Andante, the prominent falling fourth in bar 3 allies this with the theme of the preceding march where the accompaniment is also similar. These two movements also balance each other well, and the Andante transforms itself mid-way to the mood of the march without difficulty, to round off the prologue.

The Act 5 music is harmonically more subtle, and in the attractive *Air de danse* Fauré told his son Philippe (N, p. 58) that 'he wished to give the impression of a dance of antique character'. The opening chorus has a delightful modulating figure which is gradually brought to life in the orchestral prelude portraying the return of spring.

The one inferior piece is the chorus 'De roses vermeilles' which sounds dated and conventional. The melodrama that precedes it has some light and airy modulations as Caligula conjures up a mythological nature-scene. Fauré, however, resists any sort of temptation to provide a musical parallel to the 'songs cadencing in Ionian mode'. The gem of *Caligula* is the final chorus with a beautiful, mysterious prelude with distant bells that is synchronized with the melodrama text and leads into a sort of undulating motion that retains a troubled feeling until the 'door closes quietly' on the tragedy, and Messalina and the chorus lull the mad Emperor to sleep.

Fauré re-used material from *Caligula* in his incidental music for *Jules César* in the Victor Hugo translation of Shakespeare's play, produced at the Roman amphitheatre in Orange on 7 August 1905, when the conductor was Édouard Colonne. Unfortunately all that remains of this event musically is an anonymous professional copy of the full score *chez* Hamelle.

After *Caligula*, Fauré turned to a three-act comedy in seven tableaux based on *The Merchant of Venice* by Edmond Haraucourt and entitled *Shylock*. This was first produced at the Théâtre de l'Odéon on 17 December 1889 and the score (op. 57) for tenor solo and orchestra was commissioned by the director of the theatre, Paul Porel[11], to whom it is dedicated. M. Nectoux has shown in his article on *Shylock* (*BAF*, 1973, pp. 19–27) that Fauré only had a small orchestra at his disposal (5-3-3-2-2 strings; 1-1-2-1 woodwind; plus 1 horn and 1 trumpet). Doubtless remembering *Caligula*, he complained to the Vicomtesse Greffulhe on 23 November that 'for the first, second and third performances I shall have a passable small orchestra in the wings. But after the fourth performance, the economic customs of the Odéon manifest themselves: they discharge the few good musicians in the orchestra and replace them with all the impotent, infirm write-offs that they can dig up in the Luxembourg area. Then the chaos begins!' Nonetheless, Haraucourt's butchery of Shakespeare ran for fifty-six performances until 16 March 1890, though Fauré's music received few comments other than 'very delicate and vaporous'![12]

Fauré later published six movements: *Chanson*; *Entr'acte*; *Madrigal*; *Épithalame*; *Nocturne*; *Final* as a suite for full orchestra, adding two harps, timpani and triangle as well as extra brass and woodwind, and this was first performed at the SN on 17 May 1890. It has not met with as much success as it deserves, due to its tenor solo part: *Chanson* and *Madrigal* are more often heard as solos with piano accompaniment, and they appeared later in the third volume of songs published by Hamelle in 1908.

We know virtually nothing about the composition of *Shylock*, although it seems that the superlative *Nocturne* was composed in October 1889 after a short stay with the Vicomtesse Greffulhe at Bois-Boudran, Seine-et-Marne. 'I was looking for a most searching musical phrase, a Venetian moonlight, for *Shylock*, and I found it!' he told her. 'It is the air in your park that inspired it: one more reason for thanking you deeply!' The music for *Shylock* was far more of an integral part of the drama than it had been in *Caligula*, and the score in fact contained nine numbers, as the BN manuscripts (see Appendix A) show, though it took painstaking research by M. Nectoux to re-establish the original plan:

Act 1: Abduction of Jessica, Shylock's daughter, by her fiancé Lorenzo.
    1st tableau: no music.
    2nd tableau: no. 1: *Chanson* 'O les filles!': two stanzas in C separated by text.
        no. 2: *Interlude* for orchestra (see Ex. 19) 37 bars. 6/8. Allegro vivo in G.
        no. '1 bis': *Chanson:* 3rd stanza.
Act 2: Belmont. The marriage of Portia according to the wishes of her father to whichever of the three suitors (Bassanio, the Bey of Morocco, or the Prince of Aragon) chooses the casket with her picture in it.
    1st tableau: no. 3: *Madrigal* (Serenade of the Prince of Aragon). In e flat.
    2nd tableau: no music.
    3rd tableau: no. 3 bis: 3 fanfares (woodwind and brass)
        no. 4: *Entr'acte* (Casket scene). Played *pianissimo* beneath dialogue.
        no. 4bis: Fanfare, based on the entr'acte. (Opening of the caskets of gold, silver and lead.)
        no. 4ter: Interlude (this is the *Épithalame* up to letter B in the orchestral score). In B flat.
Act 3: Portia's judgement in the pound of flesh litigation between Shylock and Antonio before the Doge and Elders of Venice.
    1st tableau: no music.

2nd tableau: (Portia's garden—the love scene between Lorenzo and Jessica): no. 5: *Nocturne*

(For the general reunion at the end) no. 6: *Aubade* (this becomes the finale of the orchestral suite).

Of the two serenades (*Chanson* and *Madrigal*), the first is superior. The orchestral suite contains a prelude to the *Chanson* mostly for cello and harp that is not in the stage version. The separate third stanza 'O les filles! Vos cœurs vont mourir dans les jeûnes!' remains unpublished, being only appropriate to Haraucourt's rather ridiculous adaptation at the end of Act 1, providing ironical light relief as Jessica disappears in a gondola, willingly abducted by Lorenzo.

The first act interlude (no. 2), a lightning scherzo, serves as a perfect introduction to the scene of Jessica's disappearance, though Fauré changed his *forte* to a more appropriate *pianissimo* later on (Ex. 19). The *Entr'acte* is not an entr'acte at all, being played during the casket scene after the fanfares announce the contest with great style. It begins as a pompous march with foursquare phrasing, a little after the manner of Saint-Saëns. It is likely, as M. Nectoux says, that the two *fortissimo*

Ex. 19   **Shylock** (op. 57)

No. 2: **Interlude** (*f* altered to *pp jusqu'à la fin* on MS)

Beginning

statements of the main theme represent the entry of the noble suitors, and that the tender violin solo theme (p. 27), which recurs in the *Épithalame* (p. 46, letter B), represents Bassanio. The *Épithalame* is the first of the truly inspired movements in *Shylock*, with an unusually sonorous orchestration in the suite version (pp. 44f). It attains quite passionate heights, and the subtle rising horn entry with the main theme before letter D (p. 48) beneath rich string harmonies and harp arpeggios would fit unaltered into any romantic Hollywood film, as would the shimmering strings from D onwards. This passage is almost Wagnerian in its opulence, and shows Fauré casting aside the restraint of a tiny stage-band as he extended the *Épithalame* for full orchestra.

The *Nocturne* is perhaps the most beautiful single movement in Fauré's theatre music, and in the suite is richly scored for strings in up to 12 parts, though in the stage version the theme on the first violins was played by an unmuted violin solo (cf. the first version of the *Sanctus* in the *Requiem*). This long, haunting theme of indescribable magic haunted Fauré, too, and he used it again in only slightly varied forms

Ex. 20
Nocturne (op. 57/5) **(Shylock:** 1889)

Romance (op. 69: 1894)

Soir (op. 83/2: 1894)

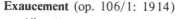

Exaucement (op. 106/1: 1914)

in the *Romance* for cello (op. 69), *Soir* (op. 83/2) and in *Exaucement* from *Le Jardin clos* (op. 106/1) in 1914 (Ex. 20 a-d).

The finale, originally titled *Aubade*, was meant to be played beneath dialogue like the *Entr'acte*, and only shines forth in the orchestral suite. The astonishing brilliance, lightness and variety of the orchestration more than compensate for the two rather undistinguished themes (pp. 62 and 67), which both undergo exciting development in this sparkling perpetuum mobile. Augmented fifth chords and sequences rising by whole tones (pp. 74–9) leading to the revised recapitulation anticipate Debussy more than once, especially the horn solo on pp. 76–7 which, as M. Nectoux suggests (N, p. 60), looks forward to Debussy's *Nocturnes*.

In 1890 Fauré set the prologue for another drama by Edmond Haraucourt, *La Passion*, for mixed chorus and orchestra. It seems only to have been performed as a separate piece, however, and the orchestration was not finished in time for the intended première at a 'concert spirituel' at the Cirque d'hiver on 4 April 1890. Fauré's music received its first performance at the SN seventeen days later under the baton of Vincent d'Indy: only the orchestral and chorus parts have survived (BN Vma. ms 915), and the modal start for strings in g is reconstructed in Ex. 21.

The 85-bar prologue is scored for a substantial orchestra including two oboes, cor anglais and timpani. The five-part chorus with divided tenors enters at bar 29: 'La terre nue et sans chemin/Où se traîne le peuple humain', and continues singing till the quiet orchestral postlude which occupies the last seven bars.

Little is known about Fauré's incidental music for Molière's *Le Bourgeois Gentilhomme* in the spring of 1893. Five performances took

Ex. 21   **La Passion** (1890) (E. Haraucourt)
Beginning of the Prologue

place in the Théâtre de L'Odéon that year, but it is not certain if Fauré's music was used. The score includes the famous *Sicilienne* for cello and piano (op. 78) of March 1893, dedicated to the English cellist William Henry Squire. Fauré's second period is rich in long-breathed modal melodies, and this is one of his most memorable. The form is rather unusual: A is punctuated by an eight-bar section with advanced falling ninth chords and cadential phrases (A$_1$), both drawn from A. A$_1$ returns after a central section (B) in E flat that turns from melodic arpeggios to scales in the piano part, with a rising tenor counter-subject on the cello. The rhythm of the counter-subject is the same as that of the start of A, and in the coda, which begins ten bars from the end, the two are fused together as the music passes deliberately into E flat but retains the texture of A. The overall arched form is thus: A A$_1$ A–B–A$_1$ A coda (A plus elements of B).

The *Bourgeois Gentilhomme* music also includes a moving serenade in f intended for Act 1 (27 February 1893), 'Je languis nuit et jour et ma peine est extrême', which fully matches its text in restless, anguished music. The voice part is expansive with an unusual dramatic vocalise and a trill at the end, and there are some unexpected cadences en route (e.g. bar 14). There also exists in manuscript a 48-bar *Menuet* in ternary form for small orchestra (flute/oboe/clarinet and strings) which may belong to *Le Bourgeois Gentilhomme*. Its use of wide melodic intervals, and its modal bias certainly suggest this period, and Fauré goes as far as he can with the Lydian raised fourth in the introductory bars (Ex. 22).

Pelléas et Mélisande (op. 80) is undoubtedly Fauré's finest and most substantial score of incidental music; M. Nectoux (N, p. 87) considers it his 'symphonic masterpiece'. It represents the first score based on Maeterlinck's drama to receive a public performance, and is also the only score not written after Debussy's opera, as were the orchestral compositions of Schoenberg (op. 5, 1902–3), Cyril Scott (*Overture* c.1912), and Sibelius's incidental music (op. 46, 1905). The London production, which enjoyed nine matinée performances at the Prince of Wales' Theatre between 21 June and 1 July 1898, arose largely through the efforts of the celebrated actress Mrs Patrick Campbell[13], her imagination having been fired by the English translation of Jack Mackail. She met Fauré at Frank Schuster's house at 22 Old Queen Street, Westminster, probably in late March or early April 1898, and read in French

those parts of the play . . . which to me most called for music.

Dear M. Fauré, how sympathetically he listened, and how humbly he said he would do his best!

His music came—he had grasped with most tender inspiration the poetic purity that pervades and envelops M. Maeterlinck's lovely play.

Ex. 22   *Menuet* (for **Le Bourgeois Gentilhomme**? — 1893)
Beginning

The music in this case came very quickly for Fauré. On his return to France on 7 April he was immediately involved in Easter duties at the Madeleine, and in a tour of inspection of the provincial Conservatoires from 18 April onwards. He wrote to his wife from Aix-en-Provence (LI, p. 32):

> I only know that it will be necessary to work flat out on *Mélisande* on my return [sic]. I shall have scarcely a month and a half to write all this music though it is true that part of it is done already in my big head!

Probably pressed for time and wishing to rescue a neglected piece he considered well written, Fauré incorporated his *Sicilienne* of 1893 as an entr'acte. A rough incomplete score for flute, oboe and string quartet of the *Sicilienne* (now BN ms 17778) shows that Fauré may have intended to orchestrate *Pelléas et Mélisande* himself. It also shows that at first he considered by-passing the middle E flat section altogether.

The bulk of the score seems to have been written in May 1898 and Fauré must have passed the pieces on as he composed them to his pupil Charles Koechlin for orchestration, as the first full score in his hand was made between 7 May and 5 June (BN ms 15458). It shows that the orchestral suite as we know it was written in the order: *Sicilienne*; *Fileuse*: *Prélude*; Molto adagio (later titled *La Mort de Mélisande*). The conducting score (BN Vm. micr. 768)[14] used by Fauré in London is also in Koechlin's hand, and comprises seventeen numbers of varying lengths, including the four pieces which form the orchestral suite.

The following list of movements shows that Fauré was directly concerned with the overall unity of his incidental music, repeating extracts from the main suite movements at strategic points, as well as repeating three other interludes (nos. 2, 3 and 14) in varying forms. Thematic material from the *Chanson de Mélisande* (Act 3, scene i), which Fauré set in his shaky English on 31 May 1898, forms the basis of *La Mort de Mélisande*. Fauré also re-used this rising figure in *Crépuscule,* the first song he wrote in 1906 for his song cycle *La Chanson d'Ève.*

ACT 1
1. *Prélude* (Suite no. 1)
2. Chorale-like passage in E (eight bars) for strings and distant muted horn which recalls the end of no. 1. Cue-*Golaud:* 'I am lost too.'
3. Slow interlude in a (twenty-four bars, originally no. 4). No. 5 to follow immediately.
4. Missing

ACT 2
5. *Sicilienne* (Suite no. 3). 'Entr'acte précédant le II Acte'.
6. Four-bar unaccompanied horn-call.

6a. Repeat no. 6.
7. Repeat no. 1 from five bars after fig. 8 to the end (twenty-one bars).
8. Repeat no. 3.
9. Repeat no. 2. Expanded to fourteen bars, which are repeated: Fauré alters Koechlin's tempo marking from 'Andante moderato' to 'Adagio'.

ACT 3
10. *Fileuse* (Suite no. 2). Used as an entr'acte.
11. *Chanson de Mélisande:* 'The king's three blind daughters.' Scored for flute, clarinet and strings.
12. Repeat no. 5, bars 1–16.
13. Missing
[14.] *Interlude* in e (twenty-three bars). To end Act 3.

ACT 4
15. Repeat no 14.
16. Repeat no. 2. Fourteen bars again (as in no. 9). Rescored for larger orchestra. Ends Act 4.

ACT 5
17. Molto adagio (*La Mort de Mélisande:* Suite no. 4). Used as an entr'acte.
18. Repeat no. 17, last eight bars only. For the changeover between scenes i and ii.
19. Repeat no. 18. Ends play.

Later in 1898, Fauré also skilfully reorchestrated nos. 1, 10 and 17 above for a larger orchestra including second oboe, second bassoon, and third and fourth horns, using Koechlin's orchestration as a basis. The manuscript in Fauré's hand is now in the BN (see Appendix A), and was published by Hamelle in 1901 and first performed at the Concerts Lamoureux on 3 February that year. The *Sicilienne* was added only in 1909, to give the four-movement suite we know today.

The *Prélude*, like that of Debussy's opera, presents the musical elements of the drama. Mélisande's theme is supple and naive at first, but soon becomes involved in a long crescendo, possibly suggesting passionate elements beyond her control. The second theme (OS, p. 8, fig. 5) suggests the inevitable tragedy with a sinister bass figure, insistent triplets in the accompaniment, and a theme on flutes that obstinately keeps returning to its tonic (D). After Mélisande's theme returns and leads to another more passionate crescendo (figs. 7–8), a distant horn-call, magically intensified at its height by the flute, announces

Golaud's entry (see no. 2 above), and the curtain rises as the tragic second theme is recalled on the solo cello (fig. 9).

The *Sicilienne* serves as an isolated entr'acte before the fountain scene in Act 2, where Mélisande loses her ring in the water in play with Pelléas. Debussy makes much use of flute and harp in this scene too, though in a more descriptive manner.

Fileuse, which introduces Act 3, scene i where Mélisande is spinning with a distaff (omitted by Debussy), is a ravishing, expansive melody for oboe with a pictorial accompaniment on muted strings: a sort of major version of the opening scene of *Pénélope*. This was published in a skilful transcription for piano by Alfred Cortot as op. 81 in 1902.

The final movement of the suite perfectly balances the high inspirational level of the *Prélude*, beginning with a sombre funereal introduction leading to a simple rising theme representing Mélisande. The staggered bass-line, the slowly rising climaxes, and the avoidance of cadences mean that the grief-laden atmosphere gains in intensity, reaching an overwhelming climax just before the end (fig. 7, p. 68) when the upper strings suddenly descend with devastating effect. Mélisande's theme returns in a coda of poignant beauty, during which the curtain rises for the final act.

Sir Johnston Forbes-Robertson's London production of *Pelléas et Mélisande* was evidently a good deal more down-to-earth than Lugné-Poë's veiled monochrome Paris original of 17 May 1893, even though this had subsequently come to London. The unnamed critic of *The Times* (22 June 1898, p. 12) noted that the effect of gauze curtains behind which the French Symbolist production took place in 'remoteness and archaic simplicity' had been replaced by Fauré's incidental music. But, he added, this was

> decidedly less transparent than the curtain it has transplanted, and if its purpose is to supply the angularity of effect which was formerly given by the gestures of the actors it must be held to have succeeded perfectly.

All the praise went to Mrs Patrick Campbell's 'poetical acting' as Mélisande and her golden dress designed by Sir Edward Burne-Jones ensured that she stole the show. Maeterlinck himself wrote to her after one of her London performances:[14]

> In a few words you, and the delightful, the ideal Pelléas [Martin Harvey], filled me with an emotion of beauty the most complete, the most harmonious, the sweetest that I have ever felt to this day.

This comes as a striking contrast to his later opposition to Mary Garden in Debussy's opera, which contributed to his refusal even to see this until 1920.

We should not make too much of the severe criticisms of *The Times* quoted here and in chapter 2. The 'continued absence of tangible form' may have been also due to inferior performance of the music and the long intervals between the pieces; it should be remembered too that Debussy's music met with even more hostile criticism than Fauré's from London critics.

Mrs Campbell approached Fauré once more for incidental music in 1908. She was planning an American tour which included a version of Hofmannsthal's *Elektra* and a sixteenth-century Japanese play translated by Robert d'Humières, called *The Moon of Yamato*, which needed incidental music. But Fauré replied that, due to pressure of work, he was 'heartbroken' to have to decline this request from the 'never-to-be-forgotten Mélisande'.[16]

One oriental project that did take place, however, was *Le Voile du bonheur* (op. 88), incidental music for a morality play by the famous left-wing politician and journalist Georges Clemenceau (1841–1929). This was first produced at the Théâtre de la Renaissance on 4 November 1901, when the conductor was Émile Vuillermoz.

In the play, a blind mandarin, Tchang-I, is pampered by his loving wife, Si-Tchun, and is surrounded by respectful children and faithful friends (see Vuillermoz, 1960, p. 185). Each day he blesses the Gods for giving him such perfect happiness ('bonheur'), and the Gods, touched by his piety, send to him a learned doctor who restores his sight. Tchang-I bids the doctor keep silent about the miracle, as he wishes to surprise his friends. But the first things he sees are his wife having an affair with his best friend Tou-Fou (scene xi), his children secretly making fun of him, and his faithful friends betraying his unquestioning trust. Overwhelmed by the cruelness of reality, he realises that his blindness was the reason for his happiness and, to avoid further disenchantment, he asks the doctor to restore to him once again his world of illusions behind the 'veil of happiness'.

Fauré's little score, recently rediscovered and now in the Bibliothèque Nationale (ms 17786), consists of 'Chinese' music for a small ensemble: flute, clarinet, trumpet, gong and tubophone (one player), strings without double-bass, and harp. The play was cast in fifteen separate scenes and Fauré contributed nine pieces, mostly brief and sparsely scored, and with a deliberately repetitive, pentatonic flavour. Scenes iv-vii and xii-xiv had no music at all, and only in scene x is its presence really noticeable, piece no. 7 being in five sections with breaks for dialogue in between. Ex. 23 shows in full score the first of these sections after Tchang-I has commanded his servants to bring goblets to drink the Emperor's health, and before he is cruelly disillusioned by reality.

There is some attempt at unity in Fauré's score: no. 1 is repeated as no. 2 and is extended from five bars to fifty-one bars in no. 3; no. 6 for

131

trumpet solo is a shortened version of no. 5; and the theme of the fourth section of no. 7 is extended in scene xv as no. 10. But there is nothing significantly Fauréan or distinguished about the themes or the harmonies, and this score is best considered as a curious excursion into the fashionable fin-de-siècle world of *chinoiserie*.

By far the most important theatrical work of the second period is *Prométhée* (op. 82). Fauré wrote it in less than six months between February and July 1900, in whatever time he could rescue between 'tooth-pulling' tours of inspection of the provincial Conservatoires. Writing from Montpellier on 20 March he told his wife (LI, p. 34), 'my hosts were bewildered by the boldness of my harmonies in *Prométhée*, but to me they seemed almost platitudinous; it is all a question of degree!' During the tours he was able to visit Béziers and meet his co-orchestrator Charles Eustace, but he was clearly worried by the tardiness of Lorrain and Hérold in delivering their text, and had still not composed much music by the end of March.

The circumstances of the highly successful first performance on 27 August have already been described in chapter 1, and Fauré was eventually satisfied after the second performance with his hastily written score (LI, p. 52). Saint-Saëns was able to write to Jacques Durand on 30 August (Nectoux, *RdM*, 1972, p. 75) that all his fears as to whether Fauré would match up to the 'breadth and nobility of character' of the subject had been put to rest. 'I know of no one else capable of achieving lines of such dimension or such simplicity within this severely contoured work, myself included'. In his enthusiasm for *Prométhée*, he also told Charles Lecocq on the same day that Fauré's score had 'that invaluable quality of being the only music suitable for the work'.

Prométhée marks a turning point in Fauré's career, with certain parts of Act 1, like the rhythmic opening chorus 'Eia, Eia', and the concerted trio for Bia, Kratos and Héphaïstos (no. 6, VS, p. 69f) looking forward to the final period. Dialogue and singing alternate in *Prométhée*, the latter being reserved for the chorus and the Gods. Pandore and Prométhée have spoken roles, though they are represented by musical motifs. The role of the messenger Hermès is also a spoken one. The five principal motifs (Ex. 24) are simple and powerful, with an amazing capacity for development and transformation in Fauré's hands. Four of them (A to D) occur within the opening prelude, and the wide melodic leaps of A, B and D again bring to mind Ulysse's royal theme (Ex. 32 B) from *Pénélope*. A represents the heroic Prométhée of Greek mythology, which combines with B, another rising theme which represents the Gods, and soon turns itself into fanfares. C, a soft but firm chorale which first appears with A as its prominent bass-line, represents the unquestioning faith of humanity in Prométhée. Finally, D, straight-

Ex. 23 **Le Voile du bonheur** (op. 88) 1901

Scene X, no. 7, section i

forward but ardent, represents fire, and is soon embroiled in chromatic modulations and descending scales.

The dynamic Prelude, in which A and D predominate, sets the tone for the whole work and leads without a break into the vigorous opening male-voice chorus. Men and women joyously rush about the rugged mountainous terrain, celebrating the arrival of the bird of fire. Andros adds 'it is Prométhée whose glorious cry will rise to meet it in the air!' 'Prométhée is power!' sing the men solidly. 'Prométhée is joy!' add the women (VS, p. 30). All humanity join together in ecstatic praise of Prométhée's virtues, as theme A flexibly develops. 'Prométhée is also

133

hope!' they shout at the end of the chorus and the music is left in mid-air on an unexpected dominant seventh on G which, after a passage in A, creates a feeling of mysterious awe for the entry of the Titan, Prométhée. Just before the end of his excited monologue about the discovery of fire, Pandore enters, her timidity in confronting Prométhée and her feminine weakness being expressed by her falling-fifth motif (Ex 24 E, Act 1 no. 2). Then Gaïa, the mother of Prométhée, rather like Erda in *The Ring*, tries to stop him (Act 1 no. 3, VS, p. 42) in a full-scale aria of commanding presence and rich harmonies. But to no avail: Prométhée climbs the hill encouraged by the chorus, whose confident theme forms a counterpoint to A and C combined (Act 1 no.

Ex. 24

Prélude (Prométhée)

Prométhée (op. 82)

Molto moderato

A

(The Gods)

B

(A)

Bars 39ff. (The Hope of Humanity)

C

(A)

Bar 77 (The Fire)

D

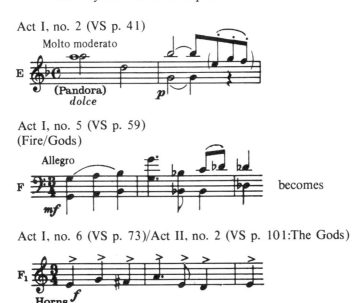

Act I, no. 2 (VS p. 41)

Act I, no. 5 (VS p. 59)
(Fire/Gods)

Act I, no. 6 (VS p. 73)/Act II, no. 2 (VS p. 101:The Gods)

4: 'Marche et poursuis ton but'). Spoken dialogue dominates the rest of the first act, with the short musical interludes raising the artistic level of the work. Prométhée is about to steal Zeus's fire (Act 1 no. 5, second fire motif F) when he is struck by lightning and hurled down. Behind the rock appear the fierce-looking God and Goddess Kratos and Bia, with Héphaïstos, the divine smith, between them to complete the trio. They cruelly spell out the details of Prométhée's punishments in a menacing development of A (Act 1, no. 6), and order Héphaïstos to lead him away to the tortures of confinement. Ex. 24 F, again in association with D, reappears in the concerted trio mid-way through this scene (VS, p. 73 bars 2–4), now assuming the association with the Gods which it retains in Act 2.

At the beginning of the second act, Fauré takes over with the long and beautiful funeral cortège of Pandore, who had been overcome by Prométhée's fate (VS, pp. 79–100). In the opening prelude, which is outdoor music at its best, distant trumpets (E) alternate with a long rising theme (which was played by the band of the 17th Infantry Regiment) in a solemn march. The chorus of Pandore's female companions offer up a tender and expressive plaint ('Larmes, coulez', VS, p. 81f), in which the rising theme of the prelude is accompanied by gentler woodwind quavers. Their lamentations are only interrupted by the aria of Aenoë, their leader (VS, p. 91), who recalls Pandore's virtues with a vocal expansiveness and harmonic élan that recalls *Puisque*

135

l'aube grandit from *La Bonne Chanson*. The chorus reply with an evocation of the silence and darkness of Hades (VS, p. 97f) and hide Pandore's body in a mountain cave. The rest of Act 2 is taken up with less impressive music for Kratos and Bia, much of it based on the unyielding F which reappears at the start of Act 2, no. 2. Here Fauré can be seen struggling against an unsympathetic and, at times, repulsive text. The Gods appear with Prométhée, and Héphaïstos is forced to chain the Titan, his brother, to the rock of the Caucasus, where Zeus's eagle can gnaw away at his liver. Only Héphaïstos has any pity, and his deeply compassionate aria 'O sublime et bon Titanide' (VS, pp. 106–9) is one of the only moving pages in Act 2, no. 2. To satisfy the needs of the drama, Pandore is restored to life, but when she comes to confront the woeful Prométhée, she is ordered back by the unrelenting Bia (Act 2, no. 4) in a purely routine aria based on B ('Pandore, arrière', VS, pp. 127–31), which M. Nectoux finds Wagnerian and redundant (N, p. 93).

In Act 3, no. 1, Pandore appears and F is transformed from its march-like severity into a gentle evocation for flute, harp and strings which melts into trills. She calls on the Océanides, feminine water spirits, for help, and they transport her to the mountain top where Prométhée is chained. Their first chorus ('Des ruisseaux et des sources claires', VS, pp. 135f) is limpid and delightful, carrying on the development of F from Act 3, no. 1, replete with trills (pp. 141f). The last of the three Océanides' choruses (VS, pp. 154–7) brings back a version of the Lydia theme on the strings, and together nos. 2–4 of Act 3 balance Pandore's funeral scene at the start of Act 2, though on a less exalted musical plane. They are spoilt through being divided by dialogue, and the continual shifting of dramatic interest from Pandore's hopes to Prométhée's fears, to the soothing tones of the Océanides, brings a feeling of indecision, of an unnecessary retardation of the dramatic action that is not Fauré's fault.

With the return of Zeus and the Olympian Gods, however, a brilliant finale begins (Act 3, no. 6, VS, pp. 161f). A terrific roll on the timpani introduces the Gods' theme (B) in a canonic fanfare. Andros announces the Gods' decision and Lorrain and Hérold without compunction play down the tragic ending of the Greek myth. Although the casket that Hermès gives to Pandore contains all the evils of the world, they concentrate on the healing balm of her pure tears, which alone can heal Prométhée's wound. His warnings to Pandore and the chorus not to accept anything from the Gods, that all his efforts will have been in vain, are retained for dramatic effect, but they pass unheeded. The chorus first welcome Hermès's gift with the hope of humanity theme (D—VS, pp. 164–6), and finally with ignorant bliss (Act 3, no. 8, VS, pp. 167f). B comes into its own in the final pages; the Gods have triumphed and there is no thought for Prométhée, whose theme (A) is conspicuously absent.

The Wagnerian comparisons, about which Fauré was so apprehensive, are obvious in *Prométhée:* Gaïa with Erda; the Océanides with the Rhinemaidens; the Olympian finish with *Götterdämmerung*. There are musical similarities too: the themes and 'leitmotifs' have a Wagnerian vitality, breadth and capacity for development, especially the arpeggios of B, though Fauré uses them for complete scenes rather than for intricate musical cross-reference. Only C can properly be regarded as a theme, the rest are motifs. However, the Wagnerian influence in the music is mostly limited to the less inspired music of Kratos and Bia in the second part of Act 2. The finest pages are pure Fauré, applying his undoubted talents for powerful dramatic music on a larger scale than before, and succeeding for the most part in providing a varied and effective score for a difficult work, which suffers both from the long passages of dialogue which put the mortals, who form the crux of the action, at a disadvantage, and from its alfresco festival conception which does not transfer easily to the conventional theatre, as its authors discovered in 1907. But the usually perceptive Émile Vuillermoz was quite wrong to maintain (*La Revue Illustrée*, 1 July 1905) that Fauré 'put more of his soul into *Soir* than into the whole of *Prométhée*', and a full appreciation of the quality of this work is vital for a balanced understanding of Fauré's genius. Powerful expression of positive, even violent feelings is as much a part of Fauré as the restrained charm and inner beauty that are better loved. His muse was not 'frightened by so much shouting and by all this instrumental violence', as Octave Seré maintained of *Prométhée* (cited in K, p. 51 nl); rather, it embraced each individual challenge and provided appropriate music, whether the demands were extrovert or introspective.

Footnotes to Chap. 4
1. Translated from J-M. Nectoux: 'Fauré le novateur', *Musique de tous les temps*, no. 18 (1974), p. 9.
2. *Correspondance générale*, vol. 4, Paris, Plon, 1933, p. 10. Letter of early June? 1894. Maurice Bagès's première took place on 25 April.
3. Léon Vallas: *Vincent d'Indy*, vol. 2, Paris, Albin Michel, 1950, p. 42.
4. See George Painter: *Marcel Proust. A Biography*, vol. 1, London, Chatto and Windus, 1961, p. 173.
5. In *L'Age d'airain*, Paris, Grasset, 1951, p. 256. Cited by Painter, id., p. 118.
6. La in the Pierpont Morgan Library, New York (Mary Flagler Cary Music Collection), probably on the 29th. The performance that Fauré envisaged was actually mounted as part of an entertainment given by the Vicomtesse in the Bois de Boulogne on 21 July 1891.

7. Id., 3pp. n.d. and no addressee.
8. Where Verlaine spent most of his time in the 1890s. The work was titled *L'Hôpital Watteau* in June 1891 and replaced the revised version of *Les Uns et les autres* proposed in April. Debussy also considered a one-act opera based on Verlaine's *Les Uns et les autres* in 1896 for the Théâtre Salon and with the singer Julia Robert in mind.
9. See J-M. Nectoux: *Gabriel Fauré: Correspondance* (Paris, Flammarion, 1980), chapter 5, for fuller details on Fauré's 1891–2 theatrical projects and the errors of Jean-Aubry. Here it is made clear (p. 160) that Verlaine had no connection with *La Tentation de Bouddha* and it also becomes obvious that the inaugural cantata à la Chabrier and *L'Hôpital Watteau* were not one and the same project as Jean-Aubry suggests.
10. Sophocles' *Antigone,* in a translation by Meurice and Vacquerie, was revived at the Comédie Française on 21 November 1893 with music by Saint-Saëns.
11. Real name Raoul Parfouru. He also commissioned *Caligula*, and there was talk of music for *Manon Lescaut* in 1892–3 though this never materialized.
12. Francisque Sarcey, *Le Temps* (23 December 1889, 'Chronique théâtrale'), cited by J-M. Nectoux, to whose in-depth article (*BAF*, 1973) the reader is directed for further information on *Shylock*.
13. For more detail on *Pelléas et Mélisande* see my article in *ML* (1975) and, more importantly, J-M. Nectoux's comprehensive article in *RdM* (1981), that includes many new discoveries about this fascinating project. The quote by Mrs Patrick Campbell comes from *My Life and Some Letters*, London, Hutchinson & Co., 1922, p. 127.
14. This is a copy of the manuscript presented to Nadia Boulanger by Robert Owen Lehman on her 80th birthday in 1967. The scoring is for 2–1–2–1 (woodwind), 2 horns, 2 trumpets, harp, timpani and strings.
15. Mrs Campbell, op. cit., p. 130. The original undated letter in French is reproduced on pp. 131–4.
16. Ibid., p. 225.

5

THE THIRD PERIOD: 1906–24

The artist should love life and show us that it is beautiful; without him, we might doubt it.

(Gabriel Fauré, quoted in Mellers, 1947, p. 71)

The third period contains no less than three distinct sub-sections. The first, 1906–14, is bordered by the song-cycles *La Chanson d'Ève* and *Le Jardin clos*, and is typified in the amazing richness, variety and power of *Pénélope*. During the second, 1915–18, Fauré, ever sensitive to current events, reflected the atrocities and upheaval of war in works of tremendous power and even violence, like the Second Violin Sonata, the First Cello Sonata and the *Fantaisie* (op. 111). This tendency, however, begins to show itself in the passionate outbursts in the heavily accented piano pieces of 1906–14, which are remarkable for their reliance on a single short motif and their inexhaustible enharmonic variety. In the final years of the third period, 1919–24, the rage cools into the philosophical wisdom of old age; the music develops a serene beauty and inner peace, coupled with a linear strength and classic restraint, both of which can be seen developing from *Le Don silencieux* onwards, through the contrapuntally alive duets for voice and piano-bass around a softening chordal centre that make up *Le Jardin clos*. If anything, the song-cycles of the final years of the third period, for there are none in the middle years, are less austere than *Le Jardin clos,* more evidently filled with the warmth of human experience. At a time when most people imagined Fauré, aged 75, to be finished as a composer, he suddenly took off in a new direction, crowning his previous achieve-ments in a manner analogous to that of Beethoven in the late quartets. Production became slower in the final years, but the quality rose, and it is a mistake to regard works like the Piano Trio, the Second Piano Quintet or the String Quartet as cerebral, austere and inaccessible; one has only to compare the First Cello Sonata (1917) with the Second (1921) to see how much more warm and approachable Fauré's final music became.

139

1. 1906–14

(i) *Songs*

Both *La Chanson d'Ève* and *Le Jardin clos* deal with gardens, a subject which renewed Fauré's inspiration each time he returned to it. For both cycles Fauré turned to the Belgian Symbolist and mystical poet Charles Van Lerberghe (1861–1907), who was to Fauré's third period what Verlaine was to his second. But here the resemblances end. Whereas Fauré knew Verlaine personally and visited him in hospital in his last years, he never met or corresponded with Van Lerberghe before his early death, as far as is known.[1] Whereas with Verlaine, the link between poet and composer was a purely aesthetic one—'De la musique avant toute chose'—and they had no common traits of character or taste, both Fauré and Van Lerberghe were sensualists, eager for freedom from restrictions, though Fauré was forced to live and dream simultaneously and remained an ever-practical escaper from reality. Both men were inclined towards pantheism and there was an imprecision in Van Lerberghe's verses that allowed Fauré to break free from the tyranny of the printed word in a way that he had not been able to do before. Indeed, Van Lerberghe wrote to Fernand Séverin in October 1901 whilst creating *La Chanson d'Ève*: 'How should I express clearly things that I imagine as indistinct and can only glimpse through a luminous fog?. . . I find that the clarity and comprehensibility that one demands from poetry belong rather to the world of science.' *La Chanson d'Ève* offers us a 'mystic participation' in the creation of the world; its message is 'Beware, lest thou mightst break anything . . . for life is sweet to all'.

As with Verlaine, Fauré turned to Van Lerberghe for the most modern poetry available. *La Chanson d'Ève*, written in Italy in the same idyllic conditions as Fauré experienced at Stresa when he set *Paradis,* was published in 1904 in four sections: First Words; The Temptation; The Mistake and Twilight. So that the emphasis remained purely with Ève, Fauré did not set any of the poems in the third part and drew nos. 1–6 and 8 from part one, no. 7 from part 2, and the last two poems of his cycle from Twilight. His settings contain some of his most experimental music in terms of both melody and harmony.

La Chanson d'Ève is Fauré's longest song-cycle, growing from an independent song *Crépuscule* (no. 9) in June 1906, to three songs with *Paradis* (no. 1) and *Prima verba* (no. 2) that September, then to five in June 1908 with *Roses ardentes* (no. 3) and *L'Aube blanche* (no. 5), then finally to ten in July 1909 as Fauré sketched the remaining songs: *Comme Dieu rayonne* (no. 4); *Eau vivante* (no. 6); *Veilles-tu, ma senteur de soleil?* (no. 7); *Dans un parfum de roses blanches* (no. 8), and *O Mort, poussière d'étoiles* (no. 10). These were completed in Paris that winter and were first performed as a cycle by Jeanne Raunay and Fauré at the inaugural concert of the SMI on 20 April 1910. The songs, written during gaps in the composition of *Pénélope*, were published independently, and the covers of the manuscripts of *Roses ardentes* and *Comme Dieu rayonne* in the BN (mss 17748 (3–4)) show that the order grew as follows: 1–3, 5 and 9; then 1–3, 4, 8, 6, 5, 9, songs 7 and 10 being the last to be written. The final order was chosen for aesthetic rather than chronological reasons, Ève's character gradually deepening as she uncovers alone more and more of the natural secrets of God's universe. She sees her days of innocence drawing to an end in *Crépuscule*[2], and finally in *O Mort, poussière d'étoiles* the mood changes again and she looks forward to death as an immortal, transfiguring and inevitable force.

Perhaps because of its long gestation, *La Chanson d'Ève* does not have quite the same sense of unity or consistency of inspiration as *La Bonne Chanson*, to which Fauré considered it 'a pendant'. Perhaps with *Le Don silencieux* in mind, in which the music simply followed the words, Fauré, when he came to add *Paradis* to *Crépuscule*, told his wife (LI, 3 September 1906, p. 127) that 'the difference in character of these two poems will necessarily bring with it the difference in the music and, from this point of view, my project interests me'. In fact, *Paradis* contains both of the main ideas of the cycle (Ex. 25). Theme A, the first notes we hear, is none other than Mélisande's motif with which *Crépuscule* began, the difference in the poems accounting for its slower unfolding and timeless expansion as we witness the creation of the world and of the soul of Ève/Mélisande. B appears in bars 21–3 as the music slides, earlier than usual, into the tonic major and Ève catches her first glimpse of the 'blue garden' of Eden. Both themes can be seen in plate XVI, which shows that Fauré later revised the third bar to make A unfold more gradually. A and B recur throughout the cycle, but can be most clearly seen in *Comme Dieu rayonne* and *Dans un parfum de roses blanches*. B produces the sort of sinuous bass-line that Fauré loved to use in supporting his enharmonic modulations (as in song no. 8).

Paradis is Fauré's longest song (139 bars) and, as M. Nectoux points out (N, p. 124), with all its changes of mood it is almost a cycle in itself. To put this in perspective, the whole of *L'Horizon chimérique* runs to only 133 bars, and the average length of the songs at the end of the second period is only about thirty bars. Fauré found the text of *Paradis* (LI, p. 129) 'difficult . . . descriptive and not at all sentimental'. The words of God and Ève proved 'even more impossible than setting

Ex. 25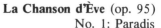

to music the voice of M. and Mme Théodore Dubois!', but Fauré finally found the answer in 'bare simplicity . . . which is always the most difficult thing to imagine'.

The words of God (p. 6, bar 73f.) provide a central C element in *Paradis,* an almost recitative-like passage beginning with a chord of F which serves as a focal point for the song, whose form is:

	A	B	A	B	C	B	A	A	B
Bars	1	21	50	62	73	91	108	126	134

The song is more subtle than this, however, for the idea of a vocal monotone followed by a rising interval recurs throughout the song, that of a third (major or minor, rising or falling) being particularly prominent and recalling the *Cinq mélodies 'de Venise'.* The vocal line also shows that one note to one syllable is the norm in Fauré's final period. And C is not really a new idea at all, for its falling piano accompaniment figure (bar 76f) is simply a compression of the first two bars of B (see B_1 in Ex. 25). The clarity is only disturbed mildly by the complex accompaniment to B, and the same feeling of contrapuntal involvement and harmonic unrest is noticeable in the more clearly motivic songs nos. 4 and 8. Paradise is only regained completely in the exquisite final bars, and the technique of having a whole song aim for a final climax or resolution onto a previously avoided tonic recurs in nos. 3–7 and 9. Final reiterations of the tonic chord (usually three times) became almost obligatory for Fauré, however far he had strayed harmonically en route. A device which arose from a desire to stabilize wayward tonality was sometimes used unnecessarily through force of habit: the repeated chords at the end of *Veilles-tu, ma senteur de soleil?*, for instance, are

142

essentially redundant. Usually in *La Chanson d'Ève*, voice and piano resolve at the same time, but this is not the case in *Eau vivante* where the vocal climax occurs two bars before the piano reaches the final tonic chord (Ex. 26). Finishing the last vocal phrase after the tonic has been reached is also characteristic of this cycle, which is made up of through-composed songs, apart from *Prima verba* which is in ternary form. The halting rhythms of *Le Don silencieux* recur in nos. 3, 5 and 8, and the final song is another long procession of slow chromatic chords in the manner of *Prison* or *Le Parfum impérissable*, though the effect here is very different.

O Mort, poussière d'étoiles derives some of its sombre blackness from the fact that most of the rest of the cycle is in the treble register and is thinly or linearly scored. For the first time we encounter a thick tenor

Ex. 26
Bar 29–end

La Chanson d'Ève
No. 6: Eau vivante

and bass texture, and the passing notes, which were all sensuous warmth and introspection in *Prima verba* (no. 2) as Ève marvelled that her voice had brought things to life, now take on an agonized feeling that is intensified in the final pages where the vocal part and the harmonies for once sink rather than rise. On this rare occasion, Fauré's confidence in an ideal world created by artistic means comes close to annihilation. The frequent recourse to the tonic chord in *O Mort* also distinguishes it from the others and helps contribute to its leaden feeling, as does the return of the winding chromaticism of B on the final page. *O Mort, poussière d'étoiles* is at the other end of the spectrum from the beauty and stillness of night as evoked in the *Nocturne* from *Shylock* or *La Lune blanche* from *La Bonne Chanson*, and from Fauré's view of death as a gentle release in the *Requiem*.

In contrast to the final song, the sixth and seventh songs, perhaps the highspot of the cycle, are all freshness and luminous grace. In *Eau vivante*, Ève rejoices in the spring water which gives life to nature, and Fauré for once turns from arpeggios to delicious rising scales in the piano part which adopt a whole-tone feeling in bars 8–11. There are obvious similarities with the contemporary Fifth Impromptu here.

In *Veilles- tu, ma senteur de soleil?* (no. 7), vibrant with inner life, Ève attempts to relate to man (Adam) whom she has not yet seen, and she wonders if he knows of her presence. The other most beautiful song is *L'Aube blanche* (no. 5), in which Ève is awakened by the sun and her innermost being becomes gradually aware of the beauty and love in all things. As the sunlight breaks through the peaceful stillness on a major ninth chord in bar 6, there is a sudden and unusual change of texture that is almost Debussyan (Ex. 27).

For *Le Jardin clos* (op. 106), Fauré turned to Van Lerberghe's earlier *Entrevisions* (1898) because, as he told his wife on 21 July 1914 (LI, p. 123), 'I can find nothing, alas, in the work of contemporary French poets which suggests music to me!' The eight songs of *Le Jardin clos* were written within six months in Ems, Geneva, Pau and Paris; they form a cycle through style and content rather than thematic links. The mood is one of contemplation, tenderness and inner peace. As M. Nectoux says (N, p. 132), the cycle differs from *La Chanson d'Ève* in that 'mystic love gives place to human love'. When the war broke out during the composition of *Le Jardin clos*, Fauré kept writing to try to keep his mind off current events, but the cycle does not reflect the force that characterizes most of the other wartime works, and so belongs to the first part of the third period rather than the second. The cycle was first performed at the Concerts Casella by Clare Croiza and Fauré on 28 January 1915, but is sadly little performed now. This most sparsely scored of Fauré song cycles, the introverted opposite to *La Bonne*

Ex. 27 **La Chanson d'Ève**
Bars 1–6 No. 5: L'Aube blanche

Chanson, needs repeated hearings and a sympathetic audience for its intimacy to be fully appreciated.

The line between *Le Don silencieux* and *Le Jardin clos* is a clear one, for the majority of the 'enclosed garden' songs appear as themeless contrapuntal duets between the voice and the piano bass-line which surround a less austere chordal centre. Sometimes this centre is less fragmented than in *Le Don,* as in *Exaucement* (no. 1), whose long harmonic voyage of exploration is only resolved when the tonic is unequivocally regained with the last syllable of the text three bars from the end. But, as in *Dans le pénombre* (no. 6), the staggered effect is as evident as it was in *Le Don silencieux* and there is not a great deal of difference between Ex. 28a and Ex. 28b, except that the vocal line in the latter is less like a recitative. The later song also has a contrasting and often quite discordant falling idea in block chords (bar 14). If the lean and economical *Jardin clos* appears simple, it is only its sparse texture that gives this impression. The virile interaction between treble and bass, from which the strength and tension of the third-period songs derive, means that the outer parts rarely move in honeyed thirds, sixths or tenths.

Only *La Messagère* (no. 3) and *Il m'est cher, Amour, le bandeau* (no. 7) are at all extrovert, and something of the passionate ardour of *Veilles-tu, ma senteur de soleil?* (op. 95/7) is visible in the latter. *La Messagère* is another evocation of spring, but the joy is more contained

145

Ex. 28
a: **Le Don silencieux** (op. 92)
Bars 18–20

b: **Le Jardin clos** (op. 106)
No. 6: Dans le pénombre
Bars 25–31

than it was in *La Bonne Chanson*. Complementary or independent melodies in the right hand of the accompaniment disappear by the time we reach *Le Jardin clos*; the uppermost piano part follows the vocal line during much of the third period. There are still only the merest piano introductions or postludes, their functions being simply to establish or confirm the tonic. The long, often sequential, harmonic climbs are still present, but, as in the early third period piano works, the motifs for repetition are shorter and the ascents more difficult. At times *Le Jardin clos* becomes genuinely discordant (Ex. 29).

The gentleness of *Je me poserai sur ton coeur* (no. 4) is almost self-effacing. The syncopated bass-line provides the rather uncertain foundation for a rarefied evocation of delicate beauty, and the enharmonic transition to G flat (bar 17) for the second stanza is as unexpected and poetic as the too-early return to the tonic (E flat) at its close ('Des flots et de l'espace', bar 28).

Dans la nymphée (no. 5) is yet another in the long line of songs stretching from *Le Secret* to *Diane, Séléné* (op. 118/3) in which a slow

Ex. 29   **Le Jardin clos** (op. 106)
Bars 24–30   No. 3: La Messagère

chain of meditative chords reflects Fauré's innermost feelings. The moving ascent to the final climax (p. 20) as the fascinating 'garden is illuminated in the depth of the night', and the rapid descent to the end, as we realise that it all took place 'in the flash of light of a dream', are of a remarkable luminous intensity: bars 20 to 23 are really an enormous neapolitan sidestep to D from the tonic (D flat) that was expected at the start of bar 20.

The final song *Inscription sur le sable*, like *O Mort, poussière d'étoiles*, is a meditation in the face of death, here that of an unnamed young girl, possibly an exotic princess. All that remains on the sand are the diamonds of her crown: only the eternal stones tell where she once lay. But there is nothing tragic or mournful in Fauré's view of death here, indeed the harmonic vocabulary is, for once in the cycle, diatonic rather than chromatic. There is nothing tortuous about the restrained, almost philosophical progressions, and Fauré faces up to tragedy with calm detachment. The manuscript in the possession of Durand et Cie in Paris shows that Fauré added a *tierce de picardie* to the final chord of the cycle, turning e into E. Perhaps he wisely thought better of it, for it does not appear in the printed copy.

(ii) *Piano Music*

The wealth of piano music Fauré wrote in his third period is relatively little known, especially the nine Preludes (op. 103), perhaps because there is a certain gravity, an almost angry feeling to much of it. This is the case with Barcarolles nos. 8 to 11 and the Ninth and Tenth Nocturnes, which carry further the tendency begun in the Seventh Barcarolle of 1905 towards short themes over-used sequentially in long, climbing, often tortuous, chromatic sequences, and which show a similarity in the type of syncopated or staggered accompaniment figures used unaltered for long periods. Most of the pieces are heavily accented and are prone to dramatic outbursts and intense climaxes rather than sustained lyricism. This last is encountered only in the deeply moving elegy for Noémi Lalo, wife of the critic Pierre Lalo, in the Eleventh Nocturne (op. 104/1) of 1913. This hovers 'on the edge of scarcely utterable grief' (Northcott, 1970, p. 36) and is perhaps the best of Fauré's varied requiem movements which, through the final movement of *Pelléas et Mélisande,* Pandore's funeral scene in Act 2 of *Prométhée,* the final songs of *La Chanson d'Ève* and *Le Jardin clos* to the *Chant funéraire* of 1921, reflect Fauré's increasing interiority and depth of spiritual focus. Although in reality the Eleventh Nocturne is constructed from a single two-bar cadential phrase that is repetitive within itself (bars 4–5), the effect is altogether different. It is conceived in long paragraphs, and the occasional expansions of the main motif make it feel like a continuous song. The narrowness of the intervals used, the throbbing inner pedals, and the parts which are always converging on each other, all contribute to the mounting intensity. The tension is only released on the final page where the accompaniment turns first to arpeggio semiquavers, and then to an undulating texture which looks forward to *La Mer est infinie* from *L'Horizon chimérique*. It is as if the soul of Noémi Lalo is being gently borne out to sea.

Most of the single ideas in the early third-period piano works use rhythms dotted across the middle of the bar, as in the Ninth and Tenth Nocturnes and the Tenth and Eleventh Barcarolles. The Ninth Nocturne (op. 97) of 1908 repeats its first bar almost to the point of monotony and is only rescued by a rich and expansive coda in the tonic major. The main idea of the Tenth Nocturne (op. 99) of the same year is even shorter (Ex. 30). This offers the same treble/bass duet around a staggered accompaniment as *Le Don silencieux,* and is only different from the song in the range and instrumental nature of its upper line. Fauré's penchant for imitation in this period is revealed in the long rising sequential climax that begins in bar 23 (Ex. 31) and collapses only when a new development of the main idea begins seventeen bars later. The second climax (bar 51f.) is disappointing, for even though it was made more gradual and sustained and nearly doubled in length in a revision, Fauré meanly cuts the piano back to a single note at its zenith (bar 58, p. 6 bar 7). This is the equivalent of the *subito piano* effects that occur at similar moments elsewhere (bars 46 and 50), and was Fauré's way of keeping a passionate piece within strictly controlled limits. The conventional perfect cadence and the static bar before the beginning of the coda (bars 61–2) in the Tenth Nocturne are unexpectedly weak for Fauré; this Nocturne is again rescued by its coda, which alternates between major and minor like that of the Tenth Barcarolle. In the coda

Ex. 30   **Tenth Nocturne** (op. 99)
Bar 1
Quasi adagio

Ex. 31
Bars 23–30

the undulating semitones of the main motif turn into a rising octave
and a semitone incorporating triplet rhythms, both of which suggest
the contemporary Ulysse theme from *Pénélope*.

Barcarolles nos. 8 to 11, together with no. 5, form a powerful and
impressive series. The Eighth Barcarolle (op. 96) of 1906 has a violent
ending that is unique in the later piano music, and its hemiola effects
(bars 6, 8, etc) recall the Fifth Barcarolle. Again the search for total

unity results in a single idea developed in a multitude of ways, and both the Eighth and Ninth Barcarolles make extensive use of scales in a decorative, counter-subject capacity. The Ninth Barcarolle in a (op. 101) has a particularly undistinguished main subject, a sort of 'sailor's song' (N, pp. 126–7) that produces a series of exercises in cadencing in the dominant. This feature is carried over into the weaker Tenth Barcarolle (op. 104/2) of October 1913 in the same key, which is also an exercise in descending harmonic sequences. The Eleventh Barcarolle (op. 105) in g is a more extended and interesting piece and has a beautiful limpid coda, which begins like modal Grieg but soon develops along purely Fauréan lines. What might have been a *scherzando* ending in the treble in the earlier periods has an extra five bars added here to bring it to a more sober and profound conclusion.

In contrast to these serious and concentrated pieces, the Fifth Impromptu (op. 102) of 1909 is a light perpetuum mobile in the same category as the Second Prelude (op. 103) and the scherzo of the Second Piano Quintet. The opening section is the nearest Fauré came to a proper study in whole-tone writing, though it never suggests Debussy as the melodic phrasing and the texture are too consistently maintained. Fauré's sense of continuity arises through the similarity of each bar within a section. The sections in this period tend to consist of sequential extension of a single development of the main motif against continually changing harmonic backgrounds, and there is no trace of the contrasting two-bar units fitted together into a mosaic pattern that we find in Debussy. Unfortunately the Fifth Impromptu turns into brilliant variations on *Three Blind Mice* towards the end, but after the staccato coda and the featherweight scales and arpeggios, we cannot be certain that Fauré has not had his tongue in his cheek throughout.

The nine Preludes (op. 103) were all written inside a year (1909–10) and this is their only point of direct comparison with Debussy's contemporary first book of Preludes. Fauré's have only their keys as titles and are extremely diverse, though he almost certainly intended them to be played together as a single work, for the Seventh Prelude recalls first the triplet theme of the Fifth in inversion (bar 8) and then the B and A ideas of the First Prelude, much as they occur on p. 3 in bars 11–12. Preludes nos. 2 and 8 are studies, 3–5 could be taken for Barcarolles, and the last two together, a flying triple-time scherzo followed by a serene chorale, strongly resemble the plan at the end of the highly unified *Thème et variations*. The order of the Preludes must have been important to Fauré, since the manuscripts in the Pierpont Morgan Library, New York show that Prelude no. 6 originally came before Prelude no. 5.

The First Prelude resembles the earlier Nocturnes in having a self-contained A section, and a more troubled B section that turns into A at the end, giving it the function of an intermezzo. In mood, key and figuration, however, A recalls *C'est l'extase* (op. 58/5); only the staggered rhythms in B and the whole-tone touches put this prelude into the third period.

Preludes nos. 4 to 9 are in freer but no less logical forms than Preludes nos. 1 to 3, and bars 9–10 of the Fourth Prelude recur reharmonized as bars 10–13 of the *Menuet* from *Masque et Bergamasques* suite (Op. 112/2) in 1918–19. This gentle pastoral prelude has all the charm of the *Pelléas et Mélisande* music of 1898.

Side by side with this, the chromatic sequences and powerful conception of the Third Prelude and the dynamic, angry Fifth are pure third period Fauré, in the same family as Barcarolles nos. 8 and 11. The Fifth Prelude, however, like the Second (a whirling perpetuum mobile in 5/4 time), has a long and unexpected coda. That of the Second Prelude is a series of slow arched sequences over a tonic pedal; that of the Fifth is strikingly similar to the *Libera me* from the *Requiem* (bars 124–6).

Prelude no. 6 in e flat carries on the contrapuntal feeling, being a tranquil three-part organ-like chorale prelude with a strict canon at the 15th between its outer parts at a distance of one crotchet. The Seventh Prelude is ambiguous: a mixture of revolt and resignation written in the first days of September 1910 as Fauré's anxiety over his father-in-law Emmanuel Fremiet's final illness grew. 'I try to work', he told his wife (LI, p. 189), 'but inevitably I am vibrating with anxiety.' For once we can see Fauré's innermost feelings directly reflected in music which rises almost to the point of exasperation before sinking to a tender but brief farewell. Fauré leads us to expect that the piece will resolve in the relative (f sharp) minor till the very end, and the close in A major has a particularly poignant effect.

The manuscripts of the Preludes show that Fauré expanded his conception of op. 103 from an initial group of three to a cycle of nine, like *La Chanson d'Ève,* and Marguerite Long gave the first performance of nos. 1 to 3 at the SMI on 17 May 1910. As a group of nine, the Preludes are of a consistently high quality, far above that of the *Huit pièces brèves*. Even though they are profoundly personal pieces, designed for performance far from the limelight ('en abat-jour'), they merit a place alongside the Preludes of Chopin and Debussy both in critical esteem and in the pianistic repertoire. As Jean de Solliers rightly says (*BAF*, 1975, p. 8): 'It took a paradoxical genius like Fauré's to fix these fugitive inner visions without causing them to lose any of their spontaneous freshness'. They retain an improvised quality and as a collection they represent one of Fauré's most remarkable achievements.

(iii) *Chamber Music*

The *Sérénade* (op. 98) for cello and piano in b, written for and dedicated to Pablo Casals, is the only chamber piece in the early third period. Composed in 1908, or perhaps earlier, it is Fauré's last fling in the 'galant' style stretching back to *Clair de lune* (1887), apart from *Masques et Bergamasques*. Both the A and B sections contain two contrasted ideas, the first a mock-serious call to attention and the second a more expansive and lyrical answer better suited to the cello's singing powers. Section B contains such archaic devices as turns and mordents, and is briefly developed and juxtaposed with A before the virtually exact reprise of A. There is a touch of gentle irony, almost of whimsy, about the *Sérénade* which is one of Fauré's most attractive divertissements, a sort of *scherzando* version of the *Pavane* (op. 50).

(iv) *Fauré and the Theatre:* Pénélope

Fauré's much-vaunted Hellenism is most obvious in the third period and in *Pénélope* it finds its 'classic expression' (Cooper, 1961, p. 143). The bond with classical antiquity was stronger in France than in any other European civilization and the French considered themselves to be descendants of the Greek philosophers in the clarity, logic and refinement of their art. Classical antiquity dominated eighteenth-century French literature and poetry, and it was only with the nineteenth-century 'romantics' that a brief but violently anti-classical reaction occurred, with the Gothic, the medieval and the oriental ousting the supremacy of Greece and Rome in almost deliberate revenge. Shakespeare, whose disorderly genius had so shocked Voltaire (*Lettre à l'Académie*, 1776), became virtually the patron saint of Romanticism and translations of Goethe and E. T. A. Hoffmann gained immense popularity in France. But the classical spirit persisted through the reaction, as can be seen in Berlioz's strong attachment to, and mixture of, both traditions in works like *Harold in Italy* or *The Trojans*. The clarion call for a return to classicism came in the preface to the *Poèmes antiques* (1852) of Leconte de Lisle, later the leader of the Parnassian poets. As in polytheistic Hellenic times, art, science and morality were to unite in the cultivation of pure beauty, far removed from the realism of politics and from everyday life and passion. Art assumed the role of a religion, with the poet as high priest, and 'art for art's sake', propounded earlier by Victor Cousin (1792–1867) in his *Cours de philosophie* at the Sorbonne in 1818, became the doctrine of Parnassians such as de Banville, Sully-Prudhomme and Baudelaire, via the writings of Théophile Gautier (preface to *Mademoiselle de Maupin*,

1835 etc.). The call for a return to the reason and pure art of the ancient Greeks came also from historians like Ernest Renan, whose *Prayer on the Acropolis* was conceived in Athens in 1865.

This classical revival soon affected music. From the 1850s came operas like Gounod's *Sapho* and *Philémon et Baucis,* which presented antiquity in a romantically humanized form. At the other extreme, classical mythology was used as a mask for political satire in Offenbach's *Orpheus in the Underworld* (1858) and *La Belle Hélène* (1864). In the 1870s there were the symphonic poems of Saint-Saëns like *Phaëton* and *La Jeunesse d'Hercule,* and Gounod's *Polyeucte* of 1878, after Corneille. As an antidote to the Wagnerism that swept France in the later 1880s, there also came a rediscovery of the Hellenistic charms of Alexandria, with Anatole France's *Thaïs,* set by Massenet in 1894, and Pierre Louÿs' *Chansons de Bilitis* of the same year. The influence of the Alexandrine revival can be seen in Debussy's *L'Après-midi d'un faune,* his Louÿs settings, and his later Preludes like *Danseuses de Delphes* and *Canope.* It can also be seen in the works of Ravel (*Daphnis et Chloé*) and Roussel (*La Naissance de la lyre*) amongst many others in the first quarter of the present century.

Fauré was associated with the Parnassian poets from Gautier onwards, and it is significant that his de Lisle settings are among his best, *Lydia* providing a Hellenic thread linking all three periods. But the key to Fauré's art is that he 'remains constantly and sincerely *himself*'. His music is 'inwardly Greek' in its bases and ideals, but it could assume 'the form of modern harmony and melody, without the least disparity, in the most complete unity of conception and style' (K, p. 56). The interior nature of his art meant that Fauré was able to resist external influences such as Wagnerism and impressionism; and, in the case of Hellenism, the religious zeal of de Lisle and the moral ambiguity and hedonism of the Alexandrine revival were irrelevant. The world of Fauré's *Pénélope* is the primitive and instinctive world of Homer's epics, but as viewed through the eyes of a sophisticated and reflective later civilization. The religious connotations of Greek tragedy are replaced by a philosophical humaneness, though Fauré does not shrink when the occasion demands from portraying the brutality and powerful life-forces that were an integral part of Greek civilization.

The genesis of *Pénélope* is described in detail in chapter 6, as it sheds considerable light on Fauré as a composer. His longest project slowly took shape during the summers of 1907–9 and 1911–12 after Lucienne Bréval, the first Pénélope, had suggested the subject to him in 1907. René Fauchois provided the well-shaped three-act libretto, which was superior to and less literary than that of *Prométhée,* and in it Fauré found the nobility, grandeur, variety and humanity that he had been seeking. For want of a better system, he consciously adopted Wagner's idea of leitmotifs though, like Debussy in *Pelléas et Mélisande,* he used relatively few. As with Debussy and Wagner, the thematic material is mostly in the orchestral part which accompanies and participates in the action but leaves the voices to expand freely. There is little or no symphonic development as such outside the Act 1 Prelude, though the five main motifs or, more properly, themes (Ex 32) are made to serve a variety of uses through skilful transformation. The derivations of the shroud and the bow of Ulysse motifs (B_1 and B_2) from Ulysse's theme (B) are particularly subtle. Apart from Đ, all the themes appear in the orchestral part. There are others, like those in Act 2, scene ii (VS, p. 126 (Ex. 35), or p. 145), but they do not recur as linking ideas across the opera.

Fauré orchestrated about four-fifths of *Pénélope* himself, only entrusting the parts that interested him least (Act 2 from the duet 'O mon hôte, à présent' to the end, VS, pp. 135–78, and the end of Act 3) to Fernand Pécoud, a composer and violinist in the orchestra of the Concerts Hasselmans, as he ran short of time. The scoring of Act 1 is remarkable for the sonority it achieves with apparently slender combinations of instruments. The extent to which Fauré relied on the strings as a basis is evident in the increased prominence of the brass and woodwind as independent or antiphonal bodies when Pécoud takes over during Act 2, scene ii (N, pp. 110–11).

There are no formal arias as such in *Pénélope*, but there are frequent flights of lyrical melody without introduction, development or reprise, as well as sections of arioso and unaccompanied recitative. In *Pénélope*, Fauré's vocal lines sing forth even more freely than in *La Chanson d'Ève*, and with far greater lyrical expansiveness than in Debussy's *Pelléas et Mélisande*. On the other hand, as Suckling points out (p. 166), much of the recitative tends to pivot around single notes in a manner that might suggest Debussy 'were it not that the orchestral part is less attenuated' (see VS, pp. 92–4). In this trio in Act 1, scene vi, the lack of differentiation (extending to overlaps in pitch) between the vocal parts of Pénélope, Euryclée and Ulysse, skilfully suggests the common bond between them. The character of Pénélope is drawn with great mastery and economy of means: her humanity, dignity and tenderness 'colours the whole work and her self-control and imperturbable sense of fitness find reflection in the music' (Cooper, 1961, p. 143).

Pénélope is the story of the eventual triumph of faithful love in the face of grief and adversity. It is different from *Tristan und Isolde* or *Pelléas et Mélisande* in that it does not involve impossible or guilty love, and its characters do not abandon themselves to inevitable fate, but use their cunning and intelligence to defeat all opposition to their

Ex. 32   **Pénélope** (themes)
(Pénélope)

Prélude, bars 17–18 (Pénélope's grief)

Prélude, bars 42ff. (Ulysse's 'royal' theme)

The Suitors (VS p. 18)

Love theme (VS p. 72) —sung by Pénélope

Ex. 32 (contd.)
Ulysse as beggar (VS p. 77)

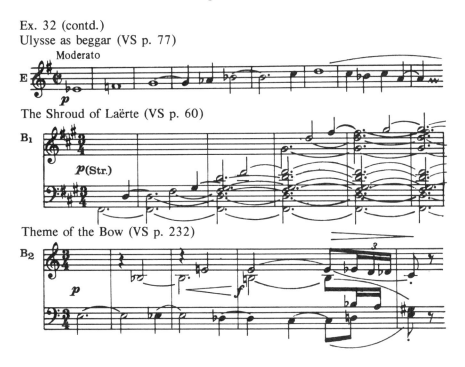

The Shroud of Laërte (VS p. 60)

Theme of the Bow (VS p. 232)

eventual happiness. Pénélope's cunning in unpicking her daytime weaving at night to thwart her vulgar and selfish suitors is paralleled by Ulysse's return to Ithaca in the disguise of a beggar and his suggestion to Pénélope in Act 2 of the contest to string and shoot his mighty bow. Only the theatrically contrived scenes in which Pénélope does not recognize her own husband in disguise (though his old nurse Euryclée does) seem a little artificial, as they did to Fauré, and the ending with the shepherds and herdsmen singing 'Gloire à Zeus', instead of leaving the reunited Pénélope and Ulysse in peace after the slaying of the suitors, does not quite come off. Fauré's interest lay not in conventional endings but in dealing with credible human situations, and for this reason he also found the traditional spinning chorus, and indeed all the first-act preparation for Pénélope's entrance, something of a chore.

Fauchois eliminated the Gods and Ulysse's son Télémaque from Homer's *Odyssey,* as well as Ulysse's multifarious adventures, in order to simplify his plot. This allowed Fauré to concentrate in a human context on the dramatic action, which has no need of mythological characters in order to develop. That is one reason for its superiority over *Prométhée,* and the ruses of the main characters add an extra dimension. For Fauré, *Pénélope* was an incarnation of conjugal fidelity, an ideal love story, a sort of 'new *Bonne Chanson* on a mythical scale' (Fauré-Fremiet, 1945, p. 17). His ancient Greece was imagined through a transfiguring mirage: the dry and dusty Ithaca became the sun-drenched Italian lakes and the luxuriant Mediterranean coast of the south of France.

Since Monteverdi's *Il ritorno d'Ulisse in patria* (1641), the story was used less often in opera than might be imagined. Operas simply titled *Pénélope* were written by Reinhard Keiser (Brunswick, 1696), Baldassare Galuppi (London, 1741), Niccolò Piccinni (Fontainebleau, 1785) and Domenico Cimarosa (Naples, 1794); but in the nineteenth century the only musical reference seems to be Gounod's incidental music for François Ponsard's tragedy *Ulysse,* first produced at the Comédie Française on 18 June 1852. In writing his *Pénélope* in free verse, Fauchois tells us (*Comoedia,* 2 March 1913) that he 'endeavoured to find prosodical lines that were both supple in the classical tradition, and suitable for an equally "pure" musician'. He considered Fauré's score 'a great step forward for French music! All the mastery and delicacy of Fauré is reunited here with a luminous purity of style . . . and fluid sonorities which turned my dream into a reality.'

In the Prelude to Act 1, Fauré suggests Pénélope's long wait for Ulysse's return and her faith that he will come back to her. The main motifs of Pénélope (Ex. 32 A) and Ulysse (B) are presented, later combining in development (figs. 5–6) as those of Golaud and Mélisande do in Debussy's far briefer prelude. Both composers use strongly differentiated rhythms to help in character identification. A is desolate yet loving, the bass rhythms ensuring that it never gets dreamy or sentimental. Perhaps Fauré had the double dots of the French baroque overture in mind here, which he adapted to suit his purposes. A_1, a passionate outburst at bar 17 representing Pénélope's grief, is none other than the Tristan chord in a very different (*fortissimo*) context and with a very different resolution (to G^7 instead of Wagner's E^7). B is Ulysse's royal theme, whose intervals of an octave and a major second recur frequently in the music of the third period. B divides into three parts (Ex. 32a–c), each of them used separately or in combination during the opera. In c, the ninth is divided into two luminous and positive rising fifths, the exact reversal of Pandore's feminine motif in *Prométhée* (Ex. 24 E.). The last two bars of B reveal its careful arched construction (abcba) centering on the high f″, a clear case of art concealing art, for the royal theme always seems simple, confident and inspiring in performance. The subtlety with which it is used can be seen in B_1 and B_2, and in the extension to D (c plus b) with which it fits quite naturally. D, representing Pénélope's love for Ulysse, is in fact the Lydia theme in yet another guise, with its raised fourth degree and its beautiful modal cadence. Its links with B (b) and E, the theme of Ulysse disguised as a beggar, are obvious. On a mundane level, these are simply Fauré's favourite rising scales, variously decorated.

The first three scenes of Act 1 are on a lower level of inspiration than the Prelude. Fauré found it particularly difficult to fit in all Fauchois' text for the weary, disheartened servants of Pénélope spinning away in the antechamber of her palace apartments. Scene i has none of the airy lightness of the *Fileuse* from *Pelléas et Mélisande*, the minor key and the syncopated, dragging bass-lines conveying the picture of the 'heavy spindles' and the 'gloomy palace'. Their activity is interrupted by the suitors' theme (C), swaggering and self-confident, and the long shouts of laughter in the silences dramatically provided by Fauré (VS, p. 18) suggest that they are getting drunk yet again in some nearby hall. Much story-telling takes place in these opening scenes and, in the third, Euryclée tries to prevent the suitors Antinoüs, Eurymaque, Léodès, Ctésippe and Pisandre from getting to see Pénélope. The long timpani roll and the stark use of C furiously accented on the strings, which brings Euryclée rushing in, recall the appearance of the Gods in Act 3, no. 6 of *Prométhée*. Preceded by B(c) and A_1, Pénélope at last makes her entry in scene iv (VS, p. 42), and the noise and blustering activity of the suitors is suddenly stilled by her dignity and humanity. The music reflects this perfectly, and a beautiful modal cadence subdues the suitors into quiet respect (Ex. 33). This is the first of many such plagal cadences associated with Pénélope, and in particular with theme D which first appears in one of her confident lyrical airs: 'Ulysse! fier époux!' at the end of scene iv (VS, pp. 70–5). Pénélope, whose music alternates between grief, love and anger throughout the act, has told the suitors that she will finish weaving her shroud for Ulysse's father, Laërte, before choosing one of them as a second husband. The suitors, annoyed at her lack of visible progress, insist on supervising her work and they call dancers and flute players to entertain her. The graceful and beguiling little ballet for flute and pizzicato strings (VS, p. 65f), with its colouristic touches on antique cymbals and tambourine, continues naturally under 'Ulysse! fier époux!' Both fit together in such perfect, living counterpoint that it is difficult to tell which is the counter-subject. After Pénélope's air ends in a climax of passionate longing for Ulysse, B in the bass leads to his entrance disguised as a beggar (scene v, VS, p. 76). Pénélope for an instant imagines that she recognises him, but Ulysse's humble music (E) convinces her that she is mistaken, and she asks him to stay and rest when the suitors would expel him from the palace. The mysterious air 'Les Dieux ouraniens' (VS, pp. 81–3) has 'a genuine feeling of antique fate' (N, p. 116) about it. Not for the first time is Pénélope cast in the contralto range, and the halting rhythms and the overlapping phrases of the voice and bass-line duet anticipate *Je me poserai sur ton coeur* from *Le Jardin clos*.

The rest of the first act is filled with wonderful moments, Fauré maintaining a consistently high level of inspiration. Against mysterious tremolando strings (VS, p. 97), Euryclée recognises Ulysse, but he warns her to say nothing as he is set on revenge. At the start of scene vii it is easy to imagine Fauré coming to a full stop in October 1908 and

Ex. 33
Pénélope, Act I, scene iv (VS p. 42)

Ex. 34
Pénélope, Act I, scene vii (VS p. 102)

160

restarting in September 1911 (VS, p. 100 line 2), and as Pénélope sets out to unpick her daytime weaving, there is a limpid Debussyan descending flute phrase through the middle of a hushed, sustained string chord (cf. B_1) which suggests her unpicking and pulling out a thread, or perhaps letting one fall to the floor (Ex. 34). The held chord (VS, pp. 102–4) is particularly magical, as the bass-line is otherwise hardly ever still throughout the opera, and Fauré wisely realised that this had more to do with a feeling of musical continuity than any other single factor. The suitors tiptoe in and catch Pénélope in the act; they insist on her choosing a husband from their ranks on the following day. In scene viii, in which D passes into the strings, the beggar suggests that Ulysse may return that very night, and Pénélope is filled with hope as she goes to her nightly clifftop vigil for her husband's ship. Ulysse is overjoyed at her faithful devotion and, in the two short scenes that conclude the act (VS, pp. 114–9), his ecstatic joy is balanced with Pénélope's tenderness and touching faith. Scene x, in which E, D in canon and B are subtly fused together on the strings as Ulysse, Pénélope and Euryclée take up watch together, seems all the more intimate and poetic after the powerful extroversion of scene ix.

The start of Act 2 is again bound to recall Wagner; perhaps this was the reason for its recomposition in 1909. The sound of the shepherd's pipe, 'low and a little melancholy', was, he knew, bound to be compared to Act 3 of *Tristan,* though in the final version the soft undulating woodwind pastorale is as un-Wagnerian as can be imagined, seeking to create a general atmosphere rather than anything descriptive. The faithful shepherd Eumée and his homebound colleague would need to be multi-instrumentalists to manage all this!

In scene ii Pénélope enters with Euryclée and the disguised Ulysse to begin her watch. Pénélope's 'C'est sur ce banc' (VS, pp. 126–30) shows how much Fauré could achieve with very little. A new theme (Ex. 35) on the strings, devised for this air only, traces a similar line to Pénélope's theme A, with the last two bars providing a light falling cadence figure. The vocal phrasing, through which Fauré lifts Fauchois' rhyming couplets on to another level, is remarkably varied, forever crossing and complementing that of the slight orchestral accompaniment. Pénélope dreams of times past and of Ulysse's return; the roses on the clifftop column are to be a sign of her undying love. Most of the act is taken up with the long duo 'O mon hôte, à présent' (VS, pp. 135f.), in which Pénélope questions the beggar about her husband, whom he claims stayed at his house in Crete (!) He almost gives himself away as he assures her of Ulysse's continued devotion, and Fauré's struggle against this contrived scene is to some extent evident in the sectional music it contains. By any standards it is a most unusual operatic

Ex. 35
Pénélope, Act 2, scene ii (VS p. 126)

Ex. 36   cf. Ex. 42A
Pénélope, beginning of Act 3 (VS p. 179)

love duet. As Pénélope greets the sea for the last time, resolving to die rather than yield to the suitors, the mournful music from the start of Act 2 returns (VS, p. 159), this time more tortured and chromatic, and the general level rises. Ulysse reminds her of his mighty bow (VS, p. 164) and suggests that only he who is able to draw it should win her hand. Left alone in scene iii, Ulysse reveals himself to Eumée and a conveniently assembled chorus of shepherds, and asks them to come to the palace at dawn to assist him in his revenge on the suitors. The chorus have only five brief passages in *Pénélope* and their music contains few rewards. Here in Act 2, scene iii the musical interest is centred in the exciting orchestral part based on B, and Fauré keeps the tension mounting throughout this short scene until the very last modal cadence.

The dynamic and concentrated prelude to Act 3 maintains and intensifies the powerfully aggressive mood with which Act 2 finished. It has the feeling of a primitive and instinctive life-force and exhibits a surging dionysian anger that links it with the later wartime compositions. The virile theme (Ex. 36, bars 2–3) which derives from B, is a clear antecedent of Ex. 42 A from the First Cello Sonata. The pounding syncopated chords hark back to Act 1, scene iv (VS, p. 48) and

Pénélope's first confrontation with the suitors, whose eventual doom is strongly suggested in Ex. 36, bar 1.

A series of short scenes follows. First, Ulysse vents his anger and hides his great sword of Hercules beneath Pénélope's throne for later use (VS, pp. 180–83). He then tells Euryclée to remind the distressed Pénélope of the bow; all will be well if his plan is carried out and he can remain incognito. In scene iii (VS, p. 190), Eumée tells Ulysse of the suitors' elaborate preparations for the forthcoming marriage feast, and Ulysse bids him and his friends be ready with swords beneath their cloaks. The music here at times feels like a more powerful version of Bia's Act 2 aria in the same key in *Prométhée* (VS, pp. 127–31: 'Pandore, arrière' cf. *Pénélope* VS, pp. 194–7), and shows the extent to which Fauré had developed as a composer in the intervening years.

A strange sinuous chromatic link on the violins leads into scene iv, and a light, almost 'galant' madrigalian air for Antinoüs: 'Qu'il est doux de sentir sa jeunesse' (VS, p. 198). However much he disapproved of this body of suitors who were in reality only a single person, Fauré gave them some exquisite music. Eurymaque's gentle air, 'Depuis qu'en ce travail piété s'absorbe' in Act 1, scene iv (VS, p. 59) also belongs to this category, with its whole-tone touches characteristic of the 1905–9 period. The suitors demand that Pénélope make her choice and command the feast to be prepared, and scene iv is really a long diversion, containing a second ravishing dance for flute and orchestra with harp and antique cymbals, which emerges (VS, pp. 210–11) after Ulysse has once more given vent to his rage in an aside. The motif which prefixes this outburst reveals that Ulysse's scheme will work after all, for the Ulysse theme B(b) has by now (VS, p. 209, Ex. 37) almost reached the final stage in which it emerges as the theme of the bow (Ex. 32 B_2).

In scene v Pénélope enters, and the suitors are temporarily abashed by her obvious grief (A_1). They soon return to their threatening mood however and Pénélope confronts them with the challenge of the bow

Ex. 37   cf. Ex. 32B_2

Pénélope, Act 3, scene iv (VS p. 209)

Più moderato

(VS, pp. 219–20). In a wonderful passage that is all mystery and anticipation, with striking scoring by Fauré for divided violins, the scene darkens, and Pénélope foretells coming disaster and death (VS, p. 223f). The heavy chords from the start of Act 3 underline her words 'La mort est ici', but the thick-skinned suitors take no heed. As the bow is brought in and each suitor tries his hand at drawing it, the string effect of p. 223 is cunningly transferred to the bass of the orchestra and from it swells the final theme of the bow (Ex. 32 B_2, VS, p. 232), with its almost comic little whimper at the end as each suitor pathetically fails! The beggar humbly asks to be allowed to try (theme E) in music that is too serene for the circumstances, and the suitors treat him as a ridiculous cabaret to their boozy celebrations. But when the beggar draws the bow, everything changes, and themes B and B_2 are dissonantly forced together to signify that the impossible is now taking place (Ex. 38, VS, p. 241). The high tremolando strings from p. 223 return to evoke their astonishment and incredulity. All realise at last that the beggar is Ulysse and he takes his merciless and bloody revenge, with Eumée and the shepherds cutting off the suitors' retreat.

Ex. 38
Pénélope, Act 3, scene v (VS p. 241)

In scene vi (VS, p. 252), Pénélope and Ulysse are reunited and A, B and D appear side by side and in combination, with B naturally predominant. In the final thanksgiving scene (VS, p. 259), Fauré tries to maintain a feeling of deep inner joy rather than create a noisy, conventional finale. To some extent he succeeds and the luminous, shimmering orchestration does its best to compensate for the ecstatic shouts of the chorus and Pénélope and Ulysse.

Fauré's only opera is one of his most accessible later works, though it has sadly never 'caught on'. For those that expect formal arias and ensembles, and lots of chorus action, *Pénélope* inevitably comes as a disappointment, and it must be admitted that Act 3, scene vi ('Justice est faite!') is an anticlimax after Fauré's exciting music for the slaying of the suitors. I cannot agree with Martin Cooper, however, when he complains (1961, p. 144) that 'what is wanting in *Pénélope* as an opera, is simplicity and broad lyrical sweep', for these are surely its primary attributes. Rather, the answer lies in Norman Suckling's view (p. 169) that *Pénélope* 'is not sure enough of its own direction to be a supreme masterpiece'. Fauré clearly had difficulty maintaining the tension in the last act, and was far more at home in dealing with short scenes of marked contrast as at the end of Act 1, or suddenly raising the tension for a dramatic finish to Act 2.

Apart from Pénélope herself, the characters lack depth and variety: Eumée is over-enthusiastic in his zeal; Euryclée is the prototype of the solid and faithful nurse; Ulysse is too preoccupied with his thoughts of revenge, though when the faithful gather together early in Act 2 Fauré gives them some wonderfully humane music. By the same token, Fauré miscalculates in trying to give some semblance of human emotions to the suitors, in the two airs mentioned above for Antinoüs and Eurymaque. The suitors need to be cardboard characters and Fauré's warmth is inappropriate for them. But the opera as a whole is soundly constructed, despite occasional feebleness in the text, and it is far superior in its musical unity and integrity to many operas that have survived for one reason or another. Perhaps *Pénélope* is not performed as often as it should be because it has no spectacular feature by which a fickle public can identify it—no mad scene or soldiers' chorus. But if it made musical concessions it would not be by Fauré, and it would not be a masterpiece of French Hellenism that stands as the crowning achievement of his dramatic career.

2. 1915–18

(i) *Songs—None*

(ii) *Piano music*

There are only two, very different, piano compositions in the war years, the Twelfth Barcarolle (op. 106bis) and the Twelfth Nocturne (op. 107), both composed in St-Raphaël in August-September 1915. Neither uses short motifs like the piano music of the *Pénélope* years. The Twelfth

Ex. 39
Bars 15–20

Twelfth Barcarolle (op. 106 bis)

Ex. 40
Bars 31–7

Twelfth Barcarolle

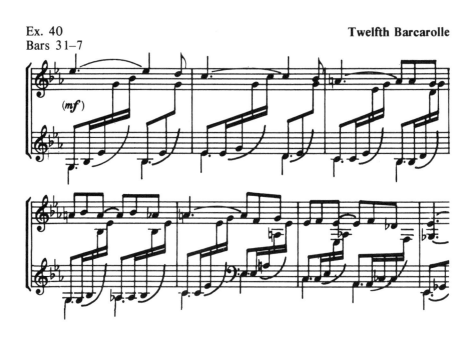

Barcarolle is a refreshing return to an extended theme in a clear ternary structure with coda. Theme A, almost certainly written much earlier, and its simple accompaniment, take us back even past the uncomplicated world of the Sixth Barcarolle in the same key to the first period and the *Romances sans paroles*. But the start is deceptive; the major seconds that formed an integral part of the Ulysse theme are evident from the second half of bar 1 onwards. Beyond theme A, the Twelfth Barcarolle is exclusively third period, especially the rhythmically halting B (bar 44), the canonic return of A (bar 62), and the restless accompaniment that erupts into continuous troubled semiquavers in bar 38 in a sort of coda to the first section. The Twelfth Barcarolle also provides some of the clearest examples of Fauré's elliptical harmonic and melodic progressions. The continual and unexpected returns to the tonic in Ex. 39 are paralleled by the elliptical nature of the melody in Ex. 40, which is simply another extension of A which restarted in bar 28. In Ex. 39, Fauré's subtle effect arises from harmonic ambiguity: the final bar could be either E flat or g. Knowing Fauré, it feels like E flat, but g is in fact confirmed on the third quaver of this bar, and we do not reach another definite chord of E flat until bar 27.

The Twelfth Nocturne is restless and sombre throughout, like an angry sea continually surging upwards. It does however look back to the early third period: its constant major/minor ambiguity recalls the Tenth Nocturne and the Tenth Barcarolle; its sudden abandoning of the bass at the peak of climaxes (bars 6, 11 etc) recalls the Tenth Nocturne again; and the whole-tone touches and minor seconds, evident especially in the more agitated B section (bar 21f), suggest the earlier period generally. The opening of the Twelfth Nocturne is perhaps the nearest Fauré comes to Brahms, and M. Nectoux is right to call this (N, p. 136) a 'piece in the romantic spirit, but in a modern style', for the sustained intensity that rises to a terrific pitch in the *più mosso* section (p. 10) is Brahmsian in its hemiolas, but far beyond anything conceived by Brahms in its rising parallel harmonies. Unfortunately, Fauré releases the tension in the final bars and this exciting and energetic piece, otherwise one of Fauré's most successful compositions for the piano, ends almost apologetically, unable to decide whether it is major or minor to the last.

(iii) *Chamber Music*

The Second Violin Sonata (op. 108) and the First Cello Sonata (op. 109) represent Fauré's most substantial wartime achievement. Both works are richly contrapuntal, favouring close canon between the outer parts; both use syncopation extensively, and are harmonically auda-

cious. With the *Fantaisie* for piano and orchestra and the Second Violin
Sonata, Fauré leaves the classical sonata-form plan to experiment with
more complex structures that are nonetheless clear and logical in themselves. All three works are remarkable for their vitality, and for their
powerful, elevated conceptions.

The Second Violin Sonata in e, superior to the First but far less often
played, was conceived at Évian in the summer of 1916 and finished in
Paris over the following year. Fauré evidently set great store by these
complex and powerful pages for, when in March 1922 Alfred Cortot
was about to accompany the sonata before Élisabeth, Queen of the

Ex. 41   **Second Violin Sonata** (op. 108): themes

Belgians to whom it is dedicated, Fauré lamented to his wife (LI, p. 279) that 'this poor sonata is so very seldom played! So much time is needed before music becomes widely known!' Again, in July 1924, he wrote of the way Thibaud and Cortot had 'woken' his sonata from its 'long, sad sleep', almost as if it were a fairy-tale.

The first movement plunges straight into the accented and syncopated A (Ex. 41), the restless, surging mood being intensified by the rapid crescendo from the quiet piano start to the wide-ranging violin entry in bar 4. A softer rising phrase in fig. 1 is simply a development of A, but the expansive new idea at fig. 2 (B), with its curious rhythmic hiatuses so characteristic of Fauré's third period, cannot be dismissed as another adjunct to A as it recurs independently later on and is developed as a theme in its own right. The real second subject (C) at fig. 3 is a calm and tranquil descending scale, but its halting bass links it inseparably with A, as does its inner quaver accompaniment. In Fauré's previous outer movements, a change of texture from semi-quavers to quavers would point to C being the main second theme, but in the Second Violin Sonata even this reliable criterion does not hold good, as C returns on p. 15 with the arpeggio semiquavers that accompanied A and B. And more surprises are in store! Fauré's earlier large-scale movements invariably began development immediately after the exposition of an individual theme, but in the Second Violin Sonata there are two expositions, each containing the three themes in the same order, and each containing development. The second exposition begins on p. 5 line 3. The third appearance of A in the tonic, imitated by the violin a minor third higher, clearly begins the recapitulation (p. 12, fig. 7) lest anyone should think Fauré was returning to the repeated exposition plan of the First Violin Sonata. Development begins again almost immediately, reference to a theme in the appropriate key being sufficient to indicate a formal divide in Fauré's third period. But again the same thing happens. After C has returned in the tonic major (p. 15), another complete recapitulation begins with different instrumentation of A and C (fig. 9), before an ecstatic imitative coda (fig. 11) rounds this continuously developing four-section movement off. The overall plan is thus:

```
1st exposition/development  ——  2nd exposition/development  ——  1st recapitulation/development  ——

A       B       C (+A)   ——   A       B       C (+A)   ——   A              B (+A)   C
Pno     Vln     Vln           Pno     Vln     Vln           Pno/Vln        Vln      Vln/Pno bass
                                                            (imitation)             (canon)

——  2nd recapitulation/development  ——  Coda

——  A               B       C    ——   A
    Vln/Pno bass    Vln     Pno/Vln     Vln/Pno
    (canon)
```

The central Andante in A major sings all the while like the first movement and is no less expansive or harmonically complex. Like the first movement of the First Cello Sonata, it derives its first theme (D) from the abandoned Symphony in d (op. 40). D is tender, almost naïve, but its apparent innocence is not matched in its sophisticated accompaniment. After D has appeared on the piano, a second, less stable, theme (E) produces alternate bars of E major and side-stepping f minor harmonies at fig. 2. The overall form is:

D−E−(development of E)−D−E−D + E (further development)

with the second appearance of D being a rather curious reprise in C major. The tonic is only regained with great difficulty two bars after fig. 6 for the second appearance of theme E (N, pp. 138–9).

The finale is as complicated as the first movement, again involving a four-part plan, but this time introducing a rondo element in theme F (Ex. 41), and cyclic recall of A and C from the first movement. One would never guess what lay in store from the fresh and alluring opening theme (F), a second childhood creation of Fauré's old age. The syncopation is still there, but a regular rhythmic piano accompaniment with a stable bass gives it a forward propulsion at the outset that comes as a delightful contrast to the involvement of the preceding movements. However, it is only nine bars before Fauré can no longer resist cross-rhythmic imitation in the bass, and only half that time before the graceful E of the start is clouded by a modulation to C major. Development begins straight after the more expansive and lyrical G has appeared on the violin (p. 32 bar 1), and it leads straight to a third theme (H, p. 33 bar 1) which is smooth and lyrical but has rhythmic affinities with the syncopated F.

In the second part (p. 34 bar 8f), each theme is freely developed in the same order, as in the first movement. Then the recapitulation (fig. 8) brings back F in imitation between piano and violin, leading to G in the tonic. But all our forecasts based on the first movement's thematic order are upset by the reappearance of A in the piano bass (fig. 9, p. 40) beneath a cross between F and H on the violin. In addition, a new accompaniment in triplet quavers announces C in augmentation just before fig. 10. This begins the fourth and final section in which F and G return, and the last appearance of G (fig. 11) develops its whole-tone aspect in rising sequences that involve F as well (p. 43). G dominates in the brilliant, luminous coda making the overall form:

F G H—F G H—F G A—C F G (+ F)

The First Cello Sonata was composed at great speed for Fauré, mostly at St-Raphaël in July-August 1917 in the darkest period of the war. It is no less full-blooded and powerful than the Second Violin Sonata, but more compact and formally straightforward. The accents and cross-rhythms of the first movement approach violence at times and exploit the rugged side of the cello, completely at odds with the public image of Fauré and his more popular *Élégie*. For this reason, the First Cello Sonata is sadly the least played of his cello pieces and is over-shadowed by the mellower and more easily accessible Second Sonata of 1921, even though this exploits fewer of the instrument's technical resources.

The two subjects of the opening Allegro in d in sonata form (Ex. 42 A and B) represent the same opposition between strength and sweetness that we find in the *Fantaisie* the following year. Ex. 42 (2) shows the link between A and the opening theme of the Symphony in d (op. 40). A is remarkable for the brusqueness of its accompaniment, a factor accentuated by its frequent and unpredictable silences. B (fig. 2), on the other hand, is dreamy and sensuous with a regular quaver accompaniment. The development continuously opposes the two themes, never allowing the harmony to settle as it did on the first appearance of B. In the recapitulation of A, Fauré provides a jazzy, imitative accompaniment at fig. 8, and the coda (fig. 11) develops A to exciting new levels, still managing to incorporate aspects of B after fig. 12 (N, p. 142).

The inner peace of the Andante in g provides a perfect contrast to the first movement and is limpid, without ever becoming slack or uninteresting. The two themes C and D appear in quick succession at the outset, and the rest of the movement is a long, singing dialogue between the two complementary ideas. C is unusual in that it is a duet from the very beginning, both elements recurring as the piece develops, with the piano providing an answer to the questionings of the cello. The calmly poised D is perhaps the nearest Fauré comes to Ravel's combination of purity and melancholy. C and D return in the tonic near the end, and this makes ternary form the best broad definition of this movement. As in the outer movements of the Second Violin Sonata, however, there are several statements of C and D in their original order with development en route. The fourth such statement rises to a passionate intensity that spills over into the fifth and final statement in the tonic (fig. 5).

The finale in the tonic major, 'after these heights of pure music . . . provides a diversion' (N, p. 143). E is graceful and with an almost nonchalant air that looks back to the world of *La Bonne Chanson*; the bold but brief second theme (Ex. 42 F) leaps around more energetically, covering all three cello registers in its two acrobatic bars. Its whimsical humour is complemented by flying arpeggios and scales on the equally liberated piano. The rest of the movement is one long development; the themes are so clearly differentiated that simple recapitulation would be redundant, and all Fauré needs to do is to gravitate skilfully back to the tonic to close. The harmonic direction is easier to follow than usual, and the interest

Ex. 42

First Cello Sonata (op. 109)

cf. Ex. 36

Symphony in d (op. 40)

172

Ex. 42 (contd.)

III

is centred on the canonic treatments of E. The best of these employ Fauré's favourite canon at the octave at a distance of one beat, though for once he miscalculates at fig. 4, when the piano right hand in single notes is expected to balance both the cello and the piano left hand in octaves, as well as provide the accompanying semiquaver pattern. But the movement bubbles extrovertly on, and achieves the seemingly impossible by welding E and F together. By the end of the finale the anger of the first movement has been transformed through the quiet contemplation of the Andante into joyous optimism, which is Fauré's real wartime message.

Une Châtelaine en sa tour . . . written for the harpist Micheline Kahn in 1918 (op. 110) is included here because it would otherwise need a section of its own. Mlle Kahn had been active in playing and publishing arrangements of Fauré's piano works, with his approval and assistance, like the *Sicilienne* (op. 78) and the so-called Eighth Nocturne. For the solo piece dedicated to her, Fauré chose a line from Verlaine's *Bonne Chanson* that he had previously set to music in September 1892 (op. 61/1). He compressed this extract from *Une Sainte en son auréole* into the two-bar modal and non-modulating motif upon which the piece is based (Ex 43). *Une Châtelaine en sa tour* . . . has a more agitated

Ex. 43   **Une Châtelaine en sa tour . . .** (op. 110)

a: **Une Sainte en son auréole** (op. 61/1), bars 8–10

b: **Une Châtelaine en sa tour**, bars 1–2

central section (pp. 4–5) deriving mostly from the last three notes of Ex. 43b, and the main theme recurs in canon at a bar's distance in the varied shorter recapitulation. This relatively slight piece, whilst sensitive and practical harp music, belongs rather to the world of the divertissement *Masques et Bergamasques* than with the great wartime sonatas. These two works inspired by Verlaine are the only instances of instrumental pieces to which Fauré added descriptive titles of his own choosing.

(iv) *Orchestral Music*

The *Fantaisie* for piano and orchestra in G (op. 111) represents the other summit of Fauré's wartime achievement and was mostly written during the summer of 1918 at Évian and finished in its original two-piano format in Nice that winter. Alfred Cortot, to whom the work is dedicated, revised the piano part to make it more easily accessible (see chapter 6), though sadly this did not have the desired effect, for this compact and original masterpiece has been little heard since its initial airings in 1919: first in Monte Carlo by Marguerite Hasselmans on 12 April, then in Paris by Cortot on 14 May.

Fauré found writing the *Fantaisie* easy once he got under way. 'It seems that the older I get, the quicker and easier composition becomes', he told his wife on 8 September 1918 (LI, p. 244–5), though as usual he had trouble with the end, for 'endings are always prickly!' (13 September, LI p. 245). The orchestration of the second piano part he entrusted to Marcel Samuel-Rousseau, though Fauré checked his work carefully and made a few minor alterations himself.

The three-in-one form of two slower movements around a central faster one has obvious affinities with the *Ballade* of 1879, though the dionysian energy of the *Fantaisie* is worlds away from the romantic lushness of op. 19. For sustained intensity the 15-minute *Fantaisie* is unsurpassed in Fauré's output and, with works like the Second Prelude (op. 103), it shows his skill in juxtaposing very different sections within a unified whole.

The solo piano announces the wide-ranging and virile theme A (Ex. 44) without any introduction, its feeling of excitement being enhanced by its off-beat accompaniment in thick chords. A is constructed around the interval central to Fauré's third period, the major second. This is also evident at the start of the warmer and more lyrical B, and it often finds itself compressed into a minor second in the aggressive middle section. Both A and B use the Lydian raised fourth degree, and both provide dramatic contrasts with the short, narrow-ranged motifs which dominate the piano music of the first years of the third period.

Ex. 44   **Fantaisie** for piano and orchestra (op. 111)

B appears in the orchestra at fig. 2 after a short development of A that only begins to explore its rhythmic and motivic possibilities. The first part of B belongs to the same noble category as Ulysse's royal theme from *Pénélope* (Ex. 32 B), whilst its second part is more expansive and scalar, with a favourite third-period rhythm in the fourth bar. Development begins with a restatement of A in the tonic at fig. 4, a device Fauré borrowed from the finale of the First Cello Sonata (N, p. 145).

After a dramatic silence, the central Allegro molto begins with one of Fauré's most surprising and acerbic accompaniment figures based on the harsh interval of the diminished fifth, but emphasizing the minor second between E and F natural. This turns out, however, to be a decorated dominant pedal. Theme C, which moves from c to e flat and then back enharmonically to the main key of e, foreshadows further harmonic complexity ahead, though it is not long before the expansive D occurs on the piano, against an insistent dominant pedal in the orchestra (fig. 9). This rhythmic ostinato complements the piano accompaniment to D which is almost as fragmented as that which begins the First Cello Sonata. But after development of D, theme B makes an unexpected return in sumptuous augmentation in the orchestra (pp. 20f.) to provide an element of continuity in the ceaseless activity, and to dominate the rest of the central section, mostly in alternation with theme C. D develops in the gaps between the two main appearances of B, the second of which (p. 28) sparks off an exciting crescendo leading to the triumphant return of A to begin the varied reprise of the opening section at fig. 15 (p. 30). The tense dialogue between soloist and orchestra continues unabated till the end with marvellous new thematic developments in which A dominates B. A series of ever-larger climaxes gradually introduce the spectacular thundering octaves which turn from whole-tone scales to something nearer to G major at the close.

3. 1919–24

(i) *Songs*

The two song-cycles of the final years are much shorter than those of 1906–14, and are warmer and less austere than *Le Jardin clos*. The dialogues between the outer parts still persist, but around a richer harmonic centre and with less syncopation and fewer textural gaps. Substantial climaxes and long sequential climbs are replaced by a restrained beauty and a sense of inner calm. The vocal part becomes more like a recitative, the wider melodic intervals vanish, and the accompaniment more clearly doubles the voice. As in *Le Jardin clos*, the songs of *Mirages* (op. 113) are all in major keys with the last in the minor, the reverse procedure to the omnitonic chamber music where minor leads to tonic major at the end. In *L'Horizon chimérique* (op. 118) all is finally major, but as with the two later cycles, the unity stems from mood and style rather than from any sort of thematic recall or tonal plan.

Mirages, written in July–August 1919 for Madeleine Grey, begins the collection of works of Fauré's Indian summers with the Maillots at Annecy. Fauré owed his introduction to Renée de Brimont's poetry[3] to Gabriel Hanotaux, and the discovery of *Cygne sur l'eau* came as such a 'deliverance' from indecision that he dedicated *Mirages* to Hanotaux's wife. 'I haven't the least idea what I shall do next', he told his wife on 17 July 1919 (LI, p. 256), but by 23 July he had 'slowly sketched' *Cygne sur l'eau*, and less than a month later the cycle was complete, the exquisite *Danseuse* (no. 4) taking a mere five days (15–19 August). The first two songs are images of water and for the third, *Jardin nocturne*, Fauré returns to the favourite subject of his two previous cycles. Even if, as René Chalupt says (*ReM*, 1922, p. 31), these feminine verses are 'a little too adorned with epithets that are nothing but decorative filling, they have elegance and variety and show an awareness of the Verlainean seduction of irregular metres'.

With *Cygne sur l'eau* we are back in the key and mood of *Lydia* once more as the black swan 'glides slowly to the shores of weariness on the bottomless waters of the dream, the mirage, the echo, the fog, the shadow and the night'. Fauré's timeless limpid chordal accompaniment and virtually unbroken line, ever rising up to the dominant and falling back again, fits de Brimont's illusory world to perfection. Nothing is allowed to distract from the words, though for one brief moment, before the final stanza brings a return to the opening bars, the slow forward progression is suspended in mid-air and left oscillating around a nebulous harmonic sequence (bars 41–5) as the singer tells the swan that 'no Chinese miracle, or strange America will welcome you to safe harbours from your slow voyage towards inevitable doom'.

Ex. 45   **Mirages** (op. 113)
Bars 33–9   No. 2: Reflets dans l'eau

In *Reflets dans l'eau* (no. 2), the mood could not be further from the virtuosity of Debussy's *Image* of 1905 or Ravel's *Jeux d'eau*. The singer peers into a pond and imagines herself submerged, lost in the world of memory. The accompaniment is deliberately repetitive and on the vague, shadowy side, which makes the points where it changes harmonic direction all the more effective. As she remembers past love ('J'aime vos caresses de soeur', p. 8), the piano starts a long descent, with the bass falling in whole tones. As she then imagines herself drowning silently in the pool ('Si je glisse . . . '), the accompaniment stops, a *very* rare event in Fauré, and we have three equally rare descriptive passages as an object slides into the water in the bass and the ripples spread gradually across the pond, slow down, and stop (Ex. 45). But the waters quickly return to their former timeless existence, and the overall impression is one of their indifference to the events imagined by the unknown singer (N, p. 151).

Jardin nocturne 'is a poem of shadow and secrecy' (Jankélévitch, 1974, p. 219). Instead of the customary progression falling by whole tones, the start offers us a rising one. I cannot agree with M. Nectoux (N, p. 151) that the garden 'shivers in the breeze and palpitates with tiny noises' for, to my mind, the accompaniment perfectly matches the poem which describes a moonlit garden where all is stillness and peace. The background is rather one of calm mysterious beauty, rising to a restrained climax as the singer complains that she knows only too well the charms of the garden that are 'disturbed by desires and weariness' (p. 15). Despite the crescendos, the loudest marking is *piano*, and the song continually falls back to the melancholy repose of its tonic (E flat).

If there is a criticism of *Mirages*, it is that as a cycle it is too veiled and reserved. The first three songs are cast in the same mood of slow, nocturnal stillness. Only *Danseuse*, one of Fauré's most impressive creations in its absolute simplicity, is different. Here a dotted falling figure persists from beginning to end as the singer exhorts a mysterious being to dance, so much so that the whole song has a mechanical, yet antique feeling. The variations of the motif are fascinating in themselves, especially when it becomes a sinuous low flute-figure filling the whole bar at 'Danse, danse au chant de ma flûte creuse' (p. 19). In contrast to the other three songs, the vocal line is more spread out, and even contains a rare melisma on 'ailes *nues*' (p. 18 bar 3) which Fauré with his customary skill makes the vocal peak of the song.

Fauré was probably trying to recapture something of the mood of *Danseuse* when he wrote the rising dotted bass figure which begins *C'est la paix* (op. 114) and which is its only redeeming feature. He had agreed to set the poem of the winner of a competition organized by *Le Figaro* on the theme of post-war peace, and Mlle Georgette Debladis's uninspired verses were finally given musical shape at the Hôtel de la Terrasse, Monte Carlo between 6 and 8 December 1919. The ultra-sensitive Fauré complained to his wife (LI, p. 260) that what was worst about the 'horrible little poem' was the word '*Poilu*,[4] that was so heroic in conversation but terrible when associated with music!' The only way he could get over the problem was to change 'Poilus' to 'soldats' at the climax of the second verse (bars 18–19).

If *Mirages* gives a monochrome impression, then *L'Horizon chimérique* is all ardour and forceful directness. Fauré chose for his last cycle in the autumn of 1921, four poems by Jean de La Ville de Mirmont (1886–1914)[5] who had been tragically killed in the war. The cycle is unified by its rich harmonic style and by its subject matter, for the three outer songs: *La Mer est infinie*, *Je me suis embarqué* and *Vaisseaux, nous vous aurons aimés* are varied seascapes completing the long line of inspired arpeggio-based pieces stretching back sixty years to *Les Matelots* (op. 2/2). The third song *Diane, Séléné* is a contemplative chordal hymn to the moon (N, p. 157).

The accompaniment of *La Mer est infinie* perfectly matches the forceful poem and maintains its restless energy from first to last, the voice forming a continuous line with only the minimum of breathing space. Throughout, 'the sea sings in the sun, beating against the cliffs', and just before the end Fauré introduces into the accompaniment a rocking hemiola figure in sustained crotchets that is echoed in the following song (bars 26–7) as the singer asks the wind and sea to 'rock me like a child'. In *Je me suis embarqué*, Fauré seeks rather to portray 'the vessel which dances' than the sea on which she sails. The main rising figure, accented on both the first and second beats (in triple time), is over-used. But there are some forceful moments, like the sudden outburst near the end ('O ma peine, ma peine', bar 40), which redeem this otherwise rather sullen song.

Vaisseaux, nous vous aurons aimés, like *La Mer est infinie*, is one long expansive vocal line over a restless rising accompaniment figure repeated without alteration throughout. The mood is one of nostalgia mixed with yearning for the unattainable. The singer, a creature of the land, sees the ships he has become attached to set sail, and he is powerless to affect their destinies. But the call of the sea makes him despair, for he has unfulfilled desires to travel. Fauré does not attempt to match in the music the changes in the subject's moods, but maintains the same declamatory vocal style throughout. As usual there are no *rallentandos* or *accelerandos* marked and, in order to work, the final climax on 'inassouvis' either needs a *rall.* or the high d'' extending by half a bar, with the resolution to the tonic delayed until the final word 'moi'.

(ii) *Piano Music*

Fauré may have been tempting providence when he wrote his Thirteenth Barcarolle and Nocturne in 1921, and the latter's completion on 31 December that year closed the door on his last great productive cycle stretching from the beginning of the war.

The Thirteenth Barcarolle (op. 116) of February 1921 with its transparent, almost naïve opening theme in C is deceptively simple. The whole piece is a fascinating enigma, and it seems that Fauré is smiling at us from the wisdom of old age as we try to discern something in it that was never intended. The similarity with the diatonic Twelfth Barcarolle is obvious, though the left-hand semiquavers are cast in more distorted and unexpected patterns. The neo-classical Thirteenth Barcarolle is in ternary form, though its more expansive and dramatic B theme in 9/8 time (p. 5) uses the same iambic rhythms as A. A develops in a wealth of different harmonic directions with complete effortlessness, and there is a beautiful variation in the texture on its reprise (p. 6) with a decorative turn that recalls the second theme of the Third Barcarolle (bar 27f.).

The noble and deeply introspective Thirteenth Nocturne (op. 119) is in a world of its own, a combination of profound meditation and surging energy scarcely intended for the concert-hall. It begins like an austere Bach chorale, with audacious harmonies full of retardations and passing notes that can only be explained, as is often the case in Bach, by the supreme logic of the part-writing. A brief but restrained chromatic development leads to a more forceful theme B in octaves (Ex. 46) which ends with an important whole-tone figure B_1 (bar 29). The development of B_1 becomes almost Ravelian just before the return of A (bars 38–9), recalling the *Toccata* from *Le Tombeau de Couperin* of 1914–17 (cf. Exx. 47 a and b).

Ex. 46   **Thirteenth Nocturne** (op. 119)
Bars 22–3

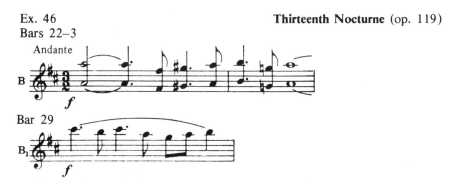

Ex. 47
a: **Thirteenth Nocturne**, bars 38–9

b: Ravel: **Le Tombeau de Couperin**
VI: Toccata, bars 57–8 and 63–4

B₁ acts as a bass to A and the tension builds powerfully into an impulsive central Allegro in the tonic major (p. 5). What appears to be a new theme (p. 5 bar 6f.) is really a luminous, forceful transformation of the sad opening theme. This is fused with B₁ in the bass in the passage leading to a long virtuoso climax of terrific intensity for Fauré (pp. 8–10), but in which the virtuosity is an integral part of the development. A sudden hiatus and a rare rallentando swiftly bring us back to A. The first fourteen bars are an exact reprise of the start, but after passing through the worlds of doubt, passion and anger, their effect is now one of tranquil appeasement. The various ideas combine in a visionary coda which is like that of the Eleventh Nocturne: both pieces close in the minor mode in which they began, gradually lulling themselves into silence after a brief heightening of the emotional intensity just before the end (N, p. 161).

(iii) *Chamber Music*

Fauré began work on the Second Piano Quintet in c (op. 115) on 2 September 1919, only a fortnight after completing *Mirages* (LI, pp. 257–8). As with all his post-war chamber works he composed the middle movements first, and this is his last four-movement work, with its scherzo coming second as in the Piano Quartets. But composition was becoming a slower process for the infirm Fauré, although after 1920 he was at last able to devote all his professional energy to it. The manuscript of the Quintet bears a date as late as March 1921, but was probably completed in Nice early the previous month (LI, p. 267). It is a full-blooded work, singing throughout almost as if its life depended on it. The finale is superior to that of the First Quintet though, to my mind, it is still its least successful movement. Similarities with the First Quintet extend to the strings entering one by one over a pulsating accompaniment at the outset, and an intense B theme announced by the quartet alone, all playing on their lowest strings.

The Second Piano Quintet extends Fauré's experiments into the realm of continuous development in four sections in its opening movement, and into the developing rondo in its rhythmic finale, though there is no cyclic recall of themes as there was in the Second Violin Sonata. Fauré's deliberate avoidance of the lowest bass-register is most noticeable in the Second Quintet out of all the chamber works of the last years. So much so that when a deep-lying passage does appear at fig. 8 in the slow movement it feels like a totally new departure. This results in the Quintet appearing luminous and incandescent, the feeling of spiritual elevation being intensified by its chosen pitch.

The opening theme (Ex. 48 A) on viola is confident and self-contained; the bare fourths and fifths in the accompaniment and the first two bars of A give the start an elemental feeling, which warms immediately the dominant pedal ceases and the familiar major sevenths appear in bar 4. At no time before we reach the aggressive B is a straightforward root position tonic chord of c minor sounded, and the first two statements of A are concluded by Fauréan plagal cadences in E flat and A flat. This process is repeated in B flat and D flat on pp. 7–9, after some development of B and its more restful secondary piano theme A_1, which characteristically derives from A, and not from B as one would expect. A_1 gives rise to Fauré's favourite progressions descending in whole tones which help to link the movement together and also recur in the scherzo. After this second exposition of A, imitative development begins (fig. 6, p. 9), leading to an abrupt contrast between B in full intensity on the strings and a quiet development of A_1 beginning on the piano, which reveals its origins by fusing at once with A.

The third section (fig. 10) opens with another recapitulation of A, this time at its original pitch but with harmonies beginning and ending in E flat. The movement then plunges straight back into development in which A and A_1 dominate. Our formal expectations are confused at fig. 15 however: what feels like the beginning of the final peroration in the tonic major turns out to be the start of a fourth section of development which includes a restatement of B in the tonic minor. The

Ex. 48 **Second Piano Quintet** (op. 115): themes

I: Allegro moderato

cf. Ex. 17B

III: Andante moderato

Ex. 48 (contd.)

IV: Allegro molto

coda does not begin till fig. 18, and this time the music soars joyously
to a plateau and stays there. By the close, however, there has been too
much C major, and Fauré rather overstates his case at the ends of both
the outer movements.

The lightning scherzo is one of Fauré's most miraculous inventions.
As in the Second Prelude (op. 103) and the central section of the
Fantaisie, we are confronted with something totally unexpected. This
is as far from 'pure' music as is imaginable, being all texture and effects,

with fascinating half-chromatic/half-diatonic scales on the piano setting off pizzicato and spiccato effects and cross-rhythms on the strings in a foretaste of the scherzo of Bartók's Fourth String Quartet. There is no trio as such, but a more lyrical theme (D) is extended melodically and harmonically alongside ingenious developments of the whirling C. The ideas are combined after fig. 9. In the staccato grace-notes descending into the bass in the final bars it seems as if Fauré is laughing gently at us as he did at the end of the Fifth Impromptu (N, p. 153).

In the Andante moderato, a tender arch-shaped theme on the strings (Ex. 48 E) is answered by a short dotted figure on the piano (E_1, bar 9). This is complementary to E, even if it has its own separate accompaniment texture in semiquavers. The second theme proper (F) appears at fig. 3, and is a quintessential third period idea with an off-beat accompaniment, and a graceful, aspiring melody which frequently straddles the middle of the bar. As such, it resembles *Roses ardentes* (op. 95/3) or theme H from the Second Violin Sonata (Ex. 41), and looks forward to E (Ex. 50) from the Piano Trio. Theme F is novel because it is introduced from a full stop in G major in the nearest Fauré gets in the third period to a traditional modulation (Ex. 48 F). There are yet more references to the Lydia theme after fig. 4 (p. 44), and what looks like another premature recapitulation in the tonic (fig. 5) proves to be the starting point for a development of E and E_1, which leads to the unusually low-pitched statement of F at fig. 8. E_1 is extended through a most beautiful succession of chromatic modulations between figs. 9 and 11, before the third return of E in the tonic begins the final development section. As this is never very far from the tonic (G), it has the feeling more of a coda than a development or recapitulation.

In the rhythmic and exuberant finale, the hemiola figure in the bass (G_1) which accompanies theme G turns out to be as important to the development of the movement as A_1 and E_1 did previously. There are obvious affinities between the arch shapes of all the opening ideas in the Second Quintet (A, E and G), which are matched by the arched piano scales at the start of the scherzo. Both outer movements also begin on the viola, and it was probably for this reason that Fauré began the slow movement with a rising sixth on the viola rather than the cello. Whereas Fauré had trouble with the form of the first movement ('As Saint-Saëns says, in the ordering of ideas, the difficulties do not smooth themselves out with age')[6], in the finale he told his wife (LI, p. 268) that he was 'working with continuity and pleasure'.

Theme G and its vital bass accompaniment G_1 make up another rondo idea, with secondary themes H (fig. 2) and J (fig. 8) entering on the piano to provide episodes around the developments of G and G_1. J is essentially a compression of G, which appears for the last time in its original form at fig. 7 in what feels like another of Fauré's early reprises, but again proves to be the start of a new development leading to J. Both H and J are varied later on, and G_1 turns out to be the main rondo element, though it disappears in the final section from fig. 17 onwards, as elements of G, H and J combine in a long, precipitous coda in the tonic major.

The Second Quintet enjoyed an overwhelming success at its first performance at the SN on 21 May 1921 by a distinguished group of devoted Fauréans including Robert Lortat (piano), Victor Gentil (second violin) and Gérard Hekking (cello). Poor Fauré could only hear the applause properly, and when he took his bow (FF, p. 122) 'he appeared extremely frail, emaciated and unsteady beneath his heavy winter overcoat'. When he got home, he told his assembled family from his bed: 'Naturally a successful evening like tonight pleases me greatly. But what is *disturbing*, is that afterwards it is not simply a question of coming down to earth again, one must try to do even better.'

This Fauré did to the amazement of all in his Piano Trio and String Quartet, but in the meantime he was commissioned by the State to compose the *Chant funéraire* for the commemoration of the centenary of the death of Napoleon at the Hôtel des Invalides on 5 May 1921. His elegy, orchestrated and conducted by Guillaume Balay, leader of the Orchestre de la Garde Républicaine, met with considerable acclaim. So as not to waste this moving occasional piece, Fauré resolved in March 1921 to use it as the basis around which to build his Second Cello Sonata (op. 117) in g. This he finished on 10 November 1921, and the equally successful first performance by Gérard Hekking and Alfred Cortot took place on 13 May the following year.

In the Second Cello Sonata the close imitation characteristic of the third period returns, after having been less in evidence in the Second Quintet. The first movement is a remarkable example of sustained lyrical force, and its use of sonata form is relatively straightforward. A, another arch-shaped theme of scalar origins, even starts in imitation, and its restless nature, accentuated by the off-beat accompaniment, contrasts strongly with the broadly passionate B on the piano (fig. 4). In between is a secondary motivic idea A_1 (Ex. 49), linked to A by the descending cello scale that accompanies it. All three ideas develop separately, with the scale figure derived from A playing a linking role.

The central Andante in c invites comparison with the *Élégie* (op. 24) and shows how far Fauré had travelled musically since 1880. Whilst the climax of the *Élégie* is ostentatious in its cello cadenza and thundering piano part, the Andante for Napoleon preserves its noble gravity and profoundly meditative mood throughout. It has greater contrapuntal strength too, and its restrained passion makes the grief it expresses

Ex. 49   **Second Cello Sonata** (op. 117): themes

I: Allegro

III: Allegro vivo

seem all the heavier. A more lyrical theme D provides a degree of appeasement after fig. 3, and the main climax comes at fig. 5 in mid-development of the end of the first phrase of C (bars 4–5), rather than at the start of the recapitulation, as in the *Élégie*. The tension drops very suddenly as the unexpected key of b minor shifts, without slowing, back to c minor for the return of theme C (fig. 6). This time the second part of C is by-passed, and D appears in the tonic major in canon between bass and cello at a minim's distance (fig. 7). This is skilfully transformed into the same descending phrase from C used for the climax at fig. 5, which ends the plaint in a most moving manner (N, p. 156).

The finale is a light and joyous scherzo; an inexhaustible fund of invention in the same class as that of the Second Quintet. The elusive rising idea (Ex. 49 E) on the piano is only identifiable as a rhythmic unit 'x', and the descending scale on the cello that answers it proves equally important, and often includes whole-tone excursions. F is a sort of chorale in four-part harmony (fig. 2, p. 25), whose first four bars are the most important, the rest being scales again. Fauré's part-writing is so smooth here that the dissonances pass almost unnoticed. After development of E, a false recapitulation in the tonic at fig. 4 suddenly gives way to a stranger, colouristic episode, a sort of feverish trio. Here a three-note rising figure (G) just before fig. 5 is followed by a flashing arch of semiquavers on the piano, together with pizzicato interjections on the cello. This returns briefly (p. 34) after further development of E and F, before an extension of E leads into an exciting coda using the repeated-note idea on the cello from the trio.

Overall, the Second Cello Sonata is simpler and easier to come to terms with than the First. All its movements pass from the minor into the tonic major, and the central Funeral Elegy lends it a special memorability, as well as providing one of the best examples of Fauré's 'pure' music. It matters little what this movement is scored for, its impact is still the same.

The idea to write a Piano Trio came from Fauré's publisher Jacques Durand, and gradually took shape between August 1922 and the spring of 1923. The logic of the first movement provides a good opportunity to clarify Fauré's modified classical sonata-form plan as it appears in the most important third period chamber works. On a general level the Allegro ma non troppo is a slow controlled climb from a limpid start to the incandescent coda. The two main contrasting ideas: A, a long singing cello theme (Ex. 50) which seems to have all the time in the world; and B, an oscillating phrase on the piano, are linked, or rather, separated by the brusque A_1 on the piano. This is shown to be a derivative of A as it is answered by 'x' on the strings, which is an important development motif taken from the end of A (bars 15–16). Development of A and B in separate paragraphs, either by extension or motivic cross-play, begins immediately after the exposition, and it is always difficult to tell what is theme and what is extension, so continuous is the musical flow. In B, for instance, the repeat of the start on the strings immediately incorporates A_1 (p. 4), which sends the music off in a totally new direction, and Fauré was a past master at fusing apparently incongruous ideas into one continuous thread in his long, organic developments.

After each idea has been exposed and initially developed, the 'development' proper begins, in which themes are juxtaposed, or more often canonically or imitatively treated. This 'development' invariably begins with a re-exposition of all or part of A in the tonic. This was Fauré's way of stabilizing the tonality, for harmonic development always went hand in hand with thematic development in his invariably sequential approach. It also provided the listener with a feeling of security, a reminder perhaps of the repeated exposition that was a hallmark of classical sonata form. In the Trio the re-exposition of A occurs at fig. 4, characteristically rescored and with a new bass-line. The movement proceeds, singing sequentially, renewing A, A_1 and B in ever-changing patterns, and climbing towards the third section (fig. 8), which looks

Ex. 50   **Piano Trio** (op. 120): themes

like another recapitulation in the tonic, but turns out to be the start of yet another development of A, this time making more use of 'x'. The feeling of a recapitulation recurs when B appears in the tonic major (fig. 10), but this again reverts to development of 'x'. Long rising whole-tone sequences (fig. 11) lead to the fourth section (fig. 12), a second recapitulation of A and B in the tonic (minor), which makes this movement like a simpler version of the Second Violin Sonata. The 'x' figure from A returns for the last time to dominate the jubilant coda, in which there are none of the customary dips down to *piano*, but a powerful assertion that the logic behind the movement has triumphed at last. We even get Fauré's late version of a dominant pedal, and a bell-like accented bass which recalls the end of the opening movement of the Second Quintet (N, p. 162).

The long slow movement must surely rank amongst Fauré's most inspired, an effortless contrapuntal duet, sometimes a trio, around a chordal centre on the piano, which in the first two movements scarcely stops for even a quaver's rest. Theme C, with violin answered by cello against a procession of slow chords, starts the dialogue off in an atmosphere of modal beauty. The elliptical D appears soon afterwards on the piano (fig. 1), indulging immediately in the sort of melodic and harmonic chromaticism that only Fauré could handle. As it happens, D provides just the right sort of passionate balance to the melancholy C, and its similar cadence rhythm to the rhythm which began C allows the two to fuse naturally in development. There are similarities too in the shape of the opening bars of C and D. But, as in the slow movement of the Second Quintet, there is a third, slowly rising theme (Ex. 50 E, p. 18) on the piano. The extensions to this are exquisite, with a duet between strings and piano in overlapping phrases building slowly to a powerful climax (p. 20), and incorporating C in the process at fig. 4. The suspense is maintained until the very last second (p. 21), when the music veers suddenly into a recapitulation of C with less than half a bar's harmonic preparation. Even Fauré is forced to add a *poco rit.* here. C and D develop further, often in genuine three-part dialogue: E reappears in conjunction with C, but is mostly saved for the final pages (N, p. 163).

The violence of the finale comes as a complete shock. Emmanuel Fauré-Fremiet tells us (*BAF*, 1972, p. 17) that the *fortissimo* string announcement of Leoncavallo's 'Ridi Pagliaccio' (Ex. 50 F) was a 'pure coincidence'. It is odd all the same that Fauré did not notice the similarity and reconsider the movement for, in an interview on modern Italian music (*Comoedia*, 31 January 1910), he relegated *Pagliacci* to the bottom of the list as 'provoking the indignation of all those who care about music'. He did not, however, go as far as Debussy in the same enquiry, and compare *verismo* opera with brothels!

The piano's irregularly phrased answer (G), an accented rustic dance tune, establishes that the finale is in fact a scherzo, like the finales of the Second Cello Sonata and the String Quartet; also that the principle of a dialogue between strings and piano will continue. A third strident and accented theme (G_1) appears in canon at a bar's distance on the strings at fig. 4, and this has affinities with bars 2–5 of G. The long piano answer to G_1 almost justifies calling this third theme 'H', as both parts feature in the subsequent development (after figs. 5 and 7) and in the recapitulation (after fig. 9). Following development, the three themes return in reverse order, which allows Fauré to return naturally to G_1 for the final pages. It also makes F something of a rondo theme, though it is closely rivalled in this role by the first two bars of G_1.

The extrovert ends of the outer movements of the Second Quintet and the Piano Trio contrast strongly with the quiet endings that dominate the later piano music, and makes nonsense of the myth of Fauré retiring into an ivory tower to compose introverted music that was either serene or austere. The relative straightforwardness of the harmonies and the clearer textures of the Trio in particular arise from a sense of inner peace and confidence, and put across an optimistic message of hope and of a vibrant inner life that represents the triumph of mind over matter.

The Trio was first performed on 12 May 1923 by Tatiana de Sansévitch (piano), Robert Krettly (violin) and Jacques Pathé (cello), though the second performance on 29 June by the celebrated Cortot- Thibaud-Casals Trio was considered to be the more outstanding.

The String Quartet (1923–4) was Fauré's first chamber work without piano, and for the last time he returned to themes from the discarded orchestral works of his first period (see Ex. 8). As in the Trio, the opening Allegro moderato begins with a thematic dialogue—here between violin and viola. Such a positive start is unusual for Fauré, but the violin's expansive, softer cantilena provides a reassuring answer to the anguished questions of the viola, in a manner that recalls the slow movements of opp. 109 and 115. For once the movement is in straightforward sonata form, with even a halt in the dominant at the end of the exposition (fig. 3), and a recapitulation in the tonic (fig. 5). Here A is shortened, and the questioning viola phrase which played such a large part in the development is omitted. Midway between figs. 7 and 8 the recapitulation begins to go its own way, and blossoms forth in further development of the opening violin answer into the tonic major (fig. 9), although the recapitulation of B had already taken place in that key. The serene coda extends the opening viola phrase in imitation with an unexpectedly lush ending.

The harmonic astringency that marks certain passages in the first movement continues in the central Andante, bars 5–8 of Ex. 51 providing an example of the chains of mild unresolved discords which characterize it, and which are sweetened by the string quartet sounds and by the ceaseless song of the first violin. Ex. 51 also shows how theme C temporarily becomes a duet in bars 4–5, and how Fauré constructs one of many slow ascents to a climax (bar 9). These usually then fall to give an arch shape and complete the musical paragraph, as in bars 9 to 16. Theme D, on Fauré's favourite viola, which begins the second musical paragraph (fig. 11), is even more confident than C, recalling F from the Second Quintet. A third idea (E), undulating and

Ex. 51   **String Quartet** (op. 121): themes

II: Andante (theme C)

Ex. 51 (contd.)
III: Allegro

gently syncopated, appears at fig. 13 on the viola, providing a counter-subject for a development of D on the violin which leads to the modified recapitulation at fig. 14. Here the main ideas recur in further development in the order C–E–D, before a coda based on C rounds the movement off.

The finale is another scherzo 'of a light and pleasant character'. F is a vigorous cello theme, a series of small arched phrases making up a longer arch, with a delicious pizzicato accompaniment. F and G, another singing cello theme, are continually varied as long musical paragraphs, and there are remarkable similarities of outline between the sections: start to fig. 21, figs. 23–5 and figs. 28–30 for instance. Theme F again assumes something of the character of a recurring rondo idea and dominates the lively, almost breathless final pages, whilst G provides a contrapuntal contrast, its viola quaver figure recalling E from the previous movement, which also looks like a counter-subject. In fact in Ex. 51 G the true 'Art of Fugue' subject appears to be the second violin line in semibreves, which has a real answer ten bars later when this musical paragraph is repeated a fifth higher.

If the Quartet has a fault it is its lack of 'sufficient contrast in the character of the themes, in rhythmic vigour, in dynamic fire'.[7] Again the intensity of the soaring lyrical song of the first violin is heightened by so much of the Quartet being pitched in the treble register. But closer study reveals a wealth of difference between the outer movements, and it is only because the 'slow' movement moves along so rapidly and has so much interesting counterpoint that we sense any lack of variety overall. Rather, all the more obvious similarities, like E and the viola part in Ex. 51 G, are forces for unity, and Fauré's subtle variation of whole musical paragraphs in the scherzo/finale makes the links within the movements more than just skin-deep, the craftsmanship being so consummate that we need to listen hard even to notice the joins or the thematic counterpoint that gives the Quartet its virile strength.

(iv) *Fauré and the Theatre:* Masques et Bergamasques

Masques et Bergamasques (op. 112) is a one-act lyric divertissement to a text adapted from Verlaine by René Fauchois. The slight argument runs as follows:

> Harlequin, Gilles and Columbine, comedians from the Italian Theatre, amuse themselves on a free day amidst the rustic decor of a Cytherean island.
>
> Suddenly their fashionable theatre audience arrives—the Lindors, Clymènes, Clitandres and Lydés—and the humble performers, hidden behind the bushes, are treated in their turn to an unexpected show that the marquises and marchionesses, inspired by love, provide for them without realising it.

For this whimsical spectacle, Fauré produced eight musical extracts, of which only nos. 2 and 5 below are definitely compositions of 1918–19. The orchestral suite comprises nos. 1, 5, 7 and 2 from the following:

1. *Ouverture* (based on an *Intermezzo de symphonie* of 1867–8)
2. *Pastorale*
3. *Madrigal* (op. 35, with orchestra)
4. *Le Plus Doux Chemin* (op. 87/1, with orchestra)
5. *Menuet* (1918–19)
6. *Clair de lune* (op. 46/2, with orchestra)
7. *Gavotte* (1869)
8. *Pavane* (op. 50)

The orchestrations were by Fauré himself, though he was helped in his task by Marcel Samuel-Rousseau, who probably re-orchestrated the *Gavotte*. The *Pastorale* is by far the most interesting movement in *Masques et Bergamasques*, and Fauré significantly chose it to close the suite of previously unpublished movements in a mood of tender serenity. It contains some of Fauré's happiest melodic developments, including a reference back to the opening of the *Ouverture* which occurs twice around fig. 4.

On 1 April 1919, in the same week as the Monte Carlo première of *Masques et Bergamasques*, Fauré told his wife (LI, p. 253) that Raoul Gunsbourg also had to 'knock into shape two operas, an Italian *opera buffa*, and Saint-Saëns's *Phryné!*' It was the old *Pénélope* team of Fauchois–Fauré–Gunsbourg–Jéhin back together again in the same theatre, and Fauré reported to his wife on 10 April (LI, p. 255) after the première that 'the performance met with success. The dances were attractive, the décor and costumes excellent. (The décor is that of the famous *Swing* by Watteau.)'

On 5 April, Fauré told Albert Carré of the Opéra-Comique during rehearsals[8] that he had devised the title *Masques et Bergamasques* himself, although Fauchois had been inexplicably opposed to this. Reynaldo Hahn's two-act opera *Nausicaa*, also to a Fauchois libretto, was to precede *Masques et Bergamasques*[9], and Fauré told Carré with great delight that 'as his work finishes with the embarcation of Ulysses for Ithaca . . . the audience will no doubt be surprised to see Ulysses land at Cythère, surrounded by a company in Regency costume, to the sound of gavottes and minuets!'

On 14 April Fauré wrote home (LI, pp. 255–6) that Carré 'is in raptures over my little "piècette" ', and wanted to transfer it to Paris with *Pénélope*, which had opened at the Opéra-Comique on 20 January 1919. He added that Gunsbourg's production in Monte Carlo was a 'bit heavy and too showy', correctly supposing that Carré's would be more sensitive, and better suited to this collection of pieces of an 'evocative and melancholy—even slightly nostalgic—character', which were intended to give the same sort of impression as 'a Watteau, which Verlaine has defined so well:

"Jouant du luth et dansant et *quasi*
Tristes sous leurs déguisements fantasques!" [*Clair de lune*]'

At the Monte Carlo première Mme Marguerite Valmond played the part of Columbine to Pierre Stephen's Gilles: René Fauchois himself played the part of Harlequin. Transferring to the Opéra-Comique on 4 March 1920, with décors by Lucien Jusseaume and choreography by Mme Jeanne Chasles, *Masques et Bergamasques* met with even greater success and has since become one of Fauré's best-loved creations, achieving its 100th performance by 25 February 1948.

Footnotes to chapter 5
1. Van Lerberghe was present at the London première of *Pelléas et Mélisande* in June 1898, though he never mentioned meeting Fauré. For more detail on Van Lerberghe and *La Chanson d'Ève* see Philippe Fauré-Fremiet's article reproduced in *BAF* (1973), pp. 7–14.
2. This is appropriately a developed version of *La Chanson de Mélisande* which tells of the fate of the King's three blind daughters waiting in vain for their

rescuing Prince as their lamps burn ever lower. In *La Chanson d'Ève* the mood changes abruptly with *Crépuscule* and a sudden chill comes over the garden of Eden in the stark economy of its opening bars.

3. The Baroness Renée de Brimont (née de Beaumont; pseudonym René de Prat) was the confidante and literary champion of the mystic religious poet Oscar Milosz (1877–1939) who described her as 'the living torch'. *Mirages*, published in Paris by Émile-Paul in 1919, is divided into two sections: 'De l'eau et des paysages' (25 poems) and 'Des songes et des paroles' (35 poems). Fauré chose poems 1, 9 and 23 from section one and added to them *Danseuse* (poem 27) from section two.

4. French Infantrymen of the Great War. The original meaning of the word was 'hairy' or 'shaggy', and it implied manly bravery.

5. Published in 1920 by the Société Littéraire de France.

6. Quoted in LI, p. 264 on 23 August 1920 whilst 'in the middle of the first movement' at Veyrier-du-Lac.

7. Egon F. Kenton, sleevenote to *Turnabout* TV 37039S.

8. La in the Pierpont Morgan Library, New York (Mary Flagler Cary Music Collection). Perhaps Fauchois was opposed to Fauré's title because of its anachronism.

9. *Nausicaa* was first performed on 13 April 1919, three days after the première of *Masques et Bergamasques*.

I   Baron Louis Niedermeyer (1802–61)   (Bibl. du Conservatoire)

II   Fauré at the École Niedermeyer, 1865

III   Fauré aged about 22, 1867   (Coll. Mme Ph. Fauré-Fremiet)

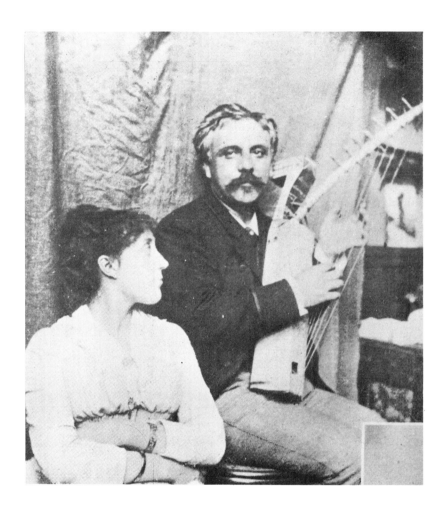

IV   Gabriel and Marie Fauré, summer 1883

V   Fauré and his father-in-law Emmanuel Fremiet, Bougival, 1889

(Coll. Mme Ph. Fauré-Fremiet)

VI   Fauré and his son Emmanuel, summer 1889

VII   Marie Fauré and her sons Emmanuel and Philippe, c. 1895

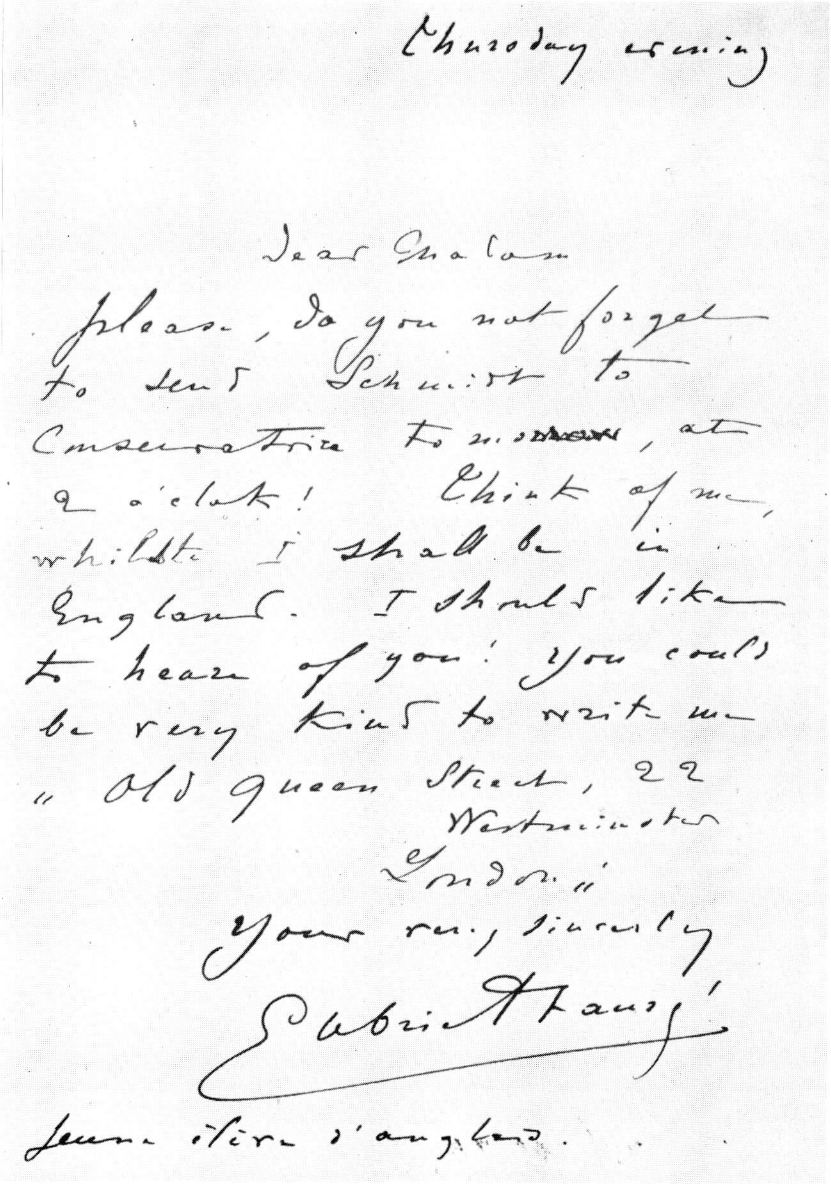

(Thursday evening)

Dear Madam

please, do you not forget
to send Schmitt to
Conservatoire tomorrow, at
2 o'clock! Think of me,
whilst I shall be in
England. I should like
to hear of you: you could
be very kind to write me
" Old Queen Street, 22
　　　　　Westminster
　　　London "
　　Your very sincerely
　　Gabriel Fauré

Jeune élève d'anglais.

VIII　　Letter to Mme de Chaumont-Quitry, probably from Paris, 24
　　　　March 1898
　　　　　　　　　　　　　　　　　(Coll. R. Orledge)

IX   Drawing of Fauré by John S. Sargent RA, made at the house
of Frank Schuster, The Hut, Bray, on 26 June 1898

(Mr R. A. Cecil, London)

X   Fauré and Mrs Patrick Campbell by John S. Sargent RA, 26 June
1898

(Richard Ormond)

Chère Madame

Je vous remercie de votre bien charmante lettre et je vous exprime de nouveau, très sincèrement, mon profond regret de vous savoir aussi longuement tourmentée par la santé de votre fils. Il ne m'a jamais semblé consolant de parler de ses propres soucis à propos des autres, cependant je puis vous dire que mon fils aîné après nous

XI   Letter to Mme de Chaumont-Quitry, early July 1899, pp. 1 and
4. The music-line is the beginning of *Le Secret*.

(Coll. R. Orledge)

et engagez le à recommencer la
bataille l'année prochaine. Je
ne suis pas convaincu que
Mesthèbe ira à Rome. Dans ce
cas il y aurait encore lieu à
décerner deux premiers prix l'année
prochaine. Pour tout ce qui
concerne Schmidt et l'Institut
et Massenet, je vous supplie de me
garder le plus profond secret !!

[notation musicale] je veux que le matin l'igno—re !!

Vous me ferez le plus grand plaisir si
vous voulez bien quelques fois me donner
de vos nouvelles. Je reste à Paris indéfi-
niment. Veuillez bien, chère Madame
agréer le respectueux hommages de votre
tout dévoué et affectionné
Gabriel Fauré

XII   Rehearsal for *Prométhée*, Béziers, August 1900
(Coll. Mme Ph. Fauré-Fremiet)

XIII   First performance of *Prométhée*, Béziers, 27 August 1900
(Coll. Mme Ph. Fauré-Fremiet)

XIV   Fauré at his desk in the Conservatoire National de Musique,
17 November 1905   (Coll. Mme Ph. Fauré-Fremiet)

XV   Pages 1–2 of the *Ave Maria*, op. 93, Vitznau, August 1906

XVI Pages 1–2 of *Paradis* from *La Chanson d'Ève* (op. 95/1), Stresa, 8 September 1906 (see also description of front cover photograph on p. xvi) (Bibl. Nat.)

qui se lè - ve des on - - - - des,

poco a poco

Un jar-din bleu se pa - rou-

crésc.

cantando

XVII Caricature from *L'Assiette au beurre*: 'Les Messieurs du Jury', 20 July 1907, no. 329

(Coll. Mme Ph. Fauré-Fremiet)

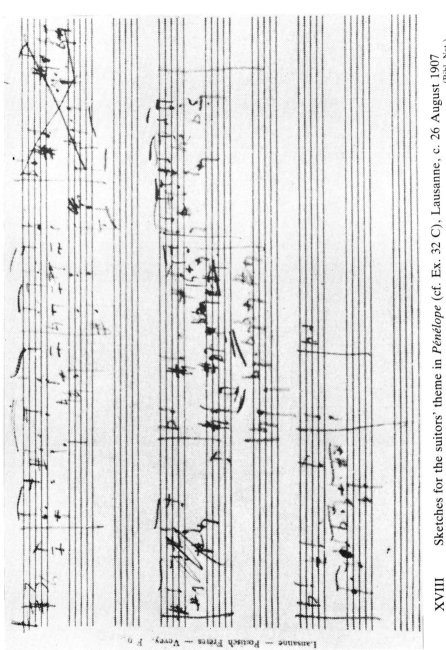

XVIII   Sketches for the suitors' theme in *Pénélope* (cf. Ex. 32 C), Lausanne, c. 26 August 1907
(Bibl. Nat.)

à aller respirer avec toi en
voiture. Mais pour le
moment aussi, lorsque tu travailles,
ne t'inquiète pas du résultat.
Expose tes idées, quelles qu'elles
soient, dans la forme la meilleure
que tu pourras. Ces idées changeront
sans doute dans la suite, elles
se modifieront dans le sens d'une
plus humaine logique, mais la
forme gardera ce que le travail
lui aura fait gagner. Imaginer,
cela consiste à essayer de formuler
tout ce qu'on voudrait de meilleur,
tout ce qui dépasse la réalité. Risque
donc ce qui te paraîtra peut-être
absurde plus tard. Tu n'auras tout
de même pas perdu ton temps.
Pour moi l'art, la musique surtout,
consiste à nous élever le plus loin
possible au dessus de ce qui est.

XIX   Letter to Philippe Fauré-Fremiet on the art of musical composition, 31 August 1908 (see p. vii)

XX   Fauré at Albéniz's house in Barcelona, March 1909

XXI   The Founding Committee of the SMI, 1910. Standing, left to right: Louis Aubert, A-Z. Mathot, Maurice Ravel, André Caplet, Charles Koechlin, Émile Vuillermoz, Jean Huré. Seated: Fauré and Roger-Ducasse   (*Musica*, June 1910)

XXII Moscow, November 1910. Seated, left to right: Raoul Pugno, Eugène Ysaÿe, Fauré, Mme
Wieniawska, Lucien Capet. Standing left to right: M. Bandoukov, Henri Casadesus, A. T.
Wieniawski, M. Ziloti, Maurice Hewitt, Marcel Casadesus   (Coll. Mme Ph. Fauré-Fremiet)

XXIII   Fauré composing *Pénélope* at the Grand Hôtel Métropole et Monopole, Lugano 1911

XXIV   Maquette for Act 1 of *Pénélope*, decor by Ker-Xavier Roussel, Théâtre des Champs-Élysées, 1913
(Private Coll.)

XXV   Fauré at St-Raphaël, summer 1915

(Coll. Mme Ph. Fauré-Fremiet)

XXVI   Fauré in front of the church porch at Annecy-le-Vieux, 1923
(Coll. Mme Ph. Fauré-Fremiet)

XXVII   End of the String Quartet, op. 121, Annecy, 11 September
         1924   (BN ms 417)

313

Dernières mesures de la
dernière œuvre: le Quatuor

XXVIII   Caricature of Saint-Saëns by Fauré   (Bibl. Nat.)

XXIX   Caricature of André Messager by Fauré   (Bibl. Nat.)

6

FAURÉ THE COMPOSER

What a pity it is that I have other things to do besides composition.
(30 August 1900, LI, p. 52)

Fauré was not particularly forthcoming in public about his music or the way that he wrote it, although he was not as reticent on the subject as his contemporary Edward Elgar. Music was Fauré's reason for existence: he never pretended otherwise and was never ashamed of his profession. Like Elgar, he was by no means averse to bettering himself socially, especially in his younger years, and was always something of a lady's man. Fauré did however write freely about his music and his compositional problems in his frequent letters to his wife, who must often have felt herself to be a 'composer's widow' when once again she was left behind in Paris as Fauré set off on his professional travels. If his manuscripts do not tell us all that much about his creative processes, then the letters and the seven carnets of sketches from the collection of Mme Fauré-Fremiet do; the latter are assessed here for the first time.

Relatively little is known about Fauré's technique of composition prior to 1885, though he tantalizingly mentions that *Le Papillon et la fleur* (LI, p. 282, 14 July 1922) was 'composed in the dining-hall of the École Niedermeyer amongst the smells from the kitchen' in 1861. His preference for sustained summer vacation writing was established by his visits to the homes of the rich industrialist Camille Clerc and his wife at Villerville and Sainte-Adresse where he composed most of the First Violin Sonata, the First Piano Quartet and the *Ballade* in the second part of the 1870s; and it was confirmed by the idyllic excursion to Venice and Florence with the Princesse de Polignac in the summer of 1891. As Fauré became increasingly involved with official duties at the Conservatoire after the turn of the century, preference became necessity, and long summer vacations, faithfully chronicled in almost daily letters to his wife, trace the gestation of several of his greatest works, including the opera *Pénélope* in the years immediately preceding the Great War.

Fauré's methods of composing and the problems he encountered are perhaps best seen in the long struggle which resulted in the First Piano Quintet (op. 89). The first sign of this comes in a sketchbook that must date from 1887 as it contains the *Pie Jesu* of the *Requiem* and *Clair de lune* much as we know them today. The first three bars of theme E (Ex. 17) of the finale can be seen unaccompanied on p. 21 and Ex. 52 shows that Fauré originally envisaged the movement in 2/4 time in F major. The different extension of the theme in bar 5 contains the rising

Ex. 52   Carnet 1, p. 21

figure 'x' which Fauré may have turned into the pizzicato string accompaniment to E at the start of the finale. The next news of the Quintet is in the early 1890s. After finishing the *Cinq mélodies 'de Venise'* in September 1891, Fauré's son Philippe tells us (FF, p. 74), he considered transforming and expanding a projected Third Piano Quartet into his First Piano Quintet by adding a second violin. The Quintet was actually announced as op. 60 by Hamelle about this time. The first two movements, Allegro and Andante, Fauré-Fremiet says,

> were sketched more or less simultaneously; however, only the exposition [of the Allegro] was completely written. Written, then rewritten; the piano arpeggios lacked the necessary lightness. Ysaÿe came to Paris with his Quartet. In Fauré's drawing-room at [154] Boulevard Malesherbes they tried through the passages already written and Ysaÿe was in raptures over the work. So much so, that Fauré promised to dedicate it to him. [But despite] the élan of the opening, its richness, . . . its profound and expansive poetry, all of which surpassed the grandeur of the exposition of the Second Piano Quartet, Fauré was not content. The sort of developments he envisaged at the time did not satisfy him, and the First Quintet was consigned to a cupboard, along with the Violin Concerto and the Symphony [op. 40].

I am indebted to Jean-Michel Nectoux for telling me that Fauré actually worked intermittently at the Quintet during the period when he was composing *La Bonne Chanson* (1892–4), before finally abandoning it until 1903.

1 August 1903 found Fauré in Aix-les-Bains for a performance of his *Pelléas et Mélisande* suite. Two days later he lamented to his wife (LI, p. 72) that he had composed nothing for almost a year, adding as an

excuse: 'I have always gone for quality rather than quantity'. The joy which the 'deliciously well played' *Pelléas* music brought him on 5 August was sadly tempered by a more serious recurrence of the ear trouble that had worried him the previous year. Nonetheless, he meticulously prepared his hotel-room table ready to begin work, but his depressed state meant that little got done before 16 August, and even then it was heavy going despite the rain which forced him to stay indoors. The breakthrough did not come until 20 August, when he told his wife (LI, p. 75) that he 'believed, *still without being sure*, that the ideas which kept buzzing around in his head, and that he was trying to write down, were for a [second] violin sonata'. He hoped anyway that it would turn out to be chamber music, although at the time he kept remembering his recent success at Béziers with *Prométhée*.

Five days later, Fauré finally identified his sketches as the second movement of the Piano Quintet, and this gradual formulation of ideas in terms of 'pure' music which gradually suggested its eventual scoring was not uncommon: the Second Violin Sonata (op. 108) only emerged slowly from sketches in August 1916; the Piano Trio began with the central episode of the Andantino, and even when this movement was finished after nearly a month's work on 26 September 1922, Fauré still referred to the Trio as being for 'clarinet (or violin), cello and piano' (LI, p. 284). The problem with realizing that his sketches were for a Piano Quintet was that Fauré knew he would have to return to the opening movement, which still lacked a satisfactory development section. He compared his Quintet with a 'Schumann Quartet' which occupied its author from '1843 to 1848' (LI, p. 77), though his memory must have played him false here for Schumann completed three String Quartets, a Piano Quartet and a Piano Quintet in 1842 without apparent difficulty. The rest of August and early September at Lausanne seems to have produced more soul-searching and philosophizing than actual music. Time and again Fauré came up against a brick wall, and he was also worried about Édouard Colonne's request for a new work for the coming Paris season, for *Prométhée* was unsuitable and *Pelléas et Mélisande* had already been performed elsewhere. His newly assumed responsibility as *Le Figaro*'s music critic did not help matters either.

During the winter of 1903–4, Fauré managed to find some time to work on the development of the first movement of the Quintet, and between 12 August and 4 October 1904 at the Pension Sternwarte in Zürich he made a supreme effort and finished the first movement (4 September) and almost completed the second. He had hoped to finish the Quintet that autumn, but the ending of the second movement caused him great difficulty and was still not completed to his satisfaction when he returned to Paris. The summer of 1904 highlights Fauré's problems as a composer struggling with 'this animal of a Quintet' (29 August, LI, p. 88). The gulf between aim and achievement is obvious; rare days of enthusiastic satisfaction alternate with longer abortive periods of artistic discontent. Fauré's most productive part of the day was the afternoon: on 30 August he virtuously told his wife (LI, p. 89) that he had worked from 1.30 to 6.30 pm, and on 1 September he composed from 2 pm to dinner-time. On days like this, usually when works were nearing completion, Fauré sometimes worked on after dinner, though this tended to prevent him sleeping properly. In the rest of the time he took long walks, often jotting down ideas en route (31 August), or copied out music sketched the previous day (5 September). Morning, like evening, composition was something that required special comment, as for example when Fauré was trying to finish *Paradis* from *La Chanson d'Ève* in Stresa on 8 September 1906 (LI, p. 130), and he later told his wife (1 April 1919, LI, p. 254): 'I have never been much good in the mornings, except at mercenary tasks like choir-training, organ-playing etc.'

Writing the music down took place in his hotel room on a large table and he compared his methods to those of Pénélope and her never-completed weaving (20 and 22 August, LI, pp. 84–5). He was forever unpicking and reworking his music, with minute concern over internal detail. This concern can be seen in his sketches for the coda to the finale of the Second Piano Quartet (1886), in which Fauré's desire for precise sequential balance extends to all the members of the ensemble (Ex. 53a). In the final version (Ex. 53b), Fauré simplified the texture by doubling the violin part at the lower octave on the viola (the suggestion for this can be seen in bars 1–2 of Ex. 53a), and giving the viola figure to the cello an octave lower, converting the falling minor third on the third beat to a falling fifth throughout in the process. The additional cello line was omitted, and it is extremely rare in Fauré to find four independent lines running simultaneously as they do in Ex. 53a. Fauré's care for detail can be seen in the revision of the enharmonic conflicts in bar 3 of Ex. 53, and in the alteration of the piano right-hand part in the final bar to bring it into exact sequential line with the two previous bars.

Fauré found the necessary self-discipline of creative work extremely difficult to achieve, and he compared his struggle with the final bars of the second movement of op. 89 to writing his *Figaro* articles to a deadline (24 and 25 September, LI, p. 98). He wrote elsewhere that he was 'slow in working, choosing and deciding' (5 September), although his consolation was that those who worked quickly often had later cause to regret their haste. At no stage, incidentally, did Fauré consider abandoning or restarting his Adagio afresh: once he had decided the sort of movement he wanted, his faith in his invention was unshakeable. 'Where there is invention, there is genius', Fauré once claimed (quoted in Nectoux, *Musique de tous les temps*, 1974, p. 7), and he always preferred talking about invention rather than inspiration. Each bar was so carefully conceived that no mere routine finish would suffice: the Adagio became so much a part of him during its composition that he could leave and re-enter its world at will, a practical ability that was particularly fortunate because of the amount of other work Fauré had to undertake for financial reasons.

Fauré did however extend his stay in Zürich by over a week in an attempt to complete the Adagio, but he had to return for a wedding at the Madeleine on 6 October. He thought that he might be able to complete the missing ten or twelve bars en route, in a bus or train, but this was not to be.

A piano was not usually necessary for composition, and Fauré wrote on 21 September that he had not needed to use the instrument to confirm passages in the second movement as he sometimes did (LI, p. 96). He worked almost entirely in his head, and seems to have been able to isolate himself from his surroundings quite easily. Fauré's particular form of deafness no doubt forced him to develop his aural imagination still further, and probably made the piano more of a hindrance than a help with composition.

The problem with being so self-reliant was that, once an idea entered Fauré's head, he could not easily rid himself of it. Leaving his work-table did not mean that he had ceased to work, and during the composition of the second movement on 21 September he became obsessed with 'a rhythmic theme in the manner of a Spanish dance', which formed in his head and 'developed, re-dressed itself in all manner of amusing harmonies, modified and modulated itself etc—that is to say, it composed itself' (LI, p. 97). Whether or not Fauré notated or later used this theme is not known; his only 'Spanish' piece is the finale to the earlier *Dolly* suite of 1897, but it affords a fascinating glimpse of the way an idea seized and dominated Fauré, sometimes when he least wanted it.

The other problem Fauré faced was preserving the spontaneity of his ideas when he committed them to paper. This was of especial concern with the opening movement of op. 89, which he wanted to be really 'splendid'. At times Fauré regretted the similarity in his music, which he wished was as varied as the weather (27 August, LI, p. 87): 'It seems that I repeat myself constantly and that I cannot find a noticeably different approach from that already expressed'. Perhaps Fauré was aware that he over-used sequence and the same kind of piano arpeggio accompaniments, and perhaps even that he over-developed his themes

Ex. 53

Second Piano Quartet: Finale

a: Carnet 3, pp. 4–5 (1st version)

Ex. 53 (contd.)   **Second Piano Quartet:** Finale
b: Hamelle, p. 90, bars 9–13

in his effort to achieve unity and a sense of continuity in his music. He never could bring himself to radically alter his approach, though the constant renewal within the limited number of movement and accompaniment types that his style permitted remains a source of wonder for Fauré enthusiasts.

Fauré did not complete the Adagio of op. 89 until the late summer of 1905. He returned to the same room at the Pension Sternwarte on 8 August and, after taking his usual few days to settle in, began by composing the 'eight beautiful pages' (LI, p. 109) of the Seventh Barcarolle between 11 and 14 August, his first work for Heugel, and a significant one in the development of his piano style. When he took up the end of the Adagio again on 18 August, he was still planning a four-movement Quintet, as he had in 1904, but by 1 September he had finished the Adagio and was third of the way through his third, and now final, movement. His gleeful anticipation of the chores he could now give up, like the Madeleine, composition classes and some of his theatre and concert reviews (15 September, LI, p. 114) was counterbalanced by his increased responsibility at the Conservatoire and the administrative burdens it entailed, though composition was on the whole less anguished than it had been the previous summer. Due to Conservatoire problems, September proved less productive than August, though by 15 September Fauré had over half his finale written. The rest he completed in Paris during the following winter ready for the first performance with the Ysaÿe Quartet in Brussels on 23 March 1906. Needless to say, Ysaÿe adored the finished article, and Fauré gives us a fascinating insight into his lax rehearsal habits in the *Lettres intimes*. The first rehearsal of the Piano Quintet only took place on the afternoon of 22 March because of Ysaÿe's other commitments! He did not return from a concert in Antwerp till 2 o'clock that morning, and did not appear until 1 pm for lunch. His wife had had the 'stupid idea' (LI, p. 117) of making this a grand celebratory affair 'à la flamande' and Fauré was 'livid, but naturally forced to smile' as the event ground slowly on. At 2.30 pm, after the guests had finally left, they got down to work on the Second Piano Quartet, and eventually between 3.30 and 6.30 pm they managed to look through the Quintet. They had a further rehearsal on the afternoon of the concert, but Fauré considered that it would not be 'played *well* until the Paris performance' on 30 April, for which the Brussels première was simply a rehearsal.

Judging from compositions like the Seventh Barcarolle or the Thirteenth Nocturne it would appear that smaller pieces gave Fauré far less trouble. However he wrote from Lugano on 2 August 1910 (LI, p. 186), whilst working on the Sixth Prelude (op. 103), that composition for the piano was 'perhaps the most difficult genre of all' because 'it was no good using padding. Everything had to be interesting and to the point all the time'. Despite this problem, the vast majority of Fauré's works involve the piano, and he had a horror of padding anyway, as he told his wife on 6 August the following year (LI, p. 197) whilst busy with Act 2 of *Pénélope.*

Perhaps the most consistently productive and least troublesome period was surprisingly the final flowering of chamber music between 1916 and 1921. Only in the Piano Trio and the String Quartet did Fauré encounter the sort of difficulties he had faced earlier. But here he was struggling against physical infirmity; his sureness in the quality of what he managed to write down even increased in his last years.

Apart from the *Ballade* (op. 19) and the slow movement of the Second Piano Quartet, Fauré did not respond directly to external stimuli in his music. In a letter to his wife on 11 September 1906 (LI, p. 132) he maintained that 'the desire for non-existent things . . . is the real domain in which music comes into its own'. In the same letter, Fauré agreed with his son Philippe's suggestion that the subsidiary idea to Ex. 4H in the finale of the First Violin Sonata did resemble a cock-crow (Ex. 54) but he claimed that he had not thought of this when he wrote it. In fact, he stated bluntly, 'I did not think of anything at all on this occasion'. The other, more famous, case regarding external stimuli reveals Fauré's strong sense of humour. When someone asked him (FF, pp. 72–3) 'beneath what marvellous sky he had conceived the start of the Sixth Nocturne', he replied: 'Beneath the Simplon tunnel!'

Ex. 54   **Violin Sonata** (op. 13): Finale
Bars 66–70

Personal problems did however influence Fauré's music, and these exterior events affected the speed and success of composition. The summer of 1910, when he needed to make progress on *Pénélope,* was troubled by memories of a recent campaign in the press against him and the Conservatoire, and by the knowledge of his father-in-law's serious illness. As a result he only managed to compose the four short Preludes (op. 103/4–7) between mid-July and 8 September. Similarly the summer of 1914 produced only the first three songs of *Le Jardin clos,* when Fauré was worried about the threatened onset of the war and about his increasing illness and deafness.

One possible indication that composition was not an easy process for

Fauré is the extent of his self-borrowing; like Handel, Berlioz or Dvořák he was not averse to this, as Appendix B shows. The borrowing was not limited to any particular period, but was mainly a case of rescuing from oblivion music written in Rennes in 1869, or re-using themes from his unsuccessful first period orchestral works. His acute self-criticism will, I hope, become clear from the evidence of the sketchbooks and the working manuscripts of the String Quartet and the *Fantaisie* for piano and orchestra.

The seven carnets of sketches in the collection of Mme Fauré-Fremiet (now in the Bibliothèque Nationale, mss 17787 (1–7)) contain the following identifiable material:

Carnet 1. c.1887. 48pp. (23pp. blank)

> pp. 1–8: Third Valse-Caprice (op. 59)
> p. 10: *O Salutaris* (op. 47/1). Vocal part bars 5–6 in D flat with accompaniment in repeated quaver chords.
> p. 15: *Pie Jesu* (*Requiem*)
> p. 19: First Piano Quintet (finale theme, Ex. 52)
> pp. 40–44, 46–8: *Clair de lune* (op. 46/2) Two versions.

Carnet 2. 1887. 12pp. (earlier than Carnet 1)

> pp. 1–4: *Introït* (*Requiem*)
> pp. 5–7, 9: *Kyrie* (*Requiem*)
> pp. 8, 10–12: *Pie Jesu* (*Requiem*)

Carnet 3. 1886–7. 20pp.

> pp. 4–5, 7: Second Piano Quartet. Finale, mostly coda (Ex. 53a)
> pp. 8–13: *Pavane* (op. 50) [pp. 11–12 originally pp. 27–8 in Carnet 1].
> pp. 16–20: *Offertoire* (*Requiem*)

Carnet 4. 1907. (Purchased in Vevey on 14 August from Foetisch Frères, see LI, p. 143.) 34 pp. (28 pp. blank). Includes themes for the suitors (p. 1) and Ulysse (pp. 2 and 5). See Exx. 32 and 69.

Carnet 5. August/September 1902, 1922. 48 pp. (pp. 35–45 blank)

> pp. 1–3, 6–7: *Dans la forêt de septembre* (op. 85/1). Two versions.
> pp. 4–5: 'Eighth Nocturne' (op. 84/8)
> pp. 8–17, 20–22: *La Fleur qui va sur l'eau* (op. 85/2)
> pp. 19, 23-32: *Dans le ciel clair* (L. de Lisle). Unfinished setting of stanzas 1 and 4.
> pp. 46–7: Piano Trio (op. 120). First movement.

Carnet 6. c.1882? 22 pp. (2 pp. blank)

> Unidentifiable sketches for a Valse-Caprice? (p. 3) and for a *Sanctus*? in g (pp. 5–11, 14–15, 19–22)

Carnet 7. 1910, 1923. 18pp. (pp. 4–18 blank)
    p. 1: Prélude in F (op. 103/4). Bars 38–9?
    p. 2: String Quartet (op. 121). Second movement.

These seven pocket-books are probably the only ones that have survived, as Fauré ordered all his remaining sketches to be burnt in his final letter to his wife (LI, p. 295). The books seem to have been partly for noting down themes, perhaps whilst in cafés or out walking, and there are many tantalizing fragments such as a lively six-bar passage for piano (Carnet 1, p. 17) simply marked 'Verlaine', which is possibly an

Ex. 55   Carnet 1, p. 17

idea for the start of a song (Ex. 55). This fragment is unusual in that it is written in black ink, most of the sketches being in pencil. It is carefully worked out, the contrary motion between the outer parts in bars 2, 4 and 6 making an effective and consistent linear contrast with the more dynamic guitar-like major ninths in the other bars. Fauré also used the sketchbooks for working out complex contrapuntal passages (Ex. 53a), or trying alternative harmonizations, as in Carnet 3, pp. 8 and 10, which contain four different versions of the first of a series of interrupted (V–IV) cadences leading into the coda section of the *Pavane* (VS, pp. 7–8). None of these harmonizations is the same as the final version, though the first of those on p. 10 comes quite close in outline.

Fauré also worked out quite extensive sections of compositions in the sketch-books, the longest being a section of over forty bars for the Third Valse-Caprice (Hamelle, p. 7 line 2—p. 8 line 4; Carnet 1, pp. 5–8) which must have been written as early as 1887, as it is followed by sketches for *Clair de lune*, and all the sketch-books seem to be chronological, each of them covering a period of less than a year. The op. 59 Valse-Caprice sketches are interesting for several reasons. First, they show Fauré beginning in the middle of a work, as in the later chamber compositions. Secondly, they show his sureness of inspiration; all these sketches lack is the repeated pedal idea which links the scale-based passages together (cf. *Romance* for cello and piano (op. 69), first version). The order of the keys in which the passages occur in the sketch, and in many cases the spacing of the piano part, is identical with the printed version. Thirdly, the sketches show that Fauré employed an alphabetical abbreviation system for repeated passages exactly like that of Debussy (identical bars are lettered 'A' to 'J' here, and only written out once in full). Lastly, the Valse-Caprice sketches show that Fauré knew instinctively what to reject, for the material on pp. 1–4 of Carnet 1, although of apparently equal harmonic interest and suitability, is not used at all. Its falling major seconds make it closer in style to the Fourth Valse-Caprice (op. 62), but this contains no direct quotations from material in the sketch-book.

Philippe Fauré-Fremiet tells us (FF, p. 43) that, in the earlier songs in particular, 'the music was born in Fauré at a single reading; the verse immediately suggested a musical plan, confused at first, then more clear. Art intervened to select, compose, order and plan as necessary to obtain the maximum clarity and emotion.' Fauré's decisiveness shows throughout the sketches, and all his manuscripts reflect the extensive planning he did in his head before committing his thoughts to paper, even in sketch form. The process was usually one of expansion of an initial idea, and whereas Fauré did some erasing and rewriting, especially in the vocal lines of song sketches, he never made more than two versions of any piece, and even this was a rare occurrence.

Carnets 1 and 2 show that Fauré made two attempts at both the *Pie Jesu* and *Clair de lune,* and that he sometimes began works in different keys to those in which they were printed. The *Requiem* for instance was originally to have been in c and not d minor; Fauré sketched most of the *Introït et Kyrie* in that key, again with remarkable sureness. Similarly, *Clair de lune* was to have been in g not b flat; *Dans la forêt de septembre* in g not G flat, and so on.

The first version of the *Pie Jesu* is in a minor (Ex. 56). Fauré wrote eighteen bars of this version in Carnet 2 (pp. 10–12) before abandoning it, probably because of its over-use of the tonic note. Bar 17 leads smoothly into a repeat of bar 1, this time with the words added. It seems likely that Fauré wrote the vocal line first, then drew his barlines, and lastly wrote the accompaniment, as that of bar 6 will not fit into its allotted space below the voice part. In Carnet 1 (p. 15) there is another extract from the *Pie Jesu* (Ex. 57), still in a, but much closer

Ex. 56   Carnet 2, p. 10
Pie Jesu (1st version)

to the printed version (bars 4–7, OS, pp. 61–2), which means that Carnet 2 could well date from earlier in 1887 than Carnet 1. Ex. 57 is set so that the stresses fall more naturally—'Dona *e*is requi*em*', but Fauré deliberately reverted to the stressing of Ex. 56 in his final version in B flat, emphasizing the words '*Do*na' and especially '*requ*iem'.

Ex. 57   Carnet 1, p. 15
Pie Jesu (2nd version)

It is hard to believe that the natural and flowing *Clair de lune,* which so perfectly matches the mood of Verlaine's poem, could ever have been different. But Carnet 1 (pp. 44–8) shows that Fauré got at least as far as 'Et leur chanson se mêle au clair de lune!' (bars 34–6) in g minor, and that the contrasting central section 'Au calme clair de lune, triste et beau' was to have been set differently in eight beats instead of ten (Hamelle, vol. 2, p. 80), with more chromatic harmony involving augmented fifths, in the relative major (Ex. 58). The changes in the vocal line leading to Ex. 58 show that all the time the music was getting

Ex. 58 Carnet 1, p. 47

Clair de lune (op. 46/2): 1st version of bars 39–42

Ex. 59 Carnet 5, pp. 23–4

Dans le ciel clair (Leconte de Lisle) 1902:
stanza 4, bars 1–4

calmer and simpler, more accurately reflecting the words, until Fauré achieved the perfection of the printed version. Fauré's tendency to cramp lines together at first, and then space them out in the final version is evident from the sketches of *Clair de lune, Dans la forêt de Septembre* and *La Fleur qui va sur l'eau*. In *Dans la forêt*, for example (Carnet 5), he first compressed the whole of the first two lines into nine crotchets worth of music in 4/4 time, whereas the final version covers twelve crotchets of 3/4 time, resulting in greater poise and a more relaxed atmosphere.

Perhaps the most interesting fragment in the carnets is the unfinished setting of de Lisle's *Dans le ciel clair*[1], which was almost certainly replaced by *Accompagnement* as the third song of op. 85 in the autumn of 1902. In Carnet 5, the de Lisle setting comes after sketches for the first two op. 85 songs, and between the two stanzas Fauré attempted are three pages of harmonic sketches for the end of *La Fleur qui va sur l'eau*. Quite naturally Fauré began with stanza one (p. 19), and a few simple chords and a rhythm on a monotone for 'Dans le ciel clair rayé par l'hirondelle alerte'. He does not seem to have got very far with it at this stage, and on pp. 23–9 he jumps straight to the fourth stanza which is virtually complete (twelve bars). Ex. 59 gives the opening of this stanza and it is easy to complete the text below Fauré's vocal line later in the stanza, even if he did not do this himself. The opening two-bar sequences, with their unexpected modulations to g and b flat, are constructed most skilfully in the accompaniment around different vocal phrases.

The problem with the poem seems to have been the palindromic nature of the lines enclosing each stanza:

A La volupté d'aimer clôt à demi leurs yeux,
B Ils ne savent plus rien du vol de l'heure brève,
   Le charme et la beauté de la terre et des cieux
   Leur rendent éternel l'instant délicieux,
   Et, dans l'enchantement de ce rêve d'un rêve,
B Ils ne savent plus rien du vol de l'heure brève,
A La volupté d'aimer clôt à demi leurs yeux.

The penultimate line was the only one Fauré did not set, and the trouble was that his music for the fifth line led straight to a repeat of the first line (line 7) and not to a repeat of bars 3–4 (line 6), as Ex. 60 shows.

Fauré's pupil, Charles Koechlin, who set the poem for female chorus and piano (op. 4/1, 1894) *before* he came to Fauré for composition lessons, solved the problem of its length by omitting the second of the five stanzas and by using slower-moving harmonies and less recitative-like vocal lines. In his version, the harmonic speed increases in the central stanzas giving an impression of development, and he does

Ex. 60   Carnet 5, pp. 28–9
Dans le ciel clair, stanza 4, bars 9–12 (end)

not bother about too exact a musical parallel between the outer lines of each stanza: the last line resembles the first melodically, but it can be at a different pitch, or reharmonized, or both. Koechlin also employs a wide-ranging key scheme during his setting. He begins and ends in A, but he starts the fourth stanza in A flat. Fauré's centering of both stanzas one and four in E flat would have presented problems of tonal development in the song, despite the modulations within stanza four. All in all, Koechlin's broader, more varied and less intimate conception of *Dans le ciel clair* proved more successful, though on the only other occasion when they both set the same text Fauré's earlier version of Verlaine's *N'est-ce pas?* is superior in its flexibility, harmonic subtlety and lyrical expansiveness[2].

After leaving stanza four virtually complete, Fauré returned to stanza one, and Carnet 5 ends with a neat setting of the first two lines (Ex. 61) which puts it mid-way between his setting of de Lisle's *Nell* (op. 18/1) and *La Mer est infinie* (op. 118/1) at the other end of his career, by the nature of its accompaniment and its implied smooth part-writing. Fauré's indecision about setting *Dans le ciel clair* in triple or common time (cf. Exx. 59–61) provides another reason why he might have abandoned this song.

Ex. 61   Carnet 5, p. 31
Dans le ciel clair, beginning (stanza 1)

Dans le ciel clair   ra - yé   par l'hi-ron-delle a -

- ler - te,   Le ma - tin   qui fleu- [rit   comme un di-vin - ro- sier]

Another fascinating insight into Fauré's process of composition offered by his sketchbooks is the harmonic conception of *La Fleur qui va sur l'eau*. Fauré soon tired of writing out in full the enormous 3/2 bars with their complex semiquaver patterns and resorted to a chordal skeleton. In other sketches he occasionally used a figured bass, as at the start of Carnet 3 for what looks like the opening of the finale of the Second Piano Quartet. As with *Clair de lune*, Fauré's original sketch for *La Fleur qui va sur l'eau* proved too compressed, and the voice part at first entered at the end of bar 1 ('Sur la mer'), instead of in bar 3 as in the printed version (vol. 3, p. 77). Carnet 5, pp. 11–13 shows the problems he had with the first main climax ('La Rose Beauté!') in bars 11–13. First (Ex. 64a), it was a question of melodic shape. Then, in Ex. 64b–c, Fauré sought a better-placed vocal climax, expanding more towards the end of the now smoothly-rising phrase. Carnet 5, p. 14 shows Fauré in haste confusing one line with another in the second stanza of Catulle Mendès' poem, writing 'L'océan hurleur' for 'L'ouragan hurleur' in the second line.

The heat of Fauré's inspiration in the final section (vol. 3, p. 81) meant that he not only wrote minim chords in place of the final quaver figuration (Carnet 5, pp. 20–22), but that he omitted most of the vocal

Ex. 64   Carnet 5, pp. 11–13
La Fleur qui va sur l'eau (op. 85/2)
First vocal climax, bars 11–13

[irri]-té, La Ro - se des Fiè-vres, La Ro - se Beau - té!

- té, _____ La Ro - se des Fiè - vres, La Ro - se Beau - té!

(Hamelle, vol. 3, p. 78)

- té, La Ro - se des Fiè - vres, La Ro - se Beau - té! _____

line as well. Thus the end of *La Fleur qui va sur l'eau* was conceived
in purely harmonic terms, and it seems as though Fauré worked out
the end of the song (bars 38–40; Carnet 5, p. 20) before bars 31–7 that
lead into them (Carnet 5, pp. 21–2). Only the first bar of the new
quaver figuration with both hands (vol. 3, p. 81 bar 1) was jotted down
later on a spare line.

The detailed care and self-criticism Fauré applied to his composition
can also be seen in the revisions he made to his final manuscripts of the
String Quartet and the *Fantaisie*. Philippe Fauré-Fremiet tells us (FF,
pp. 112–13) that in his last years all his father needed in order to
compose was manuscript paper and a table. Unlike Debussy, he did
not need to be surrounded by beautiful or familiar objects. He stopped
work without fuss for post or meals, because the music was constantly
there in his 'spirit'. Only if he had a particularly difficult problem did
he beg to be excused for 'five minutes'. He still used sketchbooks, but
his invention became surer and surer as he got older, necessitating
fewer erasures.

All this is borne out in the manuscript of the String Quartet, though
the erasures Fauré did make are of considerable interest. With the
String Quartet, he chiefly feared comparison with Beethoven and he
also remembered the fear Saint-Saëns had of the medium, which he
only tried towards the end of his life and then without the success he
achieved in other branches of composition.[3] The number of late
nineteenth- and early twentieth-century composers who completed only
one string quartet, whether or not in the shadow of Beethoven, is

interesting, and Fauré joined the distinguished ranks of Verdi, Grieg, Franck, Debussy and Ravel. He kept the composition of the Quartet secret even from his wife until 9 September 1923, four days before he finished the central Andante (LI, p. 288). On both 13 and 30 September 1923, Fauré called his Andante the first movement of the Quartet, and after he had completed the finale (18 July–11 September 1924) he considered writing a short fourth movement to place between the first and second, though 'as it is not really necessary, I shall not wear myself out trying to find it at present', he told his wife on 12 September (LI, p. 293). So, had he stuck to his original plan, the String Quartet *might* have ended up as follows: Andante—short 'fast(?) movement—Allegro moderato—Scherzo/finale. An unusual structure indeed!

Fauré did not bother to complete the last two bars of repeated E major chords in the first movement of the String Quartet (BN Mus. ms 417, p. 12). As his son Philippe says (LI, p. 290), these closing bars were 'of minimal importance' compared to the rest of the movement, 'for it was not a question of an eventual refinement to be fixed later'. But this omission is curious, nonetheless, for many of the bars in BN ms 417 that appear to be corrections are simply cases of neater recopying when Fauré slightly misjudged the spacing of a bar, or it protruded into the margin (e.g. finale p. 4 bar 1, or p. 14 bar 3). Sometimes Fauré erased his mistakes with a razor, but more often he crossed out bars that were at fault with an elaborate criss-cross pattern. This is true of all his manuscripts, early ones especially, most of which, like the Quartet, are written in black ink ready for the printer to use as a final copy.

The Quartet manuscript shows, more than any other, that Fauré's priorities were the notes themselves: the only section to which he added phrasing and dynamics came at the very start. The shakiness of the lines here suggests that this might have been his last musical act. He only got as far as fig. 3 (Durand score, p. 4), and the only performance indications in the last two movements are clefs, time and key signatures, and 'pizz' and 'arco' signs in the finale. The second movement is not even marked 'Andante'. The task of editing he confidently left to Roger-Ducasse, though he might not have been quite so happy about this had he known that his own phrasing and dynamics at the start would appear differently in the printed score, and that this would be inconsistent within itself (cf. viola part bars 1–2 and 9–10). Fauré rightly left the assertive viola phrase in bars 1–4 unbowed.

The musical revisions in the Quartet are of varying lengths and are equally spaced throughout the three movements. They mainly involve the extension, or occasionally the contraction, of the sequential patterns on which Fauré's music is based. For instance, the lead into fig. 5 in

Ex. 65
1st movement, p. 6, bars 9–11
Original lead-in to fig. 5

String Quartet (op. 121)
BN ms 417

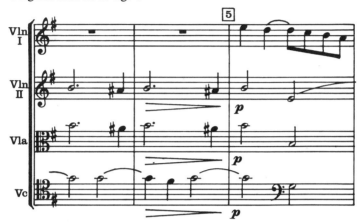

the first movement was originally as in Ex. 65, and Fauré added two extra sequential bars in the margin to produce a more gradual change, altering the tessitura of the accompaniment in the bar before fig. 5, instead of in the fig. 5 bar itself, in the process. The dynamics here are genuine, being virtually the last Fauré added.

Often he spotted a mistake after writing in only the first violin part, and he quickly converted a two-bar melodic sequence into a three-bar one by reversing the order of bars 12 and 13 after fig. 4 (score p. 5). But on other occasions he got quite a way with a full quartet texture before he realised that he was travelling in the wrong direction. The habitual change to the tonic major (fig. 9) originally came seven bars later: the seven deleted bars are shown in Ex. 66. Four bars prior to this, Fauré also deleted another eight-bar passage, showing that the exact placing of the climactic key-change caused him difficulty, and that he considered it best to have his long exultant passage once E major was attained (fig. 9) rather than detract from it by a preparatory crescendo. The final sunlit section (pp. 10–11) proved trouble-free, but it might have been very different had Fauré retained the seven bars he deleted (Ex. 66) which return to the lighter texture first used just before fig. 1.[4] Fauré wisely does not re-use the fig. 1 idea here, and a more sustained and concise climax is the result.

The alterations in the second movement are shorter on the whole; the section between figs. 14 and 18 went straight down in full quartet texture with no second thoughts whatsoever. In the finale, only one minor change occurs in the first half of the movement before the change

Ex. 66
1st movement, pp. 9–10
Original lead-in to fig. 9

String Quartet (op. 121)
BN ms 417

to four sharps at fig. 27, and from then on the ten revisions are fairly equally spaced, including the interesting extension of a three- into a four-bar sequence at fig. 30. The writing changes from page to page, reflecting Fauré's variable state of health, although the final two pages are relatively firm and assured (see plate XXVII). Two bars before fig. 34 (ms p. 23, bar 4) Fauré had some trouble continuing his melodic sequence and considered putting double-stops on the first instead of the second violin, but otherwise this exhilarating finish to a lifetime's work seems to have been the most spontaneous thing in the world.

The revisions in the two-piano working copy of the *Fantaisie* (op. 111) now in the BN (ms 17753) provide another glimpse of Fauré's compositional technique in his final years. Sketches for some parts of the *Fantaisie* are preserved on the blank versos of the fair copy; the most interesting on p. 22v concerns a modulatory passage in the central Allegro molto section after fig. 11, which leads via theme C of Ex. 44 (see Ex. 67b, bars 4–6) to the second return of theme B in augmentation in the tonic key of G (Ex. 67b, bar 9f.). Fauré's original six-bar passage

Ex. 67   **Fantaisie** (op. 111)
(p. 22v, 1st version)   BN ms 17753, pp. 21–2
(p. 21, 2nd version)

218

Ex. 67 (contd.)

(Ex. 67a) unfortunately brought him out in G flat, which would have upset the sharp-oriented tonal balance of the work, as only theme C is allowed to veer far on the flat side. Fauré completed his eight-bar statement of theme B in G flat before spotting that all was not as it should be. To correct matters (Ex. 67b), he kept the overall melodic shape of Ex. 67a but introduced an enharmonic change in bar 2 and an extra stabilizing third bar, which also converted the undulating inner figure into repeated notes. To balance this, he repeated the process with bars 7 and 8. Thus the flat and sharp roles of the modulatory and thematic halves of Ex. 67a were reversed in the final version Ex. 67b. The passage reappears as p. 23, bar 5f. in the Durand two-piano score. This example shows Fauré's strong grasp of the overall tonal direction. However complicated the enharmonic changes appear to be, they are all part of the purposeful plan, and Fauré's sequential approach allowed alterations to be made with the minimum of disruption.

If Fauré did make major mistakes in composition, he left no record of them. The hypothesis that he did is unlikely to be correct because of the long time he spent simply thinking about his more substantial works, which makes their dating so difficult. The Piano Quintet is by no means unique in this respect, it is just more fully documented.

As with the String Quartet, Fauré scored in terms of his original conception throughout. He left no gaps to fill in later, keeping both piano parts going as he composed. Most of the other changes in the manuscript of the *Fantaisie* are minor ones concerned with the spacing and texture of the piano parts, octave doublings and so on. A sketch on the verso of p. 30 for the exciting climax leading to the return of the opening at fig. 15 shows that Fauré wrote this passage at top speed, one might almost say in the white heat of inspiration, if the composer were not Fauré. According to the *Lettres intimes* (p. 244), he reached this point on 25 August 1918 at Évian, for in his later works he numbered his bars carefully, page by page, and sometimes included the numbers in his progress reports to Paris. The quavers in the main piano part at this point have no stems in the sketch, and were apparently grafted on to the thematic plan in the second piano part. Fauré did not bother with the stabbing chords below the first piano's scalar descent into fig. 15, and only wrote in the first two notes of the recapitulation in his sketch. By then he knew that the majority of his worries were over.

The later copy of the *Fantaisie* (BN Rés. Vma. 198) reveals that the spacing and practicability of the piano solo part as we know it today owes much to the revisions of Alfred Cortot, for whom it was composed. Passages like fig. 1 were made fuller by the addition of octaves, and here the only redistribution of material took place, with Fauré's solo piano left-hand chords being transferred to the second piano (or orchestra). Fauré, however, refused to accept the octave doubling Cortot proposed for the start, and wrote to him from Monte Carlo on 22 March 1919[5]: 'The theme in question [Ex. 44 A] only seeks to express sprightliness, gaiety and general contentment. I am afraid lest the octaves, and *above all* the low chords of the piano accompaniment, will result in heaviness'. Cortot was also over-ruled in the case of the recapitulation (fig. 15), where he wanted to add chords to the solo piano part in the opening bars. They remained as Fauré wrote them with the chords on the second piano. The other changes to the solo part were made in the interests of fluency and ease of performance, for Fauré had a tendency in his later piano style to omit the first semiquaver in a group in left-hand passages, even when there was no movement in the right hand on the beat. Rather surprisingly, he must have approved changes like those in Ex. 68 which make the solo part less awkward, whilst not affecting the musical content.

In the 1920s Fauré's private relations with Cortot declined, and he

Ex. 68   **Fantaisie** (op. 111)
Bars 7–8 after fig. 4
Fauré's original texture

was disappointed that Cortot preferred playing the music of Debussy, Ravel and Albéniz after he had done so much to further his early career. Cortot even neglected the *Fantaisie* dedicated to him, especially in his concerts abroad, and there is evidence[6] that Fauré considered that the letters of homage Cortot sent him were hypocritical, though he never said so publicly.

The sketches for *Pénélope* and its composition I have left till last, as the gradual emergence of the opera is fully documented and casts yet more light on Fauré as a composer[7]. Fauré had long been in search of an ideal libretto and, according to an interview published posthumously in *Comoedia* (10 November 1924), the idea of an ancient Greek subject and the employment of René Fauchois as librettist were both proposed by Lucienne Bréval during a specially arranged dinner party. Also present was Raoul Gunsbourg who, amidst the general enthusiasm of the evening, agreed to produce it at Monte Carlo. Fauré suspected a plot of some kind, and later discovered that Fauchois, far from having completed a libretto at this stage, had only sketched out a plan.

Fauré began to write *Pénélope* in the summer of 1907 at the Hôtel Mont-Fleuri in Lausanne. The opera was to occupy five summers (1907–9, 1911–12), though in reality the music took nine months actually to write down and a further two-and-a-half months to orchestrate, not including the abortive summer of 1909. Fauré began on 25 July 1907 by copying the text of Fauchois' opera into a special cloth-covered book, to familiarize himself with its content, and to put Fauchois' 'flying leaves' in a more manageable form. His letters to his wife in this year are unusually full and revealing, although Conservatoire problems, like the replacement of Antonin Marmontel by the young Alfred Cortot, were always on his mind.

By 29 July Fauré had written the first twenty-six bars of the Prelude to *Pénélope*, but by 4 August he had developed Pénélope's theme (Ex. 32A) as far as he could (forty-one bars), and had come up against a brick wall. This was the lack of a suitable theme for Ulysse, a situation he acknowledged on 16 August (LI, p. 144) but could not then overcome, and the prelude was not completed until August the following year. Fauré preferred to jump straight to the opening *Scène des fileuses*, and whereas the sketchbook purchased in Vevey on 14 August 1907 contains several attempts at Ulysse's royal theme (Ex. 69a–c), Fauré

Ex. 69   Carnet 4: Lausanne, late August? 1907
Pénélope: sketches for Ulysse's royal theme (Ex. 32B)

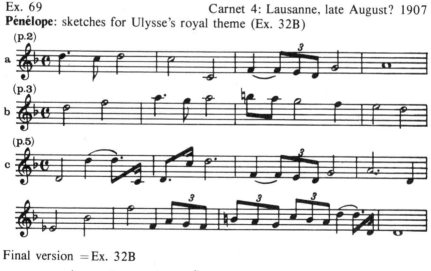

Final version = Ex. 32B

did not see that, by converting it from common to triple time and joining the bits together, he could overcome the obstacle presented by the Prelude. He even came as close as harmonizing part of the theme (Ex. 69d) with implied tremolando strings, much as it appears in bars 46–7 of the prelude (VS, p. 4 bars 1–2). In the end, he chose to continue as far as he could with the action, trying all the time to reach the entrance of Pénélope before he was forced to return to Paris.

For this he needed a regime of regular work, but was now worried by both eye and ear trouble, pessimistically envisaging his gradual paralysis through arterio-sclerosis on 9 August. But by 12 August he was absorbed by his female chorus of spinning servants, and was already imagining the scene on the stage. What the servants said was of less importance than the general atmosphere. The problem was that the ladies had too much to sing; two of their three stanzas had already covered three musical paragraphs (VS, pp. 12–15). Nevertheless, Fauré reached the loud burst of offstage laughter of the suitors on 14 August (LI, p. 143), but was then faced with finding them a suitable theme.

The problem was still with him on 16 August. Fauré already realised that he would have to use the Wagnerian leitmotif system, for want of a better one: so much had to be achieved through the music itself, and multi-purpose themes were vital. This was the case with the suitors' theme, and Fauré found his first attempt even a little too Wagnerian. His letter of 16 August (LI, p. 144) shows us Fauré's compositional mind at work:

> I have searched for something [Ex. 32C] that gives the impression both of brutality and of complete self-satisfaction. And when I say I am working at this theme, here is what goes into the process: first, I seek out all the combinations into which I shall need to mould the theme according to the circumstances of the text . . . I also look to see if this theme will combine with that of Pénélope. Then I seek out all the ways of transforming the theme, to bring about varied effects, both in its entirety and in its constituent parts . . . In a word, I make myself a card-index of its resources which will serve me for the entire work, or, if you prefer it, I make *studies,* as one makes for a painting.

Fauré obviously felt he needed to justify his apparent lack of progress with *Pénélope* to his wife, and explained that his extensive preparatory work 'made later work very much easier', and that he was by no means 'wasting time' over it. By 22 August he was using material from his sketches and was nearly at the start of scene ii where the suitors enter. Even a visit from Paul Dukas did not interrupt his work. He was preparing the start of scene ii on 26 August, and this seems to be the point at which Carnet 4 begins. The sketches in black ink on p. 1 with blue corrections (see plate XVIII) are almost identical with the opening bars of scene ii (VS, p. 32 bars 1–5), the only difference being that Fauré later lengthened the first note of bars 2 and 3 and converted the music from triple to common time. As usual, once he decided on something, it stayed, and he never returned to touch up passages in the light of subsequent developments.

The rest of Carnet 4 contains music for the suitors and Pénélope, as well as the sketches for the Ulysse theme already mentioned. Although the music does not recur exactly in the vocal score as it does here, there are some distinct similarities:

Carnet 4: p. 2 lines 1–2: cf pp. 32–3; p. 44 bars 6–7. This includes the falling sixth (Ex. 32A$_1$) symbolizing Pénélope's grief, though as a minor and not as a major sixth.

p. 3 lines 1–2: cf. VS, pp. 40–1, just before Pénélope's first entrance.

p. 4: Harmonizations of the first falling third motif of the suitors' theme, cf. VS, pp. 36–40.

p. 7: Difficult to identify, but cf. VS, p. 50 line 3.

Fauré began Act 1, scene ii on 27 August, and on 2 September he had reached a portion of the text that was 'not always very lyrical' (VS, p. 35):

Léodès: 'Nous voulons la voir . . . Qu'elle vienne!'

Eurymaque: 'De notre part, cours le lui dire, chienne!'[8]

But it was less the 'triviality of expression' which 'offended' Fauré than the 'precision of the rhythms' that 'constrained' him. In fact, neither the 'softness' of the spinning girls nor the coarseness of the suitors inspired him much and he longed for the entrance of Pénélope to lend 'nobility and elevation' to the opera. He even thought in a depressed moment during the night of 2 September (LI, p. 150) that all he had written thus far was 'very mediocre'. By 5 September, however, he had reached scene iii (VS, p. 36), and Euryclée's entrance. On 7 September he was looking ahead to the final act, and he realised that Act 1, scene iii must contain the germ of the final tragedy in its orchestral part, at the point where Pénélope was first threatened by the suitors, and before she knew of Ulysse's return.

A short break proved necessary between 9 and 11 September as Fauré, whilst 'delighted with systematic work', had made himself unable to sleep. After returning from a trip around the Lake Thun area and Interlaken, he returned to work refreshed and by 15 September announced with excitement that Pénélope had at last entered the opera (scene iv, pp. 41–2, see Ex. 33). In the previous pages the suitors had tried to pass Euryclée to get to Pénélope's chamber, and their 'obstinate theme' (C) was mixed with a fragment of Ulysse's theme, now apparently written, which served to slow their steps (VS, pp. 40–41). The whole passage (scene iii) had been a great struggle as it had to mount gradually in pitch and tension leading to the chordal explosion which, in the Prelude, had represented Pénélope's grief (VS, p. 41 bar 12, Ex. 32A$_1$).

On 20 September Fauré again complained that Fauchois had given him 'too much text' (LI, p. 153). 'He does not consider that music prolongs verses enormously, and that what takes only two minutes to read takes at least three times as long to sing'. The suitors in particular were 'never-ending arguers', and Fauré had been obliged to make some small cuts when there was no threat to the plot or to the continuity. Even Pénélope's lines were too long, though the poetry was superior and 'devoid of affectation'. But, looking back, Fauré was upset by the amount of time, effort and music that had been expended on so little action (LI, p. 153).

By 25 September Fauré was well into Pénélope's first scene (iv). He had reached the words: 'Et qu'un jour je pourrai l'adore davantage' (VS, p. 53), and was rather pleased with the last few lines from 'J'ai tant d'amour à lui donner encore', which had 'amply pathetic and expressive accents', and which used Pénélope's theme (A) in broad augmentation in the accompaniment (LI, p. 154). The section prior to this (VS, pp. 50–52) had used the 'heroic and almost joyous' part of the Ulysse theme with its strident rising octaves. During the remainder of his stay at Lausanne, Fauré worked on the final section of scene iv which he delivered to the copyist on 1 October, so that it could be 'printed immediately'. Not arrogance, but a practical sureness in his own invention.

Fauré returned to Lausanne the following summer, installing himself at the Hôtel Cecil on 31 July. After his customary few days' holiday, he returned to *Pénélope* on 4 August, and spent the next five days reacquainting himself with the music written in 1907. 'I found myself facing these pages . . . like forgotten events', he lamented to his wife on 4 August 1908 (LI, p. 162). He took up the Prelude again at the entrance of Ulysse's theme (bar 42) and, after a trip to Chamonix to see his son Emmanuel properly settled in for a mountain holiday (10–11 August), he finished the Prelude on 18 August. As usual he had trouble with the final bars and was still afraid of writing 'bad imitation-Wagner', as he confided to Pierre de Bréville around 12 August (BN, La 86). He then reverted to Act 1, scene iv, but was obliged to make a second trip to Lucerne to conduct the Kursaal Orchestra in *Pelléas et Mélisande* (op. 80) and to accompany Jeanne Raunay in *La Bonne Chanson* (23–25 August). Back with *Pénélope*, Fauré was once again finding fault with the 'vulgar verbiage' of the suitors, and on 28 August he was planning the sort of music he would write for Act 2 to 'create a nocturnal, maritime and rustic atmosphere' (LI, p. 166). Sketches for this and work on Act 1, scene iv seem to have gone well in this period, and Fauré commented that, as Saint-Saëns, Massenet and d'Indy had found, only completely uninterrupted days were really productive for creative work. But interruptions continued to appear, like the request from the Opéra-Comique for Fauré to check the vocal accentuation in a new translation of *The Magic Flute* on 1 September.

By 15 September he had nevertheless completed Act 1, scene iv (VS, p. 75) which meant the entry of Ulysse, another significant landmark. Fauré, who often patiently explained the action of the opera to his wife as he went along, announced that he hoped to complete Act 1 before returning to Paris. He reached the end of scene v with the 'gossiping' suitors and the servants around 19 September (VS, pp. 86–90), and by 4 October was into scene vii with Pénélope alone at night, unpicking her weaving. Two months' work produced slightly more in 1908 (62 pp.) than in 1907 (55 pp.) and, despite the interruptions, Fauré's rate of composition was remarkably regular, around one page of vocal score per day. Like Debussy, though, he tended to overestimate the amount he had completed and the amount he could achieve within a fixed period. For instance, he claimed on 15 September that he had only 'three scenes' left to write, when there were six (Act 1, scenes v–x), and Act 1 was not completed until October 1911, *after* Act 2.

In 1909 Fauré transferred from Lausanne to Lugano, and most of the remainder of *Pénélope* was written and orchestrated there at the Grand Hôtel Métropole et Monopole (see plate XXIII). His son Philippe considered the change to be a favourable one, as in Lugano 'his imagination was better able to evoke the Grecian world' (LI, p. 176), though this was not the case in 1909–10, which were not at all productive years as regards *Pénélope*.

In 1909 Fauré sketched the last five songs for *La Chanson d'Ève,* and the summer of 1910 produced only the four Preludes (op. 103/4–7). All the work on *Pénélope:* the orchestration of the Prelude and of the start of scene i (26 July–9 August), and the composition of Act 2, scenes i and ii (9–24 August), was completely re-done in 1911–12—a rare occurrence for Fauré. In his 1909 orchestration of the Prelude, Fauré took great pains to create 'exactly the right atmosphere for the drama' (LI, p. 178) and showed unusual interest in the task. When he had finished all the music for the opera in early September 1912, however, he found this first attempt 'valueless', though unfortunately he gave his wife no reasons for his decision. He was by then very pressed for time, and the reworking of all that he wrote of *Pénélope* in 1909 shows the extent to which Fauré was a perfectionist, and how he was not prepared simply to 'touch up' inferior passages.

The main difficulty with Act 2 seems to have been the text. 'It has virtually no action', Fauré complained on 16 August (LI, p. 179), and he found the long dialogue between the disguised Ulysse and his unsuspecting wife 'conventional', implausible and unrewarding (VS, pp. 134–70). His letter of 31 August shows that he was all the time thinking of improvements and changes in the text that Fauchois seems to have been perfectly willing to comply with, but on 7 September he was again comparing his methods of working with those of Pénélope (LI, p. 180). Towards the end of the month, he gradually became aware that his Act 2 music was no good. On 22 September (p. 181) we sense the loneliness and isolation of the composer when Fauré says that 'he has need of the advice of an artist' . . . 'I am afraid that the action is cold, and that the music reflects this'. On 1 October he finally realised that the technique of 'letting his music be guided by the simple nature of the action and the dignity of its characters' (p. 182), used with success in *Prométhée*, was not going to work with *Pénélope* Act 2, and he even resorted to the unusual step of trying his music through on the piano, which convinced him that it was 'terribly cold, giving a general impression of being stiff and formal'. Even if the public liked theatre music which *he* found inferior, and vice versa, this was no reason to compromise his standards with *Pénélope*.

1911–12 in Lugano fortunately proved as productive as 1907–8. Between 4 and 21 August, Fauré rewrote the long Act 2 duo between Ulysse and Pénélope, though he still found the contrived theatrical situation hard to handle. In the rest of August he worked on the gaps in Act 2, scene i before returning to complete Act 1 (September–3 October; VS, pp. 100–119). On 9 September he was dealing with the picturesque shroud scene and finding it very difficult and 'not to his taste', although he knew 'musicians who would write *Pénélope* for this scene alone' (LI, p. 199). His horror now was of not finishing on time, for the première was already scheduled for February 1913 at a point (25 August 1911) when Fauré did not even have the music of a single act completed.

He therefore worked hard to finish Act 2 and sketch Act 3 in the winter of 1911–12, and during an Easter vacation at Hyères in the south of France (2–24 April 1912), he wrote half of Act 3, although he had hoped to complete two-thirds. He was now working slowly and systematically, so that the vocal score could be printed by Heugel as he completed each section. Conservatoire worries still plagued him, and frustration over the construction of a vital concert hall brought some strong words against a philistine Government on 14 April (LI, p. 202).

Between 24 July and 31 August 1912, in Lugano, Fauré finished Act

3 (VS, c. p. 223f), still averaging about one page per day as in 1907–8. I am working 'like a lost soul on the finale of *Pénélope*!', he told his son Emmanuel on 25 July (*BAF*, 1972, p. 8), and he got straight down to composition and maintained a regular regime of about eight hours a day with the orchestration in September–October, which he found extremely taxing. Fauré's nervous feeling of working against the clock comes out in his letters, but his practical consideration of things like the publication of the orchestral parts, or whether the Paris première should be at the Opéra or the Opéra-Comique (LI, p. 205) shows that he was far from being an ivory-tower composer in the case of *Pénélope*.

Between 2 September and 16 October Fauré re-orchestrated the Prelude and completed the orchestration of Act 1. From the detailed progress reports he sent his wife in September 1912, and his obsession with counting page numbers, it is possible to calculate that Fauré's average speed of orchestration ranged from two to a maximum of four bars per hour. 'Often', he wrote on 6 September (LI, p. 208), 'it is necessary to spend several hours thinking about four bars!', though his speed increased slightly as he got more used to his 'enormously amusing' task during September, and he orchestrated about three times as fast as he composed. Whilst all this was going on, Lucienne Bréval was learning her Act 3 part with Alfred Cortot in the downstairs salon.

The orchestration of Act 3 and the start of Act 2[9] (VS, pp. 120–35) was finished at Monte Carlo between 19 December 1912 and 12 January 1913, where Fauré had gone to liaise with Léon Jéhin who was to conduct the première on 4 March. Jéhin was at that time occupied with conducting *Parsifal* and Fauré remarked on 10 January that he had had to change a detail in the orchestration as he was unable to leave the bass drum out of the *forte* passages as he had hoped to. 'But', he added (LI, p. 214), 'Wagner used it to good effect. So!' The only other minor changes he made to *Pénélope* after the première concern its orchestration. He arranged a conclusion to the Prelude for concert performance in early September 1913, and retouched bits of the orchestration, probably of Act 3, in St-Raphaël around 25 August 1917 (LI, p. 235).

No study of Fauré as a composer would be complete without looking at his views of other composers, as these can give an insight into what he was trying to achieve in his own music, as well as what he was at pains to avoid. In his most serious period of self-doubt during the first version of Act 2, scene ii of *Pénélope* on 1 October 1909, Fauré lamented bitterly to his wife (LI, p. 183):

> The excessive polyphony of Wagner, the chiaroscuro effects of Debussy, the vulgar, impassioned writhings of Massenet are the only things that move or attract the attention of the general public. Whereas the clear and consistent

(*'loyale'*) music of Saint-Saëns, to which I myself feel most attracted, leaves this same public indifferent. And all that sort of thing gives me a pain in the neck!

In the case of Debussy, Fauré remained on cordial terms but 'admired his work much more than he liked it' (FF, p. 91). He wrote to Albert Carré in early May 1902[10]: 'I remain rebellious to Debussy's musical procedures, but I nonetheless applaud his work, which has given me great delight in many ways; real emotions that I have enjoyed wholeheartedly in complete abandon.' But Fauré was anxious to remain on good terms with the director of the Opéra-Comique and the Princesse de Polignac tells us (1945, p. 128) that Fauré remarked to her after the 1902 première of *Pelléas et Mélisande*: 'If that was music: I have never understood what music was!' She was wrong, however, in saying that 'he was partly influenced by the fact that Debussy had married Madame Sigismond [Emma] Bardac, to whom Fauré had dedicated *La Bonne Chanson*, and to whom he had become deeply attached', as Debussy did not marry Emma till 1908. However, Lockspeiser rightly assumed that Fauré, like many others, disapproved of Debussy's extra-marital arrangements, and he gives this as a possible explanation for Fauré's complaint that the *Danse sacrée* and *Danse profane* of 1904 contained 'the same profusion of harmonic singularities . . . sometimes frankly disagreeable'.[11] In his appeal to young French musicians in 1912 (in *La Dépêche de Toulouse*), Fauré shows that he regarded the Debussyist influence as something far more serious, and transcending any personal grievances; 'a disastrous influence in the sense that it has diverted our French conception of music', and therefore one to be avoided.

Debussy, for his part, was equally critical of Fauré, caustically calling him the 'music-case ['porte-musique'] of a band of snobs'[12], and he seems to have taken Fauré far less seriously than he deserved. His irreverent public criticism of an SN concert in *Gil Blas* (9 March 1903) runs as follows:

> We afterwards heard a *Ballade* for piano and orchestra by the master of charms, Gabriel Fauré, which was almost as lovely as Mme Hasselmans, the pianist. With a charming gesture she readjusted a shoulder-strap which slipped down during every lively passage. Somehow an association of ideas was established in my mind between the charm of this gesture and the music of Fauré. It is a fact, however, that the play of the graceful, fleeting lines described by Fauré's music may be likened to the gesture of a beautiful woman without either suffering from the comparison.

Fauré and Debussy shared more dislikes than likes: notably a horror of rhetoric, sentimentality, and the superficial and showy. Their common qualities were elegance, refinement, 'sensibilité', and a highly developed feeling for sonorous beauty. But Debussy was more intellectual and universal in his tastes than Fauré, for whom a fusion of the arts was one Wagnerian facet that held no allure. If he was less concerned about texture and orchestration, less sensual, worldly and humane, then Fauré had the greater capacity for sustained, gradual development, and a supreme ability to concentrate his thought on purely musical invention.

The case of Ravel was different, for he was Fauré's favourite and most talented pupil, rather as Fauré had been Saint-Saëns's. Fauré's slow evolution contrasted markedly with Ravel's speedy and almost deliberate development, as did Fauré's profound sincerity with Ravel's often ironical and parodistic approach to art. Fauré told Louis Aubert after the première of the *Histoires naturelles* on 12 January 1907:[13] 'I like Ravel very much, but I do not like the fact that he sets to music things like that', and he found the finale of the String Quartet that Ravel dedicated to him short and unbalanced, though he loved *Jeux d'eau* and later the Piano Trio.

Both Ravel and Fauré were attracted towards songs and chamber music, and Ravel admitted 'the profound influence of Fauré's songs which showed the young composers of 1895 the smoothest path ('le plus doux chemin')' (*ReM*, 1922, p. 27). But their attitudes towards the orchestra were altogether different. Although he wrote for the piano and orchestrated afterwards, the orchestra was at the centre of Ravel's art, and he was even more of a master in this sphere than Rimsky-Korsakov or Debussy. For Fauré, orchestration was something that could easily be used to conceal poverty of musical ideas, and he wrote to his son Emmanuel on 17 March 1908 (*BAF*, 1972, p. 6) that Ravel's *Rapsodie Espagnole* was the 'result of procedures thought musical at the moment'. But Fauré, more than most other composers, was placed in a difficult position by the evolution of the orchestra in the early part of the present century, and Ravel and Stravinsky inadvertently did a great deal to detract from his reputation in this respect.

Ravel remained enthusiastic about Fauré's music, as his letter of praise after the première of *La Chanson d'Ève* shows,[14] and he knew a lot more of Fauré's music than is generally imagined, though it was the vocal music primarily that attracted him. Both composers became increasingly classical in their approach after the war, though Ravel pursued in his own individual direction the fusion of tonality and modality begun by Gounod and Saint-Saëns but opened up by Fauré. Resemblances and examples of cross-fertilization are few: there is something of Fauré in Ravel's song *Sainte* (1896), in the *Pavane pour une Infante défunte*, and later in *L'Enfant et les sortilèges* ('Toi, le coeur de la rose'); and there is some Ravel in Fauré's Second Cello Sonata and in the Thirteenth Nocturne (Ex. 47). Both composers share a common French ancestry in the eighteenth-century clave-cinistes.

In 1924, several composers were asked to set poems by Ronsard for a special supplement of *La Revue Musicale*, but Fauré significantly destroyed his sketch for what was to be his final song, *Ronsard à son âme*, when he discovered Ravel had already set the same text.

In the musical criticisms that he wrote for *Le Figaro* between 1903 and 1921, Fauré sought to praise the good points in a composer's work rather than stress its faults. His forthright statements in private letters make some of his press criticisms look bland, but this does not make his opinions any the less perceptive, and his 1907 review of Strauss's *Salome* is a masterpiece. It is interesting that many of Fauré's hardest-hitting reviews come from his early years with *Le Figaro* when he might have been expected to have been most wary. Defining his view of the critic's role in answer to an enquiry in *Le Gaulois*, Fauré wrote (30 October 1904):

> I think that the chances of judging a work of art justly are much higher when one has oneself practised and experimented in that art all one's life.
>
> I think equally that a constant battle with the difficulties of that art inclines one very naturally towards leniency. I should add, finally, that the work of the critic obliges him to look beyond his own particular medium, and that this considerably broadens his focus on the world.

The musical nadir for Fauré seems to have been Italian *verismo* opera, as it was for Debussy. Writing on Mascagni's *L'Amico Fritz* (10 May 1905)[15], Fauré complains of its 'inadequate style and rudimentary technique where, perhaps beneath a pretext of modernity, certain unskilful and disagreeable harmonic progressions take place'.

Puccini, on the other hand, Fauré recognized as having something more worthwhile to say. He thought the scene in Scarpio's chamber in Act 2 of *Tosca* far superior to the rest of the opera (14 October 1903), and even waxed lyrical over *Madam Butterfly* (29 December 1906), though he thought that its oriental cousins, Saint-Saëns's *La Princesse jaune* and Messager's *Madame Chrysanthème*, deserved at least equal recognition. If Puccini's pathetic situations were too uniformly similar, and if emphatic accents often deprived of invention occupied too important a place in his works, then he excelled in scenes of movement: 'His verve, his fondness for harmonic and orchestral experimentation, his manner of embellishing the most slender of ideas with attractive detail, are a source of real pleasure for the listener' (OM, p. 102). In fact, Puccini fares at least as well as Fauré's Conservatoire predecessor Massenet. Fauré greatly regretted the over-emotional climaxes in *Werther* (25 April 1903), as at the end of the first act. Whilst this might well represent genuine emotions on Massenet's part, he over-used the technique of taking a simple, touching theme and presenting it in an orchestral *fortissimo*. Fauré did not go in for much cross-reference or direct comparison, but he obviously had the Italian *verismo* school in mind here.

Neither was Fauré enamoured with the naturalistic symphonic poems of Richard Strauss. He was chiefly impressed by Strauss's orchestral technique, and found *Ein Heldenleben* (30 August 1903) superior to *Salome* (9 May 1907), which he aptly perceived was a symphonic poem with added voice parts. He regretted that everything was 'described in minute detail, and all this by means of often mediocre themes'. But he thought that these themes were developed and interwoven with consummate artistry, in which the magic of the orchestral technique was such that the 'themes end up by acquiring character, power and almost emotion' (OM, p. 140). Strauss's fluency and 'prodigious dexterity', and the 'transience of his always novel, curious and arresting orchestral effects . . . ends up by continually dazzling the senses, and even the eyes'. Fauré pointedly asks: 'Is it because of the particularly brutal nature of the subject, or is it just to be innovatory, that Strauss introduces so many cruel dissonances which defy all explanation?'

Rimsky-Korsakov fared little better. Fauré thought that his music lacked continuity and evenness of inspiration. The fault, as he saw it in *The Snow Maiden* (OM, p. 125, 23 May 1908), was that each small section of the opera was complete in itself, but bore no relation to its neighbours, being linked only by recitative. Nothing developed, and the series of juxtapositions resembled a 'vast marquetry' pattern, albeit full of lovely, colourful moments. On the whole Fauré was suspicious of orchestral magicians, and even Berlioz came in for reproval. Fauré disliked the staged version of *La Damnation de Faust* (OM, p. 18, 9 May 1903) in which 'interest dwindled and died, and inattention and boredom grew in proportion to the nearness of the work's dénouement'. In the following year (21 November 1904) he wrote of the 'mediocre themes, the baroque form and the vulgar sonority' of the *Benvenuto Cellini* overture, though he thought more highly of *Romeo et Juliet* and *L'Enfance du Christ* (14 and 28 December 1903).

Two rather more surprising dislikes were Mendelssohn's 'Reformation' Symphony which Fauré found austere, 'devoid of all trace of profound emotion, stripped of the seductive qualities of elegance, charm and colour (except in the second part)' (OM, p. 83, 23 March 1903); and Brahms's Fourth Symphony. He thought the opening Allegro of this symphony had 'enough movement to conceal the coldness and insignificance of the following Andante and the redundancy of the third movement' (21 March 1904), but he put much of this down to the incompatibility of temperament which separated the Latin and German races, and which he saw as an unbridgeable artistic chasm.

The Princesse de Polignac in her *Memoirs* (1945, p. 119) says she 'always found Fauré attracted by expressive music and easily bored by works of too classical a spirit . . . I have often heard Fauré, although an ardent admirer of Bach, speak of some fugues as utterly boring.' But she may have converted specific occasions into erroneous generalizations for Fauré revered Mozart without reservation. 'Is there any other music', he asked of *The Magic Flute* (1 June 1909), 'which can convey such an immediate and profound impression . . . which, without making the slightest effort, sustains the spirit in such joy, such calm restraint, and from which springs such an important message, together with the strongest and the most exquisite emotions?'

Beethoven, Gluck and Liszt he also revered, and Wagner was beyond criticism. Significantly, Fauré did a lot of homework on Wagner, looking up his writings on opera in *A Communication to my Friends* when reviewing *The Flying Dutchman* in December 1904, and his interest in Wagner is evident from his ability to compare the productions he reviewed with earlier ones. Otherwise, Fauré mostly confined himself to a précis of the plots in the cases of *The Ring*, *Tristan* and *Parsifal*. When he did briefly come to consider the music, the aspects that he liked best were its ability to withstand time and criticism, and its power to elevate its audience far above the ordinary world in which they lived. Of *Götterdämmerung* he wrote (OM, p. 149, 24 October 1908) that it had

> now reached the serene regions where it hovered sublimely, far above everyday quarrels, far above all criticism, and even far above the most exaggerated panegyrics. More moving than ever, the music becomes with time still nobler, still more spacious, still clearer, and how sublimely classical.

Marcel Proust however found it difficult to believe all this and wrote to Reynaldo Hahn:[16]

> I do not know whether Fauré is sincere in all he says, but one is a bit bewildered to see that, after talking about Wagner's *Twilight of the Gods* as a 'Titan', he produces exactly the same sort of eulogies for Serge Basset and Broussan etc. etc.

None of this deterred Fauré, however, and in January 1914 (OM, p. 154) he described *Parsifal* as 'hovering above us in the regions of peace and forbearance', precisely the qualities he sought to attain in his own compositions.

Fauré formed his musical predilections early in life, and remained loyal and without hypocrisy. In a letter to the critic Hugues Imbert on 19 September 1887 (BN, La 14) he wrote:

> In reality, the musicians who interest me most are my friends d'Indy,

Chabrier, Chausson, Duparc etc. . . . As to the elder generation . . . there is Gounod, I really admire works of his . . . and Saint-Saëns, for whom I have a passionate, blind devotion and a profound gratitude.

To this list might be added Bizet, Messager, Rabaud, Franck and Dukas, whose *Ariane et Barbe-Bleue* Fauré thought a vigorous and beautiful masterpiece which perfectly matched Maeterlinck's drama (11 May 1907). Sadly, he never wrote a full-length criticism on Debussy, and in reviewing Ravel's *L'Heure Espagnole* (20 May 1911) he made little positive comment on the music, simply remarking on its 'originality, subtle ingenuity, gaiety and spirit'.

It was above all the urbane craftsmanship of Saint-Saëns that Fauré so deeply admired. Of *Déjanire* (OM, p. 134, 15 March 1911) he writes in characteristic adulation:

> It does not seem necessary, when it comes to Saint-Saëns, to praise the continuity, the dignity of style, the superiority of the technique, the appropriateness of the expression, the orchestral interest. For there is hardly a musician, in France or elsewhere, whose works are a source of beautiful and noble thoughts to the same degree as his.

The Fauré–Saint-Saëns correspondence (Nectoux, *RdM*, 1972–3) shows the extent to which Fauré came under the spell of his celebrated teacher, but the admiration in the early days was reciprocal, for Saint-Saëns wrote of Fauré's Violin Sonata (op. 13) in the *Journal de Musique* on 7 April 1877, at a time when Fauré greatly needed reassurance and publicity:

> He combines a profound musical technique with a rich abundance of melody and a sort of unconscious naivety which is the most irresistible of forces . . . On top of all that hovers a charm which envelops the entire work and makes it acceptable to the average audience, like something completely natural . . . With a single leap, M. Fauré has taken his place alongside the great masters.

And there is no reason to suppose that Fauré's adulation of Saint-Saëns, who helped him so much, was other than completely genuine. But Fauré did distinguish between real originality and occasional pieces in Saint-Saëns's vast catalogue, reserving a special place in his affections for the Third Symphony and *Samson et Dalila*. But he was not too keen about lyric creations like *Phryné* (1893) and *Parysatis* (1902), and in his *Revue Musicale* obituary article (1922, p. 98) he perceptively pointed out that it was more correct to say that Saint-Saëns was 'the most complete musician France had ever possessed' than that Saint-Saëns was the 'greatest musician of his time', as others had done. After all, he *was* a contemporary of Berlioz and Debussy.

Although the paths of the two composers diverged widely after 1900 and Saint-Saëns was unable to comprehend Fauré's musical development after *Prométhée*, the things Fauré admired in Saint-Saëns's music were the elements he strove to perfect in his own: formal clarity and continuity, craftsmanship, elegance, charm, restraint and discretion. The two composers were closest musically around 1880, and in the genres of piano and chamber music; and it was the neo-classical element in Saint-Saëns's music that had the greatest effect on Fauré, coming to the surface in works like the *Pavane* (op. 50), the *Airs de danse* in *Caligula* and *Pénélope*, and the *Menuet* and *Gavotte* in *Masques et Bergamasques*, as M. Nectoux has pointed out (*RdM*, 1972, p. 85).

The main difference was that Fauré was a much slower and more self-critical worker. Like many great artists he found the self-discipline of composing in isolation difficult, and only towards the end of *Pénélope* did he develop a regular schedule which excluded the external distractions that he otherwise gave in to so easily. The eclectic and essentially Germanic Saint-Saëns was closer to composition 'factories' like Massenet and Czerny; his greatest music was his earliest, up to about the Third Symphony (op. 78) of 1887. The inner searching and self-doubt that Fauré admitted to his wife on occasions must have been foreign to him. The result is that Fauré's music maintains a consistently high level, developing all the time, and has much more to offer, hovering above the urbane as Fauré intended it to. As Saint-Saëns said: 'It is not the absence of defects, but the presence of merits that makes Art and men great'. As a composer, Fauré possessed merits in abundance.

Footnotes to Chap. 6

1. From the *Poèmes tragiques,* Paris, Alphonse Lemerre, 1884, from which Fauré also took *Les Roses d'Ispahan* (op. 39/4) and *Le Parfum impérissable* (op. 76/1).
2. Koechlin's setting was made in 1901–2 as the third of the *Quatre poèmes de la Bonne Chanson* (op. 24).
3. Saint-Saëns's first chamber work without a keyboard instrument was the String Quartet in e (op. 112) of 1899. Fauré probably had his second String Quartet in G (op. 153) of 1919 in mind when he made his comparison.
4. It is interesting to consider the passage around fig. 6 in the context of Ex. 66, as this inserts a similar passage between two more sustained, scalar ones.
5 and 6. La in the Pierpont Morgan Library, New York (Mary Flagler Cary Music Collection). The second dates from mid-May 1922.
7. See Philippe Fauré-Fremiet: 'La Genèse de Pénélope', *ReM*, 1945, pp. 9–26 for further details.
8. This is how the passage appears in the Heugel vocal score. Fauré either changed it in the process of composition, or misquoted it in his letter to his wife, which reads (LI, p. 149): ' "Nous voulons lui parler, qu'elle vienne, Cours de notre part le lui dire, chienne!" '.
9. The parts not confided to Fernand Pécoud (see chapter 5).
10. Cited in Marcel Dietschy: *La Passion de Claude Debussy*, Neuchâtel, Éditions de la Baconnière, 1962, p. 159 n41.

11. Cited in *Debussy: His Life and Mind*, vol. 2, London, Cassell, 1965, p. 6.
12. In a letter to Georges Hartmann on 9 August 1898. See J-M. Nectoux's article 'Debussy et Fauré' in *Cahiers Debussy*, Nouvelle série no. 3 (1979), pp. 13–30, for a fuller account of the links between the two composers.
13. Cited in J-M. Nectoux: 'Ravel, Fauré et les débuts de la SMI', *RdM* (1975), p. 313. This article (pp. 295–318) should be consulted for a fuller appraisal of the relations between the two composers.
14. Cited in Arbie Orenstein: *Ravel: Man and Musician*, New York and London, Columbia University Press, 1975, p. 62.
15. A selection of these criticisms was published in *Opinions musicales* (OM), Paris, Éditions Rieder, 1930. The Mascagni piece comes on p. 74.
16. *Lettres à Reynaldo Hahn*, Paris, Gallimard, 1956. Letter CIV, p. 163. This refers to Fauré's 1908 criticism cited above: Louis Broussan was co-director of the Paris Opéra and Serge Basset worked for *Le Figaro*.

7

FAURÉ'S MUSICAL TECHNIQUES

Fauré developed a musical idiom all his own; by subtle application of old modes he evoked the aura of eternally fresh art; by using unresolved mild discords and special colouristic effects in his instrumental music he anticipated the procedures of impressionism; in his piano works he shunned virtuosity in favour of the classical lucidity of the French masters of the clavecin; the precisely articulated melodic line of his songs is in the finest tradition of French vocal music.

Fauré's stature as a composer is undiminished by the passage of time.

(Nicholas Slonimsky)

1. HARMONY

Whilst the thought that his instrumental music might one day be regarded as anticipating impressionism would have roused the placid Fauré into vigorous denial, he would, I am sure, have proudly concurred with the remainder of Slonimsky's tribute. Fauré was first and foremost a harmonist and, as Françoise Gervais points out in her excellent comparative study of the harmonic languages of Fauré and Debussy (1971, p. 19), he 'reunited modality and tonality in such an intimate fusion that they formed a unique and perfectly homogeneous language'. In this language, melody was 'inseparable', and a 'sort of emanation' from the harmony, its *raison d'être*. Perhaps too much stress has been laid upon the modal element in Fauré's compositions, but the significant influence derived from Niedermeyer's teaching of the accompaniment to plainchant cannot be denied. But, whereas Niedermeyer left no traces of modal harmony in his own free compositions, Fauré used the modes to revitalize and strengthen the tonal system, and his mature works all contain modal traces to varying degrees.

Fauré's harmonic style thrives on ambiguity, and his modal interpolations are so subtle as often to pass unnoticed. He used modal elements to soften and facilitate transitions between two tonalities, and the modes brought fresh colouring and flexibility into a tonal system that remained intact in the process. Whereas Debussy creates chord progressions outside the tonal system, Fauré remains within it, whatever sidesteps or enharmonic transitions occur. For him, harmony is the central factor, rather than an element dependent on rhythm or melody, as it can be in Debussy. With Fauré harmony is never used purely for colour and remains strongly functional. Whilst being unmistakably personal, his harmonic conception did not allow him to begin in one key and close in another, the only exception being his favourite progression from minor to tonic major. In his approach to harmony in general, Fauré is a classicist, developing and expanding his inheritance from within, assimilating and transforming elements from the music of Mendelssohn, Schumann, Chopin, Liszt and Saint-Saëns into his own refined and original style. As Émile Vuillermoz says (*ReM*, 1922, p. 14):

> Fauré was no mere forerunner, a pioneer whose explorations were developed by those better equipped to do so: he was a musician who, a quarter of a century before the rest, spoke a prophetic language freely, with an ease, virtuosity and elegance which was never surpassed.

Fauré created no new chords and relied on the third-based tradition of Rameau rather than experimenting with fourth-based agglomerations as Satie, Koechlin and others did. His innovations lay within chord progressions, and his revolution was achieved through part-writing rather than texture. It was as much evolution as revolution: Fauré's message was a subtle and persuasive one, carried in compositions of uncompromising integrity and consistent excellence which transcend the musical fashions that were so much a part of the France in which he lived and worked.

Sufficient has been written about Fauré's use of flattened leading-notes and raised fourth degrees to give the impression that his harmonic style was the result simply of adapting ordinary major or minor scales along these lines, or using the Dorian or Lydian modes for certain passages. These factors can be seen in the 'love theme' from *Pénélope* (Ex. 32 D), which is in essence an adaptation of Fauré's favourite Lydia theme (Ex. 2), but the answer goes deeper than this, to Fauré's conception of tonality as such. He rarely wrote a traditional modulation in the sense of progressing from one tonal centre to another and staying there: the nearest he came in the third period is Ex. 48F. Rather, Fauré preferred tonal or modal transitions to temporary halts of various lengths on degrees within the scale in use. So his 'modulation' to a minor in bar 6 of *Lydia* is only a transition using chord I in F as a pivot, and he is back to the original tonic within two beats of reaching his supposed new one. Pivot chords are invariably used in Fauré's transitions, related both to the old and to the new keys. But there is more to it than this: a minor and F 'Lydian' major are in fact the same scale for Fauré, and in Ex. 2 he is simply shifting his tonic or final note within overlapping scales, and sliding to a different aspect of the same mode/scale, as Ex. 70 shows. This is rather like the idea of Satie's *Gymnopédies* being the same fixed object viewed from three different angles. The same principle operates with the transition to b minor in Ex. 32D, and besides being examples of Fauré's tonal/modal ambiguity, they also reflect his penchant for keys a major third apart, his free use of the forbidden weak chord on the third degree of the scale (Ex. 48E), and his unorthodox resolution of the dominant seventh and other 'discords' (see Ex. 2, bars 4 and 5), all of which the Niedermeyer method of plainchant accompaniment allowed but the stricter Conservatoire in the 1860s did not.

Ex. 70

Passages of any length purely in the Gregorian modes are rare in Fauré, though the two op. 87 madrigals offer some short examples, such as Ex. 71 in the Phrygian mode, as do the *Tarentelle* (op.

Ex. 71
Phrygian mode
Bars 6–9

Le Ramier (op. 87/2)

239

10/2) and the Thirteenth Nocturne, at either end of his career. Modal cadences, however, are common, and this was one of Fauré's main means of avoiding the obvious. The end of *Une Sainte en son auréole* (Ex. 72) provides one of the best examples of a Lydian cadence, with Fauré's favourite falling sixth in the bass. The end of the *Salve Regina* (op. 67/1) offers the same cadence in a falling melodic context. In effect,

Ex. 72
(End)
Une Sainte en son auréole (op. 61/1)

this means that perfect cadences tend to be replaced by plagal, with either straightforward IV—I progressions, as at the end of *Les Roses d'Ispahan* (op. 39/4) or, more frequently, cadences that are plagal by nature, remembering that dominants in the Gregorian modes are more frequently on the sixth degree than on the fifth above the tonic. Thus as well as the falling sixth in the bass, we get VI—I cadences at the ends of *Clair de lune* (op. 46/2) or *Fleur jetée* (op. 39/2), and frequent IV⁶—I cadences, as at the end of *Danseuse* (op. 113/4, Ex. 73) or *L'Aube blanche* (op. 95/5) where the bass falls a fourth, as well as II⁷—I (Ex. 72). These are all plagal in effect. At the same time, Ex. 72 is a cadence in the transposed Lydian mode, Ex. 73 is in the transposed Phrygian mode, and so on.

Ex. 73
(End)
Danseuse (op. 113/4)

Straightforward perfect cadences are by no means unknown, as at the end of *Puisque l'aube grandit* (op. 61/2) or *Comme Dieu rayonne* (op. 95/4), but these are more often replaced by cadences in which the third of the dominant seventh is altered to a fourth, as at the ends of the Second Barcarolle (op. 41), *Le Don silencieux* or *Chanson* (op. 94). *Roses ardentes* from *La Chanson d'Ève* (Ex. 74) provides a particularly extended instance. Sometimes the dominant seventh can be replaced by chord III, as at the ends of *Nocturne* (op. 43/2), *La Rose* (op. 51/4), *Mandoline* (op. 58/1) or the finale of the Second Violin Sonata (op. 108). The variety of these cadences is endless, depending on whether the bass falls by step or a sixth, or remains as a tonic pedal etc; and they occur as often during works as they do at the ends, and in piano works as much as in songs or chamber music. A few interrupted cadences appear, as in *Prison* (op. 83/1, bars 13–14), and there is a string of them in *N'est-ce pas?* (op. 61/8, bars 35–40).

Ex. 74   **Roses ardentes** (op. 95/3)
(End)

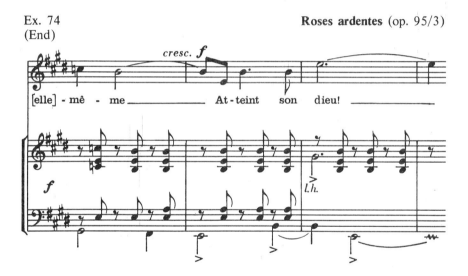

Fauré's fusion of the modes with the principles of tonality was, in a sense, the very opposite of the procedures of the Baroque era, and in his music the modes always appear in a harmonic context. If we look back to Ex. 70, weak degrees of the scale can now come in different places within the same range of notes, and so the functions of notes relative to each other can be altered. When Fauré applies these changes to the tonal system, a new conception of tonality arises which strengthens the third degree of the scale and eliminates weak progressions with roots a third apart. But it does so without destroying the importance of the now more flexible dominant. Both plagal and authentic modes are used and Fauré transfers from one mode to another as easily as between modes and keys. The start of *Prison* shows Fauré dipping into the transposed Dorian mode within a phrase in e flat minor (Ex. 75, bars 2–3), and the piano postlude to *Arpège* (op. 76/2) reveals an excursion into the Phrygian mode in both harmony and melody within an E major passage.

Ex. 75   **Prison** (op. 83/1)

Bars 1–4

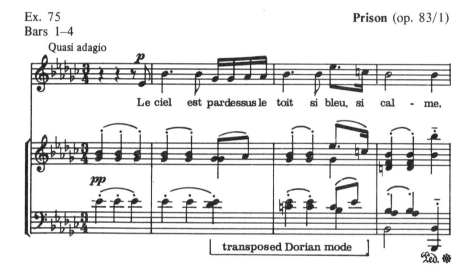

There are of course precedents for this from Beethoven's *Heiliger Dankgesang* in the Lydian mode (op. 132) onwards, through Berlioz's *L'Enfance du Christ*, Gounod's *Faust* (*Chanson du roi de Thulé*) and Saint-Saëns's *Mélodies persanes* to Duparc and Franck. But in most cases the Gregorian modes were incorporated for specific movements or for temporary coloration rather than being united continuously with the tonal system as they are in Fauré.

As Françoise Gervais has demonstrated (1971, pp. 39–43), Fauré also achieved modal effects through non-Gregorian means, using three forms of the same ascending melodic minor scale (Ex. 76a–c). Ex. 76a is the ordinary ascending form of the melodic minor scale, and its normally tonal usage is balanced by its strong whole-tone connotations, producing Fauré's favourite tritonal chord quite easily (Ex. 77 'x'), and there are numerous examples of this in *Clair de lune*, with or without raised sixth or seventh degrees. The second scale (Ex. 76b) in two Greek tetrachords is known as the mixed major-minor scale, and is really the plagal form of Ex. 76a, giving rise to the common Fauréan cadence (Ex. 78a) which

Ex. 76
Dorian mode with raised seventh degree   Major/minor mixed

Vachaspati

can be considered as VII^{7}c—I, but which has a strong plagal feeling. Ex. 78b shows it in *Pleurs d'or* (op. 72), and Ex. 78c from the *Sicilienne* (op. 78) shows how it can be used as an imperfect cadence. The third version of the minor scale (Ex. 76c) is half Lydian and half Mixolydian, and is known within the Hindu carnatic modes as the Vachaspati (a mode equally favoured by Debussy). The Vachaspati gives rise to the progression of parallel dominant sevenths with roots a tone apart (Ex. 79a) which frequently occurs in Fauré's music. Ex. 79b from *Soir* (op. 83/2) shows a rising sequential use of Ex. 79a, and it is from the Vachaspati that many of Fauré's progressions, rising or falling by whole tones in the bass, derive (cf. Ex. 60, bars 1–2).

Ex. 77   **Le Ramier** (op. 87/2)
Bars 10–12 (accompaniment)

Fauré mostly used the whole-tone scale in short passages and in a modal or tonal context. He only approached Debussy's more consistent use of the symmetrical scale melodically in the Fifth Impromptu (op. 102), and harmonically in *Pénélope* (Ex. 80), though this is a very rare example. Whole-tone interpolations are at their height during the early years of the third period, and especially between 1905 and 1909, though they occasionally appear later on as well, as at the end of the *Fantaisie*

in the hammered descending scales (p. 42). Melodic examples can be found stretching as far back as *Lydia* (Ex. 2) in the major, and the *Sérénade toscane* (vocal line, bars 12–15) in the minor. Whole-tone effects are often produced by Fauré's favourite neapolitan or augmented sixth chords, as at the start of the slow movement of the Second Piano Quintet (Ex. 48E, bars 2–3), or by chords constructed on various degrees of the chromatic scale, as shown in the same example, bar 6 (flattened sixth degree).

Ex. 78

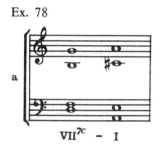

a

VII⁷ᶜ – I

Pleurs d'or (op. 72), bars 16–17

b

Pelléas et Mélisande: Sicilienne, bars 4–6

c

Ex. 79

Soir (op. 83/2), bars 8–9

Ex. 80

Pénélope, Act 2, scene ii

(VS p. 131, bars 9–12)

Altered chords are another vital aspect of Fauré's harmonic style and occur on all degrees of the scale, especially the third and sixth. These chords often add to the harmonic ambiguity by suggesting modulations that are never followed up. Ex. 81 shows an altered version of chord III acting as a secondary dominant in the *Requiem* (*In Paradisum*). Hand in hand with altered normal chords go those constructed on degrees of the chromatic scale, and Fauré was one of the first to resolve the neapolitan sixth on the flattened second degree on to a chord other than the ordinary dominant. Resolving it on to V^{7}c was one of his favourite procedures which occurs as early as the *Chanson du pêcheur* (op. 4/1, bars 31–2), but is best seen in sequence in *Puisque l'aube grandit* (op. 61/2, bars 10–11). Chords constructed on the flattened third degree are frequent and often lead to the dominant chord in a similar

Ex. 81   **Requiem** (In Paradisum)
Bars 19–21 (OS pp. 118–19)

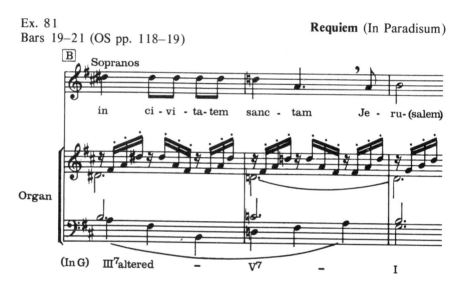

manner to the neapolitan sixth (Ex. 82), and Ex. 48E has already shown a chord on the flattened sixth degree resolving onto an altered dominant. Again, there are countless possibilities and, from the finale of the First Violin Sonata onwards, through complex mixtures of altered and chromatic chords like the Seventh Prelude (op. 103), these procedures form a vital part of Fauré's harmonic style, and most modal interpolations cannot take place within a basic tonality without using altered or chromatic chords. The two ideas overlap perfectly, as can be seen in Ex. 83 from *Le Parfum impérissable*, which ends with the celebrated return to E major that Lenepveu could not stomach, but Ravel found 'responded to a sort of ultimate and profound inner necessity' (*ReM*,

Ex. 82
Bars 1–5

La Mer est infinie (op. 118/1)

1922, p. 25). As is often the case in Fauré, Ex. 83 is open to a variety
of harmonic interpretations that reflect its subtle ambiguity. It clearly
begins and ends in E, and the tonic is used as frequent cadential
reference point in this thoroughly chromatic song. If we assume that
bars 5–9 are all in E major, then the harmonic analysis must be as in
interpretation (a), a mixture of altered chords, and chords constructed
on various degrees of the chromatic scale. If we assume that the passage
modulates, then the solution is as in (a), but with bars 6–8 passing
through G sharp major and c minor with an enharmonic change back
to E major through the third/leading note (E flat/D sharp) in the treble
part in bar 8. But if we assume that modal elements are involved, then
the solution is as in (b), using the major/minor mixed and Vachaspati
modes described in Ex. 76, the last of which provides a pivot to c minor

247

Ex. 83
Bars 5–9, accompaniment

Le Parfum impérissable (op. 76/1)

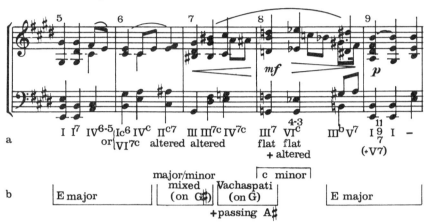

for the enharmonic change back to the tonic. Passing-notes and appoggiaturas also crop up throughout Fauré's music to add to the harmonic ambiguity. Is the main chord on the second crotchet of bar 8 in Ex. 83 c minor or E flat major, for instance? I have called it c minor because of the previous G^7, and treated the treble B flat as a passing note, but this is not the only solution. Any note in Fauré can be suspended to provide a temporary pedal or an ordinary suspension, which may or may not be resolved in a conventional manner, just as the dominant

Ex. 84
Bars 29–32

Pleurs d'or (op. 72)

sevenths are not resolved conventionally in Ex. 83, bars 6–8. In this respect, Fauré breaks down the barriers between consonance and dissonance just as much as Debussy does, and strong harmonic dissonance is equally rare in the music of both composers. In *Pleurs d'or*, for example, there is an effective resolution *from* a concord to a series of supposedly dissonant ninths and sevenths, which in Fauré's harmonic vocabulary are more lush and consonant than the triads that precede them (Ex. 84).

Other devices employed frequently by Fauré in all three periods include the circle of fifths, either flatwards or sharpwards, which invariably involve sevenths and ninths and/or sequences. From the enormous chains in the finale of the First Piano Quartet (e.g. p. 69), Fauré gradually refined the procedure as his style developed until we reach the subtle Ex. 85 from *Dans un parfum de roses blanches* (op. 95/8), where not only do the harmonic and melodic sequences overlap in the piano accompaniment, but the melodic sequences between piano and voice overlap as well.

Ex. 85   **Dans un parfum de roses blanches** (op. 95/8)
Bars 31–3

Sequence is a device perhaps over-used by Fauré, especially in the unitary piano works of the early third period. He favoured units of anything up to four bars in length, rising slowly by a semitone or a tone at a time, and his skill lay in choosing motifs or developmental variants from the main themes that were suitable for this sort of extensive repetition, and in varying the lengths of the sequences within these long rising passages (see Ex. 31). Usually Fauré's tonal goals are clear, however tortuous or ambiguous the sequences en route. Examples of his tonal control are legion, but the *Cinq mélodies 'de Venise'* provide some particularly concise instances, such as *Green* and *C'est l'extase*, which often return unexpectedly to their tonic chords whatever sidesteps crop up in between (cf. Ex. 83).

Tonal sidestepping can best be seen in *Nell* (op. 18/1) in bars 19 and 27–8, or in the Third Nocturne (bars 11–12 and 15–16). In the second period this process became more subtle. The first stanza of *La Fleur qui va sur l'eau* (op. 85/2) provides distant modulatory coloration (C sharp^7/B flat/F sharp^7) without leaving its tonic key of b minor, and the song does not settle until it reaches its final modal cadence in the tonic. Fauré is, however, most careful to end his stanzas with nearly-related

Ex. 86 **Second Violin Sonata** (op. 108)
1st movement (pp. 8–9)

Ex. 87 **Soir** (op. 83/2)
Bars 30–31

250

chords (G major in bars 13–14; D major in bar 23), though these are only part of the overall tonal plan and are not dwelt on as new tonics.

Fauré's three periods are not easy to separate harmonically; the development of his career is the story of a gradual refinement in harmonic language. Some of his most inspired moments come in his codas, like those of the slow movement of the First Piano Quartet, or of the Sixth and Seventh Nocturnes. Specific modulations occur less frequently than is generally imagined, and ambiguity exists on various levels, and can also arise from chromatic chords becoming diatonic (Ex. 86), or from diatonic chords becoming chromatic (Exx. 87 and 92, bars 1–2 [f sharp to D flat]). Fauré invents no new chords, but uses existing ones in new combinations, and his subtle chordal inversions place him in a direct line of descent from Schumann, the previous master of the dominant and secondary seventh. Second inversion triads only occur in cadential or passing contexts in Fauré's early works: later they become chords in their own right to be freely used, either to start a recapitulation (op. 108/first movement, fig. 7), or in an almost dominant function (Ex. 74, last bar). The diminished seventh is almost as rare as it is in Purcell, and this is why *J'allais par des chemins perfides* (op. 61/4), with its frequent diminished sevenths, sounds unusually anguished. Fauré much

Ex. 88

Ex. 89   Gounod: **Absence** (Songs, Vol. I, no. 18)
Bars 36–8

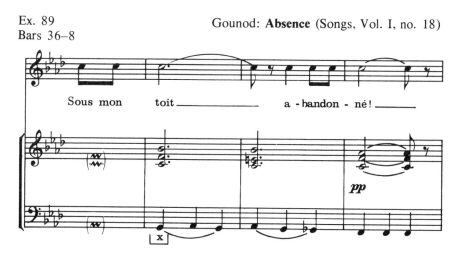

preferred the dominant, major or minor seventh, and especially the major seventh, his order of preference for inversions being second, third, then first. Ninth chords are less used than sevenths and are mostly of the dominant or subdominant variety, often made more subtle by the omission of the third of the chord. The augmented fifth, which Fauré inherited from Liszt, is most used in transitions between keys, and sometimes adds a whole-tone touch to sequences. In addition, tritone and false relation effects between chords are very frequent. Fauré obtained another whole-tone chord by replacing the fifth of the dominant seventh with a minor sixth (Ex. 88), and he also liked to use parallel dominant sevenths with their roots a semitone (as well as a tone) apart (Ex. 83, bar 7, or *Soir,* bars 20–21).

Consecutive dominant sevenths were not new to Fauré; they occur in Gounod's songs and in *Le Médecin malgré lui* (1857), for instance. Gounod also used superposed fourths and fifths at perfect cadences, although with him the fourth usually resolves onto a third to give an ordinary dominant seventh (Ex. 89). The mildly dissonant chord 'x' that Fauré used so often invariably occurs in the context of a tonic and/or a dominant pedal in Gounod.

Saint-Saëns is more important for his example and for his practical help than for any direct harmonic influence on Fauré, and the same is true in the case of Fauré's influence on his Conservatoire pupils like Ravel, Schmitt or Enesco. The fact that Saint-Saëns wrote a Piano Quartet (op. 41) in 1875, at a time when French musical priorities were firmly directed towards opera, is more important than anything it contains. Whilst Saint-Saëns's First Piano Trio (op. 18, 1869) or his Six Bagatelles (op. 3, 1855) contain some passages similar to those found in early Fauré, the first two Valse-Caprices that Saint-Saëns so much admired were composed before his *Valse Canariote* (op. 88) of 1890. As Ravel points out (*ReM*, 1922, p. 23), Saint-Saëns's main preoccupation lay in formal experiment: he 'virtually created new processes of development'. Fauré did the same thing spontaneously, though this was 'a supple means' to an end, rather than an end in itself, as it could be with Saint-Saëns.

In the case of Mendelssohn, the idea of the featherweight scherzo or the unexpected but inspired re-introduction of themes (*Songs Without Words* opp. 85/3 and 102/4, cf. Fauré: Barcarolles nos. 1 and 6) is more important than direct harmonic influence, though equally subtle recapitulations can be found in the first movements of Mozart's Symphony in g (K. 550) or Schubert's String Quintet in C (D. 956). Similarly, Schumann's rhythmic and textural consistency is more important than anything harmonic, and Fauré's arpeggio figurations often have a contrapuntal significance that Schumann's lack (see *Donc, ce sera par un clair jour d'été* (op. 61/7) etc). In any case, the early harmonic influences, like Chopin's distant coda modulations, become less and less obvious as Fauré's harmonic style develops.

The Brahmsian similarities tend to be overdone too. Although Fauré contributed towards a monument to Brahms in Paris in 1904, Emmanuel Fauré-Fremiet maintains (*BAF*, 1972, p. 15) that his father 'really knew little of his music well'. Only the Twelfth Nocturne sounds at all Brahmsian, and, there is nothing Fauréan about Brahms's Intermezzos as M. Nectoux suggests, other than a certain interior quality of thought. Fauré can only be considered as 'the Brahms of France' (Copland, 1924, p. 575) in equivalent artistic terms, and not through any direct parallels in musical content.

Fauré's harmonic idiom is, as I have tried to show, extremely rich and varied: in its capacity to renew the tonal system from within, it is also original. As Fauré's music becomes better known and appreciated, it can only be a matter of time before the misconceptions disappear. If 'extreme harmonic complexity did become almost a mannerism with Fauré in his old age' (Cooper, 1945, p. 79), we know from analyses of his harmonic style that this was a logical extension of his highly personal inventive genius, and not merely evidence of his 'delight in the posing or solving of technical problems almost for their own sake, skill being called in to supply the failing lyrical and creative impulse'. Bayan Northcott is perhaps nearer the truth (1970, p. 36) when he maintains that the 'unresolved feeling' in Fauré's later works, which 'paradoxically retain some of the strangeness of new music', arose because 'Fauré was still in transition in his own terms towards similar regions to those that the younger moderns were already conquering'. Whilst his unique style rules out the latter part of this interesting theory, the idea of Fauré being still in transition is a better way of looking at the String Quartet than Mellers' hypothesis that it is an elegy for the passing of French civilization (1947, p. 71).

There is no doubt that certain keys are rare (b, e flat, c sharp, or F sharp) and some even non-existent (g sharp) in Fauré's music, but I feel that Jankélévitch overstresses this aspect in his otherwise excellent *Fauré et l'inexprimable*. Fauré made no attempt to unify his song-cycles by key and freely permitted transposition into keys that suited his singers, as Schubert did. It was probably as a result of this that Jankélévitch was able to enthuse (1974, p. 70) about 'the luminous and smiling key of E major refuting somewhat the sadness of the subject' in *Adieu* (op. 21/3), when Fauré actually wrote the song in G flat! But Fauré did prefer multiple-flat to multiple-sharp keys and was scrupulous about correct enharmonic notation (see Ex. 53). In the early and later periods simpler keys take precedence, whereas many of the masterpieces of the middle period have several flats, and some were put into keys with more flats in during their composition (*Clair de lune, Dans la forêt de septembre*). Fauré was careful about tonal unity within pieces, and always cast his scherzos and slow movements in nearly-related keys like the subdominant (second movements: opp. 45, 89, 108, 117), the dominant (slow movement, op. 115), or the relative major (second movements: opp. 15, 115, 120).

The sketches for *La Fleur qui va sur l'eau* show that Fauré probably thought in harmonic at least as often as in melodic terms, and there is every reason to suppose that he considered chords individually and according to the degree of the scale on which they were constructed. There is evidence in the sketches too to suggest that Fauré worked in terms of a figured bass for at least some of the time, and in this he would have used the system of Abbé Vogler perfected by Saint-Saëns's teacher Pierre de Maleden and reproduced in Gustave Lefèvre's *Traité d'harmonie* (1889), which condensed the general theories behind the École Niedermeyer teaching as Fauré received it in the 1860s. This would have led to a strong sense of an overall key in a piece, rather than towards the idea of using a single note as a tonal centre of gravity, as Debussy sometimes did. This is most evident in the strong sense of tonal direction in Fauré's long sequences, and the progression from minor to tonic major that dominates his chamber music provides additional proof of his omnitonic approach. To this end Fauré even cast the Adagio of his First Piano Quartet in the tonic minor, and his increasing concern for tonal unity in the third period led him to favour partial re-exposition of his opening themes in the tonic at the start of his development sections (op. 108 etc), and sometimes to overlong reiteration of the tonic chord in root position at the ends of his movements (outer movements of op. 115 etc).

2. MELODY

If Debussy's music 'did not aspire to be other than melody', melody for Fauré was more the surface of harmony, growing from it but without a separate life of its own. This is clear in songs like *Le Parfum impérissable* or *Cygne sur l'eau* (op. 113/1), and there is no self-sufficient melody like Debussy's *Syrinx* in Fauré's oeuvre. As we have seen, many of his melodies are constructed from falling scales, from the *Sérénade toscane* through to the Twelfth Barcarolle, or Ex. 41C from the Second Violin Sonata. Even Fauré's most memorable creations, like *Clair de lune* or the *Sicilienne* from *Pelléas et Mélisande,* have scalar or arpeggio components, and both are inseparable from their piquant modal harmonies. Fauré's skill lay rather in abstracting suitable motifs for development from his themes, and for inventing themes that, through consummate craftsmanship, could be welded together until they appeared but variants from a single source (e.g. the Seventh Nocturne, op. 74). Often his later thematic extensions were elliptical, and matched by similar harmonic progressions (see Ex. 40). In the piano works of 1905–13, Fauré moves towards pieces dominated by a single short idea (e.g. Nocturnes nos. 9 and 10, Ex. 30); another possibility was for a dominant motif to evolve from the theme itself (e.g. B_1 in the Thirteenth Nocturne, Ex. 46).

But Fauré's approach to melody, in the instrumental works at least, was generally wide-ranging and expansive, as in the two violin sonatas (Exx. 4, 41) or Ulysse's theme in *Pénélope* (Ex. 32B). They involve wider intervals than his vocal lines and, in the third period, more use of cross-rhythms. In the second period, Fauré occasionally uses rising melodic sequences in vocal lines that climb slowly and chromatically to produce an almost Wagnerian spiral effect. *C'est l'extase* (op. 58/5, bars 10–20) and *Soir* (bars 12–18) are examples of this Tristanesque procedure on a small scale (cf. *Tristan und Isolde*, OS, pp. 350–4; 385–90 etc.).

In the second- and third-period songs, the interpenetration of harmony and melody can occur through the melodic line becoming embedded in the piano texture, and this can replace the melodic duets that make *En Sourdine* and *Green* so distinctive. *L'Hiver a cessé* (op. 61/9, bars 16–18) shows the melodic line carrying on beneath the words 'que le coeur le plus triste' at the top of the piano arpeggios as a duet which rejoins the vocal line at the word 'cède' (p. 41). In *L'Aube blanche* (op. 95/5) the bottom notes of the accompaniment figure in semiquavers form a bass-line around the pedal part in the left hand, which supports the vocal line in a sort of duet (Ex. 27), and so on. It should be remembered, however, that one of the songs Fauré considered his most successful was *Le Don silencieux,* precisely because it had no theme at all.

In his third-period songs, Fauré moves towards a one-syllable-to-one-note technique, which can produce the effect of recitative, but maintains a feeling of lyrical arioso because of the longer notes involved. Somehow his songs never sound hurried, although they sometimes look as if they might do on paper. The ambitus of his melodies narrows after *La Bonne Chanson*, and in the third-period song-cycles he avoids the extremes of the vocal range. In this final period, the use of intervals larger than a third diminishes and the use of repeated notes increases significantly. Fauré's melodic gift can be seen at its most expansive in *La Bonne Chanson*, and the overlaps and irregularity in the phrasing in the first stanza of *Une Sainte en son auréole*, a duet between voice and piano, show the extent to which art conceals art in mature Fauré. The left hand of the piano part, imitating the right hand, provides a further overlap to cement the structure together in bars 1–10.

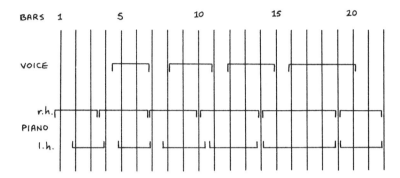

One harmonic aspect that does find a melodic counterpart in Fauré's songs is his frequent use of vocal suspensions, and these often appear as a sort of expressive Lydian appoggiatura in the songs (Ex. 90) from op. 85 onwards. Fauré takes great care in the shaping and placing of his vocal climaxes, and the saving of the high tonic (E flat) for the final word '*chan*tera' in *En Sourdine* was mentioned in chapter 4. The gradual rise in pitch of the notes that begin the anguished central phrases in *Prison* (bars 15–21) is further evidence of Fauré's craftsmanship. He also knew when to leave things simple, and wisely resisted the temptation to add a 9-8 suspension to the final word 'bas' in *C'est l'extase*, in the style of lesser composers like Massenet or Reynaldo Hahn.

Fauré's prosody is invariably excellent, apart from an early lapse like

Ex. 90   **La Fleur qui va sur l'eau** (op. 85/2)
Bars 10–11

Le Papillon et la fleur. He can however present us with some unexpected and deliberate alterations of the poet's intentions. *Les Berceaux* (op. 23/1) with its:

has already been mentioned. To this must be added *Le Ramier* (Silvestre, op. 87/2) with another unusually stressed opening:

La Fleur qui va sur l'eau has some equally unpredictable prosody, though here it contributes to the restless feeling generated by the surging, oceanic accompaniment.

Fauré told Louis Aguettant in 1902 (Fauré, 1954, p. 6) that he sought to express the general sentiments rather than individual details in his song settings. So, in *Les Berceaux* it is the rocking of the cradles or boats in the accompaniment that is all-important: in *Le Ramier* it is the madrigalian gentleness of the wood-dove's song. Fauré does, however, reflect major changes of mood in *Avant que tu ne t'en ailles* (op. 61/6) and in *J'allais par des chemins perfides* (op. 61/4), where both harmony and melody contribute to the 'anguished uncertainty' of the lover at the start, and his 'joyous reunion' through the certainty of love at the close.

It did not worry Fauré too much if he omitted stanzas or changed words in the process of composition, and he would not have agreed with Théodore de Banville that 'a poem cannot be altered without reducing it'. Neither can the changes have been all accidental, and Verlaine surprisingly suffers worst of all. Stanzas 2–4 and 6 disappear from *Puisque l'aube grandit*, and Fauré sets only stanzas 2, 3 and 6 of *N'est-ce pas?* in *La Bonne Chanson*, splitting stanza 3 between its second and third lines for another entrance of the Lydia theme on the piano (p. 36 line 3). The opp. 51 and 58 songs fare rather better, but in *En Sourdine* line 5, Verlaine's 'Fondons nos âmes' becomes 'Mêlons nos âmes', and in line 16 'de gazon' becomes 'des gazons'. Similarly in *Il pleure dans mon coeur* (inexplicably called *Spleen*), 'ce coeur' (line 10) and 'ce deuil' (line 12) become 'mon coeur' and 'mon deuil' as Fauré sets them to music.

Fauré only once set English words to music, in the *Chanson de Mélisande* for Act 3 scene i of *Pelléas et Mélisande* on 31 May 1898. He managed at least as well as Handel, and English caused him considerable difficulty, as plate VIII from the same year shows. His only obvious mistake came in bar 12 when he set 'hope' as a two-syllable word, though he corrected his mistake when it recurred in bar 25. The far more flexible and interesting setting that resulted when he expanded the song into *Crépuscule* in 1906 shows how much happier Fauré was when setting congenial contemporary poetry in his native language.

3. RHYTHM

Rhythm was another factor of less importance to Fauré than to Debussy. There is no equivalent to the attempt to use all the possible rhythmic sub-divisions of a two-bar unit as in Debussy's *Jeux,* though the opening theme of the *Fantaisie* for piano and orchestra is very varied rhythmically (Ex. 44A). Nor did Fauré show any interest in the emanicipation of rhythm led by Stravinsky, though he comes close to the systematic use of ostinato patterns in the central section of the *Fantaisie.* Fauré's chief concern was consistency and continuity, and giving a theme a distinctive rhythm enabled it to remain identifiable in development, as Ex. $46B_1$ does in the Thirteenth Nocturne. Conversely, when ideas are fused together in development, this is achieved by means of rhythmic similarities, as in Exx. 50C and D, or G and G_1.

Rhythmic variety became of increasing concern to Fauré in his third period, and his desire to avoid stressing the strong beats of the bar in common time recalls the rhythmic flexibility of the sixteenth century as much as his modal borrowings. The rhythm of the Tenth Nocturne (Ex. 30) became a favourite of Fauré (Exx. 41F and H; 44B; 50D and E; 51D; etc), as did its off-beat imitative accompaniment (Ex. 48F). Avoidance of strong beats reached its height when these syncopated rhythms were transferred to the bass-line as well, in combination with an off-beat accompaniment (Exx. 28a, 31).

The equivalent to the almost jazzy opening of the *Fantaisie* (Ex. 44A) in triple time was the hemiola, which features in its central section (Ex. 44D), or in Ex. $48G_1$. The hemiola is also principally what makes the opening movement of the First Cello Sonata seem so aggressive and insecure. Fauré also used the hemiola extensively in the first two periods, often in the form:

as in the finale of the Second Piano Quartet (pp. 63–5), the finale of the First Piano Quartet (Ex. 5H), or in the Fourth Valse-Caprice (op. 62, p. 14). Although Fauré waged war on the tyranny of the bar-line, he never abandoned it altogether as Satie and Koechlin did, and preferred to use it to his advantage in cross-phrasing and irregular musical sentences. The previous example of the first stanza of *Une Sainte en son auréole* shows how little he was in fact limited by the barline. He used irregular metres less than his predecessor Berlioz, and the only time he launched directly into 5/4 time was in a perpetuum mobile (op. 103/2) where metre was of no particular consequence. Of far greater interest is the rhythmic flexibility Fauré achieved within compound metres such as 9/8 (Barcarolles nos. 5, 8 and 9), 12/8 (Twelfth Nocturne), or even 18/8 (Seventh Nocturne). He had an odd taste for enormous bars, and his works in 3/2 time (Nocturnes nos. 9 and 13, *La Fleur qui va sur l'eau*, *Accompagnement*), or 6/4 time (Seventh Barcarolle) provide further evidence of the rhythmic variety of which he was capable, and several of the above examples reflect his penchant for iambic rhythms.

When Fauré did change metre during a piece, it was an indication of something exceptional, like the final Prelude (op. 103), the eleventh variation (op. 73), or the Sixth and Seventh Nocturnes, all of which show him at his most profound.

Harmonic rhythm is of great importance in Fauré's music, and one of his main ways of achieving metric irregularity within a conservative framework lay in prolongations of chords across barlines (see end of Ex. 28b; Ex. 60, bars 3–4 (an extension of Ex. 59, bar 1); Ex. 85), and in the prolongation of chords between the end of one melodic phrase and the start of the next (Ex. 29). The separate climaxing of voice and piano in *Eau vivante* has already been mentioned (Ex. 26), and the climax of *Je me poserai sur ton coeur* (op. 106/4) is marked by the suspension of all movement across the barline (Ex. 91, bars 1–2), followed by a harmonic recapitulation in the middle of a vocal phrase (Ex. 91, bar 4). The climax of *Vaisseaux, nous vous aurons aimés* (op. 118/4) is similarly disconcerting, with a harmonic anticipation of the tonic as the voice reaches its climax: it clearly shows the independence between the rhythm of the melody and the harmonic rhythm that is quite common in later Fauré (Durand, p. 13). The end of *Je me suis embarqué* shows an even more remarkable crossing of vocal and harmonic rhythms, the harmonic tension being released by a return to the tonic in the bass at the moment of the greatest vocal tension (Ex. 92, bar 2). The harmonic tension is then increased as the vocal tension resolves (bar 3), finally resolving itself as the vocal part tails off in bar 4.

Ex. 91
Bars 25–8

Je me poserai sur ton coeur (op. 106/4)

Ex. 92
Bars 44–7

Je me suis embarqué (op. 118/2)

The breakdown of the distinction between consonance and dissonance aided the degree of flexibility Fauré could achieve through the unexpected use of harmonic accents, and Ex. 84, showing a consonance resolving on to a dissonance in *Pleurs d'or*, provides further proof of Fauré's mature awareness of the value of harmonic rhythm to his very individual style.

4. COUNTERPOINT

The only fugues published by Fauré both date from 1869 (op. 84/3 and 6), and his favourite contrapuntal device was close canon at the unison or octave, which makes its early first appearance in the last of the *Romances sans paroles* (op. 17) of 1863. Canon is used increasingly in the third period and in the wartime sonatas in particular, and is never dry or academic, turning imperceptibly into close imitation if there is any threat to the harmonic scheme. Just how musical and natural it can be is demonstrated by *Tendresse* (op. 56/5) or the Sixth Prelude (op. 103), which both use strict canon at a crotchet's distance. The latter feels like a serene chorale-prelude and has only a single free part running between the canonic outer shell to complete the harmony.

As Fauré never runs short of ideas for development, he never has to resort to a fugal exposition to take their place, unlike Saint-Saëns, as Roger-Ducasse points out (*ReM*, 1922, p. 66). Neither does he over-use canon within a movement, as it might be claimed that Franck does in the finale of his Violin Sonata.

Canon, however, is only a logical extension of the contrapuntal strength which underlies Fauré's mature compositions. The rare absence of a firm bass-line moving by step or leap is immediately obvious, as in the shroud of Laërte music in *Pénélope* (Exx. 32B$_1$ and 34). When we say that his music becomes increasingly linear in the final period, this does not mean that its harmonic centre of chords or arpeggios ever vanishes, but rather that the linear shell that binds it together becomes tauter, and its rhythms more noticeably irregular. Austerity is a term wrongly applied to Fauré's music, except possibly to parts of the motivically concentrated piano works of the early third period or some songs in *Le Jardin clos*. No one could attribute a shortage of passion or warmth to the Piano Trio or the Second Piano Quintet.

As Wilfrid Mellers justly observes (1947, pp. 61–2):

Fauré transforms the emasculated academic idiom of the time (the idiom of Saint-Saëns) into an idiom of almost Bach-like potency by means of his virile sense of melodic line and his mastery of the bass. . . . Melody and bass are mutually independent, yet mutually fructifying.

The polarity between Fauré's outer parts has been compared to that of the high baroque and to Bach in particular, and his music is invariably more powerful than its flimsy appearance suggests (Ex. 28a). Ex. 31 shows the strictly imitative, though not canonic, link between the outer parts in the Tenth Nocturne, and this tension generated by the outer parts is shared in some of the songs in op. 106 (see Ex. 91), where Fauré can make the most ordinary and repetitive-looking rhythms seem fresh and alive through the fluidity and concentration of his counterpoint. He is easily capable of managing three lines in immaculate thematic counterpoint around an accompaniment when the occasion demands, as in the slow movement of the Piano Trio (Ex. 93), though this level of complication rarely lasts for long. Perhaps more significant is the absolute stripping down that takes place in the deceptively simple Thirteenth Barcarolle of 1921. Here the texture is reduced to two parts

Ex. 93   **Piano Trio** (op. 120)
2nd movement, bars 5–8 after fig. 7

at times (Ex. 94), and the role of the thematic or complementary bass is combined with that of providing the chordal accompaniment that is usually the textural centre.

Ex. 94   **Thirteenth Barcarolle** (op. 116)
Bars 35–6

Besides having a link with the sixteenth century through modality and rhythm, and a Bachian link with the eighteenth century in his contrapuntal approaches and his rhythmic and textural consistency, Fauré also has connections with the intervening period. As well as providing harmonic stability, Fauré's basses, like those of Couperin, are 'linearly conceived—as a melodic part' (Mellers, 1947, p. 65), and facing up to tonality after an education in the use of the modes is analogous to the dilemma faced by composers of the seventeenth century. His use of close imitation between treble and bass has close affinities with Purcell too. With the intervening experience of the Romantic composers and Wagner, it is a wonder that Fauré's harmonic approach remained so pure and restrained, his counterpoint so strong and uncluttered; the latter comes nearer to the true Bachian spirit than Mendelssohn's or Schumann's pastiches ever did.

5. TEXTURE

Perhaps the severest criticism that is made of Fauré is that he relies on a limited number of textures throughout his music; there is nothing in his figuration in the first two periods that would have distressed Saint-Saëns or even Schumann, and it was more the content than the expression of it that upset Saint-Saëns in Fauré's twentieth-century music.

Fauré remained faithful throughout his career to two principal accompaniment patterns which renew themselves continually. They reflect the extent to which he was a 'pure' musician, constructing music from harmonic foundations.

The first type is the long succession of slow chords which Fauré reserved for his most sensitive, contemplative songs from *Le Secret* to *Diane, Séléné*. As with so much of Fauré, it is easy to dismiss these chorale-type accompaniments out of hand, without realising the wealth of contrapuntal, as well as harmonic, interest they contain; the part-writing is impeccable, and the unpredictability of the bass in a song like *Le Parfum impérissable* never allows the interest to flag (Ex. 83).

In the second type, the chords of the first type are decorated through

Ex. 95   **Exaucement** (op. 106/1)
Bars 1–4, accompaniment

a variety of arpeggiated figurations. At its simplest at the start of *Exaucement* (the first song of *Le Jardin clos*), this can be a simple downward arpeggio (Ex. 95a), with the lowest note becoming a bass-line in bar 3. Ex. 95b shows the chordal basis in terms of type one, with the smoothness of the part-writing being of paramount importance, as it was in Ex. 83. Fauré did not worry about academic 'mistakes' such as parallel octaves (bar 2, although these are only apparent in Ex. 95b), or parallel fifths (*Le Parfum impérissable*, bar 11; *Requiem: Offertoire*, third bar from the end, etc). To the category of Ex. 95a belong such masterpieces as *Soir* and *En Sourdine*, whereas rising arpeggios characterize *La Messagère* (op. 106/3) or *Dans la forêt de septembre*. Often the arpeggios undulate, as at the end of *Dans la forêt de septembre*, or are shared between the hands (*En Sourdine*), and many of Fauré's songs, including those mentioned here, change en route from one category to another, especially those of the second period. It is the early songs, and late songs like those of *L'Horizon chimérique*, that tend to maintain their initial textures throughout. *La Bonne Chanson* is the apotheosis of the arpeggio in Fauré, and his sea-pictures provide good examples of arpeggio figures in both hands simultaneously, from *Les Matelots* to *La Mer est infinie* (Ex. 82), though this device also figures elsewhere (see *Nell*, end of the Eleventh Nocturne, opening movement of op. 115 etc). Staggered off-beat variants of the arpeggio texture are most common in the early third period (Exx. 28a, 31) and make full use of the intervening silences. They are a logical extension of what might almost be described as a third category: syncopated chords over a firmly moving bass, as in *J'ai presque peur, en vérité* (op. 61/5). Dramatic variants of this off-beat format, like the first movement of the First Cello Sonata, occur earlier in *Larmes* (op. 51/1), and the staggered imitation between the upper parts in the second movement of op. 109 (Ex. 42D) has an earlier precedent in *Spleen* (op. 51/3).

Thus, with texture as with harmony, there are no procedures that are exclusive to a particular period. We find Fauré playing tricks with the bass-line and the harmonic and melodic phrasing as early as 1878 in *Après un rêve*; off-beat accompaniments with pregnant silences in the *Sérénade toscane*; and so on. But only in the very earliest songs and piano pieces do we find anything of a purely routine quality, and even poverty of invention is not necessarily reflected in the texture, e.g. *Hymne* (op. 7/2) or *Aubade* (op. 6/1).

Fauré's art centred on the piano with which he felt most at ease, and there is a considerable virtuoso element in his early works. More important than the cascades of notes à la Liszt or Saint-Saëns that grace the early Barcarolles and Nocturnes are Fauré's technical experiments, like the cross-hand doubling of the melody in a different rhythm (First

Nocturne bar 39f.), or the ingenious effect with repeated notes at the start of the recapitulation of the same piece (Ex. 96). These sort of devices recur later, as in the cross-hand doubling of the canonic idea in the finale of the First Cello Sonata (seven bars before fig. 4), or the climax of the Thirteenth Nocturne where Fauré reverts to the three-hand technique of the Fifth Nocturne (p. 37f.). But in the later works, the virtuosity is always an integral part of the piece, and is never grafted on to it in order to vary or impress. The foundation of Fauré's solo piano technique is again the arpeggio in various guises, though inevitably it takes on more exuberant forms than in the songs.

Ex. 96   **First Nocturne** (op. 33/1)
(p. 9, bars 4–6)

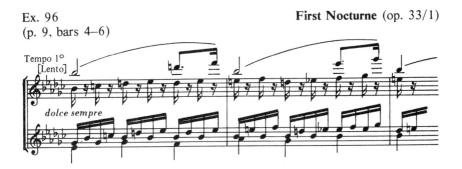

In the chamber works, the piano writing is often as extrovert as in the solo pieces, though the thematic argument is shared equally with the strings, and Fauré is extremely sensitive to the balance, the power of the piano arpeggios often being countered in the earlier chamber works by the strings in octaves, as at the start of the Second Piano Quartet. The piano tends to envelop the strings, providing the real bass more often than the cello; only after 1900 do the strings announce important thematic material entirely independent of the piano (Ex. 17B, Ex. 48B and E), and the passages where the strings play alone are very rare. This is not to say that Fauré in the chamber works was covering up unidiomatic string writing; his thorough knowledge of the instruments' capabilities is obvious from the First Cello Sonata or the scherzo of the Second Quintet, and he had a particular feeling for the viola. If he did not go in for special effects, it was because content, continuity and consistency were more important to him, and he did not place the same emphasis on colour and timbre that Debussy and Stravinsky did. Nonetheless, there is a great deal of variety in Fauré's chamber music, and textural changes assume greater importance than they do in Debussy, and serve Fauré as guides to the formal and thematic architecture.

Fauré's choral textures are more remarkable for their clarity than for their experimentation. From the *Cantique de Jean Racine* (op. 11) onwards, Fauré favoured block choral writing, with homophonic movement in four-part chords, or simple imitation that soon reverts to this. In the *Requiem* he added further devices for choral clarity: all four parts in octaves (*Kyrie eleison*; *Libera me*); soprano and contralto doubled individually by tenor and bass an octave lower (*Offertoire*, letter K); and sopranos as soloists with the three lower parts in chordal accompaniment (*In Paradisum*). Fauré's part-writing is invariably smooth and logical, his range and layout conservative: he never exceeds six parts (*Tantum ergo*, op. 55), and this only occurs in a purely harmonic context.

During his later musical evolution, Fauré reduces the number of notes in his chords to a minimum in the progression towards maximum clarity and luminosity. The Thirteenth Barcarolle reduces at times to a two-part texture and this intervallic approach can be seen equally in *Danseuse* (op. 113/4), whose accompaniment motif expands from a third to a fifth and back again, and in *Le Jardin clos*, where sparse chords in the centre of the piano are often reduced to what appears to be a two-part texture (Ex. 95a, or the start of op. 106/3). And the absence of the lower bass regions of the piano in the third period serves to make the climaxes more luminous, and the textures less 'romantic' in feeling, for this was the favourite province of Schumann (cf. *Ich grolle nicht* and *Après un rêve*). The intervallic approach is clear too at the start of *La Chanson d'Ève* (Ex. 25A), and this is one good reason for placing it at the beginning of the final period.

The other aspect which Ex. 25A and many others from the third period show is Fauré's later preference for the interval of the major second and, less often, for the minor second. The use of pedals, passing-notes, appoggiaturas or suspensions often produced quite dissonant chords by traditionally accepted means in Fauré's later works (Ex. 32B$_2$; Ex. 41C; start of the Eleventh Nocturne, etc). There can be no doubt that he took a delight in the strengthening properties of these dissonances, and that they often result from the independent logic of the parts, and in particular the outer parts, which are far more often constructed from seconds, fourths, fifths and sevenths of various types than from thirds and sixths in this final period (see Ex. 28b). That is what makes unadorned tonic chords so final and welcome when they crystallize from the continual state of mild dissonance, as at the end of *Dans le pénombre* (op. 106/6) or *L'Aube blanche* (op. 95/5), and it is in his approach to consonance and dissonance, and in the increasingly intervallic conception of his music that much of Fauré's originality resides.

6. ORCHESTRATION (original research by J-M. Nectoux, see n. 1)

Fauré is much maligned as an orchestrator who farmed his work out to others either through lack of interest, incompetence, or a mixture of both. In the introduction to a performance of *Pénélope* on BBC Radio 3 on 2 October 1975, listeners were informed that he 'left the orchestration to be done by others, as was his custom'. Rollo Myers speaks of his lack of 'real feeling for the orchestra' (1971, p. 33), and Norman Suckling comments (Su, p. 163) that 'his music often answers surprisingly well to the orchestral care taken of it by his coadjutors'.

Whilst it is true that Fauré wrote little for full symphony orchestra alone, and his two first period symphonies were laid aside after performance, he orchestrated more of his own music than is generally realised, including eighty per cent of *Pénélope*. What is more, it is clear from the *Lettres intimes* that Fauré enjoyed orchestrating *Pénélope* (pp. 206, 209), and no further proof of his competence is needed than the first act, which amazed its first conductor Léon Jéhin by the depth of sonority it achieved through such restrained orchestral means (LI, p. 214).

In the nineteenth century, orchestration did not receive the same attention in the musical curriculum as it does today. The SN was mostly involved in the performance of chamber music with only a few expensive symphony concerts each year, and the Concerts Colonne and Chevillard mostly stuck with the Viennese 'classics' and Wagner, which brought them guaranteed audiences. The main motive for teaching orchestration in France in the nineteenth century was to prepare composers for that vital success at the Paris Opéra. But d'Indy, Chausson and Saint-Saëns did a great deal to keep a symphonic tradition alive in France, and it may have been to emulate them that Fauré planned a Third Symphony in the late 1880s, just as he kept up his search for a suitable opera libretto during his second period.

Fauré studied orchestration at the École Niedermeyer with Louis Dietsch, conductor at the Paris Opéra, even though the bias of the school was towards classical and religious music. But his real teacher in orchestration was Saint-Saëns, by example and advice, though he did not take naturally to his subject as Berlioz, Richard Strauss, or his mentor Saint-Saëns did, and he belonged rather to the class of competent orchestrators like Schumann or Franck. Neither was Fauré interested enough to research into instrumental capabilities in the way that Ravel did, and Jean-Michel Nectoux perceptively observes[1] that Fauré's work in this field was done only through 'necessity', and was 'more instrumentation than orchestration'.

Unlike Debussy, Fauré's musical invention was not influenced by the orchestra, which he saw as something for which to adapt already

267

composed music, and in which the harp often replaced the more familiar piano. His orchestration is sober, without unnecessary ornamentation or experimentation; even muted strings are rare. Yet it always sounds well, and is light without being feeble, and powerful without being heavy (as Franck's orchestration often is). 'As Stravinsky said of Balakirev, his ideas are a quarter of a century in advance of their instrumentation', and Florent Schmitt drew this comparison in 1922 (*ReM*, p. 59) as a compliment, Fauré being the reverse of so many contemporary composers who attempted to cover feeble thoughts in seductive orchestral colour.

After the composition of *Pénélope*, Fauré referred to its orchestration in August 1912 (LI, p. 206) as 'a pleasure, a relief and a relaxation', even though he had foreseen it as 'hard work' that would take longer than the composition in the end. This was not the case, and Fauré orchestrated everything except the second part of Act 2 (VS, pp. 135–78; orchestral ms pp. 57–202) and the final part of Act 3 (VS, pp. 242f; orchestral ms pp. 231f), though most of the last section of Act 3 is missing in the orchestral manuscript in the Bibliothèque de l'Opéra (Opéra Rés. A. 843a (1–2)). The unnecessary doubling between wind and strings that mars *La Naissance de Vénus* disappears in *Pénélope*, and Fauré orchestrates with restraint and effect, making clear changes with the musical phrasing. He doubles a little more in Act 3 than in Act 1, preferring unison to octave doubling, and he favours the low flute as a solo instrument and the horns as harmonic fillers in the centre of the texture. There are some unusual orchestral details too, such as his use of the tuba in Act 3, scene v (Ex. 97). For the drawing of Ulysse's bow (VS, p. 232 bar 12f), he begins the figure given in Ex. $32B_2$ on the bass clarinet, adding four stopped horns as the bow expands

Ex. 97   **Pénélope**, Act 3, scene v
OS Opéra Rés. A. ms 843a[(2)], pp. 172–3
(=VS pp. 226–7)

over low tremolando cellos and basses. Fauré supervised Fernand Pécoud's work on *Pénélope*, and made a few minor changes himself to Act 2, though by and large he left his heavier and more varied scoring alone.

Strings were the orchestral centre from which Fauré worked, as they were for Ravel. Debussy, who went to the Paris première, noted how much the orchestra relied on the strings alone, and Roger-Ducasse tells us (*ReM*, 1922, p. 65) that he compared the orchestration of *Pénélope* with that of *Parsifal*. Koechlin, who had also described Fauré's orchestration in 1902 as 'classical, "resting on the strings" with some occasional touches which suggest a modern period' in a letter to Robert de Montesquiou (*BAF*, 1974, p. 11), complained to Fauré about a certain uniformity of colour in *Pénélope*. To this Fauré humbly replied[2]: 'This criticism is very just. I know myself well enough to have often considered this defect which is evidently a natural one, but which, alas, I shall not have time to correct'. Nonetheless, in Fauré's defence, there are many pages of brilliant lightness and seductive orchestral colour in his output, like the final movement of *Shylock* (op. 57), the dances in *Caligula* and *Pénélope*, and the overture to *Masques et Bergamasques*. The third act dance in *Pénélope* has some beautiful touches, such as the sinuous melody (VS, p. 210) beginning on low flute and high bassoon in unison, with accompaniment on pizzicato divided strings, harp and antique cymbals.

Only seven of Fauré's orchestrations containing symphonic development were published during his lifetime: the *Ballade* (op. 19); the *Pavane* (op. 50); *Caligula* (op. 52); the suite from *Shylock* with tenor solo; the *Pelléas et Mélisande* suite (op. 80); the Prelude to *Pénélope*, and *Masques et Bergamasques* (op. 112), in which the *Gavotte* was reorchestrated by the composer Marcel Samuel-Rousseau, who also orchestrated the *Fantaisie* (op. 111). This partly explains the popular belief that Fauré had little to do with the orchestra, though as M. Nectoux points out (1975, p. 246), most of Fauré's works composed between 1865 and 1885 were intended for performance with orchestra. The manuscripts reveal that Fauré during his first period orchestrated *Super Flumina* (1863); the Symphony or Suite in F (1865–73); *Les Djinns* (1875?); *La Chanson du pêcheur* (1876); the Violin Concerto (1878–9); the *Ballade* (1881); *La Naissance de Vénus* (1882); and *Madrigal* (1883). To these can be added the *Agnus Dei* of the *Messe basse* (1882, the other movements being orchestrated by André Messager). Also, *Les Roses d'Ispahan* (1897), the *Élégie* for cello and piano (1895), and several works probably orchestrated by Fauré whose manuscripts have not survived: *Cantique de Jean Racine* (1866, reorchestrated 1905); *Berceuse* for violin (1880); and the Symphony in d (1884).

269

In the second period, in addition to the works listed above, Fauré orchestrated the *Requiem* (first version 1892/3; second version c.1900 probably by Fauré); *Le Voile du bonheur* (1901); and probably *Clair de lune* (1888). *Prométhée*, like *Pénélope*, is a special case. Charles Eustace, conductor of the Second Regiment of Engineers at Montpellier, orchestrated the wind band music, and Fauré the music for string orchestra and harps. Opéra Rés. ms 2005, Fauré's preliminary score, shows that he conceived *Prométhée* antiphonally and carefully worked out what music was to go on the wind band, and divided this up into its component lines, though he made very few positive suggestions to Eustace as to instrumentation. BN Rés. Vma. ms 940, Eustace's final conducting score, shows that he adhered to Fauré's suggestions sent to him in ms 2005, and also that Fauré made a few minor changes in instrumentation in the final score, chiefly in Act 2, no. 1 (VS, pp. 80–82) to produce a more sustained wind band sound in Pandore's funeral cortège scene. The final score also reveals that some of the shorter scenes were cut at the first performance in 1900, or possibly at a later performance for which the score was used (viz. Act 1, no. 2; Act 2, no. 3; Act 3, no. 7; also the start of Act 1, no. 5 (VS, pp. 59–61) and the first eighteen bars of Act 2, no. 1).

Following the triumphant première at Béziers, Fauré received requests for a version for symphony orchestra to allow *Prométhée* to be performed in ordinary theatres and concert-halls. No doubt the success of *Pénélope* reminded Fauré of his intention to revise *Prométhée,* but after the enormous task of orchestrating his opera, he entrusted his earlier work to Roger-Ducasse in 1914. After he had finished revising Act 1, there seems to have been a disagreement over some of the procedures adopted by Roger-Ducasse[3], and although the three volumes of the orchestral score made in 1914–16 are in his hand, some of the numbers were also orchestrated (or reorchestrated) by Fauré, according to BN ms 17768 (1–6) and BN Vma. ms 916 (Act 1: Prelude and nos. 3 and 6; Act 2, no. 1 (VS, pp. 79–100); Act 3, nos. 4 and 5). Camille Chevillard conducted the first performance at the Paris Opéra on 17 May 1917, and this revised version is the one used today in concert versions.

Lastly, Fauré added small instrumental ensembles to some of his religious pieces composed for use at the Madeleine: *Tu es Petrus* is scored for organ and strings; *Benedictus* for organ and double bass (1880); *O Salutaris* for two horns, harp, strings and organ; and the *Tantum ergo* (op. 55) for harp and strings. Fauré also added an accompaniment for string quintet to *La Bonne Chanson* in 1898, although he thought it superfluous and withdrew it. The orchestral version by Maurice Leboucher was made against Fauré's wishes, as were the majority of the other arrangements of his more popular songs, like *Mandoline* by Florent Schmitt, and *Après un rêve*, *Notre amour* and *Le Parfum impérissable* by Henri Büsser.

7. FORM

For Fauré, form meant classical sonata form for the outer movements in chamber music and for other important movements, to be modified by cyclic references (opp. 45 and 108), or into a continuously developing form with stabilizing thematic re-expositions in the tonic, as I hope I have shown in my brief analyses. Introductions are rare, codas ubiquitous and beautiful, and Fauré approached a rondo plan in the finales of opp. 108, 115, 120 and 121, though in a developmental rather than a strict sonata-form context. Contrasts of mood and texture between sections are at least as important as contrasts of theme and key. Whereas Fauré uses nearly-related keys for themes or thematic groups and middle movements, there is no set tonic-dominant pattern as in sonata form, and the omnitonic approach, passing from minor to tonic major, is the most frequent recurring principle.

In the piano pieces, and some slow movements and scherzos in the chamber music, a ternary plan (ABA) with a self-contained A section and a coda occurs. Sometimes there is more than one theme in the A group, as in the First Barcarolle, and sometimes the structure is complicated by the introduction of a C section and thematic interrelationships between the sections (Nocturnes nos. 6 and 7); there are usually varied or developing reprises, except in the Impromptus. Fauré only used variation-form once (op. 73), but there is a variation element in all his development sections and in his invention of subsidiary ideas. His main skill lay in showing how apparently dissimilar themes were in fact closely related to one another, whilst still allowing them to preserve their identities during development.

Fauré's formal approach is thus one of experiment within limited and recognizable traditional frameworks, and he rarely springs complete surprises. His most interesting creations are the four-part opening movements to the Second Violin Sonata, Second Quintet and Piano Trio, and the attempts to fuse three movements into one à la Liszt in the early *Ballade* and the later *Fantaisie*, both significantly works for piano(s) that became works for piano and orchestra.

The unity of Fauré's creations is undeniable and the most noticeable development is one of sophistication and economy of means. As with harmony or melody, there is no clear distinction formally between Fauré's three periods, though the final chamber works do tend to be

271

more complex structurally than even the difficult Second Piano Quartet. Textural consistency has as much to do with unity as thematic repetition and, above all, Fauré's works sing from beginning to end. As Mellers observes (1947, p. 65):

> Fauré's method in his bigger chamber works is to build up movement over a regular rhythmic pulse and a consistent figuration; but the rapid enharmonic transitions of tonal centre and the manner in which the figuration lyrically *evolves*—so that the growth of figuration and the flow of the tonalities becomes inseparably the 'form', the architecture—are clearly allied to the technique of the sixteenth century in which melodic growth, polyphonically conceived, is composition.

CONCLUSION

Placing Fauré in the French musical tradition is no easy task. He lived through one of the most difficult yet exciting periods for an artist, both historically and musically, which covered everything from the romantic period to the dodecaphonic systems, via the breakdown of traditional diatonic tonality and the discovery of new horizons in rhythm through the development of music in the works of Wagner, Debussy and Stravinsky. Fauré's direct influence was and has been slight, just as he resisted influence himself, and perhaps there is a moral to be drawn from this. He was wrongly thought outdated by the neo-classicists whilst being a 'classic' in his own right, and he was a classicist deeply rooted in the music of the sixteenth century and Bach, as well as that of Mozart and Beethoven. He was also a classicist who faced up to the challenge of the twentieth century, and who did not retire behind the safety of an easily acceptable Germanic style, as Saint-Saëns did.

Fauré was conscious that, in his own way, he was adding something new to music. He was aware that he was breaking new formal ground in the *Ballade* and later in the Venetian song-cycle (op. 58), and he proudly told Vicomtesse Greffulhe in October 1893 when seeking her aid in his efforts to replace Gounod at the Institute: 'The opinion of Saint-Saëns is that I am the only one in comparison with Widor, Dubois, Joncières, Salvayre and Godard who has contributed, added something *new* to music'.[4] In 1904 he told his wife (LI, p. 85) that 'it is always natural that one wishes each work to be an advance on the last', but he never took part in the almost feverish quest for identity through novelty that so worried his post-war contemporaries, and proved so detrimental to the development of an identifiable personal style. Fauré and Ravel represent the perfection of a tonal art before the break with tonality and the massive acceleration in the evolution of musical language which made value-judgements and a sense of musical perspective increasingly difficult to achieve.

That Fauré saw his contribution to music within the perspective of the past is undeniable. In the preface to a new edition of the classics for piano by Isidore Philipp for G. Ricordi & Co. (c. 1912), he expressed his view perfectly:

> All those who, in the vast domains of the human mind, have seemed to produce new elements and thoughts and to use a language hitherto unknown, have merely been translating, through the medium of their own sensibilities, what others had thought and said before them.

In this standpoint, Fauré fulfils Marcel Proust's definition of genius[5] and its relationship with the circumstances of life:

> Genius, as opposed to great talent, comes less from possessing intellectual powers or social refinement superior to that of others than from the capacity to transform and translate these elements. Genius resides in the power to reflect and not in the intrinsic quality of the reflected spectacle itself.

Fauré's career was a long and painstaking search for perfection like that of Beethoven, and the strength and continuity of his music is synonymous with his conception of an ordered, balanced civilization. In trying to 'elevate' his pure and almost abstract art 'as far as possible above everyday existence', he was bound to face incomprehension; and he was disillusioned when third period masterpieces like the Second Violin Sonata and the *Fantaisie* were ignored for earlier creations like the First Violin Sonata and the *Ballade*. Those that call him a salon composer and 'master of charms' have never really come to grips with his very varied output. The sheer number of genres in which Fauré made a significant contribution qualify him for consideration as more than just a 'petit maître', and he did not need to write symphonies or piano concertos to demonstrate his capacity for symphonic thought. In his music, power and passion go hand in hand with suppleness and light; luxuriant sensuousness is coupled with profound spiritual depth and sensitivity, and the classical spirit can be juxtaposed with almost violent modernity, all within a single piece.

The Hellenic aspect of calm philosophical serenity has perhaps been overstressed in Fauré's case, and it is time that this took its rightful place behind the joyous strength, the sustained intensity and the supreme manifestations of diversity within unity that are the lasting contributions of Fauré's art to the present century. Novelty is no criterion by which to judge any artist and, if Fauré's music is so subtle as only to appeal initially to a cultivated and interested minority, then by its other qualities of timelessness, idealism and depth, it will eventually win through to a more universal appreciation. In the first decade of this century, when composers like Mahler, Strauss and Schoenberg

273

needed vast orchestras and a complex range of sonorities to express their innermost thoughts, Fauré was quietly pursuing his chosen path of restrained and genuine classicism in which all he wanted to say could be expressed in the 'pure' music itself, playable with two hands on a piano. In his use of smaller forces and clear chamber textures, Fauré foreshadowed later twentieth-century musical developments. His genius was one of synthesis, for the reconciliation of opposing elements like modality and tonality, anguish and serenity, seduction and force, movement and contemplation within a single non-eclectic style. His highly civilized music constantly renews itself and cannot become dated: together with that of Debussy and Ravel it represents (Mellers, 1947, p. 71) 'the most important thing that has happened in French music since Berlioz, and one of the few "imperishable" monuments of its time'.

Footnotes to Chap. 7

1. See 'Les Orchestrations de Gabriel Fauré: Légende et vérité, *Revue Musicale Suisse*, cxv (1975), p. 247, and the rest of this thorough article for further details (pp. 243–9).
2. Letter of 11 September 1913, cited in Nectoux (1975), p. 247. The uniformity of which Fauré speaks is perhaps a reflection of the consistency of texture and density that is so important to his chamber works.
3. See *Gabriel Fauré*, Paris, Publications techniques et artistiques, 1946, p. 21.
4. Cited by J-M. Nectoux in 'Fauré le novateur' (1974), p. 8.
5. In *A l'ombre des jeunes filles en fleurs,* vol. 1, Paris, Gallimard, 1928, p. 176.

APPENDIX A
CHRONOLOGICAL CATALOGUE OF WORKS
(originally compiled by Jean-Michel Nectoux)

The initial dates are those of completion of a composition. If in inverted commas, they are taken from a manuscript. Cases of a manuscript-date without a manuscript-source mean that the information comes from a sale catalogue, and that the manuscript itself now exists somewhere in a private collection: many Fauré manuscripts have changed hands frequently and demand far exceeds supply in what has become an investment market. In cases where Fauré made a copy of an original manuscript for one reason or another (e.g. op. 103/4), the earliest dated manuscript is taken to be the date of completion of the composition. Many of Fauré's works were long in gestation, and where this is known to be the case (e.g. op. 89), full dates are provided, the work being classed by its year of *completion* rather than the year in which it was begun. Letters and other documents are used to assist in the dating of compositions, and these take precedence over dates of first publication, which, with the early works especially, can be as much as a decade after the composition was completed.

The Appendix gives the following information: date of composition; title; author of text, if applicable; forces involved; opus number; key; dedication; manuscript location, where known; publisher and date of publication; date of first performance and performers, where known.

The first list includes important sketches that remain unfinished, works without opus number, but only arrangements with opus numbers (e.g. op. 81). A separate list of the more important works is provided at the end which is chronological by genre, to fit in with the subdivisions within chapters 3–5, and because the ordering of the opus numbers is by no means chronological before 1900, as has been explained in the text.

Much of this problem is due to the gap between composition and publication, and Fauré's lack of concern both with manuscript-dating and opus numbers in his first two periods. Also, much confusion has arisen from the ordering of the three volumes of songs published by Hamelle. We have already seen how opp. 1–8 were attributed in 1896 according to the ordering of Hamelle's volume 1 of 1887, itself a reprint of Choudens' collection of twenty songs and romances first published

275

in 1879—the original plates made for this are still in use today! The second volume of songs published by Hamelle in 1897 was different from the one we know today, and the reorganization took place when the third volume was published in 1908. Hamelle found that they had only fourteen songs left for their third collection (opp. 57, 58, 76, 85 and 87) and, whilst the imbalance did not bother Fauré, it worried Hamelle who decided to put twenty songs in each of the three volumes. The resulting reshuffle resulted in the four op. 51 songs being placed in volume 3, along with *Prison* and *Soir,* which had previously been published by Fromont in 1896 as op. 51, then by Metzler as op. 68, then by Hamelle in the original second volume of 1897 as op. 73, then finally by Hamelle in the third volume in 1908 as op. 83! *Soir* was also published in *L'Illustration* in 1896 without opus number at all, and chronologically the songs should be op. 67, making the usually haphazard Metzler and Co. of London the most accurate after all!

With this transfer, volume 2 now contained only nineteen songs, and *Barcarolle* (op. 7/3) was borrowed from volume 1 (no. 17) and tacked on anachronistically after *Clair de lune* (op. 46/2). *Noël* (op. 43/1) of 1886, a canticle rather than a song (like *En prière*), was then transported back in time to fill the gap left by *Barcarolle,* to complete the artistic mix-up.

The abbreviations used in Appendix A are as follows:

Forces				
	fl	flute	pno	piano
	ob	oboe	org	organ
	cl	clarinet	hp	harp
	bn	bassoon	str	strings
	hn	horn	vln (1, 2 etc)	violins
	tpt	trumpet	vla	viola
	tbn	trombone	vc	cello
	timp	timpani	cb	double bass (contrabasse)
	orch	orchestra		
	S	soprano (high voice)	T	tenor
	Mez	mezzo-soprano (middle-range voice)	Bar	baritone
	Ctr	contralto (low voice)	B	bass
	A	alto (choral works only)		

(Fauré usually wrote in terms of high voice (S or T), middle-range voice (Mez or Bar), or low voice (Ctr, not alto, or B), though he rarely specified this in the prefatory stave of his songs.)

Opus number	op. 95/5	opus 95 no. 5
	no op. no.	no opus number
Key	d flat	d flat minor
	D flat	D flat major

(The original key is given in every case)

Dedication	Ded.	dedication

(Given in French as on the original manuscript or first published edition)

Manuscript	BN	Bibliothèque Nationale
	coll.	collection of
	Cons.	Conservatoire
	f(f)	folio(s)
	ms(s)	manuscript(s)
	micr.	microfilm
	n.d.	no date
	p(p).	page(s)
	Rés.	Reserve collection
Publishers	Unpub.	unpublished
	Eng. trans.	English translation by
	repr.	reprinted

Volume numbers refers to the three volumes of songs published by Hamelle in their present available forms: vol. 2/3 volume 2, song number 3

	VS	vocal score
	OS	orchestral score
Performance	Prem.	First performance (première)
	23.3.73	23rd March 1873 (or 1973, depending on context)
	Cond.	Conducted by
	SMI	Société Musicale Indépendante
	SN	Société Nationale

(All first performances take place in Paris, unless otherwise specified)

Note: Hamelle et Cie have now been taken over by Alphonse Leduc et Cie, 175 rue St-Honoré, Paris 1, where inquiries regarding Hamelle publications and manuscripts should now be directed. The same applies to Heugel et Cie. (R. Orledge, September 1982.)

1861	*Le Papillon et la fleur* (Victor Hugo), Mez or Bar, op. 1/1, ms in D flat, pub. in C with title as above Ded. A Mme Miolan-Carvalho ms BN ms 17754, 5pp. Orig. title *La Fleur et le papillon* Choudens 1869/Hamelle 1887 (vol. 1/1) Prem. Casino de Saint-Malo, 13.8.68: Mme Miolan-Carvalho, Fauré
1861?	*Mai* (V. Hugo), Mez or Bar, op. 1/2, F Ded. A Mme Henri Garnier G. Hartmann 1871/Choudens 1877/ Hamelle 1887 (vol. 1/2) Prem. SN, 22.3.73: Félix Lévy
1862?	*L'Aube naît* (V. Hugo), no op. no. Unpub. and lost
1862?	*Rêve d'amour*— 'S'il est un charmant gazon' (V. Hugo), Ctr or B, op. 5/2, E flat Ded. A Mme C. de Gomiecourt Choudens 1875/Hamelle 1887 (vol. 1/10) Prem. SN, 12.12.74: Mlle Marguerite Baron
'8 December 1862'	*Puisque j'ai mis ma lèvre* (V. Hugo), S or T, no op. no., C Unpub.
c.1863?	Fugue à 3 (SAB), F ms Humanities Research Center, University of Texas at Austin, 3 pp. Unpub. (Probably one of the fugues written for the composition *concours* at the École Niedermeyer in 1861, 1863 and 1865. These may have been reworked in 1869 and used in op. 84.)
1863? (or earlier)	*Trois romances sans paroles* for pno, op. 17

no. 1, A flat, Ded. A Mme Félix Lévy
no. 2, a, Ded. A Mlle Laure de Leyritz
no. 3, A flat, Ded. A Mme Florent
   Saglio
Hamelle 1880
Prem. nos. 1 and 2, SN, 25.2.81: Pauline
   Roger
     no. 3, SN, 19.1.89: Mlle Kasa
   Chatteleger

'14 July 1863'

Super Flumina [*Babylonis*] 'Psalmus
   CXXXVI' for mixed choir and orch.,
   no op. no., a
ms BN ms 17781, 36 pp.
Unpub.
(Gained honourable mention in the
   composition *concours* at the École
   Niedermeyer. Two other religious
   vocal works with orchestra, 1861
   (*proxime accessit*) and 1864 (second
   prize) have since been lost.)

c.1864

Esquisse d'une fugue pour piano, no op.
   no., b
ms BN ms 17752, 3 pp.
Unpub.

1865

Cantique de Jean Racine for S A T B
   choir and org: orch. 1. 1866; 2. 1905
   by Fauré?, op. 11, D flat
(Won first prize for composition at
   École Niedermeyer.)
Ded. A César Franck
F. Schoën 1876/Hamelle 1893, and with
   orch 1905
Prem. First version for 'orch' (harmonium and string quintet) Church of
   St-Sauveur in Rennes, 4.8.66; then
   SN, 15.5.75, cond. César Franck
1905 fuller orch. version: Prem. Société
   des Concerts du Conservatoire,
   28.1.06, cond. Georges Marty

c.1865–8

Tristesse d'Olympio (V. Hugo), Mez or
   Bar, no op. no., e

279

Ded. A mon ami Adam Laussel
ms BN Vma. ms 919, 7 pp.
Unpub.

c.1865–8   *Dans les ruines d'une abbaye* (V. Hugo),
S or T, op. 2/1, A
Ded. A Mme Henriette Escalier
Choudens 1869/Hamelle 1887 (vol.
1/3)
Prem. SN, 12.2.76: Léonce Waldec

c.1865–8   *Les Matelots* (Théophile Gautier), Mez
or Bar, op. 2/2, E flat
Ded. A Mme Édouard Lalo
Choudens 1876/Hamelle 1887 (vol.
1/4)
Prem. SN, 8.2.73: Mme Édouard Lalo

1867–8   *Intermezzo de symphonie* for orch, no
op. no., F (see Appendix B)
Durand 1919 (as *Ouverture* to *Masques
et Bergamasques* suite)
Prem. Hôtel de Ville, Rennes, 8.2.68
(see J-M. Nectoux article in *19th-
Century Music*, ii no. 3 (March 1979),
pp. 239–41 for fuller details.)

Spring
1868   *Tantum ergo* for voice and org, no op.
no., g?
Unpub. and perhaps incomplete.
Theme used by Saint–Saëns as opening theme of his Second Piano Concerto in g (op. 22, 1868)
ms lost (See Nectoux, *RdM*, 1972, p.
86)

1868   *Cantique à St-Vincent-de-Paul* for voice
and org, no op. no.
Unpub. and lost
Prem. Church of St-Sauveur in Rennes,
19.7.68

'30 March
1869'   *Intermède symphonique* for pno duet,
no op. no, F (see Appendix B) (an
arrangement of the *Intermezzo de
symphonie* (1867–8) listed above)

280

Ded. A Valentine et Laure de Leyritz
ms coll. M. Malo Ceillier
Unpub.
Prem. Béziers, Festival de la côte languedocienne, 25.7.1974: Richard Philips and Mireille Varjabédian

'27 April 1869'

Cadenza for the Third Piano Concerto by Beethoven in c (op. 37), first movt., op. posth.
Ded. [A Laure de Leyritz]
ms Until recently in Robert Owen Lehman Coll.
Publ. P. Schneider 1927

'16 May 1869'

Gavotte for pno, no. op. no., c sharp (see Appendix B)
ms coll. M. Malo Ceillier
Unpub.
Prem. Maison de la radio (Paris), 15.11.1974: Louis-Claude Thirion

'30 June 1869' revised 1878–9 for Mme Clerc

Petite fugue for pno, op. 84/3, a
Ded. A Laure de Leyritz.
Hamelle 1902 (*Pièces brèves* no. 3)

'30 November 1869'

Fugue for pno, op. 84/6, e
Ded. A Valentine de Leyritz
Hamelle 1902 (*Pièces brèves* no. 6)

'31 December 1869'

Prélude for pno, no op. no., e
Ded. A Valentine de Leyritz
Unpub.
Prem. Maison de la radio (Paris), 15.11.1974: Louis-Claude Thirion

c.1870

L'Aurore (V. Hugo), S or T, op. posth., A flat
Ded. A Mlle Anna Dufresne
ms BN ms 419(c), 2 pp.
Publ. in Noske, Fritz: *La Mélodie française de Berlioz à Duparc*, Paris, Presses Universitaires de France, 1954, p. 195

c.1870

Lydia (Leconte de Lisle), Mez or Bar, op. 4/2, F (see Appendix B)

281

Ded. A Mme Marie Trélat
Hartmann 1871/Choudens 1877/
    Hamelle 1887 (vol. 1/8)
Prem. SN, 18.5.72: Marie Trélat

c.1870

Hymne (Charles Baudelaire), S or T,
    op. 7/2, G
Ded. A M. Félix Lévy
Hartmann 1871/Choudens 1879/
    Hamelle 1887 (vol. 1/16)
Prem. SN, 22.3.73: Félix Lévy

c.1870?
or later

'Andante mosso' for org, no op. no., E
ms BN ms 418, 7 pp.
Date and authenticity very dubious
Unpub.

'1871'

Seule! (Th. Gautier), Ctr or B, op. 3/4,
    e
Ded. A M. E. Fernier
ms BN ms 419(a), 3 pp.
Hartmann 1871/Choudens 1877/
    Hamelle 1887 (vol. 1/5)

'3 April
1871'

L'Absent—'Sentiers où l'herbe se bal-
    ance' (V. Hugo), Mez or Bar, op.
    5/3, a
Ded. A M. Romain Bussine
ms BN ms 419(b), 3 pp.
Choudens 1879/Hamelle 1887 (vol.
    1/11)

1871?

Chant d'automne (Baudelaire), Mez or
    Bar, op. 5/1, a
Ded. A Mme Camille Clerc
Choudens 1879/Hamelle 1887 (vol.
    1/9)
Prem. SN, 6.1.83: M. Quirot

1871?

La Rançon (Baudelaire), Mez or Bar,
    op. 8/2, b
Ded. A Mme Henri Duparc
ms BN ms 419(d), 4 pp, n.d.
Choudens 1879/Hamelle 1887 (vol.
    1/19, now 18)

'August 1871'	*Ave Maria* for male voice choir (TTB) and org, op. posth., A Ded. Hommage au Grand Saint-Bernard ms BN Vma. ms 914 (not by Fauré) Heugel 1957 Prem. Chapel of the Hospice of Mount Saint-Bernard in Switzerland, 20.8.71: Choir of the École Niedermeyer
1872?	*Tu es Petrus* for Bar solo, choir (S A T B) str and org, no op. no., C ms coll. Durand, (D & F 3148), 4 pp. by Fauré 'maître de la chapelle de la Madeleine'/BN ms 17721, parts (10) of an arr. for choir, str quintet and org by Fauré (choir alto and Bar solo parts missing). Cb part in Madeleine archives Durand 1884/Hamelle 1911 in *Musique religieuse de Fauré*
1872?	*La Chanson du pêcheur* (*Lamento*) (Th. Gautier), Mez or Bar, op. 4/1, f Orchestral version by Fauré, 1876 (Hamelle) Ded. A Mme Pauline Viardot Choudens 1877/Hamelle 1887 (vol. 1/7)/Metzler 1896 (Eng. trans. A.S.) Prem. SN, 8.2.73: Mme Édouard Lalo
c.1873	*Aubade* (Louis Pomey), Mez or Bar, op. 6/1, F Ded. A Mme Amélie Duez Choudens 1879/Hamelle 1887 (vol. 1/12)
c.1873	*Tristesse* (Th. Gautier), Mez or bar, op. 6/2, c Ded. A Mme Édouard Lalo Choudens 1876/Hamelle 1887 (vol. 1/13)

1867–73	*Suite d'orchestre* or Symphony [no. 1] in F: Allegro/Andante/Gavotte/ Finale, op. 20 (see Appendix B)
	mss BN ms 17780, first movt. only (orch) 44 pp, (c. 1870)
	coll. Mmes Ceillier and Maspéro, movts. 1–3 arr. for str à 5 and org (c. 1876)
	Unpub.
	Prem. movts. 1–3, SN, 8.2.73: Camille Saint-Saëns and Fauré (two pnos). Complete orch prem. SN, 16.5.74, cond. Édouard Colonne
1863, rev. 1873	*Puisqu'ici-bas toute âme* (V. Hugo), duet (2S) and pno, op. 10/1, C (based on earlier material)
	Ded. A Mme Claudie Chamerot et Mlle Marianne Viardot
	Choudens 1879/Hamelle 1887
	Prem. SN, 10.4.75: Claudie Chamerot and Marianne Viardot
c.1873	*Tarentelle* (Marc Monnier), duet (2S) and pno, op. 10/2, f
	Ded. A Mme Claudie Chamerot et Mlle Marianne Viardot
	ms BN ms 17783, score of orch version by André Messager (c. 1880), 16 pp. Unpub./Orch parts (22) BN Rés. Vma. ms 918 (c. 1880)
	Choudens 1879/Hamelle 1887
	Prem. SN, 10.4.75: Claudie Chamerot and Marianne Viardot
1873	*Barcarolle* (Marc Monnier), S or T, op. 7/3, g
	Ded. A Mme Pauline Viardot
	Choudens 1877/Hamelle 1887 (vol. 1/17, now vol. 2/20)
	Prem. SN, 20.3.75: Mme de Grandval
c.1874	*Ici-bas!* (Sully-Prudhomme), Mez or Bar, op. 8/3, f sharp
	Ded. A Mme G. Lecoq, née MacBrid

Choudens 1877/Hamelle 1887 (vol. 1/20, now no. 19)

c.1875   Cadenza for Mozart's First Piano Concerto (K.37) in F
Unpub.

1874/1875?   *Les Djinns* (V. Hugo), chorus (S A T B) and orch, op. 12, f
Ded. A Louise Héritte Viardot
ms BN ms 17750 for chorus and pno, 10 pp.
     coll. Hamelle/Leduc for chorus and orch, 41 pp, n.d. Orch parts by Fauré
Hamelle 1890 (VS only)
Prem. SN, 22.4.76

c.1875?   *Mazurka* for pno, op. 32, B flat
Ded. A Mlle Adèle Bohomoletz
Hamelle 1883, in coll. 1930
Prem. SN, 23.1.86: Mme Bordes-Pène

c.1875   First Nocturne for pno, op. 33/1, e flat
Ded. A Mme Marguerite Baugnies
Hamelle 1883, in coll. 1924
Prem. SN, 21.2.85: Marie Jaëll

'August 1875'   *Au Bord de l'eau* (Sully-Prudhomme), S or T, op. 8/1, c sharp
Ded. A Mme Claudie Chamerot
Choudens 1877/Hamelle 1887 (vol. 1/18, now 17)
Prem. SN, 19.1.78: Mlle Miramont-Tréogate

1875–6   [First] Violin Sonata, op. 13, A
Ded. A Paul Viardot
Breitkopf & Härtel, Leipzig, 1877
Prem. SN, 27.1.77: Marie Tayau and Fauré

1876–7   *Ave Maria* for 2S and org, no op. no. (see Appendix B)
Unpub. but reused in op. 93 (1906)
Prem. Madeleine, 30.5.77: Claudie Chamerot and Marianne Viardot

Autumn? 1877	*Libera me* for Bar and org, no op. no., d (see Appendix B) Unpub.
1877	*Romance* for vln and pno, op. 28, B flat Ded. A Mlle Arma Harkness Hamelle 1883 Prem. SN, 9.2.83: Arma Harkness. (Orch. version is by Philippe Gaubert, 1919. Hamelle 1920. Prem. Concerts Lamoureux, 11.1.20: Lydie Demir- gian, cond. Camille Chevillard.)
c.1878?	*Sérénade toscane*—'O tu che dormie riposata stai' (anon. adapt. Romain Bussine), Mez or Bar, op. 3/2, b flat Ded. A Mme la Baronne de Montagnac, née de Rosalès Choudens 1879/Hamelle 1887 (vol. 1/6)
c.1878?	*Après un rêve*—'Levati sol que la luna è levata' (anon. adapt. Romain Bus- sine), Mez or Bar, op. 7/1, c Ded. A Mme Marguerite Baugnies Choudens 1878/Hamelle 1887 (vol. 1/15) Prem. SN, 11.1.79: Henriette Fuchs
1878	*O Salutaris* for voice and org, no op. no. (see Appendix B) Unpub. Prem. Church at Arromanches, Nor- mandy, summer 1878
Completed October 1878	*Sylvie* (Paul de Choudens), Mez or Bar, op. 6/3, F Ded. A Mme la Vicomtesse de Gironde Choudens 1879/Hamelle 1887 (vol. 1/14) Prem. SN, 11.1.79: Henriette Fuchs
1878	*Poème d'un jour* (Charles Grand- mougin), S or T, op. 21 1. *Rencontre* (D flat), 2. *Toujours* (f

sharp), 3. *Adieu* (G flat)
Ded. A Mme la Comtesse de Gauville
ms coll. Durand, 5, 5, 4 pp.
Durand 1880/Hamelle 1897 (vol. 2, 4–
6)/Metzler 1897 (Eng. trans. Paul
England)
Prem. SN, 22.1.81: M. Mazalbert

1878   *Nell* (Leconte de Lisle), S or T, op.
18/1, G flat
Ded. A Mme Camille Saint-Saëns
Hamelle 1880 (vol. 2/1)/Metzler 1896
(Eng. trans. A.S.)
Prem. SN, 29.1.81: Henriette Fuchs

1878?   *Le Voyageur* (Armand Silvestre), S or
T, op. 18/2, a
Ded. A M. Emmanuel Jadin
Hamelle 1880 (vol. 2/2)

1878   *Automne* (Armand Silvestre), Mez or
Bar, op. 18/3, b
Ded. A Mlle Alice Boissonnet
Hamelle 1880 (vol. 2/3)
Prem. SN, 29.1.81: Henriette Fuchs

1876–9
(and 1883)   First Piano Quartet (pno, vln, vla, vc),
op. 15, c
Ded. A Hubert Léonard
ms of rewritten finale (completed by
10.11.83) BN ms 17770, 31 pp. (first
version lost)
Hamelle 1884
Prem. with original finale, SN, 14.2.80:
Fauré with Ovide Musin (vln), M.
Van Waefelghem (vla), M. Mariotti
(vc)
Prem. with 1883 finale, SN, 5.4.84

1878–9   *Berceuse* for vln and pno, op. 16, D
Orch version, 1880, probably by Fauré
Ded. A Mme Hélène Depret
Hamelle 1880; Orch version 1898
Prem. SN, 14.2.80: Ovide Musin and
Fauré

	Prem. with orch, SN, 24.4.80: Ovide Musin (vln), cond. Édouard Colonne
1878–9	Violin Concerto: Allegro/Andante/ Finale, op. 14, d (see Appendix B)
	ms BN ms 17749, first movt. only, 64 pp
	Sketches coll. Mmes Ceillier and Maspéro
	Unpub.
	Prem. Allegro and Andante, SN, 12.4.80: Ovide Musin (vln), cond. Édouard Colonne
	Prem. Andante with pno accomp., SN, 27.12.78: Musin and André Messager
	(The finale, sketched in 1879, was abandoned incomplete)
1879?	Sextet from *Barnabé* (comic opera in one act, text by Jules Moineaux), for Georgette, Margot, Simone, Gervais, Jeanne and Barnabé with pno reduction of orch accomp., no op. no., c sharp
	ms BN ms 17744, 9 pp., n.d.
	Unpub.
1879 (finished by July)	*Les Berceaux* (Sully-Prudhomme), Mez or Bar, op. 23/1, b flat
	Ded. A Mlle Alice Boissonnet
	Hamelle 1881 (vol. 2/7)
	Prem. SN, 9.12.82: Jane Huré
?1877–9 (finished by 17 September 1879)	*Ballade* for pno, op. 19, F sharp
	Orch version by Fauré 'April 1881' (probably made at Liszt's suggestion)
	Ded. A Camille Saint-Saëns
	ms BN ms 15136 (orch score), 74 pp.
	Hamelle 1880; Orch version 1902
	Prem. SN, 23.4.81: Fauré, orch cond. Édouard Colonne
c.1879	*Notre amour* (Armand Silvestre), S or T, op. 23/2, E
	Ded. A Mme C. Castillon

Hamelle 1881 (vol. 2/8)/Metzler 1897 (Eng. trans. A.S.)

1880   *Élégie* for vc and pno, op. 24, c
Orch version mostly by Fauré 1895
Ded. A M. Jules Loëb
ms BN ms 17751 (orch score), 22 pp. Corrections and remarks in pencil in another hand. Last 3 pp. very sketchy.
Hamelle 1883; Orch version 1901
Prem. (private) probably *chez* Saint-Saëns, 14 Rue Monsieur-le-Prince, Paris 6, 21.6.80 (see *Gabriel Fauré: Correspondance* (ed. Jean-Michel Nectoux), Paris, Flammarion, 1980, pp. 99–100) ? Jules Loëb (vc), Fauré
Prem. (public) SN, 15.12.83: Jules Loëb (vc), Fauré
Prem. with orch, Monte Carlo, 23.1.1902: Carlo Sansoni (vc), cond. Léon Jéhin

c.1880   *Ave Maria* for T and Bar soli, hp, org, str quintet, no op. no., F
ms BN ms 17723 (score for soli and org), 6 pp. Parts (4), only hp and vc by Fauré
Unpub.

c.1880?   *Ave Maria* for S and Mez soli and org, no op. no., G
Ded. A Mme Auguez de Montalant
L. Grus 1912

c.1880   *Benedictus* for SATB choir, org and cb, op. posth., B flat
ms BN Rés. Vma. ms 893. Parts (6), only org by Fauré
Unpub.

1880–81   *Le Secret* (Armand Silvestre), Mez or Bar, op. 23/3, D flat
Ded. A Mlle Alice Boissonnet
Hamelle 1881 (vol. 2/9)
Prem. SN, 6.1.83: M. Quirot

c.1881	Second Nocturne for pno, op. 33/2, B Ded. A Mme Louise Guyon Hamelle 1883
1881?	*Le Ruisseau* (anon), female chorus and pno, op. 22, E flat Ded. A Mme Pauline Roger Hamelle 1881 Prem. SN, 14.1.82: Choeur Pauline Roger
1881?	First Barcarolle for pno, op. 26, a Ded. A Mme Montigny-Rémaury Hamelle 1881 Prem. SN, 9.12.82: Camille Saint-Saëns
'September 1881'	First Impromptu for pno, op. 25, E flat Ded. A Mme Emmanuel Potocka Hamelle 1881 Prem. SN, 9.12.82: Camille Saint-Saëns
'September 1881'	*Messe* for three-part female choir, with soloists, no op. no. First version with harmonium and vln solo in collaboration with André Messager: 1. *Kyrie* (Messager), 2. *Gloria* (Fauré), 3. *Sanctus* (Fauré), 4. *O Salutaris* (Messager), 5. *Agnus Dei* (Fauré) Unpub. Prem. Church at Villerville, Calvados, 4.9.81 (for the benefit of the fishermen of Villerville)
Summer 1882	Second version of 'Messe à l'Association des Pêcheurs de Villerville' with accomp. for small orch (fl, ob, cl, str quintet and harmonium), nos. 1–4 orch by Messager, no. 5 by Fauré Pub. planned (London, 1983) by Jean-Michel Nectoux, from ms he has discovered Prem. Church at Villerville, 10.9.1882 with Mlle de Hérédia, Mlle Leudet

and Mme Amélie Duez, ?Fauré (harmonium), cond. André Messager

1881—
'30 December
1906'

Third version of *Messe*, with the title *Messe basse* (*Low Mass*), for female choir, soloists and org, minus the movts. written by Messager, and with a new *Kyrie* by Fauré: 1. *Kyrie*, 2. *Sanctus*, 3. *Benedictus* (based on the 'Qui tollis' from the previous *Gloria*), 4. *Agnus Dei*
Ded. A Mme Camille Clerc
Heugel 1907, repr. 1934

1882

Chanson d'amour (Armand Silvestre), Mez or Bar, op. 27/1, F
Ded. A Mlle Jane Huré
Hamelle 1882 (vol. 2/10)
Prem. SN, 9.12.82: Jane Huré

1882

La Fée aux chansons (Armand Silvestre), S or T, op. 27/2, F
Ded. A Mme Edmond Fuchs
Hamelle 1883 (vol. 2/11)
Prem. SN, 12.5.88: Maurice Bagès

1882

La Naissance de Vénus (Paul Collin), mythological scene for soloists, chorus and orch, op. 29, D
Ded. A M. Antonin Guillot de Sainbris; later reded. to M. Sigismond Bardac
ms coll. Hamelle, 86 pp. entirely by Fauré, n.d.
Hamelle 1883 (VS only)
Prem. 8.3.83: Choeur de la Société chorale d'amateurs, M. Quirot (bass), Fauré, César Franck, M. Maton (pnos), cond. A. Guillot de Sainbris
Prem. with orch SN, 3.4.86: Choeur Guillot de Sainbris. Soloists: Mmes Castillon and Storm, MM. Anguez and Dupas, cond. Guillot de Sainbris

1882?

First Valse-Caprice for pno, op. 30, A
Ded. A Mlle Alex. Milochevitch
Hamelle 1883

291

'Paris. May 1883'	Second Impromptu for pno, op. 31, f Ded. A Mlle Sacha de Regina ms BN ms 17755, 9 pp. Hamelle 1883 Prem. SN, 10.1.85: Camille Saint-Saëns
1883	Third Nocturne for pno, op. 33/3, A flat Ded. A Mme Bohomoletz Hamelle 1883 Prem. SN, 23.1.86: Mme Bordes-Pène
1883	Third Impromptu for pno, op. 34, A flat Ded. A Mme Eugène Brun Hamelle 1883 Prem. SN, 10.1.85: Camille Saint-Saëns
'1 December 1883'	*Madrigal* (Armand Silvestre), vocal quartet (S A T B) or chorus with accomp. for pno or orch (by Fauré, 1883), op. 35, d (see Appendix B) Ded. A M. André Messager ms coll. Hamelle Hamelle 1884 Prem. SN, 12.1.84: Choeur de la SN
1884	Fourth Nocturne for pno, op. 36, E flat Ded. A Mme la Comtesse de Mercy-Argentau Hamelle 1885
1884	Fifth Nocturne for pno, op. 37, B flat Ded. A Mme Marie P. Christofle Hamelle 1885
'20 May 1884'	*Aurore* (Armand Silvestre), S or T, op. 39/1, G Ded. A Mme Henriette Roger-Jourdain Hamelle 1885 (vol. 2/12) Prem. SN, 13.12.84: Marguerite Mauvernay
'25 May 1884'	*Fleur jetée* (A. Silvestre), S or T, op. 39/2, f Ded. A Mme Jules Conin Hamelle 1885 (vol. 2/13)

Prem. SN, 13.12.84: Marguerite Mauvernay

'30 May 1884'

Le Pays des rêves (A. Silvestre), S or T, op. 39/3, A flat
Ded. A Mlle Thérèse Guyon
Hamelle 1885 (vol. 2/14)
Prem. SN, 27.12.84: Thérèse Guyon

1884

Les Roses d'Ispahan (Leconte de Lisle), Mez or Bar, op. 39/4, D
Orch by Fauré, 1897
Ded. A Mlle Louise Collinet
Hamelle 1885 (vol. 2/15)/Metzler 1896 (Eng. trans. Adela Maddison)
Prem. SN, 27.12.84: Thérèse Guyon

'July 1884'

Second Valse-Caprice for pno, op. 38, D flat
Ded. A Mme André Messager
ms BN ms 17784, 14 (18) pp.
Hamelle 1885
Prem. SN, 16.2.89: Mme Bordes-Pène

1884?

Papillon for vc and pno, op. 77, A
Hamelle 1898

1884

[Second] Symphony in d: Allegro deciso/Andante/Finale, op. 40 (see Appendix B)
ms BN Rés. Vma. ms 954. Two first vln parts (7th and 8th desks) only, 14, 14 pp. by M. Baudoux with autograph changes by Fauré on pp. 8–9 in both parts
Unpub. and otherwise destroyed by Fauré
Prem. SN, 15.3.85: Orch des Concerts Colonne, cond. Édouard Colonne
Second perf. Antwerp, 14.10.85, cond. Vincent d'Indy
The central Andante was also performed on 23.5.89 by the orch of the Concerts Lamoureux, cond. Charles Lamoureux, at the Exposition Universelle

'Taverny. August 1885'	Second Barcarolle for pno, op. 41 (orig. op. 40), G Ded. A Mlle Marie Poitevin ms BN ms 17740, 10 pp. Hamelle 1886 Prem. SN, 19.2.87: Marie Poitevin
1885	Third Barcarolle for pno, op. 42, G flat Ded. A Mme Henriette Roger-Jourdain ms BN ms 17741, 11 pp, n.d. Hamelle 1886
1886	*Noël* (Victor Wilder), canticle for S or T with pno and harmonium ad lib., op. 43/1, A flat Ded. A mon ami A. Talazac Hamelle 1886 (vol. 1/20)
1886	*Nocturne* (Villiers de l'Isle-Adam), Ctr or B, op. 43/2, E flat Ded. A Mme Henriette Roger-Jourdain ms Library of Congress, Washington. Copy by Fauré, 7 pp., dated '4 February 1892' Hamelle 1886 (vol. 2/17)
1886	Fourth Barcarolle for pno, op. 44, A flat Ded. A Mme Ernest Chausson Hamelle 1887
1885–6?	Second Piano Quartet (pno, vln, vla, vc), op. 45, g Ded. A Hans de [von] Bülow ms BN Cons. ms 9440, 111(115) pp. n.d. Sketches (finale only), BN ms 17787 (3), pp. 4–5, 7 Hamelle 1887 Prem. SN, 22.1.87: Fauré with MM. Remy (vln), Van Waefelghem (vla) and Delsart (vc)
1886– September 1887	*Pavane* for orch and chorus ad lib. (Comte Robert de Montesquiou), op. 50, f sharp (see Appendix B) Ded. (in 1890 presentation copy of orch

score in New York) A Mme la
Vicomtesse Greffulhe, née
Caraman-Chimay
ms OS in Pierpont Morgan Library,
New York (Mary Flagler Cary Music
Coll., Catalogue no. 104b), 27 pp.,
1890
Sketches BN ms 17787 (3), pp. 8–13
Version for chorus and pno pub. in
L'Album de Gaulois, 1888, entitled
'La Danse'.
Hamelle VS 1891, OS 1901
Prem. with chorus, SN, 28.4.88
Prem. with dancers, chorus and orch as
part of an entertainment given by the
Vicomtesse Greffulhe in the Bois de
Boulogne, Paris, 21.7.91

1887   *Les Présents* (Villiers de l'Isle-Adam),
S or T, op. 46/1, F
Ded. A M. le Comte Robert de
Montesquiou-Fezensac
ms coll. Mme Henry Goüin, Royau-
mont. Copy by Fauré dated '27 Jan-
uary 1892'
Hamelle 1888 (vol. 2/18)

1887   *Clair de lune* (Paul Verlaine), Mez or
Bar, op. 46/2, b flat
Orch probably by Fauré in 1888
(unpub.) (see Appendix B)
Ded. A M. Emmanuel Jadin
ms Sketches BN ms 17787 (1), pp. 40–
44, 46–8. Two versions
Hamelle 1888 (vol. 2/19)/Metzler 1897
(Eng. trans. Adela Maddison)
Prem. SN, 28.4.88: Maurice Bagès

1878 and
November
1887   *O Salutaris* for Bar, cb and org, op.
47/1, B
Second version by Fauré with accomp.
for 2 hn, hp, str quintet in B flat
Ded. A Jean-Baptiste Faure
ms BN ms 17720. Cb part (1 p.) for first
version in B by Fauré, also indicating

possible transposition to B flat
Sketch in BN ms 17787 (1), p. 10
Hamelle 1888 (both versions)
Prem. first version, Madeleine, 21.11.87:
Jean-Baptiste Faure (Bar)

1887–8   *Requiem* 'Messe des Morts' (first version) for mixed choir (S A TT BB),
boy soprano solo, hp, timp, org, vln
solo, vlas, vcs, cb, op. 48, d
1. *Introït et Kyrie* 1887, 2. *Sanctus* '8
January 1888' (with vln solo), 3. *Pie
Jesu* 1887, 4. *Agnus Dei* '6 January
1888', 5. *In Paradisum* 1887 and/or
early Jan. 1888
ms no. 1: BN ms 410, 25 pp.; no. 2: BN
ms 411, 15 pp; no. 4: BN ms 412, 20
pp.; no. 5: BN ms 413, 15 pp.
Sketches no. 1: BN ms 17787 (2), pp.
1–7, 9
no. 3: BN ms 17787 (1), p. 15; 17787
(2), pp. 8, 10–12
Pub. planned (London, 1983; ed.
Jean-Michel Nectoux)
Prem. Madeleine during midday mass
for M. Joseph Le Soufaché, 16.1.88:
Louis Aubert? (S solo), cond. Fauré

1877,
and 1886–
90   *Requiem* (second version) with Bar and
S soloists, chorus and orch. augmented by hns, tpts and tbns (see
Appendix B)
1. *Introït et Kyrie*, 2. *Offertoire* (1886,
1889–90), 3. *Sanctus*, 4. *Pie Jesu*, 5.
Agnus Dei, 6. *Libera me* (1877,
1890?), 7. *In Paradisum*
ms as above, plus sketch for no. 2 in BN
ms 17787 (3), pp. 16–20
Hamelle VS 1900
Prem. Madeleine, 21.1.93, cond. Fauré
No. 6 first performed in an SN concert
at the Church of St-Gervais, 28.1.92:
Louis Ballard (Bar)

1877– 1900	*Requiem* (third version) for full orch, prob. by Fauré (1899–1900) with woodwind and violins (movts. as second version) Hamelle OS 1900 Prem. Trocadéro, 12.7.1900: Mlle Torrès (S), M. Vallier (Bar), Eugène Gigout (org), orch Lamoureux, cond. Paul Taffanel
c.1888	*Petite pièce* for vc and pno, op. 49, G Unpub. and lost
1888?	*Souvenirs de Bayreuth* 'Quadrille sur les motifs favoris de l'Anneau du Nibelung—R. Wagner', for pno duet (in collaboration with Messager), op. posth., G ms BN ms 17769, 4 pp., in Messager's hand Costallat 1930
1888	*Caligula*, incidental music for the tragedy by Alexandre Dumas père, female chorus and orch, op. 52 (see Appendix B) 1. Prologue: (a) Fanfares. Marche; (b) Choeurs des Heures du Jour et de la Nuit; (c) Andante (orch) 2. Act 5: (a) Choeur: 'L'hiver s'enfuit'; (b) Air de danse; (c) Mélodrame et choeur: 'De roses vermeilles'; (d) Choeur final: 'César a fermé la paupière' Ded. A Ernest Dupuy; later editions ded. A Paul Porel [Raoul Parfouru] mss BN ms 17746 (1, 3–4) Corrections enlarging orig. orchestration for publication. (1) Prologue, pp. 1–38; (3) Act 5 (c) and (4) Act 5 (d), pp. 68–101 BN ms 2465. Prologue. Concert version for larger orch c. 1889, 21ff. Title by Saint-Saëns who donated the ms

BN ms 17747. Act 5 (c) VS reduction, pp. 44–54

BN ms 17663. Act 5 (b) Reduction for pno duet, pp. 35–43

BN Vma. ms 675. Vocal and instrumental parts with autograph corrections. Harmonium part and pno reduction of Act 5 (b) mostly by Fauré

Hamelle 1888 (VS), 1890 (OS)

Prem. Théâtre National de l'Odéon, 8.11.88, cond. Fauré

'Paris.
1 March
1888'

Maria, Mater gratiae, duet for T and Bar and org, op. 47/2, E flat

ms BN ms 17757, 5 pp.

Hamelle 1888, repr. 1911 in *Musique religieuse de Fauré.*

1888

Larmes (Jean Richepin), S or T, op. 51/1, c

Ded. A Mme la Princesse Edmond de Polignac (at the time of writing 'Princesse Wynarette de Scey-Montbéliard' before her remarriage in December 1893)

ms Pierpont Morgan Library, New York (ex Robert Owen Lehman Coll.), 5 pp.

Hamelle 1888 (vol. 2/20 now vol. 3/1)

1888

Au Cimetière (Jean Richepin), S or T, op. 51/2, e

Ded. A Mme Maurice Sulzbach

ms Pierpont Morgan Library, New York (ex Lehman Coll.), 5 pp.

Hamelle 1888 (vol. 2/21, now vol. 3/2)/Metzler 1896 (Eng. trans. A.S.)

Prem. SN, 2.2.89: Maurice Bagès

1888

Spleen—'Il pleure dans mon coeur' (Verlaine), Mez or Bar, op. 51/3, d

Ded. A Mme Henri Cochin

ms Pierpont Morgan Library, New York
(ex Lehman Coll.), 6 pp.
Hamelle 1888 (vol. 2/22, now vol. 3/3)

'23 December
1888'

Il est né le divin enfant, harmonized
carol for children's unison choir with
org, hp, ob, 2 vcs, cb, no op. no., B
flat
ms BN ms 17718, 12 pp., OS
Hamelle 1920 (VS). OS unpub.
Prem. Madeleine, 25.12.88

'March'
1889

Ecce fidelis servus (for the Feast of St
Joseph, 19 March), trio for S, T and
Bar with org, hp, vc and cb, op. 54,
B flat
ms Sold Paris 14.12.79 (Bodin no. 49)
Score 3 pp., and parts for 3 soloists
(arranged for the words 'Mulierem
fortem. . .'), hp, vc and cb (1p. each).
Cb part by a copyist, the rest by Fauré
Hamelle 1893 (VS), repr. 1911 in
Musique religieuse de Fauré

1889

Shylock incidental music for the adaptation of Shakespeare's *The Merchant of Venice* by Edmond
Haraucourt, T solo and orch, op. 57
Ded. A M. Paul Porel (Raoul Parfouru)
mss BN 17777, 164 pp. 1889–90. Conducting score for smaller orch with
numerous corrections enlarging orch
for publication. Two serenades for T
and orch by a copyist, the latter
appearing in two versions (no. 2
transposed into F by Fauré for
publication)
BN Vma. ms 917. Harmonium part, 11
pp. (1889) for 3rd and 5th tableaux
by Fauré. Used to reinforce orch in
initial performances
Hamelle 1897 Suite for T and orch: 1.
Chanson, 2. *Entr'acte*, 3. *Madrigal*,

299

4. *Épithalame*, 5. *Nocturne*, 6. *Final*
The two serenades *Chanson* and *Mad-rigal* are publ. with pno accomp. by Hamelle (vol. 3/5 and 6), also *Mad-rigal* by Metzler 1896 (Eng. trans. A.S.)
Prem. Théâtre National de l'Odéon, 17.12.89, cond. Fauré
Prem. (concert suite) SN, 17.5.90: T solo, M. Lepnestre, cond. Gabriel Marie

1889–90

En Prière (Stéphan Bordèse), canticle for voice and org, no op. no., E flat
Orch version by Fauré, 1890
Ded. A Mme Leroux-Ribeyre
Durand 1890 (coll. *Les Contes mystiques*)/Hamelle 1897 (vol. 2/16)/Metzler 1897
OS Hamelle 1923

1889–90

Tantum ergo for T solo, mixed choir, hp and org, op. 55, A
Second version with str by Fauré (unpub.)
Ded. A M. l'Abbé J. Panis
Hamelle 1893, repr. 1911
Prem. SN, St-Gervais, 22.1.91: M. Warmhodt (T) with M. Frank (hp)

c.1890

Noël d'enfants—'Les Anges dans nos campagnes', harmonization for uni-son children's choir and org, no op. no., A
Hamelle 1921

1890

La Passion, Prologue to the drama by Edmond Haraucourt for mixed cho-rus and orch, no op. no., g
ms BN Vma. ms 915. Orch and chorus parts with autograph corrections by Fauré
Unpub.
Prem. SN, 21.4.90, cond. Vincent d'Indy (originally intended for a con-

	cert at the Cirque d'hiver on 4.4.90, but the orchestration was not completed in time)
August 1890	*La Rose* (Leconte de Lisle), S or T, op. 51/4, F Ded. A M. Maurice Bagès Hamelle 1890 (vol. 2/23, now vol. 3/4)
June–September 1891	*Cinq mélodies 'de Venise'* (Verlaine), S or T, op. 58 1. *Mandoline.* Venice, June 1891, G 2. *En Sourdine.* 'Venice–Paris, 20 June 1891', E flat 3. *Green.* Paris, 28 June–July 1891, G flat 4. *A Clymène.* Paris, July–August 1891, e 5. *C'est l'extase.* Paris, August–September 1891, D flat Ded. A Mme la Princesse Edmond de Polignac (see op. 51/1, 1888) mss no. 2 sold Paris, 14.12.79 (Bodin no. 52). 6 pp., dated as above; no. 5 ex Robert Owen Lehman Coll. Hamelle 1891 (vol. 3/7–11)/no. 1. pub. in *Le Figaro musical* no. 2 (November 1891) and by Metzler 1896 (Eng. trans. Adela Maddison) Prem. SN, 2.4.92: Maurice Bagès
'Monday 27 February 1893'	*Sérénade du Bourgeois Gentilhomme* (Molière)—'Je languis nuit et jour', Mez or Bar, op. posth., f ms BN ms 17776, 'Acte 1 (Sérénade)', 6 pp. Heugel 1957 (Eng. trans. Rollo Myers)
'March 1893'	*Sicilienne* for vc and pno, op. 78, g (Probably part of the incidental music for *Le Bourgeois Gentilhomme*, see Appendix B) First orch version (incomplete) by Fauré, 1893? Second orch by Charles Koechlin 'Mon-

day 16 May [1898]', preserved intact in printed orch suite from *Pelléas et Mélisande* (op. 80)
Ded. A M. W. H. Squire
mss 1. For vc and pno, BN ms 17779, 6 pp.
  2. First orch version for fl, ob, str by Fauré, BN ms 17778, 2 pp. (unpub.)
  3. Second orch version by Koechlin, BN ms 15458 no. 3, 8 pp.
  4. London conducting score no. 5. coll. Nadia Boulanger (ms by Koechlin, 15 pp): copy in BN Vm. micr. 768

Metzler, London 1898/Hamelle 1898 (vc and pno)
OS Hamelle 1909 (incorporated later as no. 3 in orch suite, op. 80)
Prem. in Koechlin's 1898 orch as part of the incidental music for *Pelléas et Mélisande*, London, Prince of Wales' Theatre, 21.6.98, cond. Fauré
Prem. as part of the orch suite, 1.12.1912, cond. Messager

1893?

Menuet for small orch (for *Le Bourgeois Gentilhomme*?), no op. no., F
Orch by Fauré (fl, ob, cl, str) (see Ex. 22)
ms BN ms 17758, 4 pp., n.d.
Unpub.

1887—
'Prunay. August 1893'

Third Valse-Caprice for pno, op. 59, G flat
Ded. A Mme Philippe Dieterlen
ms BN ms 17787 (1), pp. 1–8. Sketch c. 1887
  Pierpont Morgan Library, New York, final version (1893), 17 pp. (ex Cortot and Lehman colls.)
Hamelle 1893

1892–
February 1894

La Bonne Chanson (Verlaine), S or T, op. 61

Version with str quintet and pno by Fauré, 1898 (unpub.)

1. *Une Sainte en son auréole*, '17 September 1892', A flat
2. *Puisque l'aube grandit*, 1893, G
3. *La Lune blanche*, '20 July' 1893, F sharp
4. *J'allais par des chemins perfides*, 1892, f sharp
5. *J'ai presque peur, en vérité*, '4 December 1893', e
6. *Avant que tu ne t'en ailles*, 1892, D flat
7. *Donc, ce sera par un clair jour d'été*, '9 August 1892', B flat
8. *N'est-ce pas?*, '25 May 1893', G
9. *L'Hiver a cessé*, 'February 1894', B flat

Ded. A Mme Sigismond Bardac

ms BN ms 17745 (1, 4, 9): nos. 1 (7 pp.), 4 (8 pp.), and 9 (9 pp.)

Sibley Music Library, Eastman School of Music, University of Rochester, New York, nos. 3 (7 pp.) and 7 (7 pp.)

coll. Mme Henry Goüin, Abbaye de Royaumont. Complete cycle: nos. 1 (6 pp.), 2 (8 pp.), 3 (5 pp., '20 July'), 4 (8 pp.), 5 (12 pp., 'Monday 4 December 1893'), 6 (6 pp.), 7 (7 pp., '9 August 1892'), 8 (8 pp., '25 May 1893'), 9 (9 pp., 'February [18]94')

Hamelle 1894 (in separate volume)

Prem. private concert *chez* Madeleine Lemaire, 25.4.94: Maurice Bagès, Fauré

Public prem. SN, 20.4.95: Jeanne Remacle, Fauré

Prem. (and only performance) with str quintet and pno, 1.4.98 at a private

	concert at the London home of Frank Schuster: Maurice Bagès, Fauré
1893–4	Fourth Valse-Caprice for pno, op. 62, A flat Ded. A Mme Max Lyon ms Pierpont Morgan Library, New York (ex Cortot, Lehman Coll.), 17 pp., n.d. Hamelle 1894 Prem. SN, 2.5.96: Léon Delafosse
1894	*Hymne à Apollon,* Greek melody from 3rd century BC discovered at Delphis and transcribed by Théodore Reinach with accomp. by Fauré for hp, fl, 2 cl, op. 63bis, a Ded. A M. Théodore Homolle O. Bornemann, Paris 1894; second corrected edition 1914 Prem. École des Beaux-Arts, 12.4.94: Jeane Remacle with M. Frank (hp), Fauré (harmonium)
1894	*Romance* for vc and pno, op. 69, A Ded. A M. Jules Griset mss BN ms 17775, first version for vc and org, simply called 'Andante', (see Ex. 16), 7 pp. corrected to bring org part in line with pub. pno version BN ms 17774, second version for vc and pno, 7 pp., vc part 2 pp. Title 'Romance en la majeur ... op. 63' added by editor Julien Hamelle at start Hamelle 1895 Prem. Geneva, 14.11.94: M. Rehberg, Fauré
'Prunay. 3 August 1894'	Sixth Nocturne for pno, op. 63, D flat Ded. A M. Eugène d'Eichthal ms Pierpont Morgan Library, New York (ex Cortot, Lehman Coll.), 11 pp. Hamelle 1894
1894	*Ave verum,* duo for S and Ctr, or T and Bar with org and cb, op. 65/1, f

ms BN ms 17739, 5 pp., n.d., with cb part ms 17719
Hamelle 1894, repr. 1911 in *Musique religieuse de Fauré*

'Bas-Prunay.
14 August 1894'

Tantum ergo for three-part female choir with soloists and org, op. 65/2, E
Hamelle 1894 (as op. 65/1)

1894

Sancta Mater for T solo, mixed choir and org, no op. no.
Hamelle 1922

'Bas-Prunay.
18 September
1894'

Fifth Barcarolle for pno, op. 66, f sharp
Ded. A Mme la Baronne Vincent d'Indy
ms Pierpont Morgan Library, New York (ex Cortot, Lehman Coll.), 11 pp.
Hamelle 1894
Prem. SN, 2.5.96: Léon Delafosse

'4 December
1894'

Prison (Verlaine), Mez or Bar, op. 83/1, e flat
ms Library of Congress, Washington, 8 pp
E. Fromont, Paris 1896 (as op. 51/1)/ Metzler, 1897 (Eng. trans. Adela Maddison, as op. 68/1)/Hamelle (vol. 2 as op. 73/1 in 1897; then vol. 3/14 as op. 83/1 in 1908)

'Paris.
17 December
1894'

Soir (Samain), Mez or Bar, op. 83/2, D flat
ms coll. Mme Henry Goüin, Royaumont, dated on p. 6. Page 7 is a revision of the last 11 bars as in the printed copy (see *Music and Letters*, lx no. 3 (1979), pp. 316–22)
Pub. as *Prison,* but op. 51/2 etc. Hamelle vol. 3/15. Also publ. as a musical supplement to *L'Illustration,* no. 2773 (18.4.96), without op. no.

'Paris. 25
March 1895'

Salve Regina for T (or S) and org, op. 67/1, F
Ded. A Mme Sigismond Bardac
ms BN Rés. Vma. ms 503, 4 pp.

Hamelle 1895/1911 in *Musique reli-gieuse de Fauré*. Also publ. as a mus-ical supplement to *L'Illustration*, (4.5.95)

1894–5

Ave Maria for Mez or Bar and org, op. 67/2, A flat
Ded. A Mme Adèle Bohomoletz
ms BN ms 17738, 3 pp. n.d.
Hamelle 1895, repr. 1911 in *Musique religieuse de Fauré*

1895 (finished September)

Thème et variations for pno, op. 73, c sharp
Ded. A Mlle Thérèse Roger
Metzler 1897/Hamelle 1897
Prem. St James's Hall, London, 10.12.96: Léon Delafosse

1895–6

Sixth Barcarolle for pno, op. 70, E flat
Ded. A M. Édouard Risler
Metzler 1896/Hamelle 1896
Prem. SN, 3.4.97: Édouard Risler

'21 April 1896'

Pleurs d'or, orig. *Larmes* (Albert Samain), duet for Mez and Bar, with pno, op. 72, E flat
Ded. A Mlle Camille Landi et M. David Bispham
Metzler 1896 (Eng. trans. Paul England)/Hamelle 1896
Prem. St James's Hall, London, 1.5.96: Camille Landi, David Bispham, Henry Bird (pno), Adolph Brodsky (vln)?

1893–7

Dolly, six pieces for pno duet, op. 56
1. *Berceuse*, 1893, E
2. *Mi-a-ou* (orig. *Messieu [R]Aoul!*), 'for the 20 June 1894', F
3. *Le Jardin de Dolly*, '1 January 1895', E
4. *Kitty Valse* (orig. *Ketty Valse*, Ketty being Dolly's brother Raoul's pet dog) '20 June 1896', E flat

5. *Tendresse*, 1896, D flat
6. *Le Pas Espagnol*, 1897, F
Ded. A Mlle Hélène Bardac (Dolly)
mss no. 1 BN ms 17922, 6 pp.
no. 2 coll. Hamelle (now Leduc)
no. 3 BN ms W.13. 6.², 5ff (9 pp.)
no. 4 coll. Hamelle (now Leduc)
    Orch score by Henri Rabaud c.1906,
    BN Cons. ms 9008
Hamelle 1894 (no. 1), 1897 (nos. 1–6)/
    Metzler 1897; OS Hamelle 1906
Prem. SN, 30.4.98: Édouard Risler and
    Alfred Cortot
Orch prem. Monte Carlo, 6.12.06,
    cond. Léon Jéhin
Ballet version (Louis Laloy), Théâtre
    des Arts, Paris, 9.1.13, cond.
    Gabriel Grovlez

1896–7?

Prélude for piano, no op. no., C
Durand 1897 (Volume of octave studies
    ed. Isidore Philipp)

1897

Morceau de lecture for vc (with pizzicato
    accomp. for vc 2), no op. no.
ms BN ms 17766; 3 pp.
Unpub.
Prem. Concours du Conservatoire, July
    1897

1878–9? revised
'Paris. July 1897'

Andante for vln and pno, op. 75, B flat
    (see Appendix B)
Ded. A Johannes Wolff
ms BN Cons. W.12. 4¹, 11 pp. with vln
    part (W.12.4²), 2 pp.
Hamelle 1897/Metzler 1897
Prem. SN, 22.1.98: Armand Parent
    (vln) and Germaine Polack (pno)

'22 August
1897'

Le Parfum impérissable (Leconte de
    Lisle), Mez or Bar, op. 76/1, E
Ded. A Paolo Tosti
ms Stanford University (Memorial
    Library of Music), California

Hamelle 1897 (vol. 3/12)/Metzler 1897
(Eng. trans. Adela Maddison)
Prem. Paris, 4.11.97: Émile Engel

September?
1897

Arpège (Albert Samain), Mez or Bar,
op. 76/2, e
Ded. A Mme Charles Dettelbach
Hamelle 1897 (vol. 3/13)/Metzler 1897
(Eng. trans. Adela Maddison). Also
pub. as a musical supplement to *Le
Figaro* on 16.10.97
Prem. SN, 30.4.98: Thérèse Roger

June 1898

Fantaisie for fl and pno, op. 79, e/C
Ded. A M. Paul Taffanel
Hamelle 1898
Prem. Paris Conservatoire, 28.7.98 by
the prizewinner Gaston Blanquart
(Orch version by Louis Aubert, 1957,
publ. Hamelle 1958)

June 1898

Morceau de lecture for fl and pno, no
op. no.
ms sold Paris 14.12.79 (Bodin no. 53),
2 pp.
Unpub.
Prem. Paris Conservatoire, 28.7.98

May–June 1898

Pelléas et Mélisande, incidental music
for the play by Maurice Maeterlinck
(Eng. trans. Jack Mackail), op. 80
First version for London, orch. by
Koechlin (unpub.)
ms BN ms 15458. '16 May'—'5 June
1898'
  BN Vm. micr. 768 (coll. Nadia
  Boulanger—ex Lehman) is the
  conducting score made by
  Koechlin and used by Fauré for
  the première at the Prince of
  Wales' Theatre on 21.6.98
Second version—orch suite—by
Fauré, based on Koechlin's original
orchestration, uses nos. 1, 10
and 17 of the London score:

Prélude — Fileuse — Molto adagio (*La Mort de Mélisande*)

ms coll. Mme Fauré-Fremiet: all mss by Fauré

mss *Prélude*: BN ms 17762 (1) pno score, 6 pp., 'May 1898'

BN ms 17763 orch score, revised version by Fauré, 19(20) pp. Large format paper, n.d. but c. 1899

BN ms' 17764 (1) orch score, definitive version used for printed suite, 18 pp. Smaller paper, dated on cover 'Paris. June 1898' but probably written 1899

Fileuse: BN ms 17762 (2) pno score, 8 pp., n.d. BN ms 17764 (2) orch score, definitive version, 19 pp., n.d.

Molto adagio: BN ms 17762 (3) pno score, 5 pp., n.d. BN ms 17764 (3) orch score, definitive version, 13 (14) pp., n.d. Used for printed suite (as ms 17764 (2))

Ded. A Mme la Princesse Edmond de Polignac

Hamelle 1901. The *Sicilienne* (see op. 78, 1893) was incorporated as the third movt of the orch suite in 1909

Prem. 3-movt suite. Concerts Lamoureux, 3.2.1901, cond. Camille Chevillard

4-movt suite, 1.12.12, cond. André Messager

(*Fileuse* was transcribed for pno solo by Alfred Cortot and publ. as op. 81 by Hamelle in 1902)

'31 May 1898'

Mélisande's Song — 'The King's three blind daughters' from Act 3, scene i of *Pelléas et Mélisande* (London score no. 11), Mez and pno or orch, op. posth., d (see Appendix B)

mss BN ms 17765, 4 pp (copy by Alfred Cortot c. 1950). Also in BN Vm. micr. 768 no. 11, 5 pp. for fl, cl, str. Orch by Koechlin
Hamelle 1937
Prem. London 21.6.98? Mrs Patrick Campbell, cond. Fauré
(Orch revised by Koechlin 27.8.36 as op. 159bis. Version with larger orch first performed on 21.12.36, Salle de la Schola Cantorum, Paris)

August 1898

Seventh Nocturne for pno, op. 74, c sharp
Ded. A Mme Adela Maddison
Hamelle 1899
Prem. SN, 20.3.1901: Alfred Cortot

February–
July 1900

Prométhée, lyric tragedy in three acts by Jean Lorrain and André-Ferdinand Hérold, op. 82
1. First version (1900) orch by Charles Eustace (wind band) and Fauré (str and hps)
ms Bibl. de l'Opéra, Paris, Rés. 2005 (by Fauré). Eustace's cond. score with some changes by Fauré—BN Rés. Vma. ms 940.
Ded. A M. Fernand Castelbon de Beauxhostes
Hamelle 1900 (VS)
Four performances at the Arènes de Béziers, 27 and 28.8.1900, and 25 and 27.8.01, cond. Fauré
Also Hippodrome, Paris, 5.12.07, and Paris Opéra, 17.12.07, cond. Fauré
2. Second version for symphony orch by Roger Ducasse (1914–16), ms coll. Hamelle (now Leduc). Fauré also reorchestrated Act 1 Prelude, nos. 3 and 6, and Act 3 nos. 4–5 for symphony orch c. 1902: BN mss 17768 (1–5), 28, 26, 31, 9, 10

pp. with BN ms 17768 (6) giving a sketch of the reorch. of 17768 (5), 22 pp. Also, BN Vma. ms 916 gives a VS of Act 2 Prelude and first chorus (1900?), 28 pp. by a copyist but with corrections by Fauré

Unpub.

Prem. Paris Opéra, 17.5.17, cond. Camille Chevillard

Autumn 1901

Le Voile du bonheur, incidental music for the play by Georges Clemenceau, op. 88. 'Chinese' music for fl, cl, tpt, hp, gong, tubophone, vlns, vlas, vcs

mss BN ms 17786, conducting score, 28 pp. BN Vma. ms 920. Orch parts (10) by copyist

Unpub.

Prem. Théâtre de la Renaissance, 4.11.01, cond. Émile Vuillermoz

'15 April 1902'

Cadenza for the 24th Piano Concerto of Mozart (K.491) in c, op. posth.

Pierre Schneider 1927 (edition and fingering by Marguerite Hasselmans)

Prem. Concerts Hasselmans, 15.4.02: Marguerite Hasselmans

1869, 1878–9, 1899, 1901–2

Huit pièces brèves for pno, op. 84 (see Appendix B)

(Titles added by Hamelle against Fauré's wishes in the second printing of 1903)

1. [*Capriccio*], July 1899, E flat
2. [*Fantaisie*], 1902?, A flat
3. [Fugue], '30 June 1869', revised 1878–9, a
4. [*Adagietto*], '27 August 1902', e
5. [*Improvisation*], '9 July 1901', c sharp
6. [Fugue], '30 November 1869', e
7. [*Allégresse*], '2 August 1902', C
8. [Eighth Nocturne], '4 September 1902', D flat

Ded. A Mme Jean Léonard-Koechlin
mss coll. Mme Henry Goüin, Royaumont: no. 4 titled 'Petite pièce',
4 pp., no. 8 titled 'Pièce', 7 pp.
Dates as above
BN Rés. Vma ms 504, no. 6, 7 pp.
(pp. 2–3 blank)
Sketch no. 8 BN ms 17787 (5), pp.
4–5
Hamelle 1902. No. 1 written for Concours du Conservatoire on 22 July
1899 and publ. in *Le Figaro* on
29.7.99. The 1902 version is more
fully developed. Piece no. 5 was written for the Concours d'hommes on
19 July 1901 and publ. in *Le Monde
Musical* on 30.8.01
Prem. nos. 2, 4, 7, 8, SN, 18.4.03:
Ricardo Viñes

'28 March 1902'

Accompagnement (Albert Samain),
Mez or Bar, op. 85/3, G flat
Ded. A Mme Édouard Risler
ms Music Library, Yale University,
New Haven, Connecticut, 8 pp.
Hamelle 1902 (vol. 3/20)

'29 September
1902'

Dans la forêt de septembre (Catulle
Mendès), Mez or Bar, op. 85/1, G
flat
Ded. A Mlle Lydia Eustis
ms sketches BN ms 17787 (5), pp. 1–3,
6–7
Hamelle 1902 (vol. 3/18)

Autumn 1902

La Fleur qui va sur l'eau (C. Mendès),
Mez or Bar, op. 85/2, b
Ded. A Mlle Pauline Segond
ms sketches BN ms 17787 (5), pp. 8–17,
20–22
Hamelle 1902 (vol. 3/19)

Autumn 1902

Dans le ciel clair (Leconte de Lisle),
Mez or Bar, orig. to be op. 85/3?, E

	flat. Unfinished sketches (stanzas 1 and 4 only) ms sketches BN ms 17787 (5), pp. 19, 23–32 (see Exx. 59–61) Unpub.
July 1903	*Morceau de lecture* for vln and pno, no op. no, A Written for the Concours du Conservatoire, 24 July 1903 Publ. in *Le Monde musical*, 30.8.03
July 1904	*Morceau de lecture* for harp, no op. no. Written for the Concours du Conservatoire, 25 July 1904 Unpub.
July 1904	Impromptu for harp, op. 86, D flat (see Appendix B) Written for the Concours du Conservatoire, 25 July 1904 Ded. A Mme Alphonse Hasselmans Durand 1904 (as Sixth Impromptu for pno, op. 86bis, Durand, 1913) Prem. Conservatoire, 1904: Mlle Charlotte Landrin (Mme Jacques Lerolle); SN, 7.1.05: Micheline Kahn
1904	*Le Plus Doux Chemin* (Armand Silvestre), Mez or Bar, op. 87/1, f (see Appendix B) Ded. A Mme Édouard Risler Hamelle 1907 (vol. 3/16)
1904	*Le Ramier* (A. Silvestre), Mez or Bar, op. 87/2, e Ded. A Mlle Claudie Segond The Gramophone Company, Milan, 1904/Hamelle 1907 (vol. 3/17)
'3 November 1904'	*Tantum ergo* for S solo and mixed four-part choir and org, no op. no., F Version with str by Fauré unpub. ms BN ms 17782, 4 pp. '3 November 1904'. First version in F

coll. Durand (D & F 6512), 4 pp. 'Pour la Messe de mariage de Mlle Greffulhe'. Final version in G flat
Durand 1905/Hamelle, *Musique religieuse de Fauré*, 1911
Prem. Madeleine, 14.11.04

1905?

Piece for 2 cbs, no op. no., A
Publ. in *Dechiffrage du manuscrit*, Lemoine, 1905

1905

Jules César, incidental music for Victor Hugo's translation of Shakespeare, based on music for *Caligula* (op. 52, 1888), no op. no., orch by Fauré? (see Appendix B)
ms coll. Hamelle (anonymous copy of score only)
Unpub.
Prem. Théâtre antique d'Orange, 7.8.05, cond. Édouard Colonne

1887, 1891–4, 1903–5

First Quintet (pno, 2 vln, vla, vc), op. 89, d
Ded. A Eugène Ysaÿe
mss BN Rés. Vma 895. Instrumental parts (27, 27, 23, 23 pp.) [1906] used for first performance and printed parts. By copyist, but with last page of each part by Fauré and numerous autograph corrections
BN ms 17787 (1), p. 19 sketch for finale theme (1887)
BN ms 17772 sketches c. 1891, 2 pp. for first version?
Schirmer, New York 1907
Prem. Cercle Artistique, Brussels, 23.3.06; then Paris, Salle Pleyel, 30.4.06: both by Fauré and the Ysaÿe Quartet (Eugène Ysaÿe, Édouard Deru, Léon Van Hout, Joseph Jacob)

Zürich.
11–14 August 1905

Seventh Barcarolle for pno, op. 90, d
Ded. A Mme Isidore Philipp

314

Le Figaro Illustré, Christmas edition 1905/*Le Ménestrel* 18.2.06/Heugel 1906

Prem. Salle Érard, 3.2.06: Arnold Reitlinger

August 1905f

Fourth Impromptu for pno, op. 91, D flat

Ded. A Mme de Marliave (Marguerite Long)

ms BN ms 17756, 14 pp, n.d.

Heugel 1906

Prem. SN, 12.1.07: Édouard Risler

1876–7 rev.
Vitznau, 10–17
August 1906

Ave Maria for 2S and org, op. 93, b (see Appendix B)

Ded. A Mme Georges Kinen (Anita Eustis)

ms BN ms 17737, 10 pp. Dated p. 10: '10 August 1906' (LI, p. 121 says *Ave Maria* completed on 17 August)

Heugel 1906

Vitznau, 17–21
August 1906

Le Don silencieux (Jean Dominique, real name Mme Marie Closset), Mez or Bar, op. 92, E

Ded. A Mme Octave Maus

ms BN ms 17761, 5 pp. Orig. title '*Offrande.* op. 94'. Dated p. 5, '20 August 1906' (LI, p. 121 suggests that the song was completed on 21 August)

Heugel 1906

Prem. La Libre esthétique, Brussels, 12.3.07: Jane Bathori, Fauré

1906

Chanson (Henri de Régnier), Mez or Bar, op. 94, e

Heugel 1907

1906–7

Vocalise-étude for S and pno, no op. no., e

ms BN ms 17785, 5 pp. Printer's date 31.1.07

Leduc 1907 (no. 1 in the collection of vocalises-études by A. L. Hettich)

'30 December 1906'

Messe basse (third version): see 1881–2

June 1906–January 1910

La Chanson d'Ève (Charles Van Lerberghe), Mez or Bar, op. 95

1. *Paradis*, '8 September 1906', e: Heugel 1907
2. *Prima verba*, '28 September 1906', G flat: Heugel 1907
3. *Roses ardentes*, June 1908, E: Heugel 1909
4. *Comme Dieu rayonne*, 1909, e: Heugel 1909
5. *L'Aube blanche*, June 1908, D flat: Heugel 1908
6. *Eau vivante*, 1909, C: Heugel 1909
7. *Veilles-tu, ma senteur de soleil?*, January 1910, D: Heugel 1910
8. *Dans un parfum de roses blanches*, 1909, G: Heugel 1909
9. *Crépuscule*, '4 June 1906', d: Heugel 1906
10. *O Mort, poussière d'étoiles*, January 1910, D flat: Heugel 1910

Ded. A Mme Jeanne Raunay

mss BN ms 17748 (1–9), 13, 5, 5, 4, 4, 6, 6, 6, 7 pp. Humanities Research Center, University of Texas at Austin, no. 10 (5 pp.)

Publ. in 1 vol. by Heugel 1911

Prem. nos. 1, 2 and 9, Bechstein (now Wigmore) Hall, London, 18.3.08: Jeanne Raunay, Fauré

nos. 1–3, 5, 4, 6 and 9, Salle Érard, 26.5.09: Raunay, Fauré

Complete cycle, SMI inaugural concert, 20.4.10: Raunay, Fauré

1906

Eighth Barcarolle for pno, op. 96, D flat

Ded. A Mme Suzanne Alfred-Bruneau

ms BN ms 17742, 10 pp, n.d.

Heugel 1908

1908

Ninth Nocturne for pno, op. 97, b

Ded. A Mme Alfred Cortot

ms BN ms 17759, 6 pp, n.d.
Heugel 1908

1908? *Sérénade* for vc and pno, op. 98, b
Ded. A Pablo Casals
Heugel 1908

'November 1908' Tenth Nocturne for pno, op. 99, b
(mostly 9–15 Ded. A Mme Brunet-Lecomte
September 1908, ms BN ms 17760, 8 pp. 'November 1908'
see LI, p. 167) Heugel 1909

early 1909 Ninth Barcarolle for pno (orig. op. 100),
op. 101, a
Ded. A Mme Charles Neef
ms coll. Heugel, sold Paris 14.12.79
(Bodin no. 53), 9 pp., nd.
Heugel 1909
Prem. Salle Érard, 30.3.09: Marguerite
Long

1909 Fifth Impromptu for pno, op. 102, f
sharp
Ded. A Mlle Cella Delavrancea
Heugel 1909
Prem. Salle Érard, 30.3.09: Marguerite
Long

1909–10 Nine Preludes for pno, op. 103
1. D flat: finished January 1910
2. c sharp: finished January 1910
3. g: finished January 1910
4. F: finished 20.7.10, Lugano
5. d: 20–27 July 1910, Lugano
6. e flat: 27 July–August 1910, Lugano
7. A: finished 5 September 1910,
Lugano
8. c: Autumn 1910
9. e: Autumn 1910
Ded. A Mlle Élisabeth de Lallemand
ms no. 1 BN Cons ms 414, 4ff (3 pp.
music), '1910'
no. 2 BN ms 17767, 6 pp. n.d.
nos. 4–8 Pierpont Morgan Library,
New York (ex Lehman Coll.), 5,
6, 3, 5, 5 pp., n.d.

no. 4 (copy by Fauré) in Isabella Stewart Gardner Museum, Boston, Massachusetts, 6 pp., '1912'
no. 6 BN Rés. Vma. ms 502, 4 pp. (microfilm)
no. 7 sold Paris 20.6.77 (Hôtel Drouot, no. 32), 6 pp.
nos. 1–3 Heugel 1910; nos. 4–9 Heugel 1911; nos. 1–9 in one vol. 1923
Prem. SMI (nos. 1–3), 17.5.10: Marguerite Long

1907–9, 1911–12

Pénélope, lyric drama in three acts (René Fauchois), no op. no.
Orch Act 2, scene ii (VS, pp. 135–78) and end Act 3 by Fernand Pécoud, otherwise by Fauré 2.9.12–12.1.13
Ded. A Camille Saint-Saëns
ms Bibl. de l'Opéra Rés. A. 843a (1–2)—Vol. 1: Act 1. 477ff. All by Fauré except ff175–8 recopied in another hand; Vol. 2: Act 2. 202ff. ff81–9 and 147–53 missing and sold Paris, 14.12.79 (Bodin no. 54, ex coll. Heugel. Part of scene ii by Pécoud with corr. by Fauré = Heugel VS pp. 143–6 and 163–6). Orchestration by Fauré up to p. 57, where Pécoud takes over; Act 3. ff numbered 19–232. Orchestrated by Fauré (except ff231–2). Final section orchestrated by Pécoud missing, also ff1–18 (= Heugel VS pp. 179–84 and 242 to the end). Sketches BN ms 17787 (4)
Heugel VS 1912. OS 1913. Also Act 1 Prelude separately 1913
Prem. Monte Carlo, 4.3.13 (also 11 and 15 March): Lucienne Bréval, Charles Rousselière, cond. Léon Jéhin
Paris, Théâtre des Champs-Élysées, 10.5.13: Bréval, Lucien Muratore (Ulysse), cond. Louis Hasselmans (ten performances, four in

the October 1913 revival in the same theatre)

Paris, Opéra-Comique, 20.1.19: Lubin, Rousselière, cond. François Ruhlmann. Repeated 1922–4, 1927, 1931 (63 perf.)

Paris Opéra, 14.3.43: Germaine Lubin, Georges Jouatte, cond. Ruhlmann (performed 1943–9)

Also Brussels, Théâtre de la Monnaie, 1.12.13: Claire Croiza, M. Darmel, cond. Corneil de Thoran

Productions in Rouen (1913), Orange (1923), Strasbourg (1923), Antwerp (1924), Nice (1924), Bordeaux (1927), Lyon (1927)

1913	Eleventh Nocturne for pno, op. 104/1, f sharp Ded. En souvenir de Noémi Lalo ms Pierpont Morgan Library, New York (ex Lehman Coll.), 6 pp., n.d. Durand 1913
August– 'October 1913'	Tenth Barcarolle for pno, op. 104/2, a Ded. A Mme Léon Blum ms coll. Gregor Piatigorsky, USA, 7 pp. Durand 1913
1913	Eleventh Barcarolle for pno, op. 105, g Ded. A Mlle Laura Albéniz ms BN ms 17743, 9 pp., n.d. coll. Durand, first page (bars 1–12) only: copy Durand 1914
21 July–November 1914	*Le Jardin clos* (Charles Van Lerberghe), S or T, op. 106 1. *Exaucement*, C: A Mme Albert Mockel 2. *Quand tu plonges tes yeux dans mes yeux*, F: A Mlle Germaine Sanderson 3. *La Messagère*, G: A Mme Gabrielle Gills

319

4. *Je me poserai sur ton coeur*, E flat,
   A Mme Louis Vuillemin
5. *Dans la nymphée*, D flat: A Mme
   Clare Croiza
6. *Dans la pénombre*, E: A Mme
   Houben-Kufferath
7. *Il m'est cher, Amour, le bandeau*, F:
   A Mme Faliero-Dalcroze
8. *Inscription sur le sable*, e: A Mme
   Durand-Texte
ms. BN Cons. ms 415, 16ff (28 pp.
   music)
   Coll. Durand (D & F 9341), 30 pp.
Durand 1915
Prem. Concerts Casella, 28.1.15: Claire
   Croiza, Fauré

Saint-Raphaël,
4 August– c.15
September 1915

Twelfth Nocturne for pno, op. 107, e
Ded. A M. Robert Lortat
ms coll. Gregor Piatigorsky, USA, 11
   pp., n.d.
Durand 1916
Prem. Concerts Jacques Durand,
   23.11.16: Louis Diémer

Saint-Raphaël,
mid-August–
c.15 September
1915

Twelfth Barcarolle for pno, op. 106 bis,
   E flat
Ded. A Louis Diémer
Durand 1916
Prem. Concerts Jacques Durand,
   23.11.16: Louis Diémer

Évian and Paris,
August 1916–
May 1917

Second Violin Sonata, op. 108, e
Ded. A sa Majesté Élisabeth, reine des
   Belges
ms Ex Lehman Coll., New York. Sold
   c.1971
Durand 1917
Prem. SN, 10.11.17: Lucien Capet,
   Alfred Cortot

Mostly Saint-
Raphaël, 22 July–
17 August 1917

First Cello Sonata, op. 109, d
Ded. A Louis Hasselmans
ms Library and Museum of the Performing Arts, New York Public

320

Library at the Lincoln Center, first movt only, 20 pp., n.d.
Sold Paris 14.12.79 (Bodin no. 55), 3 pp. (last 38 bars of first movt.)
Sketch for finale BN ms 17771 (2), pp. 25–6
Durand 1918
Prem. SN, 10.11.17: Gérard Hekking, Alfred Cortot

1918

Une Châtelaine en sa tour for hp, op. 110, a
Ded. A Mme Micheline Kahn
Durand 1918
Prem. SN, 30.11.18: Micheline Kahn

Évian and Nice,
18 March–winter
1918

Fantaisie for pno and orch., op. 111, G
Orch by Marcel Samuel-Rousseau. Pno solo part revised by Alfred Cortot
Ded. A Alfred Cortot
mss 1. Original 2-pno version marked '2ᵉ piano', 39 ff, BN ms 17753. Recopied sections and sketches on versos of ff5, 10, 11, 15, 22, 30 and 31
2. Proof copy (D & F 9647) of 2-pno version, corr. by Cortot and Fauré, BN Rés. Vma 198
3. Orch score (M. Samuel-Rousseau with corr. by Fauré), 117 pp., BN Rés. Vma ms 894
4. Copy of orch score, 118 pp., with parts (30), BN Vma ms 913
5. Pierpoint Morgan Library, New York: 2-pno version, 42 pp. 'A Alfred Cortot' (Piano 1 part)
Durand 1919 (OS and 2-pno version)
Prem. Monte Carlo, 12.4.19: Marguerite Hasselmans, cond. Léon Jéhin.
Paris, SN, 14.5.19: Alfred Cortot

1867–1919

Masques et Bergamasques, divertissement in one act (René Fauchois), op. 112 (see Appendix B)

Stage version:
1. *Ouverture* (1867–8: *Intermezzo de symphonie*), F
2. *Pastorale* (1919), D
3. *Madrigal* (1883) with orch
4. *Le Plus Doux Chemin* (op. 87/1, 1904), f, with orch
5. *Menuet* (1918–19), F
6. *Clair de lune* (op. 46/2, 1887), c, with orch
7. *Gavotte* (1869), d, orch by Marcel Samuel-Rousseau
8. *Pavane* (op. 50, 1887)
Ded. A mes arrières-petites-nièces Nicole et Huguette de Réveillac
ms coll. Durand (D 9802). Orch suite (movts. 1, 5, 7 and 2 above), 29, 13, 26, 19 pp.
Durand 1919 (orch suite: *Ouverture-Menuet-Gavotte-Pastorale*)
Prem (stage) Monte Carlo, 10.4.19, cond. Léon Jéhin. Paris, Opéra-Comique, 4.3.20, cond. Fernand Masson
Prem. (orch suite) Concerts du Conservatoire, 16.11.19, cond. Philippe Gaubert

Annecy,
c.18 July–
19 August 1919

Mirages (Baronne Renée de Brimont), Mez or Bar, op. 113
1. *Cygne sur l'eau*, c.18 July–2 August 1919, F
2. *Reflets dans l'eau*, finished c.2 August 1919, B flat
3. *Jardin nocturne*, c. 2–14 August 1919, E flat
4. *Danseuse*, 15–19 August 1919, d
Ded. A Mme Gabriel Hanotaux
ms BN Cons. ms 11546
Durand 1919
Prem. SN, 27.12.19: Madeleine Grey, Fauré

Monte Carlo,
6–'8 December
1919'

C'est la paix (Georgette Debladis), S or
T, op. 114, A
ms coll. Durand (D & F 9859), 3 pp.
Le Figaro, 10.10.20 (as winning entry
in poetry competition with the theme
of peace); Durand, 1920

2 September 1919–
February 1921

Second Quintet (pno, 2 vln, vla, vc),
op. 115, c
Ded. A M. Paul Dukas
ms Houghton Library, Harvard University, Cambridge, Massachusetts
(f. MS. Mus 36: 75ff., 135 pp. music)
'March 1921'. Purchased by John
Singer Sargent and Charles Martin
Loeffler
BN ms 17773, 13ff. On rectos nearly
definitive version of finale (D & F
9964 p. 55 bar 11–p. 74 bar 20). On
versos 1–6 sketches for first movt.,
7v and 10v sketches for finale, 13
recto sketches for slow movt.
Durand 1921
Prem. SN, 21.5.21: Robert Lortat
(pno), André Toumet and Victor
Gentil (vlns), Maurice Vieux (vla),
Gérard Hekking (vc)

Nice, c.10–21
February 1921

Thirteenth Barcarolle for pno, op. 116,
C
Ded. A Mme A. Soon Gumaelius
ms coll. Durand (D & F 10028), 6 pp.
'Nice. February 1921' 'A Madame
Magda A. N. Gumaelius'
Durand 1921
Prem. SN, 28.4.23: Blanche Selva

Nice, c.22 February–
4 March 1921

Chant funéraire for the centenary of the
death of Napoleon I, no op. no., c
Orch for wind band by Guillaume Balay
(see Appendix B)
ms coll. Durand, 9 pp. by G. Balay:
'Paris, 31 March 1921'
Durand 1921

Prem. Hôtel des Invalides, Paris, 5.5.21: Orchestre de la Garde Républicaine, cond. G. Balay

c.15 March–
10 November 1921

Second Cello Sonata, op. 117, g (see Appendix B)
Ded. A Charles Martin Loeffler
ms sent to Loeffler and probably destroyed in a fire at his house in 1935. BN ms 17773 f 13 verso gives sketches for the first movt.
Durand 1922
Prem. SN, 13.5.22: Gérard Hekking, Alfred Cortot

Autumn 1921

L'Horizon chimérique (Jean de La Ville de Mirmont), Mez or Bar, op. 118
1. *La Mer est infinie*, D
2. *Je me suis embarqué*, D flat
3. *Diane, Séléné*, E flat
4. *Vaisseaux, nous vous aurons aimés*, D
Ded. A M. Charles Panzéra
Prem. SN, 13.5.22: Charles Panzéra, Magdeleine Panzéra-Baillot

Nice, 21–'31
December 1921'

Thirteenth Nocturne for pno, op. 119, b
Ded. A Mme Fernand Maillot
Durand 1922
Prem. SN, 28.4.23: Blanche Selva

Annecy, Paris,
May 1922–Spring
1923

Trio (pno, vln, vc), op. 120, d
Ded. A Mme Maurice Rouvier
mss University of Chicago Library ms 767. First version of finale in 3/4 time with fingerings added by Marguerite Hasselmans
    BN ms 17787 (5), pp. 46–7. Sketch for first movt.
Durand 1923
Prem. SN, 12.5.23: Tatiana de Sansévitch (pno), Robert Krettly (vln), Jacques Pathé (vc)
Second perf. Paris, 29.6.23: Alfred Cortot, Jacques Thibaud, Pablo Casals

Paris, Divonne, Annecy, August 1923 –11 September 1924	String Quartet, op. 121, e (see Appendix B) Ded. A Camille Bellaigue mss BN Cons. ms 417, 49 (12, 13, 24) pp. BN ms 17771 (1–2), 8 and 26 (20) pp. Sketches for finale, with sketches for slow movt. on pp. 17–18 of ms 17771 (2) and ms 17787(7), p. 2. Sketches for finale also on p. 11v of ms 17773 Durand 1925 Prem. SN, 12.6.25: Jacques Thibaud and Robert Krettly (vlns), Maurice Vieux (vla), André Hekking (vc)
1924	*Ronsard à son âme* (Ronsard) Sketch of song for *Revue Musicale* (May 1924), commemoration of the 400th anniversary of Ronsard's birth. Destroyed when Fauré knew that Ravel had set the same text

Transcriptions of the music of Saint-Saëns
1. Overture to *La Princesse jaune* (op. 30) for pno duet and 2 pnos (8 hands); transcribed 1887; Durand
2. Fourth Piano Concerto in c (op. 44) for 2 pnos; Durand
3. Suite for orchestra (op. 49) for 2 pnos (8 hands); Durand
4. *Suite Algérienne* (op. 60) for pno duet, ms coll. Durand (D & F 7867), 43 (11, 17, 5, 10) pp.; Durand
5. Septet (op. 65) for pno duet, ms coll. Durand; Durand

LIST OF WORKS BY GENRE

(i) *Songs (and duets)*

op.	1/1	*Le Papillon et la fleur* (V. Hugo), 1861
	1/2	*Mai* (V. Hugo), 1861?
	2/1	*Dans le ruines d'une abbaye* (V. Hugo), c.1865–8
	2/2	*Les Matelots* (Théophile Gautier), c.1865–8
	3/1	*Seule!* (Th. Gautier), 1871
	3/2	*Sérénade toscane* (Romain Bussine), c.1878?
	4/1	*Chanson du pêcheur (Lamento)* (Th. Gautier), 1872?
	4/2	*Lydia* (Leconte de Lisle), c.1870
	5/1	*Chant d'automne* (Charles Baudelaire), c.1871?
	5/2	*Rêve d'amour* (V. Hugo), 1862?
	5/3	*L'Absent* (V. Hugo), 1871
	6/1	*Aubade* (Louis Pomey), c.1873
	6/2	*Tristesse* (Th. Gautier), c.1873
	6/3	*Sylvie* (Paul de Choudens), 1878
	7/1	*Après un rêve* (anon. adapt. Romain Bussine), 1878?
	7/2	*Hymne* (Ch. Baudelaire), c.1870
	7/3	*Barcarolle* (Marc Monnier), 1873
	8/1	*Au Bord de l'eau* (Sully-Prudhomme), 1875
	8/2	*La Rançon* (Ch. Baudelaire), 1871?
	8/3	*Ici-bas!* (Sully-Prudhomme), c.1874
	10/1	*Puisqu'ici-bas toute âme* (duet for 2 S) (V. Hugo), 1863, rev. 1873
	10/2	*Tarentelle* (duet for 2 S) (Marc Monnier), 1873
	18/1	*Nell* (Leconte de Lisle), 1878
	18/2	*Le Voyageur* (Armand Silvestre), 1878?
	18/3	*Automne* (A. Silvestre), 1878
	21	*Poème d'un jour* (Charles Grandmougin), 1878
		1. *Rencontre*
		2. *Toujours*
		3. *Adieu*
	23/1	*Les Berceaux* (Sully-Prudhomme), 1879
	23/2	*Notre amour* (A. Silvestre), 1879?
	23/3	*Le Secret* (A. Silvestre), 1880–81
	27/1	*Chanson d'amour* (A. Silvestre), 1882
	27/2	*La Fée aux chansons* (A. Silvestre), 1882
	39/1	*Aurore* (A. Silvestre), 1884
	39/2	*Fleur jetée* (A. Silvestre), 1884
	39/3	*Le Pays des rêves* (A. Silvestre), 1884
	39/4	*Les Roses d'Ispahan* (Leconte de Lisle), 1884

op. 43/1   *Noël* (Victor Wilder), 1886
43/2   *Nocturne* (Villiers de l'Isle-Adam), 1886
46/1   *Les Présents* (V. de l'Isle-Adam), 1887
46/2   *Clair de lune* (Paul Verlaine), 1887
51/1   *Larmes* (Jean Richepin), 1888
51/2   *Au Cimetière* (J. Richepin), 1888
51/3   *Spleen*—'Il pleure dans mon coeur' (Verlaine), 1888
51/4   *La Rose* (Leconte de Lisle), 1890
57   *Chanson* and *Madrigal* from *Shylock,* 1889
58   *Cinq mélodies 'de Venise'* (Verlaine), 1891
    1. *Mandoline*
    2. *En Sourdine*
    3. *Green*
    4. *A Clymène*
    5. *C'est l'extase*
61   *La Bonne Chanson* (Verlaine), 1892–4
    1. *Une Sainte en son auréole,* 1892
    2. *Puisque l'aube grandit,* 1893
    3. *La Lune blanche,* 1893
    4. *J'allais par des chemins perfides,* 1892
    5. *J'ai presque peur, en vérité,* 1893
    6. *Avant que tu ne t'en ailles,* 1892
    7. *Donc, ce sera par un clair jour d'été,* 1892
    8. *N'est-ce pas?,* 1893
    9. *L'Hiver a cessé,* 1894
63bis   *Hymne à Apollon,* Greek melody, with accomp, for hp/ fl/2 cl, 1894
72   *Pleurs d'or* (duet for Mez and Bar) (Albert Samain), 1896
76/1   *Le Parfum impérissable* (Leconte de Lisle), 1897
76/2   *Arpège* (A. Samain), 1897
83/1   *Prison* (Verlaine), 1894
83/2   *Soir* (A. Samain), 1894
85/1   *Dans la forêt de septembre* (Catulle Mendès), 1902
85/2   *La Fleur qui va sur l'eau* (C. Mendès), 1902
85/3   *Accompagnement* (A. Samain), 1902
87/1   *Le Plus Doux Chemin* (A. Silvestre), 1904
87/2   *Le Ramier* (A. Silvestre), 1904
92   *Le Don silencieux* (Jean Dominique), 1906
94   *Chanson* (Henri de Regnier), 1906
95   *La Chanson d'Eve* (Charles Van Lerberghe), 1906–10
    1. *Paradis,* 1906
    2. *Prima verba,* 1906
    3. *Roses ardentes,* 1908

4. *Comme Dieu rayonne,* 1909
5. *L'Aube blanche,* 1908
6. *Eau vivante,* 1909
7. *Veilles-tu, ma senteur de soleil?,* 1910
8. *Dans un parfum de roses blanches,* 1909
9. *Crépuscule,* 1906
10. *O Mort, poussière d'étoiles,* 1910

op. 106   *Le Jardin clos* (Charles Van Lerberghe), 1914
1. *Exaucement*
2. *Quand tu plonges tes yeux dans mes yeux*
3. *La Messagère*
4. *Je me poserai sur ton coeur*
5. *Dans la nymphée*
6. *Dans le pénombre*
7. *Il m'est cher, Amour, le bandeau*
8. *Inscription sur le sable*

113   *Mirages* (Baronne Renée de Brimont), 1919
1. *Cygne sur l'eau*
2. *Reflets dans l'eau*
3. *Jardin nocturne*
4. *Danseuse*

114   *C'est la paix* (Georgette Debladis), 1919

118   *L'Horizon chimérique* (Jean de La Ville de Mirmont), 1921
1. *La Mer est infinie*
2. *Je me suis embarqué*
3. *Diane, Séléné*
4. *Vaisseaux, nous vous aurons aimés*

Completed songs with no opus number

L'Aube naît (V. Hugo), 1862?
L'Aurore (V. Hugo), c.1870
Chanson de Mélisande (Maeterlinck trans. Mackail), 1898
En Prière (Stéphen Bordèse), 1889–90. Canticle
Puisque j'ai mis (V. Hugo), 1862
Sérénade from *Le Bourgeois Gentilhomme* (Molière), 1893
Tristesse d'Olympio (V. Hugo), c.1865–8
Vocalise-étude (coll. Hettich), 1906–7

(ii) *Piano Music*

op. 17   *Trois Romances sans paroles,* c. 1863
19   *Ballade,* ?1877–9 (with orch 1881)

op. 25   First Impromptu in E flat, 1881
26   First Barcarolle in a, c.1881?
30   First Valse-Caprice in A, 1882?
31   Second Impromptu in f, 1883
32   *Mazurka* in B flat, c.1875
33/1   First Nocturne in e flat, c.1875
33/2   Second Nocturne in B, c.1881
33/3   Third Nocturne in A flat, c.1881
34   Third Impromptu in A flat, 1883
36   Fourth Nocturne in E flat, 1884
37   Fifth Nocturne in B flat, c.1884
38   Second Valse-Caprice in D flat, 1884
41   Second Barcarolle in G, 1885
42   Third Barcarolle in G flat, 1885
44   Fourth Barcarolle in A flat, 1886
56   *Dolly*, suit for piano duet, 1893–7
   1. *Berceuse*
   2. *Mi-a-ou*
   3. *Le Jardin de Dolly*
   4. *Kitty Valse*
   5. *Tendresse*
   6. *Le Pas Espagnol*
59   Third Valse-Caprice in G flat, 1893
62   Fourth Valse-Caprice in A flat, 1893–4
63   Sixth Nocturne in D flat, 1894
66   Fifth Barcarolle in f sharp, 1894
70   Sixth Barcarolle in E flat, 1895–6
73   *Thème et variations* in c sharp, 1895
74   Seventh Nocturne in c sharp, 1898
84   *Huit piéces brèves* (no. 8 is the so-called 'Eighth Nocturne'), 1869, 1878–9, 1899, 1901–2
86bis   Sixth Impromptu in D flat, transcribed from Impromptu for harp (1904) in 1913
90   Seventh Barcarolle in d, 1905
91   Fourth Impromptu in D flat, 1905
96   Eighth Barcarolle in D flat, 1906
97   Ninth Nocturne in b, 1908
99   Tenth Nocturne in e, 1908
101   Ninth Barcarolle in a, 1909
102   Fifth Impromptu in f sharp, 1909
103   Nine Preludes, 1909–10
104/1   Eleventh Nocturne in f sharp, 1913
104/2   Tenth Barcarolle in a, 1913

op. 105   Eleventh Barcarolle in g, 1913
  106bis   Twelfth Barcarolle in E flat, 1915
   107   Twelfth Nocturne in e, 1915
   111   *Fantaisie* for pno and orch in G, 1918
   116   Thirteenth Barcarolle in C, 1921
   119   Thirteenth Nocturne in b, 1921

Piano Music with no opus number

Cadenza for Beethoven's Third Piano Concerto in c (op. 37), 1869
Cadenza for Mozart's First Piano Concerto in F (K.37), c.1875
Cadenza for Mozart's 24th Piano Concerto in c (K.491), 1902
Fugue in e (op. 84/6), 1869
Gavotte in c sharp, 1869
Intermède symphonique for pno duet in F, 1869
Petite fugue in a (op. 84/3), 1869
Prélude in e, 1869
Prélude in C, 1897?
Souvenirs de Bayreuth—'Quadrille sur les motifs favoris de l'Anneau du Nibelung—R. Wagner' for pno duet in G, 1888?

(iii) *Chamber Music* (including music for harp and music for one instrument and piano)

op. 13   First Violin Sonata in A, 1875–6
   15   First Piano Quartet in c, 1876–9, finale rewritten 1883
   16   *Berceuse* for vln and pno in F, 1878–9
   24   *Élégie* for vc and pno in c, 1880 (with orch 1895)
   29   *Romance* for vln and pno in B flat, 1877
   45   Second Piano Quartet in g, 1885–6?
   49   *Petite Pièce* for vc and pno in G, c.1888 (now lost)
   69   *Romance* for vc and pno in A, 1894
   75   Andante for vln and pno in B flat, 1878–9?, rev. 1897
   77   *Papillon* for vc and pno in A, 1884?
   78   *Sicilienne* for vc and pno in g, 1893
   79   *Fantaisie* for fl and pno in e/C, 1898
   86   Impromptu for hp in D flat, 1904
   89   First Piano Quintet in d, 1887, 1891–4, 1903–5
   98   *Sérénade* for vc and pno in b, 1908?
  108   Second Violin Sonata in e, 1916–17
  109   First Cello Sonata in d, 1917
  110   *Une Châtelaine en sa tour* for hp in a, 1918
  115   Second Piano Quintet in c, 1919–21

op. 117 Second Cello Sonata in g, 1921
  120 Piano Trio in d, 1922–3
  121 String Quartet in e, 1923–4

Chamber Music with no opus number

Morceaux de lecture (sight-reading pieces) for Conservatoire exams:
1. For vc (with second vc accomp.), 1897
2. For fl and pno, 1898
3. For vln and pno, 1903
4. For hp, 1904
Pièce for 2 cbs in A, 1905?

(iv) *Secular choral music* (excluding duets)

op. 12 *Les Djinns* (V. Hugo) for mixed chorus and pno or orch, 1874–5?

  22 *Le Ruisseau* (anon) for two-part female chorus and pno, 1881?

  29 *La Naissance de Vénus* (Paul Collin) for soloists, chorus and orch, 1882

  35 *Madrigal* (Armand Silvestre) for vocal quartet or chorus with pno or orch, 1883

  50 *Pavane* (Robert de Montesquiou) for mixed chorus and orch, 1887

(v) *Religious Vocal Music*

op. 11 *Cantique de Jean Racine* for mixed choir and org, 1865

 43/1 *Noël* (Victor Wilder). Canticle for voice, pno and harmonium *ad lib*, 1886

 47/1 *O Salutaris* for Bar, org and cb, 1878 and 1887

 47/2 *Maria, Mater gratiae*, duet for T and Bar and org, 1888

  48 *Messe de Requiem* for S and Bar solo, mixed choir and orch, 1887–8 (second version: 1877 and 1886–90; third version 1877–1900)

  54 *Ecce fidelis servus* for S, T and Bar solo, org, hp, vc, cb, 1889

  55 *Tantum ergo* for T solo, mixed choir with hp and org, 1889–90

op. 65/1   *Ave verum* for two-part female choir, org and cb, 1894
    65/2   *Tantum ergo* for three-part female choir, soloists and org, 1894
    67/1   *Salve Regina* for T (or S) solo and org, 1895
    67/2   *Ave Maria* for Mez (or Bar) solo and org, 1894–5
    93   *Ave Maria* for 2S and org, 1906

Religious Vocal Music with no opus number

Ave Maria for three-part male voice choir and org, 1871
Ave Maria for 2S and org, 1876–7 (reused in op. 93, 1906)
Ave Maria, T and Bar soli, hp, org, str quintet, c.1880
Ave Maria, S and Mez soli, org, c.1880?
Benedictus for mixed choir, org and cb, c.1880
Cantique à St-Vincent-de-Paul for voice and org, 1868 (lost)
Il est né, le divin enfant, harmonized carol for unison children's choir, org, hp, ob, vcs and cbs, 1888
Libera me for Bar and org, 1877 (used in *Requiem,* second and third versions)
Messe basse: 1. For three-part female choir with harmonium and vln solo, 1881 (collaboration with Messager)
            2. Accomp. by small orch, 1882 (with Messager)
            3. Accomp. by org, 1906 (by Fauré only)
Noël d'enfants—'Les Anges dans nos campagnes', unison children's choir and org, c.1890
En Prière (Stéphan Bordèse), canticle for voice and org, 1889
O Salutaris for voice and org, 1878 (used in op. 47/1, 1887?)
Sancta Mater for T solo, mixed choir and org, 1894
Super flumina (Psalm 136) for mixed choir and org, 1863
Tantum ergo for S solo, mixed choir and org, 1904
Tu es Petrus for Bar solo, mixed choir, str and org, 1872?

(vi) *Orchestral Music*

op. 14   Violin Concerto in d, 1878–9 (see Appendix B)
    16   *Berceuse* for vln and orch in F, 1880
    19   *Ballade* for pno and orch in F sharp, 1881
    20   *Suite d'orchestre* or Symphony in F, 1867–73 (see Appendix B)

op. 24   *Élégie* for vc and orch in c, 1895
  40   Symphony in d, 1884 (see Appendix B)
  50   *Pavane* for orch and chorus, 1887
  111   *Fantaisie* for pno and orch in G, 1918
  112   *Masques et bergamasques,* orch suite, 1867–1919 (see Appendix B)

Orchestral Music with no opus number

Chant funéraire for wind band, for the centenary of the death of Napoleon I, 1921
Intermezzo de symphonie, 1867–8 (see Appendix B)
Menuet in F for small orch (for *Le Bourgeois Gentilhomme?*), 1893?

(vii) *Fauré and the Theatre*

op. 52   *Caligula,* incidental music for the tragedy by Alexandre Dumas père (Prologue and Act 5 only) for female chorus and orch, 1888
  57   *Shylock,* incidental music for Edmond Haraucourt's adaptation of Shakespeare, 1889
  80   *Pelléas et Mélisande,* incidental music for the drama by Maurice Maeterlinck (Eng. trans. Jack Mackail), 1898
  82   *Prométhée,* lyric tragedy in three acts by Jean Lorrain and André-Ferdinand Hérold, 1900
  88   *Le Voile du bonheur,* incidental music for the play by Georges Clemenceau, 1901
  112   *Masques et bergamasques,* divertissement in one act by René Fauchois, (see first part of Appendix A, and Appendix B), 1867–1919

Theatre Music with no opus number

Barnabé, sextet from a comic opera in one act by Jules Moineaux, 1879?
Jules César, incidental music for Victor Hugo's translation of Shakespeare, (based on music for *Caligula,* op. 52), 1905

Gabriel Fauré

Le Bourgeois Gentilhomme (Molière), incidental music?, 1893 (see *Menuet* and *Sérénade*, 1893 and *Sicilienne* for vc and pno, op. 78, 1893)
La Passion, prologue for the drama by Edmond Haraucourt, for mixed chorus and orch, 1890
Pénélope, lyric drama in three acts by René Fauchois, 1907–12

APPENDIX B: FAURÉ'S SELF-BORROWINGS

FIRST USES:	LATER RE-USED IN:
Intermezzo de symphonie (orch) (1867–8)	*Intermède symphonique* (pno duet) (30 March 1869)
Intermède symphonique (piano duet) (30 March 1869)	1. Symphony (or Suite) in F (op. 20) as finale? 2. *Masques et Bergamasques— Ouverture* (op. 112/1, 1919)
Gavotte for piano in c sharp (16 May 1869)	1. Symphony in F as third movement 2. *Masques et Bergamasques* (op. 112/7)
Petite fugue for piano in a (30 June 1869)[1]	*Huit pièces brèves* (op. 84/3, 1902)
Fugue for piano in e (30 November 1869)	*Huit pièces brèves* (op. 84/6)
Lydia (op. 4/2, c.1870)	There are many references to the opening of this song (Ex. 2), some more explicit than others. See: 1. *Le Secret* (op. 23/3, 1880–81) 2. *La Bonne Chanson* (op. 61/1–5, 8, 9, but chiefly nos. 3 and 5, 1892–4) 3. *Prométhée* Act 3 no. 4 (1900) 4. *Pénélope*: love theme (Ex. 32 D) VS, p. 72, line 1 (1908) 5. *Cygne sur l'eau* (op. 113/1, 1919) 6. Second Piano Quintet: slow movement (op. 115, 1919–20). Start (Ex. 48 E) and around fig. 4
Symphony (or Suite) in F (op. 20, 1867–73) 1. Allegro	*Allegro symphonique* for piano duet (transcribed Léon

Boëllmann, op. 68). Published 1895

3. *Gavotte* (1869) — *Masques et bergamasques* (op. 112/7)

4. Finale (1869?) — *Ouverture* (op. 112/1) ?

Ave Maria for two sopranos and organ (1876–7) — *Ave Maria* (op. 93, 1906)

Libera me for baritone and organ (1877) — *Requiem* (op. 48, 1893 version)

O Salutaris for voice and organ (1878) — *O Salutaris* (op. 47/1, 1887) ?

Concerto for violin and orchestra (op. 14, 1878–9)
1. Allegro — Themes re-used in String Quartet (op. 121, first movement, 1923) See Ex. 8

2. Andante — Themes probably re-used in Andante for violin and piano (op. 75, 1897)

Messe basse (1881)
Movements by Fauré: 2. *Gloria*
              3. *Sanctus*
              5. *Agnus Dei*
— 1. *Messe basse* (second version, 1882)
2. *Messe basse* (third version, 1906) re-uses 1881 *Sanctus* and *Agnus Dei,* and has a *Benedictus* based on the 'Qui tollis' section of the 1881 *Gloria*

Madrigal (op. 35, 1883) (vocal quartet or chorus and piano) — *Masques et Bergamasques* (op. 112/3) with orchestra

Symphony in d (op. 40, 1884)
1. Allegro deciso — Themes re-used in First Cello Sonata (op. 109, 1917), first movement See Ex. 42

2. Andante — Themes re-used in Second Violin Sonata (op. 108, 1916), slow movement

Requiem[2]: *Offertoire* (1886–9) — Start of Ninth Prelude (op. 103, 1910)

Clair de lune (op. 46/2, 1887)	*Masques et Bergamasques* (op. 112/6) with orchestra
Pavane (op. 50, 1886–7)	*Masques et Bergamasques* (op. 112/8)
Caligula (op. 52, 1888) Incidental music	*Jules César* (1905) Incidental music
Theme of *Nocturne* from *Shylock* (op. 57/5. 1889)	Reappears in various guises in: 1. *Romance* for cello (op. 69, 1894) •2. *Soir* (op. 83/2, 1894) 3. *Exaucement* (op. 106/1, 1914) See Ex. 20
Requiem: Libera me (1890?) bars 124–6	Fifth Prelude (op. 103, 1910) bars 45–7
Sicilienne for cello and piano (op. 78, 1893) Probably composed as part of the incidental music for Molière's *Le Bourgeois Gentilhomme*	*Entr'acte* before Act 2 of *Pelléas et Mélisande* (1898) Score no. 5. Added to the orchestral suite (op. 80) in 1909
Chanson de Mélisande (31 May 1898)³ for Act 3 scene i (no. 11) of *Pelléas et Mélisande*	*Crépuscule* (op. 95/9, 1906)
Impromptu for harp (op. 86, 1904)	Sixth Impromptu for piano (op. 86bis, 1913). Transcription
Le Plus Doux Chemin (op. 87/1, 1904)	*Masques et Bergamasques* (op. 112/4) with orchestra
Fourth Prelude (op. 103, 1910) bars 9–10	*Masques et Bergamasques* (op. 112/5), *Menuet* bars 10–13
Chant funéraire (1921)	Second Cello Sonata (op. 117, 1921), slow movement

Footnotes to Appendix B
1. Probably written as a fugue on an original subject for the composition prize at the École Niedermeyer around 1863.
2. The three versions of the *Requiem* (1888, 1893, 1900) involved a gradual expansion of forces and conception rather than specific self-borrowing.
3. The main rising 'Mélisande' theme at the start recurs elsewhere in the incidental music, notably in the final movement of the orchestral suite known as *La Mort de Mélisande*. Transformed slightly, it became the main theme of the song-cycle *La Chanson d'Ève* in 1906 (see Ex. 25 A).

APPENDIX C: SELECT BIBLIOGRAPHY

This is arranged in three sections:
1. Fauré's own writings and interviews with Fauré (chronological)
2. Books or theses on Fauré (short sections within more general reference books are in brackets, the most important books are starred)
3. Articles on Fauré (the most important are starred)

(Abbreviations of journals as in main text)

1.

Interview with Louis Aguettant, 12.7.02 (publ. in *Comoedia*, 3.3.54)
'Critique musicale' section in *Le Figaro*, 2.3.03 weekly till the end of the 1905 season, then first performances and important revivals of operas in Paris, Brussels and Monte Carlo till the summer of 1914. Also two isolated articles in 1921 on Dukas' *Ariane et Barbe-bleue* (4.5.21) and Berlioz' *Les Troyens* (9.6.21). (Selection reprinted in *Opinions musicales*, 1930)
'Lettre à propos de la réforme de la musique religieuse', *Le Monde Musical* (15.2.04)
'Réponse à une enquête' (on criticism), *Le Gaulois* (30.10.04: reprinted in the preface to *Opinions musicales*, 1930)
'Les Réformes du Conservatoire', *Musica* (November 1905)
'Joachim', *Musica* (April 1906)
'Lucienne Bréval. Jeanne Raunay', *Musica* (January 1908)
'Édouard Lalo', *Le Courrier Musical* (15.4.08)
'André Messager', *Musica* (September 1908)
Preface to Jean Huré: *Dogmes musicaux*, Paris, Éditions du Monde Musical, 1909
'Réponse à l'enquête sur la musique moderne italienne' by L. Borgex, *Comoedia* (31.1.10)
'La musique étrangère et les compositeurs français', *Le Gaulois* (10.1.11)
'Sous la musique que faut-il mettre?', *Musica* (February 1911), p. 38

Preface to Henri Auriol: *Décentralisation musicale*, Paris, E. Figuière, 1912 (also publ. in *Comoedia*, 26.12.12)

Preface to a new edition of the classics for piano prepared by Isidore Philipp, Paris, Ricordi, c.1912?

Preface to Georges Jean-Aubry: *La Musique française d'aujourd'hui*, Paris, Perrin, 1916

'Appel aux musiciens français', *Le Courrier Musical* (15.3.17)

'Camille Saint-Saëns', *ReM* (1.2.22)

'Entretien', *Le Petit Parisien* (28.4.22)

'Entretien' with Roger Valbelle, *Excelsior* (12.6.22), republ. in *BAF* no. 12 (1975), pp. 9–11

'Souvenirs' (of the École Niedermeyer), *ReM* (1.10.22), pp. 3–9

Hommage à Eugène Gigout, Paris, Floury, 1923 (57 pp.)

Preface to Émile Vuillermoz: *Musiques d'aujourd'hui*, Paris, G. Crès, 1923

'Les grands hommes quand ils étaient petits, VIII: Gabriel Fauré' by Jean Nohain (alias Jaboune) in an unknown journal in the Fauré-Fremiet archives (8.3.24)

'Souvenirs sur *Pénélope*' (Interview with Jean Gandrey-Réty), *Comoedia* (10.11.24)

Preface to Joseph de Marliave: *Les Quatuors de Beethoven*, Paris, Alcan, 1925

'Lettres à une fiancée (1877)', presented by Camille Bellaigue, *Revue des Deux Mondes* (15.8.28), pp. 911–43

Opinions musicales (selected criticisms from *Le Figaro*, 1903–21, with a preface by P. B. Gheusi), Paris, Éditions Rieder, 1930

'Entretien', *Candide* (9.12.37), p. 19

Letters on theatre projects in the early 1890s in G. Jean-Aubry: 'Gabriel Fauré, Paul Verlaine et Albert Samain ou les Tribulations de "Bouddha"', Le Centenaire de Gabriel Fauré (1845–1945), special ed. of *ReM*, May 1945, pp. 39–58

'Quelques souvenirs sur Gabriel Fauré, *Revue de Languedoc* (Albi), no. 6 (June 1945)

Lettres intimes (1885–1924) to his wife, Marie, presented by Philippe Fauré-Fremiet, Paris, La Colombe, 1951. (See section 2: Lockspeiser, E.)

Interview with Louis Aguettant, *Comoedia* (3.3.54)—see 1902 above

'Deux lettres de Gabriel Fauré à Claude Debussy (1910–17)', ed. F. Lesure and A. Verchaly, *RdM*, xlviii (1962), pp. 75–6

'Cinq lettres inédites de Gabriel Fauré à son fils Emmanuel [1908–14]', ed. J-M. Nectoux, *BAF* no. 9 (1972), pp. 6–10

'Gabriel Fauré et Camille Saint-Saëns: Correspondance inédite', ed. Jean-Michel Nectoux, *RdM*, lviii (1972), pp. 65–89 and 190–252; lix

(1973), pp. 60–98: reprinted in one vol. by Heugel, Paris 1973, second revised edition 1978

'Autour de quelques lettres inédites de Robert de Montesquiou, Charles Koechlin et Gabriel Fauré' by Jean-Michel Nectoux, *BAF* no. 11 (1974), pp. 7–11

Gabriel Fauré: Correspondance (presented and annotated by Jean-Michel Nectoux), Paris, Flammarion, 1980 (Collection 'Harmoniques' no. 1)

2.

Aguettant, Louis: *Gabriel Fauré*, Lyon, Aux deux collines, 1924

Aguettant, Louis: *La Génie de Gabriel Fauré* (conference given 17.10.24), Lyon, Aux deux collines, 1924

(Aguettant, Louis: *La Vie intellectuelle*, Paris, Éditions du Cerf, 1949)

(Aguettant, Louis: *La Musique de piano des origines à Ravel*, Paris, Albin Michel, 1954)

Alstadter, Judith: 'The Life and Works of Gabriel Fauré', unpubl. thesis, Yale University, 1966, 72 pp.

(Astruc, Gabriel: *Le Pavillon des fantômes*, Paris, Bernard Grasset, 1929)

(Bellaigue, Camille: *Études musicales* (3e série), Paris, Delagrave, 1907)

(Bellaigue, Camille: *Notes brèves* (2e série), Paris, Delagrave, 1914. Section on *Pénélope*)

Beltrando, Marie-Claire: 'Les mélodies de Gabriel Fauré', Ph.D. diss., Université de Paris, 1982

Benevides, Walter: *Compositores surdos; Beethoven–Smetana–Fauré*, Rio de Janeiro, 1970

(Bernard, Robert: *Les Tendances de la musique française moderne*, Paris, Durand, 1930 (pp. 61–73; 89–102)

Beydts, Louis and others: Collection of articles, listed in section 3, publ. as *Gabriel Fauré*, Paris, Publications techniques et artistiques, 1946

Bland, Stephen: 'Form in the songs of Gabriel Fauré', Ph.D. dissertation, Florida State University, 1976 (108 pp.)

(Boëllmann-Gigout, Marie-Louise: see Ginot-Gachet, Jacqueline below)

Borgman, Jean Pawley: 'The Fauré Requiem', Master of Music thesis, Eastman School of Music, Rochester, New York, 1948

(Boschot, Adolphe: *Chez les musiciens du XVIIIe siècle à nos jours*, Paris, Plon-Nourrit, 1922)

Boulanger, Nadia and others: Collection of articles, listed in section 3, publ. in special ed. of *ReM*, 1.10.22

(Bruneau, Alfred: *La Musique française*, Paris, Fasquelle, 1901)

Bruneau, Alfred: *Notice sur la vie et les oeuvres de Gabriel Fauré*, Paris, Charpentier et Fasquelle, 1925 (34 pp.)

Brussel, Robert and others: Collection of articles, listed in section 3, publ. in special Fauré ed. of *Musica*, no. 77, February 1909

(Coeuroy, André: *La Musique française moderne*, Paris, Delagrave, 1922)

(Colette (Sidonie Gabrielle Gauthier-Villars): *Maurice Ravel par quelques-uns de ses familiers*, Paris, Éditions du Tambourinaire, 1939)

(Cooper, Martin: *French Music* (From the death of Berlioz to the death of Fauré), London, Oxford University Press, 1951)

(Cortot, Alfred: *La Musique française de piano* (vol. 1), Paris, Éditions Rieder, 1930; repr. Presses Universitaires de France, 1948. Eng. trans. Hilda Andrews: *French Piano Music:* series 1, London, Oxford University Press, 1932 (see pp. 109–39)

(Cossart, Michael de: *The Food of Love. Princesse Edmond de Polignac (1865–1943) and her Salon*, London, Hamish Hamilton, 1978)

Crouch, Richard: 'The Nocturnes and Barcarolles for Solo Piano of Gabriel Fauré', Ph.D., The Catholic University of America (Washington D.C.), 1980 (220 pp.)

(Danwell, Wilfrid: *The Evolution of Twentieth-Century Harmony*, London, Novello, 1960)

(Davies, Laurence: *The Gallic Muse*, London, J. M. Dent, 1967)

(Demuth, Norman: *French Piano Music: A Survey with Notes on Its Performance*, London, Museum Press, 1959)

*Dommel-Diény, Amy: *L'Analyse harmonique en exemples de J. S. Bach à Debussy; contribution à une recherche de l'interprétation*, Neuchâtel, Delachaux et Niestlé, 1967f. *Fauré:* Fascicule 13 (mélodies), Neuchâtel, 1967. Fasc. 12 (piano music), Paris, Centre de Documentation Universitaire, Bärenreiter et Ploix, 1974

(Dumesnil, René: *La Musique contemporaine en France*, Paris, A. Colin, 1930)

(Dumesnil, René: *Portraits de musiciens français*, Paris, Plon, 1938)

Faure, Gabriel Auguste: *Gabriel Fauré*, Grenoble, B. Arthaud, 1945

*Faure, Michel: 'La Nostalgie du 18e siècle chez Fauré, Debussy et Ravel', Doctorat du troisième cycle, University of Paris IV, 1975 (2 vols., 367 pp.)

*Fauré-Fremiet, Philippe: *Gabriel Fauré*, Paris, Éditions Rieder, 1929. Second enlarged edition, Paris, Albin Michel, 1957

*Fauré-Fremiet (ed.): *Lettres intimes* (1885–1924) from Fauré to his wife, Marie. Paris, La Colombe, 1951

*Favre, Max: *Gabriel Fauré's Kammermusik*, Zürich, Max Niehans, 1948 (270 pp.)

Ferguson, David Milton: 'A study, analysis and recital of the piano quartets of Gabriel Fauré', Ed. D. Dissertation, University of Columbia, 1969

(Gavoty, Bernard: *Les Souvenirs de Georges Enesco*, Paris, Flammarion, 1955)

*Gervais, Françoise: *Étude comparée des langages harmoniques de Fauré et de Debussy*, Paris, Richard Masse, 1971 (*Revue Musicale*, two vols. nos. 272–3). Doctoral thesis at the Sorbonne, Paris, 30.6.54

Ginot-Gachet, Jacqueline: 'L'École de musique classique et religieuse et Gabriel Fauré' (Mémoire pour la classe d'histoire de la musique au Conservatoire national supérieur de musique de Paris), Paris, BN, 1959 (typed copy only). Formed the basis for Marie-Louise Boëllmann-Gigout's article: 'L'École de musique classique et religieuse. Ses maîtres, ses élèves', in *Encyclopédie de la Pléiade. Histoire de la musique*, Paris, Gallimard, 1963 (Vol. 2, pp. 841–66)

*Ginot-Gachet, Jacqueline: 'Les Représentations lyriques aux Arènes de Béziers de 1898 à 1911', Doctoral thesis (3e cycle), Université de Paris IV, 1976 (357 pp.)

(Gray, Cecil: *A Survey of Contemporary Music*, London, Oxford University Press, 1924)

(Hill, Edward Burlingame: *Modern French Music*, Boston and New York, Houghton Mifflin Co, 1924)

(Imbert, Hugues: *Profils de musiciens*, Paris, Librairie Fischbacher et Librairie Sagot, 1888 (pp. 57–78, and see section 3 below))

(Inghelbrecht, Désiré-Émile: *Le Chef d'orchestre parle au public*, Paris, Julliard, 1957)

*Jankélévitch, Vladimir: *Gabriel Fauré et ses mélodies*, Paris, Plon, 1938, revised and enlarged to become *Gabriel Fauré, ses mélodies, son esthétique*, Plon, 1951. Re-edited as *Fauré et l'inexprimable*, Paris, Plon, 1974

*Jankélévitch, Vladimir: *Le Nocturne, Fauré, Chopin et la nuit, Satie et le matin*, Paris, Albin Michel, 1957

(Jean-Aubry, Georges: *French Music of Today* (trans. Edwin Evans), London, K. Paul, Trench, Trubner & Co Ltd, 1919. Preface by Fauré to 1916 Paris edition (see section 1))

*Jones, John Barrie: 'The Piano and Chamber Works of Gabriel Fauré', PhD, University of Cambridge, 1974 (PhD 8799)

Kelsay, Gene Wilson: 'An analytical study of the solo and choral works of five composers in preparation for performance', University of

Missouri-Kansas City, 1969 (176 pp.)

*Kidd, James: 'Louis Niedermeyer's system for Gregorian Chant accompaniment as a compositional source for Gabriel Fauré', D.Phil dissertation (Musicology), University of Chicago, 1974 (317 pp.)

Kinsinger, Dan Howard: 'The seven song collections of Gabriel Fauré', University of Illinois at Urbana–Champsign, 1971 (211 pp.)

(Koechlin, Charles: 'Les tendances de la musique française contemporaine' and 'Étude sur l'harmonie moderne' in *Encyclopédie de la Musique*, Paris, Delagrave, 1925)

*Koechlin, Charles: *Gabriel Fauré*, Paris, Félix Alcan, 1927/2. Plon, 1949. Eng. trans. Leslie Orrey, London, Dennis Dobson, 1945

Kurtz, James Lawrence: 'Problems of tonal structure in songs of Gabriel Fauré', PhD (Theory), University of Brandeis, 1970 (124 pp.)

(Lalo, Pierre: *De Rameau à Ravel, portraits et souvenirs*, Paris, Albin Michel, 1947)

(Landormy, Paul: *La Musique française de Franck à Debussy*, Paris, Gallimard, 1943)

(Landormy, Paul: *La Musique française après Debussy*, Paris, Gallimard, 1943)

(Landowska, Wanda: *Frédéric Chopin et Gabriel Fauré*, Paris, Richard Masse, 1946)

*Lefèvre, Gustave: *Traité d'harmonie* (à l'usage des cours de l'école de musique classique, fondée par L. Niedermeyer), Paris, A l'école, 1889

(Lefèvre, Gustave and Heurtel, Vve Henri: 'L'École de musique classique Niedermeyer' in *Encyclopédie de la Musique*, Paris, Delagrave, 1931 (Part 2, vol. 6))

Lesure, François: Catalogue de l'Exposition Gabriel Fauré, Paris, BN, 1963

*Lockspeiser, Edward: *The Literary Clef*, London, Calder, 1958. (Trans. of some of the *Lettres intimes*, 1896–1924, pp. 140–59)

Long, Marguerite: *Au piano avec Gabriel Fauré*, Paris, Julliard, 1963

*(Mellers, Wilfrid: *Studies in Contemporary Music*, London, Dennis Dobson, 1947 (Chap. 3: 'The Later Work of Gabriel Fauré', pp. 56–72))

(Milhaud, Darius: *Études*, Paris, C. Aveline, 1927)

(Myers, Rollo: *Modern French Music — Its Evolution and Cultural Background from 1900 to the Present Day*, Oxford, Basil Blackwell, 1971 (Chap. 3, pp. 21–34))

*Nectoux, Jean-Michel: *Fauré*, Paris, Éditions du Seuil, 1972 (Series: *Solfèges* no. 33)

*Nectoux, Jean-Michel (ed): *Soixante ans d'amitié. Gabriel Fauré et*

Camille Saint-Saëns: Correspondance inédite, Paris, Société Française de Musicologie, Heugel, 1973

Nectoux, Jean-Michel: Catalogue de l'Exposition Gabriel Fauré (1845–1924), Paris, BN, 1974

*Nectoux, Jean-Michel (ed.): *Gabriel Fauré: Correspondance*, Paris, Flammarion, 1980 (Collection 'Harmoniques' no. 1)

*Nectoux, Jean-Michel: *Phonographie de Gabriel Fauré* (*1900–77*), Paris, Bibliothèque Nationale, 1979

Nectoux, Jean-Michel: 'Fauré et le théâtre', Thèse d'État (Esthétique musicale), Université de Paris 1, 1980

*Niedermeyer, Louis and d'Ortigue, Joseph Louis: *Traité théorique et pratique de l'accompagnement du plainchant*, Paris, E. Repos, 1857/2. Heugel, 1878

Noske, Fritz: *French Song from Berlioz to Duparc*, Paris, Presses Universitaires de France, 1954. Trans. Rita Benton, New York, Dover Publications Inc, 1970

Orenstein, Arbie: *Ravel: Man and Musician*, New York and London, Columbia University Press, 1975

Owyang, Lily Siao: 'The solo pianoforte works of Gabriel Fauré', Boston University School of Fine and Applied Arts, 1973 (95 pp.)

Painter, George: *Marcel Proust. A Biography* (two vols, 1961 and 1965), London, Chatto and Windus

*Pennington, Kenneth D: 'A historical and stylistic study of the melodies of Gabriel Fauré', Mus.D, Indiana University, 1961 (374 pp.)

Pési, Jacques: 'Le Concept de musique pure d'après l'oeuvre de musique de chambre de Gabriel Fauré', Maîtrise (d'ésthétique musicale), Université de Paris 1 1977 (107 pp.)

(Pitrou, Robert: *De Gounod à Debussy*, Paris, Albin Michel, 1957)

Rebber-Dodge, Mary Lee: 'The Piano style of Gabriel Fauré', M. Mus thesis, University of California, 1963

(Robert, Frédéric: *La Musique française au XIXe siècle*, Paris, Presses Universitaires de France, 1963)

(Rohozinski, Ladislas (ed): *Cinquante ans de musique française de 1874 à 1925*, Paris, Librairie de France, 1925f. Collection of articles by Coeuroy, Koechlin, Laloy, Vuillermoz, etc)

Rostand, Claude: *L'Oeuvre de Fauré*, Paris, J.-B. Janin, 1945

Saint-Saëns, Camille: *Portraits et souvenirs*, Paris, Société d'Édition Artistique, 1900

(Samazeuilh, Gustave: *Musiciens de mon temps*, Paris, M. Daubin, 1947)

(Schouten, Hennie: *Drie Franse Liederencomponisten—Duparc, Fauré, Debussy*, Amsterdam, Uitgeversmaatschappi, 1950)

(Schmitt, Florent: Article in Cobbett's *Cyclopaedic Survey of Chamber Music*, London, Oxford University Press, 1929)

(Séré, Octave (Jean Poueigh): *Musiciens français d'aujourd'hui*, Paris, Éditions Mercure de France, 1911)

Servières, Georges: *Gabriel Fauré*, Paris, H. Laurens, 1930

(Shattuck, Roger: *The Banquet Years: The Arts in France 1885–1918*, New York, Doubleday & Co Inc, 1961)

Sommers, Paul Bartholin: 'Fauré and his songs: the relationship of text, melody and accompaniment', Doctor of Musical Arts dissertation, University of Illinois, 1969 (175 pp.)

Soulard, Michel: 'La Bonne Chanson, du poème à la mélodie (Verlaine-Fauré)', Mémoire de maîtrise, Faculté des lettres de Poitiers, 1975 (171 pp.)

Stonequist, Elisabeth: 'The musical entente cordiale: 1905–16', PhD, University of Colorado, 1972

*Suckling, Norman: *Fauré*, London, J. M. Dent, 1946 (Master Musicians series)

Vuaillat, [Abbé] Jean: *Gabriel Fauré—musicien français*, Lyon, Emmanuel Vitte, 1973

Vuillemin, Louis: *Gabriel Fauré et son oeuvre*, Paris, Durand, 1914

*Vuillermoz, Émile: *Gabriel Fauré*, Paris, Flammarion, 1960; Trans. Kenneth Schapin, Philadelphia, Chilton Book Co, 1969

(Vuillermoz, Émile: *Musiques d'aujourd'hui*, Paris, G. Crès, 1923 (with preface by Fauré))

*Wegren, Thomas James: 'The solo piano music of Gabriel Fauré', PhD, Ohio State University, 1973 (301 pp.)

(Wenk, Arthur: *Claude Debussy and the Poets*, Berkeley and Los Angeles, University of California Press, 1976)

3.

*Aguettant, Louis: Interview with Fauré, 12.7.02 (*Comoedia*, 3.3.54)

Aguettant, Louis: 'Les Mélodies de Gabriel Fauré', *Le Courrier Musical* (1.2.03)

Almeida, Vieira de: 'La Chanson d'Ève', *Gazeta Musical e de todas as Artes* (Lisbon), ix (July–August 1959), pp. 333–4

Alstadter, Judith: 'Recollections of Gabriel Fauré', *Music Clubs Magazine* (Chicago), xlix (1969–70), pp. 12–13

Alstadter, Judith: 'Fauré: the man and his music', *Music Journal* (New York), xxix (1971), p. 152f.

Alstadter, Judith: 'Gabriel Fauré, my father' [sic], *Triangle* (Campbell, California), lxvi (1972), pp. 9–11

Amerongen, Alex van: 'Gabriel Fauré's laatste scheppings-periode', *Mens en melodie* (Utrecht), iii no. 7 (July 1948), pp. 204–7

Amerongen, Alex van: 'Brieven van Gabriel Fauré', *Mens en melodie*, vi (April 1951), pp. 115–18

Amerongen, Alex van: 'Het Festival—Gabriel Fauré te Foix', *Mens en melodie*, xiii (September 1958), p. 264

Amerongen, Alex van: 'Parijs: Fauré—herdenking', *Mens en melodie*, xx (January 1965), pp. 24–5

Amerongen, Alex van: 'Gabriel Fauré et les Pays-Bas', *BAF*, no. 14 (1977), pp. 14–19

Aprahamian, Felix: 'Rare Fauré', *Opera* (Autumn 1970), pp. 85–6

Aubert, Louis: 'Entretien avec M. Guitard', *Table ronde*, no. 165 (October 1961), p. 144

Auclert, Pierre: 'A propos de deux malentendus: Brahms et Fauré', *BAF*, no. 10 (1973), pp. 15–17

*Auclert, Pierre: 'La Ballade, op. 19, de Fauré', *BAF*, no. 15 (1978), pp. 3–11

Auric, Georges: 'Gabriel Fauré', *ReM*, vi (1.12.24), pp. 100–103

Bathori, Jane: 'Les musiciens que j'ai connus', *Journal of the British Institute of Recorded Sound*, i no. 5 (1961–2), pp. 146–7

Beaunier, André: 'Festival Gabriel Fauré' (lecture), *Journal de l'Université des Annales* (Paris, 15.2.12)

Bellaigue, Camille: 'La Bonne Chanson', *Revue des Deux Mondes* (15.10.1897), pp. 933–6

Bellaigue, Camille: 'Pénélope', *Revue des Deux Mondes* (1.7.13), pp. 217–24 (see same journal, 15.2.19 and 15.5.23 for reviews of revivals of *Pénélope*)

Bellaigue, Camille: 'Gabriel Fauré' (lecture), *La Revue Hebdomadaire* (Paris), xxxiv no. 10 (7.3.25)

Benoît, Camille: 'Le Requiem de Gabriel Fauré', *Le Guide Musical*, xxxiv, nos. 32–3 (9 and 16.8.1888)

Berger, Jean: 'On accompanying Fauré', *Bulletin of the National Association of Teachers of Singing*, Chicago, xxvi no. 4 (1970), pp. 18–21

Berger-Levrault, Mathilde: 'Les musiciens-compositeurs vus à travers leur écriture: Gabriel Fauré', *Musica* (Chaix), no. 82 (January 1961), pp. 50–51

Bernard, Robert: 'Fauré vu de l'étranger', *La Revue Française de Musique*, iv no. 1 (January 1935)

Bertschinger, Walter: 'Gabriel Fauré', *Schweizerische Musikzeitung*, xciv (1.10.54), pp. 363–6

Beydts, Louis: 'Les Mélodies' in *Gabriel Fauré*, Paris, Publications techniques et artistiques, 1946

Boulanger, Nadia: 'La Musique religieuse', *ReM* (1.10.22), pp. 104–11

Bourgeat, Fernand: 'Festival Fauré' (lecture), *Journal de l'Université des Annales* (Paris, 10.6.08)

Bowman, Robin: 'Eight late songs of Fauré; an approach to analysis', *Musical Analysis*, i no. 1 (1972), pp. 3–5

Boyd, Malcolm: 'Fauré's Requiem; a reappraisal', *MT*, civ (1963), pp. 408–9

Brussel, Robert: 'Les "lieder" de Fauré', *Musica* (Paris), no. 77 (February 1909)

Bruyr, José: 'Les Mélodies qu'il faut savoir chanter: "Clair de lune"', *Musica* (Chaix), no. 84 (March 1961), pp. 33–7

Bruyr, José: 'Les Grands Requiem et leur message', *Musica* (Chaix), no. 116 (November 1963), pp. 4–10

Calvocoressi, Michel-Dimitri: 'Modern French Composers: 1. How they are encouraged', *MT*, lxii no. 938 (1921), pp. 238–40

Calvocoressi, Michel-Dimitri: 'Obituary', *MT*, lxv (1924), p. 1134

Carraud, Gaston: 'L'Âme harmonique de Gabriel Fauré', *Musica* (Paris), no. 77 (February 1909)

Carraud, Gaston: 'La Musique pure dans l'école française', *SIM Magazine* (August–September 1910)

Carraud, Gaston: 'Gabriel Fauré', *Le Ménestrel*, lxxxii no. 15 (1920), pp. 149–51

Carter, Elliott: 'Gabriel Fauré', *Listen*, vi no. 1 (May 1945)

Chalupt, René: 'Gabriel Fauré et les poètes', *ReM* (1.10.22), pp. 28–33

Chandler, Theodore: 'Gabriel Fauré, a re-appraisal', *Modern Music*, xxii no. 3 (1945), pp. 165–9

Cooper, Martin: 'Some Aspects of Fauré's Technique', *Monthly Musical Record*, lxxv (May 1945), pp. 75–9

*Copland, Aaron: 'Gabriel Fauré, a Neglected Master', *MQ*, x (1924), pp. 573–86

Corte, Andrea Della: 'Le Vacanze di Fauré', *La Scala* no. 89 (April 1957), pp. 24–5

*Cortot, Alfred: 'La Musique de piano', *ReM* (1.10.22), pp. 80–103

Dauphin, Léopold: 'Gabriel Fauré et le Prométhée', *La Vogue* (Paris, 15.10.00)

Demuth, Norman: 'Gabriel Fauré', *Musical Opinion*, lxxi no. 845 (1948), pp. 165–6

Dukas, Paul: 'Prométhée', *Revue Hebdomadaire* (Paris, 6.10.00)

Dukas, Paul: 'Adieu à Gabriel Fauré', *ReM*, vi (1.12.24), pp. 97–9

Dumesnil, René: 'Le Centenaire de Gabriel Fauré, *ReM*, special ed. 1945, pp. 29–35

*Fauré-Fremiet, Philippe: 'La Genèse de Pénélope', *ReM*, x (May–June 1929), pp. 53–8. Expanded in *ReM*, special ed. 1945, pp. 9–26. Repub. in *BAF* no. 11 (1974), pp. 13–24

347

*Fauré-Fremiet, Philippe: 'La Pensée fauréenne', article in *Gabriel Fauré*, Paris, Publications techniques et artistiques, 1946

*Fauré-Fremiet, Philippe: 'La Chanson d'Ève (de Van Lerberghe-Fauré)', *Synthèses*, nos. 196–7 (September–October 1962). Repub. in part in *BAF* no. 10 (1973), pp. 7–14

*Fortassier, Paul: 'Le rythme dans les mélodies de Gabriel Fauré', *RdM*, lxii no. 2 (1976), pp. 257–74

Gauthier, Édouard: 'Fêtes de Béziers. Prométhée.', *La Rampe*, vi no. 27 (16.8.00)

Gauthier-Villars, Henri: 'M. Gabriel Fauré', *Revue Éolienne*, no. 17 (September 1900)

Gavoty, Bernard: 'Sur Fauré', *Journal Musical Français*, no. 176 (January 1969), pp. 16–17

Gervais, Françoise: 'Cinquantenaire: 1924–74', *BAF* no. 12 (1975), pp. 3–4

Gervais, Françoise: 'Gabriel Fauré traditionaliste novateur', *BAF*, no. 15 (1978), pp. 12–15

Hahn, Reynaldo: 'Gabriel Fauré. Préambule pour un Festival', *Journal de l'Université des Annales* (Paris, 15.7.14)

Henderson, Archibald Martin: 'Personal Memories of Fauré', *Musical Opinion*, lxxx (October 1956), pp. 39–40

Hill, Edward Burlingame: 'Gabriel Fauré's Piano Music', *The Musician*, xvi (1911), pp. 511 and 561

Hirsbrunner, Theo: 'Gabriel Fauré und Claude Debussy, oder das Ende der Salonmusik', *Schweizerische Musikzeitung*, cxv no. 2 (1975), pp. 66–71

Hirsbrunner, Theo: 'Musik und Sprache bei Gabriel Fauré und Claude Debussy', *Melos: Neue Zeitschrift für Musik*, i no. 5 (Mainz, 1975), pp. 365–70

Huré, Jean: 'Celui qui vient: M. Gabriel Fauré', *Le Monde Musical*, xvii no. 12 (30.6.05)

*Imbert, Hugues: 'Profils de musiciens. Gabriel Fauré', *L'Indépendance Musicale et Dramatique*, nos. 14–15 (15.9.1887 and 1.10.1887). Also publ. with a preface by Édouard Schuré, Paris, Librarie Fischbacher et Librairie Sagot, 1888

Indy, Vincent d': 'Gabriel Fauré', *Tablettes de la Schola* [*Cantorum*], (November 1924)

*Jankélévitch, Vladimir: 'Pelléas et Pénélope', *Revue du Languedoc* (Albi), no. 6 (June 1945), p. 123f

Jarocinski, Stefan: 'Fauré en Pologne', *BAF*, no. 14 (1977), pp. 12–13

*Jean-Aubry, Georges: 'Gabriel Fauré, Paul Verlaine et Albert Samain ou Les Tribulations de "Bouddha"', special 1945 edition of *ReM*, pp. 39–58

(*Journal Musical Français*, special number on Gabriel Fauré, 10.10.64)

Journel, J. Rouet de: 'Un Maître de la mélodie: Gabriel Fauré', *Études* clxxxi (1924), pp. 705–9

Klingsor, Tristan: 'Les Musiciens et les poètes contemporains', *Le Mercure de France*, cxlii (November 1900)

Koechlin, Charles: 'Prométhée', *Le Mercure de France*, cxliii (November 1901), pp. 550–4

Koechlin, Charles: 'Pénélope', *Gazette des Beaux-Arts* (July 1913), pp. 78–81

*Koechlin, Charles: 'Conférence sur Gabriel Fauré', *Le Ménestrel*, lxxxiii nos. 21–2 (27.5.21 and 3.6.21), pp. 221–3, 233–5

*Koechlin, Charles: 'Le Théâtre', *ReM* (1.10.22), pp. 34–49

*Koechlin, Charles: 'Gabriel Fauré, musicien dramatique', *La Musique Française* (Revue de la SIAMF), ii no. 3 (July 1933), pp. 175–86

Koechlin, Charles: 'Prométhée de Gabriel Fauré', *Eaux Vives* (August–September 1945), pp. 3–7

Ladmirault, Paul: 'La Bonne Chanson', *Le Courrier Musical*, vi no. 3 (1903), p. 34

Lafagette, Roger: 'Promenade au pays de Gabriel Fauré, *Revue du Languedoc* (Albi), no. 6 (June 1945)

Laloy, Louis: 'Gabriel Fauré', *Music Lovers' Calendar*, ii (1906), pp. 77–80

Landormy, Paul (transl. M. D. Herter Norton): 'Gabriel Fauré (1845–1924)', *MQ*, xvii no. 3 (July 1931), pp. 293–301

Lockspeiser, Edward: 'Fauré and the Song', *Monthly Musical Record*, lxxv (May 1945), pp. 79–84

Lockspeiser, Edward: 'The French Song in the 19th Century', *MQ*, xxvi (1940), pp. 192–9

Lockspeiser, Edward: 'Gabriel Fauré and Marcel Proust', *The Listener*, lxv no. 1679 (1.6.61), p. 985

Lorrain, Jean etc: 'Prométhée'. Special ed. of *Le Titan* (25.8.01)

Mangeot, André: 'Gabriel Fauré', *Le Monde Musical*, xxxv (November 1924), pp. 359–62

Malherbe, Henri: 'Le Génie de Fauré', article in *Gabriel Fauré*, Paris, Publications techniques et artistiques, 1946

Mare, Jeanne de: 'Gabriel Fauré', *Pro Musica* (The Franco-American Musicological Society Quarterly Bulletin), (March 1925), pp. 6–10

Marliave, Joseph (Saint-Jean) de: 'M. Gabriel Fauré', *La Nouvelle Revue* (July 1905), pp. 102–4

Marliave, Joseph de: 'La Musique de piano de Gabriel Fauré', *Musica* (Paris), no. 77 (February 1909)

Marliave, Joseph de: 'La Musique de piano de Gabriel Fauré', *La Nouvelle Revue* (January 1910), pp. 252–72

Matter, Jean: 'Brahms et Fauré', *Schweizerische Musikzeitung*, xcix no. 2 (February 1959), pp. 58–9

*Mellers, Wilfrid: 'The Composer and Civilization', *Scrutiny*, vi (1938), pp. 386–401. Expanded and republ. in *Studies in Contemporary Music* (no. 3), London, Dennis Dobson, 1947

Milhaud, Darius: 'Hommage à Gabriel Fauré', *Intentions*, ii no. 11 (January 1923). Republ. in *Études*, Paris, C. Aveline, 1927

(*Musica*, special Fauré edition, no. 77, February 1909)

*Nectoux, Jean-Michel: 'Proust et Fauré', *Bulletin de la Société des amis de Proust*, no. 21 (1971), pp. 1102–20

*Nectoux, Jean-Michel: 'Cinq lettres inédites de Gabriel Fauré à son fils Emmanuel [1908–14]', *BAF* no. 9 (1972), pp. 6–10

*Nectoux, Jean-Michel: 'Gabriel Fauré et Camille Saint-Saëns: correspondance inédite', *RdM*, lviii (1972), pp. 65–89; 190–252, and lix (1973), pp. 60–98. Republ. in one vol. by the Société Française de Musicologie, Paris, Heugel, 1973

*Nectoux, Jean-Michel: 'Entretien avec Emmanuel Fauré-Fremiet (14.1.71 and 11.2.71), *Scherzo*, i no. 8 (December 1971). Fuller version in *BAF* no. 9 (1972), pp. 12–18

*Nectoux, Jean-Michel: 'Gabriel Fauré ou Les Contraires Réconciliés', *Scherzo*, ii no. 17 (November 1972), pp. 7–10

*Nectoux, Jean-Michel: 'Shylock', *BAF* no. 10, (1973), pp. 19–27

*Nectoux, Jean-Michel: 'Autour de quelques lettres inédites de Robert de Montesquiou, Charles Koechlin et Gabriel Fauré [1902]', *BAF* no. 11 (1974), pp. 7–11

*Nectoux, Jean-Michel: 'Fauré le novateur', *Musique de tous les temps*, no. 18 (September–October 1974), pp. 7–11

*Nectoux, Jean-Michel: 'Les Orchestrations de Gabriel Fauré: Légende et vérité', *Revue Musicale Suisse*, cxv no. 5 (September–October 1975), pp. 243–9

*Nectoux, Jean-Michel: 'Ravel, Fauré et les débuts de la Société Musicale Indépendante [SMI]', *RdM*, lxi no. 2 (1975), pp. 295–318

*Nectoux, Jean-Michel: 'Flaubert, Gallet, Fauré ou Le Démon du Théâtre', *Bulletin du Bibliophile*, no. 1 (1976), pp. 33–47

Nectoux, Jean-Michel: 'Fauré vu de l'étranger', *BAF,* no. 14 (1977), pp. 3–4

*Nectoux, Jean-Michel: 'Albéniz et Fauré', *Travaux de l'Institut d'études ibériques et latino-américaines*, xvi–xvii (1976–7), pp. 160–86

*Nectoux, Jean-Michel: 'Works renounced, themes rediscovered: Eléments pour une thématique fauréenne', *19th-Century Music*, ii no. 3 (March 1979), pp. 231–44

*Nectoux, Jean-Michel: 'Debussy et Fauré', *Cahiers Debussy*, Nouvelle série no. 3 (1979), pp. 13–30

*Nectoux, Jean-Michel: Entry on Gabriel Fauré in *The New Grove Dictionary of Music and Musicians*, ed. Stanley Sadie, London, Macmillan, 1980 (vol. 6, pp. 417–28)

*Nectoux, Jean-Michel: 'Le "Pelléas" de Fauré', *RdM*, lxvii no. 2 (1981), pp. 169–90

Nohain, Jean (alias Jaboune): 'Les grands hommes quand ils étaient petits, VIII: Gabriel Fauré', unknown journal in the Fauré-Fremiet archives (8.3.24)

*Northcott, Bayan: 'Fauré our Contemporary, *MM*, xviii no. 8 (April 1970), pp. 32–6 (with a copy of *Le Parfum impérissable* on pp. 38–40)

*Orledge, Robert: 'Fauré's "Pelléas et Mélisande"', *ML*, lvi no. 2 (April 1975), pp. 170–79

*Orledge, Robert: 'Fauré en Angleterre', *BAF* no. 13 (1976), pp. 10–16

*Orledge, Robert: 'The two endings of Fauré's *Soir*', *ML*, lx no. 3 (July 1979), pp. 316–22

*Orrey, Leslie: 'The songs of Gabriel Fauré', *Music Review* no. 6 (May 1945), pp. 72–84

Orrey, Leslie: 'Gabriel Fauré, 1845–1924', *MT*, lxxxvi (May 1945), pp. 137–9

Orrey, Leslie: 'Gabriel Fauré: 1845–1924. 1. The Songs', *Musical Opinion*, lxviii (April 1945), pp. 197–8; id. '2. The Chamber Music', *Musical Opinion*, lxviii (May 1945), pp. 229–30

Parker, D. C.: 'Gabriel Fauré. A Contemporary Study', *The Monthly Musical Record*, no. 48 (October 1918), pp. 225–9

Patier, Marie-Claire: 'Fauré et le Wagnerisme', *BAF* no. 13 (1976), pp. 5–9

Pioch, Georges: 'L'Oeuvre dramatique de Gabriel Fauré', *Musica* (Paris), no. 77 (February 1909)

Pioch, Georges: 'Gabriel Fauré', *Conservatoires et Théâtres* no. 1 (Paris, 1.12.10)

Pioch, Georges: 'L'Homme', article in *Gabriel Fauré*, Paris, Publications techniques et artistiques, 1946

*Polignac, Princesse Edmond de: 'Memoirs of the Late Princesse Edmond de Polignac', *Horizon* no. 68 (August 1945), pp. 110–41

Pontalba, M.: 'Le Centenaire de Gabriel Fauré', *Canada Français* (September 1945), pp. 26–38

*Ravel, Maurice: 'Les Mélodies de Gabriel Fauré', *ReM* (1.10.22), pp. 22–7

*(*Revue du Languedoc* (Albi) no. 6 (June 1945) Special Fauré ed.)

*(*Revue Musicale* Special Fauré ed. 1.10.22. Includes seven pieces

based on the letters of his name by ex-pupils: Maurice Ravel, Georges Enesco, Louis Aubert, Florent Schmitt, Charles Koechlin, Paul Ladmirault, Jean Roger-Ducasse, publ. as a supplement entitled 'Hommage à Gabriel Fauré'. Also, special centenary ed. May 1945)

*Roger-Ducasse, Jean: 'La Musique de chambre', *ReM* (1.10.22), pp. 60–79

*Roger-Ducasse, Jean: 'L'Enseignement de Gabriel Fauré', article in *Gabriel Fauré*, Paris, Publications techniques et artistiques, 1946

Rowley, Alec: 'The Pianoforte Music of Gabriel Fauré', *Chesterian*, xii no. 96 (July 1931), pp. 224–7

Ryelandt, Baron: 'Gabriel Fauré et l'évolution musicale', *Académie Royale des sciences, des lettres et des beaux-arts*, xxiii (1941), pp. 90–95

Saint-Jean, Joseph de: See Marliave, Joseph de.

*Saint-Saëns, Camille: 'Une Sonate [op. 13]', *Journal de Musique* (7.4.1877). Republ. in *Au Courant de la vie*, Paris, Dorbon, 1914

Saint-Saëns, Camille: 'M. Gabriel Fauré', *L'Eclair* (23.1.93)

Saint-Saëns, Camille: 'Louis Niedermeyer', *La Nouvelle Maitrise*, no. 19 (12.6.02)

Schmitt, Florent: 'Les Oeuvres d'orchestre', *ReM* (1.10.22) pp. 50–59

Schmitt, Florent: 'Gabriel Fauré', *Chesterian*, vi no. 43 (December 1924), pp. 73–8

Schuhmacher, Gerhard: 'Fauré und Bach', *Musik und Kirche*, xxxix no. 5 (1969), pp. 235–6

Servières, Georges: 'Compositeurs modernes. Gabriel Fauré', *Revue pour les jeunes filles* (Paris, 5.4.98)

Sievers, Gerd: '"Pelléas et Mélisande": Sibelius, Debussy, Schoenberg, Fauré', *Musica* (Bärenreiter, Kassel-Wilhelmshöhe), xv (April 1961), pp. 171–4

Siguitov, Serge: 'La Musique de Fauré en Russie', *BAF*, no. 14 (1977), pp. 5–11

Sivry, A. de: 'Gabriel Fauré', *Le Monde Musical*, xvii no. 12 (30.6.05)

*Solliers, Jean de: 'Les Neuf Préludes, op. 103', *BAF* no. 12 (1975), pp. 5–8

Suckling, Norman: 'Homage to Gabriel Fauré, *Monthly Musical Record*, lxxiv (July–August 1944), pp. 121–8

Suckling, Norman: 'The Songs of Fauré', *The Listener*, xxxiii no. 844 (15.3.45), p. 305

*Suckling, Norman: 'Gabriel Fauré, Classic of Modern Times', *Music Review*, vi (May 1945), pp. 65–71

Suckling, Norman: 'The Unknown Fauré', *Monthly Musical Record*, lxxv (May 1945), pp. 84–7

Thibaud, Jacques: 'La Musique de chambre', article in *Gabriel Fauré*,

Paris, Publications techniques et artistiques, 1946

Tiersot, Julien: 'Gabriel Fauré', *Zeitschrift der Internationalen Musik-gesellschaft*, vii (1905), pp. 45–52

Tinan, Mme Gaston de: 'Memories of Debussy and his Circle', *Journal of the British Institute of Recorded Sound*, no. 50–51 (April–July 1973), pp. 158–63

Torchet, Julien: 'La Vie de Gabriel Fauré', *Musica* (Paris), no. 77 (February 1909)

Vierne, Louis: 'Silhouettes d'artistes. Gabriel Fauré', *L'Echo Musical*, i no. 12 (5.12.12)

Vuillermoz, Émile: 'Gabriel Fauré', *Le Courrier Musical*, viii no. 13 (1.7.05)

Vuillermoz, Émile: 'Gabriel Fauré', *La Revue Illustrée*, xx no. 14 (1.7.05)

Vuillermoz, Émile: 'La Musique de chambre de Gabriel Fauré', *Musica* (Paris), no. 77 (February 1909)

*Vuillermoz, Émile 'Gabriel Fauré', *ReM* (1.10.22), pp. 10–21

Wiseman, Daniel: 'Gabriel Fauré and the French Musical Renaissance', *Contemporary Review*, cxxvii (1927), pp. 333–40

INDEX OF FAURÉ'S WORKS

GENERAL INDEX

Aguettant, Louis, 83–4, 115, 257
Aix-les-Bains, 198
Albéniz, Isaac, **23**, 221
Albert, François, 31
Albert I of Monaco, Prince, 28
Alexandra, Queen, 24–5
Annecy-le-Vieux, 28, 29, 30, 176, 322, 324–5
Astruc, Gabriel, 26, 118
Auber, Daniel, 59
Aubert, Louis, 23, 113, 230, 296
Aubry, Georges Jean (see Jean-Aubry, Georges)
Auric, Georges, 42

Bach, J. S., 7, 12, 28, 36, 38, 44, 70, 180, 233, 261, 272
Bad-Ems (see Ems)
Bagès, Maurice, 17, 36, 291, 295, 298–304 *passim*
Balakirev, Mily, 268
Balay, Guillaume, 186, 323
Ballard, Louis, 113, 296
Banville, Théodore de, 153, 257
Barcelona, 23
Bardac, Emma (Mme Sigismond), **15**, 18, 36, 83, 89, 93, 229, 303, 305
Bardac, Dolly (Hélène, later Mme de Tinan), 15, 93, **96**, 306–7
Bardac, Raoul, 96, 306
Bartók, Béla, 185
Basset, Serge, 233, 236n16
Bathori, Mme Jane (Jean-Marie Berthier), 23
Baudelaire, Charles, 3, 50, 51, 91, 153
Baugnies, Mme Marguerite (later Mme de Saint-Marceaux), 12, 13, 18, 36, 82, 285, 286
Bayreuth, 13
Beaunier, André, 20
Beauxhostes, Fernand Castelbon de, 18, 310
Beethoven, Ludwig van, 3, 8, 21, 29, 49, 139, 214, 233, 272, 281; *Ode to Joy* (Ninth Symphony), 109; String Quartet (op. 132), 242
Bellaigue, Camille, 11, 30, 86, 115, 325